IN ANY CASE

Books by Richard G. Stern

GOLK

EUROPE: *or Up and Down with Schreiber and Baggish*

IN ANY CASE

IN ANY CASE

a novel by

RICHARD G. STERN

McGRAW-HILL BOOK COMPANY, INC.

New York   Toronto   London

IN ANY CASE

Copyright © 1962 by Richard G. Stern.

Printed in the United States of America.
All rights reserved. This book or parts thereof may not be reproduced in any form without written permission of the publishers.

Library of Congress Catalog Card Number: 62-17648

First Edition

61205

for Christopher, with love

ACKNOWLEDGMENTS

The characters, scenes, and details of this book are fictional, but some were suggested by Miss Jean Fuller's account of the Prosper Network in *Double Webs* (London: Putnam, 1958). Since a few of the people about whom Miss Fuller wrote are alive, I want to make it very clear that this novel is not about them or about any real people, alive or dead. Furthermore, it does not attempt to offer an interpretation of any actual events.

The story cited on page 34 was written by Miss Kate Stern, and is used here with her permission.

We have scotch'd the snake, not kill'd it;
She'll close and be herself, whilst our poor malice
Remains in danger of her former tooth.
But let the frame of things disjoint, both the worlds suffer,
Ere we will eat our meal in fear, and sleep
In the affliction of these terrible dreams
That shake us nightly. Better be with the dead
Whom we, to gain our peace, have sent to peace,
Than on the torture of the mind to lie
In restless ecstasy. Duncan is in his grave;
After life's fitful fever he sleeps well;
Treason has done his worst: nor steel, nor poison,
Malice domestic, foreign levy, nothing
Can touch him further.

MACBETH, ACT III, SCENE 1

PART ONE

"Every fact is related on one side to sensation, and, on the other, to morals. The game of thought is, on the appearance of one of these two sides, to find the other . . ."

"There is in international relations a public world and there is also an underworld. The relationship between the public world and the underworld—between the governments in office and the spies, has never been codified."

CHAPTER 1

I was a terrible father to my son, at least until it was too late for him to know otherwise. I always loved him—I nearly said "of course" —but what is love? An erratic continuum in which any feeling can exist, envy, pride, antipathy, passionate affection, hatred. Love isn't a fixed relationship, only a kind of fund that underwrites all sorts of behavior. And fathers differ as much as saints from killers; after the biological half-second, the genetic transmission, everything depends, just depends.

My son and I were not the same sort of person at all. He was shut in, I'm open; and this was true when he was four years old. Or six, anyway, when his mother died, and I was forced to regard him closely. Which brings up something else: I had to raise him by myself. Even though there were nurses and maids around, this was no easy job. In the twenties, psychologists began backing parents up against the wall. You couldn't swat a child's behind without being reminded that you were shaping generations: sons roving gutters with knives in their fists, grandsons swiping brassieres off laundry lines. Raising a child was quite a strain on a man, and for a freewheeler like myself, it was sand in all my parts.

1

Here's the way it would go. It'd be a late morning after a long night; I'd be pouring coffee into my throat, steaming, an operation in my head, when clump, dump, boom down the stairs, Bobbie's clod-hoppers, you'd think they'd shod a rhino. He'd trickle in, a small, dark, round-headed tough, nose-stuff on his non-mustache.

"What in the name of God are you doing exploding down here at nine-thirty?" Chin, nose, eyes, down, away from my look. "What's the matter? Forget your papa's native tongue? Dig down, brother, and get up with a response."

"No school today."

"Why not?"

"Saint's day."

"Saint's day. No, it's Thursday. Thursday. Your grandfather ought to get a load of 'Saintsday.' Nuns. On their fat knees sixty hours a week while the working parents of their charges suffer the ignorance they're paid to eliminate. All right, laddie. Upstairs, and write me a five-page description of the Château de Versailles. Without misspellings. And the next time you cavalry down here like that, I'm going to bat the living hell out of you as sure as you're standing there picking your nose. Dis-gusting. Now get out, till I am. *Débarrasse-moi le plancher*," to hammer it home in his own language.

But late that night I couldn't get off to sleep thinking of the way I'd treated him. "You lousy brute," I'd tell myself, "how can you abuse that motherless boy who's got only you in this world?" and I'd go down the long hall to his room, sit on his bed and take his little blacktop head in my arms.

He'd come awake groaning, knowing who it was. "What's the matter, Papa?"

"I was awful this morning, Bobbie. I'm sorry."

"You were hung over."

"No excuse," I said. "I was awful. Please forgive me. You know you're the only thing in the world I care about."

"I know."

I kissed his head. "I wish I brought more happiness into your life."

"You bring enough." He patted my hand and got his head back on the pillow.

"I hope you'll remember me with love."

"Well, I'll sure remember you," but with a smile unlike any I'd ever seen, so sweet you'd pardon a mass murderer if he showed it.

That's the way it would go, and after, I would go back to my room again, my heart liquid. There, as often as not, I'd look down at some body curling out of the sheets, someone whose name I might not recall for a second, nor where I met her, but who now, everything juiced up again, was what I wanted with the most familiar want of my life.

It wasn't so long ago that that seemed the only sure thing in the world, though God knows how it can pendulum away from what you want, how it can mute, alter, trip over itself. But what can rival it as sheer force? I've wondered if it might be the decrease of that force in me which accounts for my paternal reformation. A few years ago, I saw a book by a Spanish doctor named Marañon which explained how tenderness increases in men as their sexual power wanes. Though I have by no means thrown in that towel, I can understand this as an explanation for the change in my feelings for Bobbie, though of course the change also came from my growing awareness of what he did and what happened to him. The awareness came largely after reading Father Trentemille's book, but it started before that and was certainly in existence when Bobbie visited me for the last time in his life, down in the country in 1943. It was only the third time since the war that I'd seen him. There'd been a day back in 1940 during the *drôle de guerre* when I'd gone over to London, and then an encounter in early 1942 on Boulevard Clichy when, with a look, he'd let me know I wasn't to recognise him, and I walked by, wondering what he, a Franco-American member of the Royal Transport Corps, was doing in French clothes in the occupied streets of Paris, and then had noticed, beneath a patch of whitish gunk under his right eye, the snagged tissue of a recently bloody wound.

2

When the United States entered the war in 1941, I would have been interned if I hadn't acted like a number of Americans who'd spent most of their lives in France, and disappeared from my normal haunts to blend as a Frenchman into the countryside. In 1940, I'd exchanged my country shack just east of Poitiers for that of my dear friend, Georges Sensmesnil, whose place was in the Sarthe country near Le Mans. In effecting the bills of sale, I sold out to Georges in my own name, but bought his under the name Maurice Pouillat, the name I lived under for five years. Georges even addressed me as Maurice before the clerk to whom I showed the expensive papers which confirmed the false identity.

It turned out that Georges' place was in the Occupied Zone, my old one in the *Zone Libre*. I had some bad nights about this, but I think now that I was better off where I was. During those early years, the men who were later called Vichy Miliciens were worse than the Germans, and, being Frenchmen, they might have spotted one of my stray inflections. Then too, the Sarthe region south of Le Mans is real country, so there are fewer flannel-mouths around ready to throw you and their grandmother into the drain for a slice of dog meat. Wars are against cities, and farmers know it. No one can hate invaders as farmers can, and the few natural rats among them are restrained by fear from peaching. Also farmers are usually too tired to think much; conscientious betrayal requires a lot of thinking.

I don't know how Bobbie found me under my pseudonym down in the country, but I've long since stopped marvelling at the ways men have of getting information about other men, and too, I know now that Bobbie was one of the world's experts in such enterprise.

I was drinking the local dynamite in the fifteen feet of cleared ground between my beans and strawberry beds just at the back of that airy paperweight of a house. A bicyclist was coming around the road curve, and I half-saw him as he approached, feeling that there was something there, fifty yards away, that I knew. He went on out of sight, and then five minutes later he'd swung back and was there in the garden with me. Smallish, round, tough, his hair under the Basque beret even blacker than I remembered it, he put his hands on my shoulders and kissed my cheeks. "It's so nice to see you, Papa."

It was the first English sentence not off the BBC that I'd heard in months, except when I talked to myself. That was enough to blur things, but I was also groggy from surprise and the dynamite. "It is you, Bobbie. It really is. What a surprise," and so on, while he led me back to the bench and sat down with me.

"I've only got an hour," he said. He'd had an appointment in Le Mans, and had gone without sleep to see me. "Maybe in a month I'll come back and stay longer." He went to the bicycle and started taking things out of the leather pouches which straddled the back wheel, two large chocolate bars—he knew I loved it, and our ration was four ounces a month—a big packet of points, and, marvel of marvels, a slab of beef which would have cost an arm and a leg on the *marché noir*. He brought all this to the bench and said, "Merry Christmas, Papa."

At which, I'm sure I reddened. Few things brought my paternal inadequacy home to me as our Christmases. When Hélène was alive, we often left Bobbie with his nurse to go off skiing or swimming, and after her death, I was almost always off for the Riviera or the States. I'd have left behind thirty or forty dollars worth of francs for presents and a tree, and occasionally, I'd telephone on Christmas day, remorse slipping through the vacation daze of pleasure. Once I called from Chicago, but there was no answer. I think the cook had taken him to her home in Drieu. Then, when he was at Winchester, and later at Oxford, he spent the holidays with friends in England.

But maybe I didn't react, except to the grandeur of the presents. "Are you in the black market?"

Bobbie's answer was about the closest he ever came to playing with me. "Better not question loaves and fishes."

I'd been away from Paris too long to palaver with anyone, let alone Bobbie, and at such a time. "Are you?" Though the array looked as much a divine as an earthly dispensation to me.

"That's the least of my connections."

"What are the others?" for I had no real notion yet of what he was doing.

"It wouldn't do you anything but harm to know," he said. "But my papers are as clean as Laval's."

I cooked the meat on a skillet—though he wanted me to have a solitary roast later on—and opened one of the few non-toxic bottles of wine left in the house, a blush-pink Montrachet for which I'd given up a repairable safety razor in a rash exchange at the weekly market. Looking back, it was worth an automobile. I'm no celebrant of the palate, but every swallow of that wine was special for me. It made that hour seem almost spacious, but it was only an hour, time to feel but not to express alteration; and it was an hour on the nose when, without looking at his watch, Bobbie got up, his face abstract to the point of abandonment, a blown flag, put his arms around me, and got on his bike. I went out in the road and waved till he was smaller than a bug in the afternoon's grainy dazzle.

3

The first notion I'd had that Bobbie was involved in something other than the Royal Transport Corps came in January, 1941. I was down in the country in one of the forty or fifty thousand solitary hours during which my mind nearly faded out of existence. All day, my head buzzed with a kind of static out of which every few hours some clear thought would come as if by evolutionary accident. At night, another miserable day gotten by, I'd know a kind of liberation through the night broadcasts of the BBC. Lying back in the dark, I'd listen to my own language exhibiting the world for me, three hours of conviction that I wasn't the last Neanderthal looking blankly at the great glacier. News, music, lectures, and even—thank God, as it turned out—a program called *Messages Personnels*, a crazy-colored fog of disconnected sentences, each of which was bait for a particular fish across the channel. One night, so cold the nerves annulled themselves in your flesh, my message hooked me:

If the pongist sees the pinger in Paree, don't rock the boat.

I stared at the gold dial blinking in the dark. The message was repeated, and there was Bobbie talking to me as personally, as intimately, as he'd ever talked to me in his life.

You see, ping-pong was about the only thing we ever did together for fun. We had one of the first tables in Paris, sent over from Fields by my parents just a couple of years before they smashed themselves up on the Outer Drive coming home from a genealogy trip. With the set had come one of the pretentious manuals of those days, a treatise on the game couched in the terms of a guide to chivalric behavior. The player was called the "Pongist," and the ten-year-old Bobbie apparently discovered in this elegance the proper label for some feeling he had about me. I responded in kind, and so, for our whacking collisions, we chalked up scores to Pongist and Pinger.

That's why I didn't just pass out on the street when I saw him three months later on the Boulevard Clichy. After the message, I'd started taking the train to Paris twice a month, indicating on the travel permission forms that I was going up to collect my pension from my former "employer," Armand Boisdevres. The first few trips were an ordeal: the SD men gave your papers a real going-over, ration cards, passport, identity card, invalid's certificate; a man weighed less than his dossier in those years. I'd hand the papers over, my heart rattling on my ribs, thinking, "He'll flick the lies off this in twenty seconds, and that'll be it." But there was no trouble. I looked, I was, innocuous. In fact, the only time I had a serious scare in those years was when my name showed up on the Todt Labor Battalion list in 1944—which I took care of by handing a month's income to the local quisling, who then rendered me the complex service of drawing two lines through my name.

Paris was miserable, stupid, even ugly; the only thing you noticed was the smoky green of German banners and uniforms. There was lots of guzzling and café life; in fact, for whores, butchers, and vacationing German hausfraus, it was, I suppose, the most festive

6

time ever. All around were the little bicycle taxis that made you think you were in Shanghai. There were fields of posters full of handsome Wehrmachters handing chocolate to smiling children, though half the time you'd see a little white sticker pasted on the corner inscribed with brilliant resistance slogans and couplets. I remember one that went "*L'aspirateur hitlérien/Vide le pays en moins de rien.*" A world of debris, a morose doll-world, trivial and gross. Old lover of Paris, I felt like a flooded engine. It would take me two apéritifs to gather myself for the walk to Armand's; finally, I'd amble up there in my wartime stance, a cramped, cocoon-like slither aimed at invisibility. Then, one afternoon, the single dividend of those walks and trains and searches and icy lunches with my foxy brother-in-law, Armand: the mute, ten-second look at Bobbie, staring through me as I walked by him.

Less than a year before, I'd crossed the Channel in a blacked-out —but merry—ship and met him upstairs at Simpsons-in-the-Strand for lunch. He looked about twelve years old, swamped by a uniform in which an antiaircraft gun could have been concealed.

"I thought there was a textile shortage here," I said.

"It'll fit soon. I'm putting on weight riding a desk all day."

"That's all you're old enough to do. At nineteen, I wouldn't have been up to that, and I was more mature than you. Which is odd, considering that I was under your grandmother's loving care. Of course, you had Miss Worthington, but I've never been sure how much sympathy lay in that bag of sterling."

"She was fine to me."

"Eat up," said I, slightly miffed at what might have been a backhand rebuke to me. "Simpson's beef is better than ever. Or is it that war sharpens one's taste?"

"It's very good, Papa," but he just stroked it. A great oozing slab of beef, and he faced it like a debutante meeting the queen.

"What do they think about Churchill's taking over here?" I was trying to give us the air of men talking about general questions of importance. A shrug from Man Number Two. I pushed on. "I used to see him down at Cannes eight or nine years ago. He was staying in Maxine Elliot's chateau. Every afternoon he'd waddle down to the beach and porpoise around. Used to float around with a cigar in his mouth, looked like a volcanic island. Spoke the worst French I ever overheard." I detected a blue twitch from an old cavalier at the next table. "Of course, he's a first-rate man," and then under my breath, "give or take a Gallipoli or two."

7

"I like him," said Bobbie. He was not exactly a person with whom one enjoyed talking.

After lunch, we crossed the street to the Savoy and heard Ivar Novello sing farewell to the "dancing years." A thirst-provoking two hours. When we got out, I proposed the Carleton Bar.

"I have to get back, Papa. My train's at six-thirty from Wellington."

"I'll taxi you. Have one glass with me. It's going to be a little while before I see you again."

"Yes. I don't know how long Channel trips are going to be safe."

"They won't block the Channel, but still, I'm going down to the country for a few months. I had one war. I'm going to sit this one out. Actually, I need a rest. You can imagine what the steel business has been like since the summer."

"You do look a little tired."

"Peaked, is more like it. I've been having a run-around from a little chum," and I winked, although I detest intimations of this sort, frown on boasts of conquest, never tell a dirty story. But Bobbie looked so accessible to injury, I thought he needed toughening.

We had had ale in a filthy pub, and then, by sheer luck, I got hold of a taxi and put him in it. I reached in the window and took off his cap to rub his head. "Goodby, my boy. Take care of yourself. Stay put. War is the worst time to think of heroics. There are too many opportunities."

He smiled that smile of his, that sourceless, irresistible smile, and then leaned over to kiss my cheek goodby, there in the middle of the least emotional capital in Christendom.

4

Father Trentemille's book came in the mail unannounced and unsolicited. November, 1948, thirty years and two months since I'd come to France as an artillery officer just out of the Student Army Training Corps at Chicago, and three-and-a-half years after my return to Paris from my four-and-a-half-year snooze in the country.

The three-and-a-half years had been terrifically busy ones for me. Picking up one's life is harder than beginning it: choice has been pared, and it's harder to work up good habits. More than loss of energy, this marks age. I had a five-room apartment a block from the Parc Monceau, and was looked after by an old Pole, Madame Zdonowycz, whom I'd picked up from the Refugee Employment Agency just a few days after I'd gotten the telegram from the British War Office about Bobbie. She had more bristles than a pineapple, crooned Polish hymns half the day, and smelled like a caged grizzly bear, but she was, she is, right for me.

We were working to get our plant pulled together again. Armand had been forced by the underground to help put the place out of commission back in 1943. The explosions, timed with a feint raid of the RAF, were designed to cripple the plant for German use but not permanently; a delicate job. Those first months were miserable for all of us. I never worked harder. Half the time I'd come home too tired to eat. Zdonowycz buzzed around crucifying hymns, drowning vegetables in cream, electrocuting our roasts, but she kept me going, that old pineapple. She left me alone when I needed to be alone, and made no rumpus about my occasional visitors. In return, I decamped every Wednesday morning when, after a night's romp at the Polish Exiles' Club in Montmartre, the pineapple turned porcupine, and pinned to the wall with hangover snarls anything that crossed her path. I took my chocolate and croissants down the street out of wrath's way, and returned in the evening to the peaceful restoration of vegetable rule.

"There's this book came for you today I didn't open, this electric bill, thieves, they charge us like for four 'frigerator boxes, and some note from one of your ladies you can smell."

"Thank you, Madame," and handed her my coat. If she were twenty years younger, took a bath on Saturdays, and shaved twice a week, it would simplify my life no end.

I never read the scented note. I suppose the electric bill was paid—our lights didn't go off—but I'm a book bug and opened the package first. *84 Avenue Foch* was the title, Paul Trentemille, S.B., the author. One of the middle pages was folded at the corner. I opened to it and read the sentence which changed my life.

It is clear that the Chaleur Network was betrayed into the hands of the *Sicherheitsdienst* by Gruyère, the young American, Robert Curry.

I sat down in an armchair and opened my shirt collar.

"Heart attack?" asked Zdonowycz.

I waved her off and reread the sentence. Its meaning didn't change. For what must have been an hour, I was nothing but an ear: I heard water cruising in pipes, cars in the street shifting gear, toilets flushing, my neighbors pushing back their dinner chairs. I could write down a hundred things I heard. It was the most disembodied hour of my life.

Even the telegram from the War Office three years before had

9

been easier. I had not been unprepared for that, and not only because I hadn't heard from Bobbie since his visit to me in the country, but because those years of isolation had evaporated expectation out of me, made me a day-to-day, hour-to-hour liver, someone to whom hope meant it was time for dinner, and whose mental life consisted of the discovery that garden mud could be used for shaving cream. When I read that Bobbie had died in the Auschwitz extermination camp, my first thought was, "So at last, I'm alone." Fifty-two years old, I had no child, no wife, no parents. It was a condition for which I'd now and then wished. Every attachment weighs against every other one, and I had visions of weightlessness, of complete availability. Now that it seemed my condition, what was there to do?

One thing I did do, and that was bury Bobbie miles deep in my head where only dreams would nudge him. And then, as I'd done with Hélène's death twenty years before, I converted Bobbie's into a medal I wore on my prowls, one stamped with the bereavement which needed comforting, and which could give some in return: "Here I am," it said, "a responsible, marrying-type man who's taken part in the world's enterprise of continuity, but who is, at the moment, available, and grieving." So my losses haloed my prowls, and I had big successes, which, with hard work, piled oblivion where I needed it. Bobbie's death joined the other war debris. Until Trentemille's book.

I read it that first night as if it were reading me. Like fever, do you have it or it you? And what a book it was, what a world it uncovered to this non-reader of spy stories, a world within the world I walked in every day.

Falsity has lost its peach fuzz for me. For five years, I lived under a pseudonym, and camouflaged perhaps more than my name for longer than that, but the depth of falsity which the brave men in Trentemille's book took as the condition of their days, a falsity not only of names and papers, but habits, actions, even motives and thoughts, this was an epic mendacity that seemed too large to be anything but its own end. Though it wasn't, of course, at least as far as I could see then.

That night-world metamorphosis which makes a Metro station a homicidal rendezvous, a chocolate bar a coastal fortification, this was flat denial of the naturalness and freedom which were supposedly the ends of the whole business. As I saw him in Trentemille's book, the agent was stripped of everything that identified him as himself, of everything but that which enabled him to keep falsifying, and this minimum he gave into the hands of two or three people. Which was his fear, because knowing his own weakness, he knew that of those who held his life, knew the force which could transmute virtue, the treason which lies beneath allegiance, and which, under such force, breaks through and masks as it. And lastly, as I saw it, the agent no longer exists as an individual, but as a function of a cause; the pressures directed at him are really aimed at the cause, so that he suffers as an individual without being regarded as one. This, it seemed to me, was what people meant by hell on earth.

I finished reading at four in the morning. The swan lamp poured interrogating wattage on the blank end page; a grilling. I shook my head loose and got up; it was like building something. I went to the bathroom, but there was no toilet paper in the container. Usually I'd have called Zdonowycz right then and there. That is one of the few household items which I insist upon taking for granted, but now I suppressed my small need, washed my face and headed for my bed, my extra-size double bed with its deep Sellboua mattress. Yet I couldn't flop into it and go to sleep. A cord was tugging and hopping in me, saying, "Hold it, hold it." What a weight in the room. "I'll decide tomorrow," I said. "No," tugged the cord.

Old business-report reader that I am, my head laid out the pros and cons in double columns.

A	B
1) Bobbie's dead	1) I'm alive
2) He can't be helped	2) I can; and he can
3) Nobody will connect him with me	3) Everybody will
4) I'm too old to start tangling with priests	4) Fifty-five is young enough for younger things than that
5) What can I do?	5) Do it and see

This went on for minutes, but I knew from the beginning that something in me had said "I will," not "I don't want to." The mountain turned cloud. I went to bed.

The next morning, I watched the Number 16 bus go by the corner without me and telephoned the office to say I would not be coming in. I unscrewed the gold pen which was my father's last present to me, and wrote the following letter to the British War Office:

Sirs:

I have just learned that my son, Flight Lieutenant Robert Curry, BF-6253-5749-1961, was a member of an English intelligence group identified by the name Chaleur. According to information in the book *84 Avenue Foch*, by the Abbé Paul Trentemille (Bourges: Editions du Maquis, 1947), Chaleur is the code name of an English officer named George Towne. I would very much like to communicate with Mr. Towne's survivors. Would you be so good as to send me their names and addresses? If, in addition, you have information pertaining to the aforesaid group, I would greatly appreciate your sending it to me.

Very truly yours,
Samuel E. Curry

I jogged down the street with the envelope, delighted with myself and what I'd done. I was going to find out about Bobbie, and I was going to have help from the Townes, whoever they were. Young Towne, like most of the Chaleur agents Trentemille wrote about, had been killed by the Germans. Grief would be the common ground his parents and I would tread, and together we would ferret out the source of the calumny and set the record straight.

I hadn't done much for Bobbie in his life—had, indeed, done a great deal to him. While he lived he was largely an unknown quantity to me, yet I felt surer than I felt anything about myself that he was incapable of betrayal, that he had bravery built into him, that the virtues I lacked, he had. He had left nothing behind him, no child, no wife, no book, nothing but unfulfillment and my memory of him. It was like midnight, and I was back in his room kissing him. Except that now I was going to do more than that.

CHAPTER 2

For my father, life was a series of typical events which could be labelled, if not faced down, by a series of antique maxims. Few of our family dinners were unseasoned by stitches in time, early birds, rolling stones, or unhatched chickens. The favorite was "Opportunity knocks but once." Why my father should so frequently distribute this synopsis of his own miscalculations, I don't know, except that, like most of us, he was gaga for the strengths he lacked.

I grew up choking on these bromides, but I suppose they have formed my decisions and whipped my delinquencies more than all the Bibles in the world. No gobbet of antiquity is so stony a rebuke to my life as that favorite of his. For I had an opportunity, one which in the light of my ambition, need, and self-appraisal would have pulled me out of the swamp of self-indulgence and evasion which is the underside of the Eden of Pleasure where I've dispensed my days. There have been minor opportunities, but in 1935 the big one came. I had a chance to go back to my own country and enter a life which throughout my school years was one for which I'd yearned and prepared. A life in public affairs.

I was born in the panic year 1893 when fifteen thousand businesses and six hundred banks failed, born in Chicago, a city whose Pullman strikes, Haymarket rioters, wheat pits, and railroads made it the breeding ground for the populist reformers and muckrakers who saw the need for putting a federal bit into the wild industrial horse. My father's ignorant contempt for my idols, Henry Demarest Lloyd, Governor Altgeld, Teddy Roosevelt—"a traitor to his own class," said my East-Tennessee, dirt-farmer father—Gifford Pinchot, and La Follette (whose magazine was my Bible), fed the opposition which broke out openly only in 1916 when I cast my first and only vote for Wilson. There I was, safe in the Rockefeller-financed University which had cradled Veblen and Dewey, my father footing my bills as Rockefeller footed theirs, and I voted against the cold New Yorker, Evans Hughes. My father, whose own father would have punched him into the wall for voting Republican, came as close to tears as I ever saw him. If I'd sailed to Europe on the *Admiral Dewey* then in 1916, instead of in 1918, he might even have been happy in the justification of his correct prediction—"You're voting a war, Samuel, sure as shooting."

How could I have thought, back then, that the next thirty years would be spent coasting along the minor hazards and advantages of the expatriate?

It was seventeen years after I first saw France that I had a real chance to come back home. The American Depression had touched my old reform passions and the great overhaul of '33 had fired my public-affairs zeal, when my old roommate at the University, Justin Showalter, wrote me to come home. Justin worked in Richberg's law office in Chicago, and had followed him down to Washington when Richberg went to head the NRA. Justin wrote that they needed someone in steel who knew currency problems, foreign markets, concrete reinforcement techniques, and had a nose for cartel manipulation. He had talked about me, and they wanted to see me. I came over in May, and went down to Washington to talk with Ben Watterson, one of Frankfurter's lawyers. It was the week before the Court handed down the decision that the government had no right to tell the Schecters how to sell their chickens, but nobody that I saw in Washington really believed that the old men were going to ground the Blue Eagle for good this time.

Washington was hot, with that famous white heat which makes you wonder why the country isn't as messed up as a South American banana state. Mist, haze, blur, God, it was miserable. Watterson and I faced each other through the drizzle off our faces. Coats off, then ties, craning toward an electric fan as it creaked toward us, and I wondering how you could run a country with your brain boiling out of your skull.

Watterson was about thirty-five, six years younger than I, but his face was carved by fatigue and he looked ten years older—and talked that way, which was the first thing that threw me.

"Justin has spoken highly of you."

"He's a good fellow."

"He says he's outlined what we're looking for. At least as far as he's up on it. None of us is sure about anything at this point."

"I can imagine."

"You know, the suicide rate jumps twenty percentage points in heat like this?"

This stopped me, but I said that I sympathised. "I could use a prolonged immersion right now myself."

"You're not going to get much vacation time down here."

"I didn't mean—"

"We might get you seven thousand, but that's absolutely tops."

"The climate'll make up for that," I said.

The fan had the floor for a few seconds.

"Well, I think you can have it if you want it."

There it was, but it was very hot, Watterson was an unpleasant specimen, and my life in Paris was extremely easy. "Can I call you tomorrow?"

"That'll do." And he waved a wet handkerchief at me, which I correctly read as "goodby."

I was staying with the Showalters, and that night we drove over to the Cosmos Club for dinner. Justin and his wife look like models for American life. They're rosy, clean, handsome, and are saved from sheer inanity of good looks by a glaze of melancholy. They're hypochondriacs, and cleanliness fanatics. If the sun were about to boil the earth, they wouldn't forget to brush their teeth at eight A.M., but they'd serve a week in jail rather than use each other's toothbrush.

14

"If Watterson's the temper of the times down here, I'm not made for it."

A pause, for they were chewing their grapefruit slices.

"Don't let him get you, Sammy. They're going to send him over to the Solicitor General's anyway. They've been losing four out of five cases, and they need some good, nasty lawyers. Richberg's fed up. That's why he's arguing the chickens himself."

"Washington's a dream, Sammy. I can't tell you how lovely it can be. Bobbie will just love the schools, and things are always happening. We're going to find a nice girl for you."

"I've got nice girls right now, Ellie. I came here for something else."

"It's a bad week, Sammy. People are more scared of the Court than they'll let on. Watterson was probably on edge. Brandeis has been sharpening the axe for two years."

"What happens if the government loses? Doesn't that sink the whole ship? It was a hell of a time to come down."

"It won't affect you. They need a steel man anyway. If not for the codes, at least to keep tabs on markets. Maybe at State. I can almost guarantee that you're covered. I wish they'd turn these damn fans off. It's the worst thing about a hot town. You get cross drafts every time you enter a room. Instead of sweating the filth out, you get it driven back into you. Winter's all right, but you have to stay away from parties. Whole departments are wiped out by grippe every year. If I were Roosevelt, I'd outlaw more than three people sitting in the same room during the winter months."

"That would settle the Court," I said.

That night I broiled in the cot the Showalters had set up in their son's room for me. A full moon, yellow and angry with heat, shone right in my face. There was a hole in the screen which let in a couple of mosquitoes I couldn't go all out after because of the kid. It was one of the worst sleeping nights of my life.

I called Watterson the next day and told him I wasn't going to take it.

"I get you, and I don't blame you. If I could line up with a decent law firm, I'd get out of this Congo myself. I read an item today about ten thousand horses out in Arizona who contracted dourine. It's a spirochaete which dries them out. They drove 'em into water holes and slaughtered ten thousand of 'em. They'll package 'em for dog meat. Watch out, if you have one."

15

"I don't, Mr. Watterson. Thanks anyway. And thanks for taking time to see me. I'm just not the man for the job."

"I get you," said Watterson. "Call me Ben."

The Court brought down the guillotine on Monday, Black Monday, and two days later, as if NRA needed an epitaph, they fished Watterson out of the Potomac, drowned dead as one of his spirochaeted horses.

Or as dead as my opportunity, for there never was another one. Until the very different one which Father Trentemille's book gave me, which is to the other as a megaphone is to La Scala. I wasn't up to more than that by then. In fact, I'm lucky that I could regard the private mission as a knock on the door.

2

The letter from the British War office arrived within a week of mine to it. Bless the civil civil servants of the crown. They regretted their inability to supply information about the "group," but they would be happy to give me the name of Captain Towne's uncle and guardian, Mr. Herbert Towne, not—to my surprise—of London, Liverpool or Brighton, but of Biarritz, Les Landes, France. Another hyphenated Frenchman, though almost certainly an English one. (Bobbie was one of the few Americans in the British Service, and it had taken a good deal of finagling from Winchester and Oxford connections to get him in.)

I wrote Towne asking if I could come see him about Bobbie, and sent Zdonowycz to the post office with the letter. It wasn't until I saw her rolling along the street clutching wrinkles into it that I realised a letter from me might not be welcome in Biarritz. If Herbert Towne had seen Trentemille's book, he might consider Bobbie his nephew's betrayer. "Madame," I called uselessly.

"I'll telephone and explain everything," I told myself, and actually picked up the receiver. Again useless. If he thought Bobbie a traitor, I couldn't alter his opinion by phone. If he didn't, there'd be no reason to phone.

The businessman's credo has something: efficiency spawns its replicas. Towne's answer came in three days. From Trentemille's book, to me, to the War Office, to Towne, and then back to me in two weeks. Were all the events of the next five years this easy— well, no, it would have been loss more than gain, or, at least, there would be nothing to report but an item for the newspapers.

HOTEL DES LANDES
BIARRITZ

Manager: W. Herbert Towne Esq.

30 nov., 1948

My dear Curry,

Knowing your boy only indirectly, we (my late wife and I) regarded him
with esteem. I am sure that George thought of him as a brother-in-arms.
On George's single visit to us during the war, he told us of the fine calibre
of the men with whom he worked.

As for what you tell us of Pere Trentemille's accusations, I regard them as
a blemish which time will erase.

Of course I welcome the opportunity of meeting you, and as soon as you
find it convenient. I do not travel much, but if you come to Biarritz, I
can offer you the modest hospitality of our little hotel, where, I hope, you
will stay as our guest as long as possible. Until that time then, I am

Very truly yours,
Herbert Towne

3

Three years after Hélène's death, I'd spent ten days in Biarritz with
Bobbie during his Easter vacation. I'd leased an ugly villa with a
name something like Bagatelle from one of our clients, a French
count, but the glory of those days was not my sleeping in a peer's
bed—cold on lineage, in reaction to my father, I couldn't distinguish
an Empire title from a Capetian—but a beautiful girl from Buenos
Aires with whom I slept there, a dark chunk of diamond weeping in
a summer palace and ravenous for someone to show her *le pays*. We
watered around in her uncle's forty-foot power boat, drove one of his
three Daimlers (he was a company director) down to San Sebastian
or Bayonne, horsebacked cautiously on backpaths, and then made for
La Bagatelle. She had been eight years in a convent school, and I used
to think "God help the poor church in Argentina." Bobbie would
thunder into that little echo chamber of a house with a gang of
professional noisemakers a few hours after we'd closed our eyes,
and two or three times I drove him out with a riding boot and a
curse. The holiday collapsed one morning when the gang trooped
through a French window into our bedroom; the miscalculation cost
Bobbie a three-week bruise and me my Argentinian *sueño*.

I was full of this memory going down to Biarritz, and it helps
explain my patronising treatment of Herbert Towne. Here I was

remembering myself as a man of thirty-five or six, and bounding like one off the train and into a tiny white-haired old fellow with a great bulging head whom I nearly patted on the shoulder instead of shaking the hand he put out to me. He was all in white, including a pith helmet held in his left hand, and I wondered if he had been hired to meet all incoming trains. A boy in a red and gold uniform— taller by six inches than Towne—took my bags and put them into a rickety-looking Peugeot for which I headed.

"Would you rather walk?" asked Towne. "It's less than a kilometer, and you might want to stretch your legs after the train."

Well, I thought, as long as I don't have to scoop you up on my shoulders, old fellow.

It was a beautiful day. Over Towne's head, I could see some of the great hotels flowering off the cliffs, looking as if the only thing that held them back from falling into the bay were plugs of sunlight. We walked along the shore road, and for ten minutes, I continued to feel springy and benevolent. Then my heart started rapping like a toy drum, and my tongue felt like the beach below us. I'm a Paris walker, and no walking is supposed to be harder, but here was vacation-land sun, and unfamiliar terrain. Also, Towne had, in true British fashion, understated the length by half. Every thirty seconds a question issued from the pith igloo at my right. I could hardly grunt, let alone re- spond to inquiries about post-war Paris and the price of food, drink, hotel rooms and fishing tackle.

The hotel was a little stucco article, depressed and pink, as if it were both blushing about and mourning its lost status as a family villa. I managed the one flight up behind Towne's churning pins, and came into a small, fine white and gold room which led to a stone terrace bedecked with parasols and summery chairs. Two hun- dred yards away was a stretch of white sand blistered with rainbow shadows from the hanging buildings and four glorious beach um- brellas. It was good to be back where the look of things counted more than their usefulness.

The red-and-gold boy appeared, and Towne told him to bring something whose name I missed, but which, half an hour later, turned out to be one of the best drinks I've ever had, a kind of Planter's Punch with two or three types of Spanish rum soaking into fruit and glittering on hills of chopped ice. Half a glassful, and I resigned myself to my age and lost the fatigue which came from denying it.

"And now," said Towne, "how can I help you, Curry?"

A perfectly civil beginning, almost too civil, for I felt like someone

18

applying for a visa. There was this thumb of a man with the huge glass of liquid orange sitting back waiting for me to pour my appeal out, while I wanted him to be trotting out bandages and cold compresses for my family wound. "Well," I said, "my boy's been slandered. He was a brave boy, like your nephew, absolutely true-blue, and now he gets a load of priestly mud flung at him."

"Post-war bile," said Towne, as if this were another product whose Paris price he would like to know.

"But spilled over me. I'm thinking of a suit against him and his publishers. Not for the money, of course. Apology is what I'm after. Retraction."

Towne disengaged from the rum and said that it was his belief that in France the libelled person must be the litigant. "Your litigant is dead."

"I'm libelled because he is," I said, refraining from comparing paternal and avuncular affection. Armand had come as near to blowing up as his orderly temperament permitted when I'd told him why I wouldn't be down at the office very much, and he was an uncle whose work and fortune would have gone to Bobbie. Towne was clearly brandied out of any sense of connection with the world beyond his glass; still I resented his backspin which deflected my forward motion.

He was saying that it seemed twenty years since the war, and he had no desire to have it any closer. "I remember George as he was before he went away. That's how I protect myself against what might turn up." Did he too suspect something was wrong, or was this just the ubiquitous caution of the coward? "I've seen enough violence to know that it changes men and values and everything one believed unchangable." Yes, I thought, some combatant. I can see you hauling cannons toward the fight, a tiny snow-capped peak that'd melt at a struck match. "I hold to George as I knew him, and I can go to sleep on that."

"I sympathise with your view, Mr. Towne. I only wish I could feel that way. But remember, there's a difference. George died violently, but he rests peacefully; Bobbie has been raked out of his grave by slander. There's every difference in the world there, isn't that so?"

"Do you need anyone's confirmation for your own belief in him?" There he sat, lumped with the sediment of a thousand bottles of rum, inviting the defamed and lashed of the world to ignore their defamers and lashers, as if the world were nothing beyond a beach terrace and a glass of fruited rum.

But I was his guest, and more, had an ounce or two of the self-seeking virus which formed him. And I was on no war mission, but a private, civil one. "I don't," I said. "But all my life I've been in a business that lives by paying and getting paid its debts. I owe Bobbie something. Above and beyond love. And the world. I owe it a straight statement of my accounts. I've avoided public duty all my life. Now my private need is to see that the public books are cleared. So I don't want to go to sleep on this."

Towne picked up a pitcher a fifth his size and refilled our glasses. It was probably as hard work as he ever did. "Suppose, just suppose, the world being what it is, you find that somehow or other the evidence is against your son?"

I suppose I blinked, but partially because out on the beach, a girl, a marvellous-looking girl in a bikini suit, an absolute wonder of flesh just pinked with cloth, had leaped from a beach umbrella into the waves and was swimming out wildly, her arms depositing themselves with an opulence of movement that made me twitch with need.

"Wouldn't it be better to stay as you are, absolutely confident?"

A tub of muscle was booming over the waves toward the girl. She saw him, and they went underwater together. I could feel their bodies displace the interposing water, their feet touching. "I've only instinct, no evidence. What can I do but trust it?"

Towne tipped the glass toward his lips, his eyes shut with pleasure. Behind him trembled the stone rainbows of the hotels Miramar and Belle Vue, the golden stripes on the dark apricot bay, and the sporting lovers. I tried to work myself out of the hot beauty of the place, tried to rile myself up for what counted. Where, I asked myself, where was that powerhouse now assaulting my tower of flesh under the water, where was he when my son, his age and equal, had burst his lungs in the gas chamber? But the scene picked at the thought and blew it away. I wished it were raining.

I tried again with Towne. "I've come to you because I wanted whatever knowledge you might have about any of these agents. Your nephew's code name was the name of the group. He was its chief. Do you know anything more than that?"

"I know that George's will left his Christ College ring to a girl named Jacqueline Bargouille, whose code name was Montespan. She was the courier between George and Gruyère, between George and your son. We got her address as you got mine, from the War Office, and she acknowledged the ring gratefully, but not in a fashion that made any of us, George's brother and sister or myself, feel that we should write her again."

"She's alive then," I said. George's lover. I had visions of a uniformed version of the girl in the waves and my thirty-five-year-old self disguised as George Towne holding onto each other in the underground's imperilled nights.

"Jessica has her address. She'll give it to you, if you wish. And she can tell you more than I. She's read something about the network. It's been the subject of a number of books and films, but I do not read or see them."

He was back into his rum. It was clear he had to be written off; but I'd wait for the girl. He asked if I minded hearing a story he hardly ever thought about any longer, but which he felt explained his attitude, and I said, "Please," though it no longer mattered to me how he felt or why. Hand in dripping hand, the muscle and the girl, eying each other for pleasures given and to be given, walked out of the sea. A pact made in the water would be fulfilled before the day was through, if I knew bodies. Towne talked, lost in his story as if it were as substantial as his glass of rum. "Back in 1940, I was asked to be a link in the escape route over the Pyrenees. There wasn't much to it. A few times a month, a man would come through with the right message, and we'd keep him until it was time to slip him through to the next link. There was never any real trouble, a search or two, a few veiled threats, but that's all. Toward the end a fellow came through in the remains of RAF togs and said he'd been shot down in Belgium. A merry, pleasant chap, recited poems a lot. He said he had a degree from Oxford, had been at All Souls'. It took me less than a second to catch the mistake. I knew All Souls' had only dons and fellows; I put a gun at his ear, and that did it. He broke down. He knew he'd made a mistake too, said he must have subconsciously wanted to give himself away, he loved England so much. He'd spent two years before the war studying and teaching German at Leeds. Did I have to shoot him, he asked me. Yes, I had to shoot him. I had an absolute order to do that. I'd shot rabbits before, that was the limit of my killing. I didn't believe I could do it till it was done. He was down on his knees, his forehead to the ground.

"I'd gotten his real name and address and promised to write his wife. He was from Darmstadt. I wrote, but there was no answer. I suppose she'd been killed too. He's buried over there," and Towne waved toward a screen of grape trellises, purple and gold in that jewelling sun. "Most men can kill in a situation as clear as the war made this one, and most will not let it upset them, but that was it for me. I cleaned up the mess—it was unbelievable—and that was it. I buried him and that was it. I went on doing the work till the invasion the next month, but if there'd been another one, I would have let him shoot me and escape. I think. What I mean to say, Curry, is that things like this must have happened all the time to your son, and to George. What do you think it may have done to them? Who knows what the best of us can become under such conditions? It might be wise to stop looking."

The boy and girl from the beach had come to the edge of the terrace and called up. Towne introduced them as Jessica and Peter, "George's brother and sister. They'll be able to tell you more about him than I."

But I had lost my appetite for knowledge. The sun was going down, and we sat there, till the boy, dressed in sports clothes, appeared with glasses of Madeira. Half an hour later, Jessica brought in a lovely supper, that angelically tender veal which only the French know how to rear and cook, the thin, winy beans of the south, and a chocolate mousse, light as the air in the dome of an Italian church. We sat on the terrace, and Jessica and Peter talked about their brother, who'd been a brilliant ecologist, and had worked out a series of equations for predicting the growth of digits in mammals based on some analysis of the bacterial content of soil. Jessica was up on this because a professor from the University of Leiden had asked her to search for a paper George had written before the war to deliver there. She'd found some notes and sent them, and a few months later the professor sent her an offprint of an article on George's work.

"Your uncle says that you also know about his work in the underground," I said.

Jessica leaned back in her lounge chair. She was in pale blue, and few movie stars could have looked the way she did there. I pressed a thumb into my stomach for diversion. "I don't know much," she said. "I read a book by one of the agents which described the training and the organization. It was not a regular intelligence group. It was organised under one of the other ministries, I think Economic Warfare, and it ran special groups that weren't concerned with actual espionage, but with sabotage, blowing up trains and factories and the like. The RAF dropped arms and agents from England every month by the full moon. George's group, *le réseau* Chaleur, had its headquarters in the Paris area. It was the largest of all the groups, but it was also the least successful. The Germans took it over, and you know what happened. There are other books, but I've gotten a little like Uncle Herbert. I haven't read them. When Mademoiselle Bargouille wrote to thank us for sending George's ring to her, then was the time to find out. We should have asked her here."

"Jessica feels we owed her something if she was George's fiancée," said old Towne. "I think it would have just stirred up difficult memories in all of us."

"It's too late now," said Peter. "Maybe Mr. Curry would like to see her himself."

I wondered if the boy could have seen me looking at his sister and deduced my feelings, but I was in no position to resent, let alone act on such deductions. I said that I'd very much like the woman's address, and so Jessica fetched it for me.

Later, her fiancé came over, a smiling young man who owned the garage down the road. The five of us walked down the beach to watch a cold-looking sun, almost as silvery as a five-franc piece, slip down into a slot of sea.

I left the next morning, not unhappy with the small pickings of the visit. I had at least a point of entry and an address. The main thing was that I'd started. As for Biarritz, I had had that drink, had seen Jessica Towne, enjoyed the terrace, and, finally, learned that I was in no ghostly enterprise, that there were other people and families thinking over the residue of that underground dreamworld, however far they might be from doing anything about it.

CHAPTER 3

Different as I am from my father, as different as Bobbie was from me, I must have some of that arterial glue which kept him forty years at a LaSalle Street desk checking the risks of Midwesterners against their actuarial expectations, and which sent him nightly home to legs of lamb and his genealogy charts with the conviction that he had helped the earth twirl once again on its official sweep, no apologies and no explanations in order. I too went to work nearly every day for a quarter of a century. No engineer, I learned the contour threads of lifting eye bolts and the strength data of spider assemblies, learned how to persuade buyers in Rouen and Brussels that the screed systems of Boisdevres S.A. were as reliable as any in the world. Even painful ruts may be paths of evasion, insulations from decision, but there is the hard fact of a job done day after day, a useful job in a useful industry. If this doesn't stake claims in pride, it doesn't need apology either.

Except that beyond, underneath, within the cracks, I always knew that life held something else. Down in the country, in those crazily lonely years, unable to get on the Number 16 bus for the office, I had to live in the cracks, and think of what counted in the long run. I'm almost certain that my father had never seen them, although he felt the winds coming through them, boredom, envy, inexplicable discontent; but his life was a series of barricades against them. Without the *Tribune*, piquet, pinochle and rummy, without the legs of lamb, the insurance appraisals, and his genealogy charts, my father would have been more abandoned than a Cairo beggar lying on a doorsill with flies crawling up his nostrils.

My mother was chief guardian of the barricades. If my father were twenty minutes late coming home from the Loop, she'd be out the window like a tongue in a thirsty mouth. If anything were late or out of place, she would lose the one thing that really counted for her, equilibrium. When I came in off the streets, her relief whirled in our hothouse; things were restored, safe, between the walls. In church, in a carriage, in a theater, her attention was not on what she heard and saw but on the fact that the three of us were hearing and seeing. She would have been as happy in a tent on the Sahara, as long as no day took from or added to its predecessor anything but itself.

Yet I cannot write her off this simply. I remember finding a picture of her sitting in riding clothes on a horse that, under her, looked as big as the Trojan one. "My God," I said to her. "When did you ever ride?"

"I won a cup," she said, without pride or humor. "It's probably in the attic. We used to ride out in Wilmette every weekend."

Even the "we" was a strange fact, as my father didn't ride; that I knew. I didn't know, though, that he had been a reader of verse. Up in the attic, instead of the riding cup, I found twenty fifth-rate books of poems, and heavily underlined volumes of Keats, Thomas Moore and Byron. By the line "Her yellow hair which gleams like lamps in fog," he'd written "my Annette"; I'd never heard of Annette.

I suppose that this is the most ordinary sort of discovery, a man realising that his parents lived before he knew them, and in ways

24

he hadn't suspected; and there was nothing particularly startling about my discoveries. The startling thing was my own surprise, and that stands for how much was absent from their lives by the time I was conscious of them, how little there was beyond the commanding voice, the sufferance, the exhaust gases of routine.

For years, I regarded my own life as an incendiary repudiation of the cyclic weariness of theirs. Then, in the country, I saw that my own had been nearly as mechanical and repetitive.

Yet there is in me a streak which I have never been able to relate to this pragmatic spine of my life, something which may derive from the thoughtless devotions of my parents, but which differs a great deal from them.

Since my first years in France, I have been, now and then, enticed over the edge of the natural. I adhere to what there is no rational reason for adhering to. (I use "adhere" instead of "believe" from a mixture of caution and self-distrust.) Even as I say "over the edge of the natural," a countering voice says "There is no edge to the natural. What happens is natural, and nothing is ultimately mysterious or even paradoxical." Yet, not infrequently, despite my "belief" in this, I have found myself letting coincidence seem unnaturally persuasive, have made important decisions on the basis of hunches, of instincts. The attraction of horoscopes, palm reading, Ouija boards, table-rapping, and numerology is only half amusement for me. The attraction may be a backwash of a need for assurance, and a consequence of the laziness—or is it stupidity?—which has prevented my carrying any investigation or study to some sort of conclusive depth. For though I'm confident that the investigation of molluscs or impressionist painting or sub-atomic particles leads to no overwhelming certainties, such investigations do occupy a man's mind, engage it in relations, detail and formulations which satisfy that energy which spins at the threshold of life, threatening to enter and consume it. With certain adventurer types, like Arastignac, whose beings are stretched only by activity and danger, a halt in such activity strangles them with fear, and they leap like panicked fish out of the nets of their discipline into the choking atmosphere of the mystic. Though I can analyse the tendency dispassionately, nonetheless, I have faced Arastignac over dinner tables and happily spelunked with him in those whirling, sulphurous caverns.

Back in the last years of our marriage, Hélène and I tried one brand of airy flight after another, almost always confused about how much of what we were doing was for our "amusement." Steinerism was the first. Someone had given us a copy of *The Philosophy of Spiritual Activity* as a joke after we'd led a drunken table-rapping session at a party. We only skimmed it, but its odd notions calmed us, second sight and the rest. With our heads rocketing like the Metro, even Steiner's injuctions about wine had certain force. We could see that wine dimmed second sight—it didn't do too well by first—and so for two anthroposophical months, we went on the wagon. At Christmas time, we stopped at Basel to hear the man speak at the auditorium he'd had constructed out of the seven types of wood used in making violins. A well-groomed crowd sat on wooden benches while Steiner, a cross between Savonarola and Nehru, rattled off a German speech which we took on faith till a regal Irishwoman whispered a rapid-fire version of it in our ears. It didn't hold up too well in that enthusiastic brogue, and that cleared the clouds for us. Then, back in Paris, we read a piece of Keyserling's and were off again, questioning our opinions, diets and burdensome egos. But Keyserling was too earth-shaking, and suckers of our sort need the most personal sort of care. That didn't come again till Gurdjieff. Or it may have been after Hélène's death that I took up Gurdjieff, learned some of the exercises and did them—shall I say religiously?—for months until discovered by Bobbie one day working myself out of my own half-nelson in a sweat of self-consciousness. Later, there were other excursions, for all of which I had the affection one might have for beautiful but illegitimate and unacknowledged daughters.

As for churches, I have had little to do with them since the Danbury Park Presbyterian Church of my boyhood, except be married in one. Yet something itches when I go near churches. My old absolutist nerve ends tingle, and the heady warmth of 'belief' clouds around me, even as I tell myself that the need for belief is a human weakness like vanity or the inability to hear high frequencies.

This is what happened when I went down to see the Abbé Trentemille at the monastery in Vauven where his publisher had forwarded my letter, and where he had requested me to come. Never did I have stronger moorings in the world than on my return from Biarritz, as I moved around the country in my son's behalf. I was getting genuinely curious about this odd network which had apparently not caught Germans but only the baby-faced spiders who had spun it themselves. Never was I less disposed to count what I couldn't put my hands and eyes on, yet there, with the abbey walls looking like a thickened extension of the evening fog, transient solidifications of nothing, I felt my moorings shift and my head go on a dizzy expedition after some absolutist wisp.

In sunlight, as I saw it the next morning, it looked less weird; the gray stretch had become a garden of mullions shading traceries of bays and screenwork. In bed, a whiff of sun had opened my eyes to the green fire of the French cypress, a cluster of whose leaves was actually leaning through the open window into my room. "Friends," I said, "good morning to you." This nosy beauty brightened my whole trip. Ten hours ago, just before the Compline service, I had spoken with Trentemille on the phone. His shrill, unwelcoming harshness had sent me to bed thinking, "This priest hates me. I'm the tree which bore the poisoned fruit. I'll get nothing from him." I had an uneasy sleep, filled with dreams of the fog which swirled over the Saône Valley. Now, the flaming green of the winter cypress had leaned in with morning sun to signal the beauties of arboreal transmission. "Come on," I said to it, dressed, shaved, a preventive aspirin in my mouth, "let's have breakfast."

It would have enjoyed it. This two-by-four hotel offered a cheese omelette the like of which I hadn't eaten since 1940. Surprise augmented pleasure, and I could hardly stop wolfing down the quilted gold. The *patronne*, large, bright, and shiny as the cypress, came out of the kitchen to watch me. I was the hotel's only guest. "Monsieur must have left his wife in the Nunnery," she said. There was one a kilometer down the river. "He eats as if he's setting off on a crusade to the North Pole."

"The North Pole would become a popular place to crusade if Madame would open a restaurant there." Which brought a marvellous grin from this splendid woman. I could have settled in with her then and there.

I was to see Trentemille at ten, which meant that I had an hour to walk off the intake. I went down along the river road, my overcoat buttoned up more against the calendar time than the firm, sunedged cold. Half a mile down the road at the juncture of two dirt lanes, a ten-foot crucifix dangled a green Christ in grainy stupor. All over European countrysides, you come upon such monuments to redemptive misery. They're so familiar to me that I haven't noticed them for years, but this one held me. I stared up at the green submission and found myself wondering whether Bobbie had been a believer, and wondering why I had no notion of an answer. Hélène was nominally Catholic, but in the old French way, which, to my mind, is Protestant in attitude, if not in sacramental observance. Now and then, she took Bobbie to mass with her, and then, until he was eleven, he went to a school run by nuns. But I don't know whether he went to mass or church later on, and I found myself in front of that green weight wishing that he had, that at least he had some sort of certainty in those last years, either something official or something as special as my own traffic with the absolute.

Not an intense wish this, for I was too full of omelette and sun, and I suppose my unformed heart was just paying a quick tribute to the day; but it was a part of me as I went to Trentemille.

At the Abbey, I got shown by an ancient Père Portier into a small cloister, more Spanish than French. The ribbed arches were laced with blood red vines, and I sat on a stone bench next to a basin in which a two-foot-high St. Christopher bore a six-inch child over the waters. The water sounds were something like "drp, drp, drp, drp," and they seemed sonorously fulsome till I saw the priest.

"Jo-Jo" had been his underground name, but no clown this clump of power. Famous for strength, he had turned over automobiles by hand, kicked down oak doors, heaved two-hundred-pound men into gutters. When he strode out of the cloisters, I felt myself shrink to rabbit size. My heart walloped its sides, and I thought, "This man could crush me like a mustard seed, as he crushed Bobbie, without pausing for breath or thought." And then it came to me that he had sent me the book, turned down the page, wrapped it, mailed it, and probably cursed its route. His head, a basketball, like Balzac's without the mustache, nodded twice, four feet from mine, but did not crease for any welcoming smile. His voice was raw, not harsh. He apologised for not seeing me the night before. Compline was the most difficult time in monasteries, and he had to muster his strength to meet the dangers of the night. Poor dangers, thought I. "Your letter tells me what you feel. I understand. I didn't write to wound you. I don't live by drawing blood, but my own blood was risked in a way that tested everyone and spared no one. No one," and he sat down, the great round head like an immense period to the assertion. "God Himself cannot alter what's been. And *what's been* is the author of my book, and it has brought me here." An arm like a log swung up toward the gray walls yawning over the cloister. He was quite a priest. Then, "Children's sins aren't visited upon fathers. You are not responsible for your son's actions in scripture or in law."

"I understand that, *mon père*, but I need another understanding from you." I told him that I knew in my heart of hearts, deep inside, with the knowledge not only of Bobbie, but of the family whose last member he was, that he could not, simply and absolutely could not have betrayed anyone in this world. Yes, maybe something had happened, some misunderstanding which would account for his interpretation of whatever facts he had. I knew that he did not begin with malicious bias.

He put two fingers, two fillets of beef, against my wrist and said, "Two members of the Chaleur Network deposed at length about the events. They implicated your son. He sold out to *Sturmbannführer* Teichmann of the *Sicherheitsdienst* and was seen with him at the Avenue Foch headquarters by these two men—"

"What are their names?"

"Rampigli and Debrette. I have no hesitation in telling you. Their testimony is in the public record. Rampigli is a barber who's lived in France twenty y—"

"What did they say?"

"At Avenue Foch, your son, in the anteroom of the *Sturmbann-führer's* office, told them to reveal to the Germans the location of the arms caches under their protection. He claimed that the Germans already knew every agent in the network and controlled the codes, the radio codes and the mail codes. And he was right, Monsieur Curry, because he had revealed those codes and names to them."

"No," I said. "You are wrong, Father."

"Not 'no,'" he said. "Yes," and his fingers curled in a monstrous fist about as priestly as a Sten gun. The fist cracked into his left palm and the cloisters whipped the sound into a terrible echo around our heads. His head lowered; it looked as if air had leaked from it. He sat back, his little mud eyes sloshing back and forth in a reddening face. "Forgive me," he said, far down in his throat.

Over the "drp, drp, drp" of the splashing water, I said, "Rampigli and Debrette had reasons for saying that, special reasons."

"What were they?" Almost a whisper.

"I don't know," I said. "But I'll learn. I only know that my son was no Judas."

Assurance came as much with my words as before them. The assertions were a way of provoking information from the priest. They sprang from a role as classic as his, the parent protecting his child, an unassailable role, and I became it. I "believed" what I said, though it was an *ad hoc* belief; it worked in and for the occasion. "Why would he have volunteered for such a mission in the first place, if he was a man who could do what you claimed he did?"

"I respect the courage of his volunteering."

"Then how can you—"

But he snapped the back of this, maybe to remind me that he could indeed say what he said because he'd had his great fingers smashed by clubs, his nose punched to splinters. "The bravest yielded if their bravery was an adventurer's bravery, if it didn't spring from love of the good. Body cowards, and I am one of them,"—the words quivered amazingly from that terrific head—"can be the greatest heroes, unyielding even as their flesh whimpers and begs. Without love, without spiritual love, bravery was naked before force, and broke before it. I wish to high heaven that your son had not broken, Mr. Curry, but I am positive that he did, and neither man nor God can alter his having done so."

It shook me. A surface can reflect a depth, and a weak man understands strength because he feels its effects so quickly. Yet from the time I watched Bobbie's head on the sheets and remembered my own boyhood nights under blankets, hiding from thieves and hawks afoot in the room, I knew his bravery. But what did I know of his commitment? Less than of his attendance at mass.

I wasn't finished. Perhaps I had taken in some of Trentemille's power. "I don't want to alter the past, *mon père*. I want to discover it. I've read your book carefully"—and I looked to see if this dented the ball; it didn't—"and I do not reach the conclusions you do on the evidence you present there or here. I have nothing to add, no new evidence, but you have taken a step that no court of which I have experience would justify."

"All right," he said. "Find out something more. Deduce to your own taste. I weighed what I heard, and with a knowledge trained by a world you know only remotely. You find something else. I claim no absoluteness. But you've got to find something to change me. If that's what you want to do."

He got up. I touched his sleeve to hold him for a moment, but drew back as I would have from a grinding motor, such power exhaled from that priestly arm. Still, I managed to sound stronger than I felt. "I didn't come to change you. Only to tell you what I'm going to do. But also to ask your help, ask you to help me get in touch with those who know about the network."

"Drp, drp, drp, drp," slurped the water out of a stone oriole's mouth over St. Christoper's boots. Trentemille looked at the statue and gargled a great laugh. "If Christopher supports the Universe on his back, where does he get his footing? So you need me. All right.

Come on," and he walked out of the garden into the corridor, and I followed him, this chugging tank, past refectories, small chapels, monks, and brothers to a row of cubicles, the last of which we stepped into, his own closet which you'd think could not hold him. He flopped to the floor on his great belly, and I thought, "My God, he's had a fit," but no, he was stretching for something under the canvas cot, for a burlap bag which he dragged out and from which he took a small, blue leather address book with the gold-letter inscription *Geburtstagsbuch.*

"I don't know German," I said.

"There are only addresses here. The words mean birthday book, saint's day book, but the names here are secular saints. I took the book from a German soldier in the Givry wood. You'll want Rampigli. He's gone back to barbering Parisians. I hope he remembers he's paid to razor the outside only. Ha, ha, ha." He was some man of the cloth.

I nearly said the barber seemed to have done a throat-cutting job on my son; perhaps restraint earned me what might not otherwise have come. "He may not know that your son once saved his life. I didn't tell him, because by that time your son had tried to give the life away." The noose hung in the air, stretched for my neck. I said nothing. "Gruyère was ordered by London to give Rampigli a cyanide pill. London distrusted him. After all, he was only an Italian barber; naturally, Anglo-Saxon gentlemen concluded he was a double agent. Your son, however, didn't give him the pill. Whether from cowardice or guilt I don't know. You'd think murder would be an easy transition from treachery." The noose swung for me. I kept still. I am a manager. I will not throw my skin after the banality of insult. I was on top now. He took my disengagement for strength. Maybe it was. He stood by the glassy circlet of window and yielded. "Anglo-Saxon insularity. It saves you. But I don't know. Could I have administered a pill myself? I never had to kill a man. Can you think what it is for me here"—and he opened his hands to the walls he grazed with them—"not to know whether in the interests of the universe I could have killed a man? Not to know even now when I'm finished with it." His hand broke two wands of sun coming through the barred glass. Then it dove for mine, picked it up in an iron palm, and slapped it with the blue leather. "Now it's yours. I'm absolutely finished with it." And then in a voice depleted, filtered, "Forgive me, Mr. Curry, for burdening you. With myself." Attenuated by reflection, he hunched over. His fingertips made an arch before his face—was he praying?—and I, my moorings slipped, visualised him in a flash, nailed, hanging, penitent, redemptive, Jo-Jo, the hangman god, hanged, and brought low. I touched his stilled arm for goodby and got away.

CHAPTER 4

Bobbie spent the summer between graduating from Winchester and matriculating at Oxford in Paris. I gave him a small allowance, but his needs exceeded it, and he worked for six weeks at the plant, clerking in the accounts office and doing special errands for Armand, who, in his chilly way, was beginning to see him as his successor. Bobbie quit in September when his Winchester roommate, a fellow with a name that had something to do with a car part, came over. Manifold or Gear. I'll call him Gear. Gear bought a twenty-year-old Peugeot, and he and Bobbie tooled around town picking up American girls and entertaining them back at our apartment. (I was seldom there.) The entertainment was, at least for legal purposes, innocent, but the night before Gear was to go back to England, they picked up a couple of rampant girls from Smith College, cavorted with less innocence and more than usual noise, and then lit out in the Peugeot for the Bois de Boulogne, Bobbie driving. Where the Rue Pergolese crosses Avenue Foch—how bland a name that was then—they skidded around a pedestrian into a Citroën parked at the curb. The driver was inside, sleeping off a drunk. He sobered rapidly, called the police, and the four celebrants were hauled off to the police magistrate, before whom they swore up and down it had been an accident. Neither car was insured, and the Citroën was pretty banged up. I was at Deauville for the weekend. The magistrate called me, and I took the train back to Paris. Armand had bailed the youngsters out, and there wasn't much to do. Bobbie had a driver's license, and he'd been let off with a reprimand. I was most relieved and promised the magistrate that I'd give both boys a serious talking to. I never did get to Gear, for he left before I got up in the morning, but Bobbie waited in his room till I called him from the breakfast table.

"You're quite a man-about-town," I began.

He hung his head. He didn't look the sort of person to whom states should be handing out driver's licenses.

"Eighteen years of age, and you're a practised fornicator, drunkard, reckless driver, and potential murderer. That's no mean list of accomplishments."

He kept his head away, but his voice was controlled. "I'm ashamed, Papa."

"Shame is inexpensive."

"I'd like to pay more."

"That's novel," I said. "What do you suggest?"

"I'd like to pay the guy's damages."

That set me back a little. I'd talked to the victim, and he was a mighty unsavory specimen, a drunkard whom I wouldn't have put past planting himself in front of cars as a source of steady income. "The sentiment's decent, Bobbie, but it is sentiment. I don't think you face problems squarely by sentimentalising them."

"The fellow did get banged up, and it wasn't his fault. He was parked legally enough."

"He was drunk," I said.

"But not driving."

Bobbie had a very exasperating manner. It wasn't stubborn in anything but words. He seemed to apologise even as he contradicted. It had never failed to infuriate me. "Bobbie, I think you're trying to buy off your conscience. With my money."

"I've still got most of my plant money."

"Which means that I'll have to give you money at school to replace that."

"I thought you wanted me to bank whatever I earned."

This was what I had said. "Bobbie, if the incident teaches you that there must be no repetition of it, then it will have served its purpose. The other man is as guilty as you, but he's a man and can't expect to get out of things by deriving lessons in improvement from them. He'll have to pay for real."

"O.K., Papa," said Bobbie, and without looking at me, he left the room.

I've never liked what I did then. I had stood by Bobbie, but I do not like the way I stood by him. I don't mean that sweetness and light are the core of a father's instructions to his son. A father has to initiate his son into the world, but I am not satisfied. The incident was just the sort for which Trentemille would have indicted me, and coming back on the train with my hand around the blue *Geburtstagsbuch*, it seemed a tiny court of judgement, a weight on me. When I got home, I put it in Bobbie's desk along with notes on my talk with Trentemille.

At the back of the desk was an envelope I hadn't seen. In it were some newspaper pictures of American cities which must have been one of Bobbie's school projects. Then there were two school note-books, drafts of thank-you letters in French and English, and then something I remembered—a little English story which he wrote at the age of seven about a clown who worked in "a curious" but who one day "dinnt do his doteys." Instead of being funny, he was "serous" and the man who owned the "curious fiered him."

Why dinnt you be funny? asked the man. The clown said I thought you told the pepple what was to come next so I deceided to not do what I was told to do becuase then it would be more funny. So they told the clown the real way to be in a curious and he was a good clown then.

I put the story back under the *Geburtstagbuch*, and thought as I hadn't really thought before about what I'd lost, and how I'd lost it while I had it. And I hadn't anything to show but these lines scrawled up and down and over the ruled lines of the French exercise book. Then I thought, what would my father have found in my drawers, rummaging for memorials, if I had died in 1918. I'd written no lecture notes on the prediction of fingers and toes, didn't even underline books, hadn't won any cups, and never produced anything on the order of Bobbie's "curious" story, which already talked of duty in a way I wouldn't have been capable of as I mustered a company off the *Admiral Dewey* in 1918. Maybe my father could have dredged from a Tuley High School science notebook some of the limericks which Rattler Gordon and I passed back and forth throughout our school career, such as the one my memory will supply me with till my death.

ON MISS LIDDELL

There's a piece of French twot named Liddell,
Who says "Eh, bien" for "Well, well."
If you pinched her behind
She would prob'ly remind
You that *fesse*-pinchers go straight to hell.

A handsome legacy.

2

The fillet which twines the barber's pole stands for the arm bandage with which these ex-surgeons bound up those they bled, the ball on top, for the basin which caught the blood. Bloody symbols for this ancient profession. and ones which, it seemed to me, had burst from their modern swaddlings of decoration and pleasure to flag Rampigli's murderous drive.

A social man who lives alone gets close to those whose services he buys. He anticipates a visit to his tailor, regards the grocer, the local gendarmes, and his barber as beings with histories and futures, not as social landscape. I'm naturally well-disposed toward barbers, as toward elevator operators, so tame in their rocketing cages, actresses, dancers, florists, dental technicians. These are unofficial civil servants, filling in the cracks of the state. Barbers have another measure of my esteem: they represent one of the few professions which hasn't been engineered out of its classic lines. A barber spends fifteen or twenty minutes cutting another man's hair as his counterpart did a thousand years ago; he uses more or less the same implements, and probably enjoys the same relationship, a combination of intimacy, prideful courtesy and patronage. The barber holds his dangerous implements next to your head because you permit him to; you trust him to do the ancient job. And the pleasure of this honorable work: the hot towel on the face, the gorgeous aromas of hair tonic and lather, the ease of semi-recumbence, your head in ministering, knowledgeable hands.

But the barber Rampigli had subverted his peaceful profession, as he perhaps had subverted the network. London had suspected him and there may well have been something to the suspicion. Bobbie had saved him, and after Bobbie's death, perhaps he used Bobbie to save him again, accused him to cover his own bloody spoor.

I got my first look at him through the window of his shop on Rue Legendre, walking distance from my own apartment. He was bent over a little boy's head, studying and snipping. The first thing you saw in that face was a nose like a bomb, an avocado bomb, the fat end ballooning over large, fig lips. He was small, and looked unkempt, till later on, up close, it was clear that this black mop must have been daily tyrannised by clippers to achieve that sculptured raffishness.

I went down the street to a brasserie until I saw the boy leave. When he did, I walked back. Rampigli was nose-deep in *Combat*, but at the turn of the door handle, he was up, as if there'd never been a paper, all sparks, teeth, eye points, gleaming cheeks. "*Bon jour, monsieur, bon jour, bon jour, entrez, je vous en prie,*" in an accent that would have alerted even Miss Liddell to its deficiencies and which must have imperilled his underground existence; unless it had been protected by the Germans. The barber's sheet was flourished in a showman's *paseo*, and I, the bull, was pointed to the chair.

I raised a hand. "Monsieur, I am here on other business."

"Ah so," he said, undimmed, peculiarly incurious. He waggled a finger at my scalp. "Couldn't we combine it, your business and mine?" And then, before I could say "No," he'd stepped over, removed my hat and peered at my head, the avocado grazing me en route. "Yes, a few kisses from the shears would not be out of order." A sideshow con man, but what did I do but sit down and take it. I did need a trim.

The sheet arched and embraced me, the shears were at my head. "So, my friend," said the barber, *"en brosse?"*

"Fine," said I.

"En brosse is a necessity for the box-head. It relieves rectangularity. Or pompadour. For the round head, one arrows, triangles, frames. For bumps, one shapes inch by inch. That's work. Sweat. But not musculature. Here," he tapped a temple, "the barber composes. There is a general form: sonata, box-head; symphony, roundhead; opera, bumps. Note-by-note is cut-by-cut. My friend, you have not been composed; you have been butchered, assassinated. A pig-slicer."

"That is your view. I have no complaints." My barber was a fine old man, a great reader of Zola.

"Naturally, you have no complaints. You only face yourself twice a day over a toothbrush. It's we who study you who see the damage. Basically you've a decent, well set up head. You're graying very well. Of nature, you have no complaints to make." And so on, all the time rocking and crouching, and then lunging at this nature's delight of a head with the bright steel. I had a vision of the sword in his hand plunging toward my neck.

Then, somewhere in mid-trim, he said, "Now, what is your other business?"

"It had better wait."

"It's your tongue." He put a shaving brush under hot water, churned it in a soap mug, and began creaming my face with the crud.

"You're shaving me as well?"

"Necessarily." And my face was buried in the gunk, thicker than the mud from my garden. Yet it must have seemed protective to me, for against what I'd thought was my intention to wait until the shears were out of his hand, I said, "I am Gruyère's father."

I hardly heard the mug crash on the floor. Pounce, he was on me, the avocado smashing through the crud, the great fig lips on mine. The mad wop was kissing me, all over my face, his arms holding me in the chair. "Oh, oh, oh, oh, oh, oh, oh," came out of him. "Poor fellow. Poor old fellow."

I broke his hold and pushed him off. Shaving cream was in my collar, my nostrils. I wiped it off with the sheet while Rampigli looked on, tears in his eyes. "Poor old boy," and he went for me again.

"Stop," I said. "Hold off."

"Unbelievable," he said, subsiding. "Amazing." He slapped a towel against my face. Water sloshed in my underwear. "*Le père de Gruyère.*" It sounded like a Massenet aria. Then the towel was snatched off, and once again I had the repulsive honor of his lips on mine.

Judas kissing Jesus, no, a cow licking the stockyards slaughterer as the axe whines in the air. Some men could not complete the stroke at such a moment; I am one of them. And while I tried to adjust, I heard my intended victim shotgunning the tongues of Molière and Dante. "*Quella eroe. Un héros della mia cuore. Tel dont je tiens per tuttavia una affezione immense.*" Babble, babble, babble.

I got out of the chair. "Listen," I said. "Listen to me, my boy. I want to talk to you. Listen."

The sawed-off barrels roared again. I held off, till, in thirty seconds, it was over.

"You remember Père Trentemille? Jo-Jo? What he says of my son, of Gruyère? He says that you accused Gruyère of betraying the network to the *Sicherheitsdienst.*"

Aloft in the steamy air, the great nose zeppelined back and forth. And then, from the polylingual factory, thunder. "No, no, no, no. Not Gruyère. Gruyère was my heart, my blood. He knew it was all up. The *Messieurs Verts* knew everything. They told him what they knew, showed him letters. He did what was best." He tossed up the sheet, let it fall over his head, then drew it off, the head tilted skywards, and then, as if an operation had been performed under the sheet, the clot dissolved in his throat, and he poured out what I more or less transcribe here.

3

What was wrong, said Rampigli, was that agents were being dropped into the territory and getting picked up by the Germans within days of coming in. Somebody was in on something. We didn't really know this till a month or so before the end. Chaleur made a trip to England in the summer of forty-three and he came back knowing it was all over. It may have been London itself which had something wrong. Very, very close to the source something was happening. But

37

you see, it's a strange business. Someone might have known that the Germans were tapping a leak, so he begins supplying them with information, half-real, half-phony, thinking that the harm of the phony is worse to them than the good of the real. It's a professional problem. I have it right here with bald men: do you disguise with stretched hair from the sides, or do you go all out and trim frankly? It depends, if it's distinction that's wanted, or youth, or boldness, or whatever. Once I was down in Puy-Laurennes, it was a question of getting a little boom-boom to put out a train we knew about. There was a cache down there, not a million miles from where we would do the work, and Pol—my courier, a high school boy—and I were the only ones who knew where it was. So we thought. It's in a meadow behind an orchard on the farm of an inactive but friendly man. Good, and I am digging it out one night when—and there was no sound in the world, I swear, but grasshoppers and, you know, night noises—a light is on me. I spin over, go for my gun, when—and what luck for her—a girl says, "I wondered what's been going on around here." She'd spotted me the other time I'd been down and had nothing better to do than watch for me every night. No moon, and I could not make her out. "Get that light off," I said, "and quick." If she'd taken an extra second, I'd have shot her. You can not quite guess what a shock it was, even in that work, to find the night turned inside out so you're at the wrong end of a torch. My heart was rocking like a grasshopper's legs. "This is nothing to do with you," I said, "but if you want to be a good patriot, get down here on your ass and help me." Down she came, and really on her ass, her legs up in the air, and I did finally see her—a pretty good-sized cow she was. So I made for it, right there in the meadow. What a tug, I tell you, on the heart. From month to month, I lived like St. Francis, and my God, I had a job of driving twenty kilometers to the train, mounting the stuff on the tracks, laying the fuse, and hiding over the hill praying the train would beat the sun there; and here I was looking down at this nice cow of a girl when I hadn't seen such a sight for weeks. And who knew? She could have been a Gestapo trap; she didn't know exactly what I'd been doing, but she'd been sent maybe to find out. I'd be a thread to tear out the whole group. For a moment I thought, "I'll lay her right here in two minutes, then shoot her in the head," but it was too much. It took a few extra minutes—I'm no brute—and then I tied her dress in her teeth and roped her to a tree. I kissed her goodby, loosened the rope, and told her she could get free in an hour if she worked, I couldn't take any chances. And

38

what happened? Ha, ha, ha, ha. A maniac came by on a horse twenty minutes before the train time, the horse kicked the stuff against the tracks, and they blew themselves out of the universe. I got some brain in my eye. But I was telling you what problems we had in the network. You never knew where you stood nor where anyone else did. Gruyère I never doubted. Chaleur also. But somebody who knew where most of us hung out was in on it, or else the Germans had a remarkable control of our radios, remarkable because it's not easy to untangle fifty-five different codes the way we scrambled them. As for the end of it, that's something I'd like to know too. From where I stood, nothing much different seemed to be happening. Naturally, the whole Resistance was bigger then. You seldom lacked help; in fact, now and then you'd be crossing up some fellow who'd turn out to be a maquis from another cell. I'm sure not a few people lost their heads that way. Mostly you learned in time—you could smell the right ones—and then what a grasshopper in the heart. At the end though, here's what was happening: we were asked to knock out a little steel plant, and to knock it out to make it seem that bombers had done it as part of a raid. We worked with the air people all the time that way. Fine, but we needed help from someone who knew steel plants, who knew where to stick the boom-boom just right, and so on. The patron was more or less with us, but he was a tight fellow, we did not trust him, though we had something close on him; so London let us know someone was going to come from Holland, some Dutchman who'd been working up there for years but who knew French well enough to get by at least for a time. Like me. He was to make contacts, and I was to bring him to Chaleur and Gruyère. He was to walk past the Café Orléannais every hour from eleven on and clean his ear as he passed the end table. Fine. When I spotted the ear-cleaning, I was to put the paper to my chin and go toward Metro Valmy, where we would go right on to the cache which was in Meudon-Val-Fleury. This so the Dutchman could see what we had. What happens? I'm sitting there at eleven when the Dutchman goes by one way and Gruyère the other. "Could I have made a mistake?" I ask myself. Impossible. But there's Gruyère coming along when nobody tells me he's supposed to be there, and I'm so surprised I don't put the paper to my chin. Everyone goes by and we have to wait until twelve. I don't wait long though, because a man comes out of the restaurant and takes me by the arm, and the next thing I know, I'm in Avenue Foch, and this fellow is telling me all the names of everybody in the group, including those I know, and asking me where the caches are, and pretty soon Gruyère and the Dutchman are brought in, and Gruyère tells me that the Germans are in on everything—which is clear to me by now—and that we'd better give up the location of the caches for which we were responsible, because Teichmann, the German commander there, had agreed to trade lives for the caches, which were no good to anyone any more anyway. I asked Gruyère why he was at the rendezvous, and he said Pol told him to be there. That was that. I never saw him again. I told where my caches were, and the next day I was in a truck for Germany, where I vacationed for nineteen months, four days, and sixteen hours.

4

This was the sum of what he had told Trentemille. I could hardly credit it at first. "Is that all?" I asked him. "Is that all you told him?"

"Why not? Of course. The facts didn't change. Why should I change what I say about them?"

"If Debrette said no more than that, the priest is more slanderous than seems possible."

"Ah, Debrette," said Rampigli, and there was no gleam in his head now. "A pig in slime. Anything, that one could have said. I have some inklings how he lied about me. Sick, up here," and he tapped the same temple which had figured in his own high accomplishments. "And how I could have nailed him to the wall. No, I've told you just what I told the TMP."

"What's that?"

"The *Tribunal Militaire Permanent de Paris*. It conducted hearings. All of us who lived spoke before them, and a few like Debrette got sent up for a while. They gave him a tough time. You can find the whole story there. You could get hold of August through the records."

I repeated this. "Ow-goost?" It sounded like a Norwegian demon.

"Teichmann's interrogator, an Austrian. August Mettenleiter. A decent fellow. He had a going-over from them. He'd lived in France most of his life, worked in hotels on the Riviera. He may be back there. You can get Debrette's address in the records too. We haven't been exchanging billets-doux, so I can't give it to you."

"I have his address, but I'll look for August. Thank you, Monsieur Rampigli. I feel you've knocked the props out from the accusation. You've been a great help to me."

Rampigli shook his head. "Monsieur Gruyère," he said. "I wouldn't look forward too much to anything. It's the only way to live and smile. I live on my feelings, but I have to hold them down too." He picked up a brush and slowly took the dust from my topcoat, then helped me into it. "Come back here when you need a haircut. I treat you for nothing. That's how I feel for your son. But listen, old friend, though what one knows through the feelings is more true than what one knows through any other way, some times, some places, there are contradictions."

CHAPTER 5

Contradictions. Things can't both be and not be. A much older staple of life than barbering. I left Rampigli's shop more altered than my scalp revealed. Three views of Bobbie's world had offered themselves with the warning to stay out or I would find something worse than what had started my looking.

Well, I did stay out for a while. Though not willingly, for I intended to write Debrette right after I left Rampigli. But I decided I'd first get a surer grip on the whole situation by reading the reports of the Military Tribunal of Paris. I telephoned Felix Sensmesnil, Georges' younger brother, who was a *sous ministre* in the Department of Bridges and Roads, and he got permission for me to look at the records down at the Palais de Justice. I spent four days on the medieval benches in the Reading Room and developed the spinal cyst which laid me up for weeks and then brought me back to America for an operation.

Why America? It's because I've never really felt at ease with French doctors, not even with our good family doctor, Robichaud, now dead and succeeded by his cold fish of a son, Robichaud *fils*. This is another irrationality: French doctors are every bit as good and bad as the American crop, yielding the same ratio of medicine men and scientists, but my discomfort is a form of regression, a childish need for the antiseptic hocus-pocus of my cleanliness-is-godliness roots. Except for the war, I've had my check-ups back home in Chicago and used the Doctors Robichaud only in emergencies. So I went back to Chicago and had the cyst removed by a fine young surgeon, Dr. Cherkushnevski, who looked a little like Bobbie, though somewhat more open and easy in manner. After he'd first looked at the cyst, he'd said, "This thing is older than you are."

An extraordinary remark, which, though it meant little more than that I had a congenital condition which gave rise to the cyst, struck me as a flashing sign of the way in which Bobbie's life was bound to mine. In this way: if, say, Bobbie had stumbled into what I knew was an un-Bobbien action, might it not be an action that was older than he himself, one that was mine? Was there not in my life a streak of treason, one which appeared under the private forms of betraying my wife and romping over Bobbie? Official treason, like disease, is but the hot version of the war whose hostilities existed for years without official recognition. It's only then that the cyst is cut out of the family tree, the traitor shot, the heir of the criminal line imprisoned. Could Bobbie's public "treason," if it turned out that there was actual treason, be the spilling out into his life of the evasions which characterised mine, coupled with the extra-legal violence of my grandfather's, just as my evasions may be the spawn of my father's insularity and that violence?

That South which my father charted on the lined paper sheets with which he spent his evenings, the South of his blood line, was a cauldron which could have held Bobbie's world without boiling over a drop. My grandfather had been ambushed by a "Northerner" from the neighboring Tennessee county on his way back from the Battle of Lookout Mountain; he literally crawled back to his father's farm and recovered. After the war, he tracked the man down, found him standing on a ladder in his feed store and answered his " 'lo Sam'l" by shooting him dead on the spot. There was no trial. He walked home and raised his family of four classically named sons, the oldest of whom, Ausonius, was shot to death twenty-five years later by the son of the man whom he'd killed. These were but two of the bloody stories which my Great-aunt Zilpah told my mother, father and me when we drove our air-cooled Franklin with the life-saver tires down the silvery trail of our bloodstream into the hills of East Tennessee.

The fatal clump of protein which drove the fiat of destruction through the lucky chromosomes of my father and myself into the gas chambers of Auschwitz had had no Aunt Zilpah to warn and avert; Bobbie had been uninstructed in violence. Perhaps nothing would have helped. In the Michael Reese Pavillion, I'd read a book of Darwin's letters, including one which speculated that the principle of life was but a specific form of some more general principle.

Dr. Cherkushnevski's remark was a modest customer beside this one. Where did that locate the violence and treason of Bobbie Curry? Drift of blood was lost in drift of stars: Bobbie's treason was but an aspect of the warp of space. Adam's sin. But then, there is no end, all is equal, and neither act nor punishment matters. One must take a stand. Lying in bed, looking over the throbbing lake while the innocent auxiliary tissues breached the hole in my backside, I took my stand, freed myself of Dr. Cherkushnevski's remark and readied myself for the return trip.

2

The week of my return to Paris, I wrote Debrette to say that I was the father of the Chaleur agent Gruyère and wanted to come to Caen to see him about what happened to my son and to the network. Two days later, I received the following telegram:

> YOUR SON TOOK EVERYTHING ELSE FROM ME. HE MIGHT
> AS WELL TAKE UP MY TIME THROUGH YOU. EXPECT YOU
> THURSDAY ON THE SIX P.M. EXPRESS FROM PARIS.
>   JULES-HENRI DEBRETTE

It was what I should have expected, but it shook me nonetheless. Even professional fighters cannot habituate anxiety out of their careers; nothing could prepare me to put down the trembling which crude specimens like this put in my blood. I was glad I had a piece of him by telegram before I encountered him in person.

He'd had quite a time, this fellow, at least as I saw it in the records at the Palais de Justice. He was one of the victims of André Maginot's steel pipe dreams; his chest sheltered a piece of shrapnel which that fluent cripple—whom I used to see boozily lording it in Maxim's Bar—claimed would never pass his Line. After six months in a hospital, he fell in with one of the earliest resistance groups which, in 1941, made contact with the London agent "Peugeot," a professional thief who proved to be an outstandingly brave agent especially proficient at arranging the moonlight drops of arms and agents. It was due to a mix-up in one of the drops that a rivalry began between him and Debrette, and then between Debrette, Rampigli and Bobbie: an agent due to drop one night and be met by Peugeot, was, due to fog, dropped the next and met by Debrette. Two days later, the agent was picked up by the Abwehr boarding the train to Paris. It seemed that the man had hit his knee getting on the train and had cried out in English, but at the time, Peugeot suspected

Debrette of turning the man in and sent Rampigli, his radio operator, to London for instructions about the matter. Rampigli returned with a cyanide pill which Peugeot was ordered to administer to Debrette. Peugeot couldn't bring himself to do it and requested Bobbie to do it for him. Bobbie, however, did not distrust Debrette, and suggested a compromise, namely, that Rampigli should take over Debrette's Air Operation duties and Debrette be given innocuous ones and observed carefully. He thereby both saved Debrette's life—the origin of the twisted story Trentemille gave me about his saving Rampigli's—and earned his hatred for ordering him off Air Operations. When Peugeot contracted pneumonia after a night out in the snow, Bobbie asked London for a new Air Operations man, one who had more experience with planes than Rampigli and could better estimate landing distances. (This turned out to be Arastignac, but I didn't know that then.) Debrette's hard times had by no means ended. He was captured with the other Chaleur agents in the round-up of September, 1943, and sent first to Dachau and then to the extermination camp at Treblinka. He survived, and then, two weeks after his release, was seized by the French, charged with "collaboration with the enemy," and sentenced by the Cour de Justice at Lyons to two years' hard labor with "attendant penalties and indignities." It was during these hearings that he first blamed Bobbie for betraying the network, and it was these charges which Trentemille transcribed and which I discovered in the TMP records as I developed my cyst.

Masochism may be as strong a motive in research as curiosity, or even self-interest, of which it is a perverse form. I mean that even before the telegram, I didn't expect to get from Debrette much more than what I got from the records. I expected to be vilified, perhaps even hurt, and I think I went ahead with the trip partially because of the expectation. I was placing myself in a situation whose dangers, for all that the brave might think of them, were, in my world, equivalents of those which Bobbie himself had faced. It may have been that a disposition to bravery could have been transmitted to Bobbie by the brother genes of those that transmitted treason to him. I was, I suppose, trying to rival him. It was not the first time.

The trip began badly. I stood on the line twenty minutes while a mongoloid ticket clerk debated the proper route to Antwerp with a two-hundred-pound Medusa who kept stepping back toward my feet. Once I was too slow, and she came down on my right foot like a trip-hammer. Furious, I shoved her into the counter and prepared to defend my honor with a right hook if she turned, but the two hundred pounds was cream puff, and she beat it without a belligerent word. I, however, was disturbed enough to mispronounce my destination and was sold a ticket to Cannes by the mongoloid. By the time I discovered it, I was on the right train, but had to buy a new ticket, a first-class one at that, as I'd gotten into the wrong compartment. By Caen, I was in a state of black self-pity that readied me for homicide; whether as victim or killer, I hardly cared.

Debrette was waiting at the station but, unlike Towne, who in his white suit and beside the red-and-gold page boy made up a real review troop, Debrette was Admonition Itself in a black suit whose shine signalled a consciousness of itself as a unique specimen. When the other passengers moved out of the way, he came up and shook my hand. Slender and fair, there was a hard weight in his look, a lead whose radium had long departed. He was flushed, partially I think with the embarrassment by which self-conscious good looks underline themselves. "I'm surprised," he said right off, "to find myself shaking hands with Gruyère's father. I do so only as a gentleman."

Ridiculous little insurance clerk byroning before a cracked mirror, he was a gentleman as I'm the Prince of Wales. But the posturing helped me ease the sourness in my insides. "I appreciate your doing so, and your coming to meet me. It's not only gracious, but it makes me feel that you understand my feelings."

He stooped for my overnight bag, took it out of my hand and started walking. "There won't be a bus for fifteen minutes. It's less than half a kilometer to my place."

"Isn't there a hotel near the station? I'm planning to catch the eight-thirty back to Paris."

"I have room," he said, walking again. "And there's lots you may want to hear. Unless you won't stay with me." He stopped and looked at me full in the face.

"That's very decent of you, but I don't want to—"

He was underway. It was dark, and fog was rising in the streets. It was a depressing walk. We passed almost no one. All around were the ashlar piles left by the Allied need to extract this kingpin of the German continental defense. It was as if the materials of a city had been assembled, and then a plague had wiped out the workmen. It was the worst-shelled town I'd seen in France. I walked next to this melancholic through block after block of this dreamy, unfinished world. "What do you do?" I asked him.

"I'm a reconstruction worker."

"You've picked a good place."

"Unless they abandon it," he said. "Five hundred Halifaxes dropped twenty-five hundred tons here four years ago. These old buildings were made out of blocks of stone quarried in the Orne Valley. They hadn't needed reconstruction workers for four hundred years. Unemployment isn't one of my worries." He pointed to a fog-cancelled rise half-condensing in a street light. "That's the site of Guillaume le Bâtard's castle, the one he left to take over your *pays*."

"Not mine," I said. "America wasn't part of England or anything else then."

He stopped, put down the bag and stared at me as if a quick phrenological examination might contradict my claim. "Gruyère was English," he said, puzzled. I suppose if it were wartime, this would have meant the sort of slip which old Towne had spotted in the German agent's story, and Debrette or I would have had a gun at each other's head. "I'm American and so was Bobbie. He was only attached to the British Forces." His mistake meant that he hadn't read Trentemille's book. Which meant furthermore that Trente-mille hadn't sent his book to his informers. Is it that he didn't want his distortions challenged by their ostensible sources? The rubbled dark was no place to work this out, a street like mid-ocean, with a madman at the wheel of my skiff. For dry land, I said that William was important to Americans also, but that we referred to him as the Conqueror, "bastard" being an improper term for us.

Debrette kept looking at my face; I began to feel that some of it had worn off in the fog. Then with a restorative shake of the head, he picked up the bag and moved on. "Puritan influence," he said. "A good one." It was a relief to be in the realm of influence, and I continued in equally enlightening fashion, "Yes, I believe you could ascribe it to that."

Which exhausted the world of intellect. Nonetheless, there was less lead in the air around us. "Are you holding up all right?" It was almost a cradle song. "I live just down to the left, Rue Teinturier. I thought Gruyère a perfect English type." Even this tone was easier.

"There was much that was English about him." Nothing could have been further from Bobbie than the English manner or look. "And I'm coming along fine."

"You know, it was right of you to come here, and right of me to meet you. We've had a lot to do with each other's lives, one way or another." We walked by a church whose backbone had been twisted by some gigantic mylitus. "Église de Saint-Pierre," said Debrette, as if this were the bridge in our lives. "The tower's thirteenth century, the apse one of the masterpieces of Hector Sohier." Was he smiling? I couldn't see or guess. "Sundays, I'm a guide to ruins. A ruined guide to ruins."

"I'm sorry."

"Don't melt away," and with this knightly retort, he turned in to a small brick house which, had we walked by, I would have taken for more rubble. I followed him up a flight of stairs to a room with a small bay taken up by a cot. There was another bed in the room, a couple of chairs, a bureau and a wash basin. An uncovered bulb hung from a cord in the bay. This was the room's light, and a sizable portion of its ornamentation. Yet, after that dark walk, it was like coming into a ballroom.

Debrette took my overcoat, directed me to the WC down the hall, and when I returned, held a towel for me by the basin.

One of the chairs was a lopsided beige armchair, the right armrest wounded and showing dirty cotton stuffing. By the left arm was a bottle of Calvados and a glass. He sat on the cot facing me, holding another glass and a bottle of Vichy water. "My stomach's limit," he said. So the Calvados had been purchased, or, at least, had been opened, for me. I took a swallow, and had a lightning spasm of terror that it was poisoned and that I'd look up into Debrette's triumphant grin, but I didn't look up, and drank again, and again, my insides ironing out with pride in my steadfastness.

"I've thought and thought about all this," he said, "but I haven't said a word since the trial. Perhaps because the only real friends I ever had are back in my town. Rochepot, Route 12 to Lyons. Since the trial, I haven't had the town or the friends. Not that it's so bad here. I make my way. I'm not looking for excitement." He pushed the back of his hand across his mouth. His eyes were down. "I want to tell you that personally, I mean as a man, Gruyère was fine. He was decent and brave. I won't take that back because of what I know of the rest of him; that part I hardly understand. It may be that he was turned round by Rampigli and Peugeot. But a man is what he does, and what Gruyère did was terrible." Under that bulb, this fair Byron looked like a clot of dark, so sombre he was, so dour and soaked in misery. "For somebody who's suffered from what he did, that wipes out everything else. What he did must be remembered as his character."

"It's not how I remember him," I said, mostly to let him hear another voice, a sign to him that his complaint could no longer be an unchecked monologue, that he was now obliged to make statements that would be submitted to more objective tribunals than his own suffering memory.

Yet he seemed sheer lead, unreachable. "I was arrested driving a Canadian agent to the north. He was assigned to rally some scattered groups up there, some Gaullist, some local. Twenty-five kilometers north of Paris, we were stopped at a roadblock and asked to show our papers. The Canadian didn't even speak a decent Canuck French. I should have known what would happen. The Germans ordered us out of the car. I gunned it into the stone wall of the station house and came to three days later in Avenue Foch. The Canadian had been killed. My head felt like they were boiling water there. I could hardly speak. They had an interrogator showing me photostats of the mail Chaleur and Gruyère had sent to London. The interrogator said the whole network was penetrated. All they needed was the location of the arms caches, which, he said, Chaleur had asked us to give up in return for our lives. I asked to see Chaleur, but Gruyère came in instead and repeated what the interrogator had said, almost in the same words, as if he'd been fed the story. He ordered me to give up the caches. Which I did. He was my superior. I didn't question him."

"Why not?" I said. "You had a tongue in your head. You were quick to see he was using words the Germans put in his mouth. Why didn't you ask him? Maybe you'd have learned something that would have kept you from claiming he'd sold out to the Germans."

"There is more to it than that. I didn't think like that then, or I would have kept my caches to myself till they tore them out of my skin. But you're right, Mr. Curry, I could have talked more to Gruyère. I didn't, because by then we were not on the best of terms. We'd had a fight, a bloody fight about some trouble in the Air Operations. You see, there was this thief, I mean literally a thief, Peugeot—"

"I know about that from the records. What about the fight?" I could see this sullen maniac throttling Bobbie in some blast of hatred.

"I was the only one getting agents down safely. Gruyère didn't like that. Since the agents arrived safely, London naturally blamed the accidents on something other than Air Operations. Which Gruyère did not want, so he replaced me with that louse Rampigli. I wasn't going to let that go by. I told Gruyère I was on to his lousy game, and he socked me in the eye. I picked up a bottle and nearly lopped off his head. He was lucky. The worst he got was a little cut under the eye that I stitched up myself with a needle and skin from his arm. I never spoke to him again, except when necessary. That's the way it was. I didn't change in Avenue Foch." He looked like a child who's sick for the first time and can't imagine what's going on inside himself. This poor bum. He'd put that cut on Bobbie's face which I saw on Boulevard Clichy. I'd thought Bobbie'd broken away from a Gestapo beating or had crashed in a car. "I don't like telling you this," said Debrette. "I don't know why it should matter, but it does. What have you got to do with his selling me out? Which he did. That's not a cut in the eye. And then, what happens? After Treblinka, two weeks of breathing, and then boom, the police pick me up, and I'm taken to the TMP and told I'm the one who sold out the agents to the Germans. Why? Because I was picked up two days earlier than the others. Unconscious every second of the time, and they accuse me of passing out the names of a hundred agents. As if I knew them. Does Gruyère leave some kind of paper saying he ordered me to surrender the caches? You guess. Does my colleague Rampigli raise a syllable in my defense? You can bet not. I'm hooked by them all, alive or dead. I could have found myself in Hell after that and not been surprised. Collaborating. Why? To get myself put in a concentration camp? I had a gun. I could have shot off my head if I was looking for such benefits. So that's it, Mr. Curry. Now do you want me to make a statement that your son was a fine fellow who stood up for me and saved my life?"

"My son's dead, Debrette. He's been dead since nineteen forty-four. You've lived five years longer than that already."

"Hitler's dead. Goebbels, Himmler, Darlan. They're dead. Lots of rotten people are dead."

I got up, all the day's anger at my throat, "You've got nothing to go on. Nothing. Your mind's so twisted, you can't see a straight line. The sun is blazing on the whole business, and you've got your nose in a sewer. An imbecile could see what happened." Like Trente-mille, I slapped my fist into its brother's palm and explained, "The Germans made a pact. That's true. They knew everything. Bobbie and Chaleur knew they knew it. They were saving the only thing that counted then, lives. Theirs, yes, but yours too. That's what happened."

Debrette was rolling up his sleeve, and pointed to a number inked on his forearm. "Here's my sun, Mr. Curry. That's the light I see by."

I have sat in the logic classes of my day and know there is a name for the fallacy of such demonstration; but experience carries an odor which paralyses logic. I sat back in that ruined armchair.

"There's more," he said. "Do you want to hear it or not?"

"Yes," I said. "Yes, anything." He could hit me with a bottle, too. I'd wear the scar in my head as my son did. That was my noble thought.

"In forty-three, the last week in September, Colonel Wynn-Wyndward, the second-in-command in London came over to Paris with a deputy, Major Ravenscroft. There was a rendezvous with Gruyère. Only Ravenscroft went. Gruyère wasn't there, but the SD was. Ravenscroft was gassed at Treblinka. He'd broken an ankle and was thrown into the chamber. How do I know that? Personally. Here," and he held out his inked arm. "With four other prisoners, I lifted him and threw him in."

Demonstration Two, but what did it have to do with Bobbie? "Bobbie was in the hands of the SD. That's why he couldn't make the rendezvous."

"Exactly. He'd given away the rendezvous. How else could they have known?"

I shook my head. "There's an explanation. Even if it's that they tortured it out of him." A new thought. Bobbie's head, punched bloody and pushed into a bathtub of ice water. The pear of light, sweating light in the black of Debrette's cave. Bobbie's pain. Five years ago. My foot, where, five hours before, that Medusa had stepped on it, throbbed.

A hand on my shoulder. Debrette's voice. "I'm sorry, Mr. Curry. I saw Gruyère right after this, you remember, and he hadn't been touched. I don't say that he was malicious or cowardly. Maybe mistaken, or foolish. But that's what happened. I've lived years with it."

His hand on my shoulder. There was something to what he had said.

3

Maybe the worst part of isolation is confinement with the worst part of yourself. No outside interference, while self-excoriation works on your body. Debrette must have known it. His hand was a grace, breaking my isolation as I'd wanted my voice to break his twenty minutes before. Then he offered another antidote. "The fog's clearing. Why don't we go out a while. There's a restaurant a few blocks away. It would do us both good."

He washed out the glasses, put away the Calvados, helped me on with my overcoat—he didn't wear one—and we walked down what seemed like populated streets and across a little field, rat-gray and silver, cold and handsomely bleak. On its edge was the restaurant, an ugly but lively little place with tables outside. We went inside for dinner. He would not allow me to pay. I suppose it was *the* entertainment of his post-war life.

After dinner, we walked back to his place, and I got my bag, for I'd had enough of this crippled town. Which Debrette again understood. He took a bus with me to the station, and despite the fact that he had to get up at six in the morning, he waited with me for the one o'clock train.

CHAPTER 6

I was tired to death when I got back from Caen. The stuffy locomotion of a French night train carted me into a first-class cold, and I let it take me. Mme. Zdonowycz cooked up a gallon of Polish lentil soup, and I poured bowlful after bowlful down my throat. Huddled under quilts, gulping steam from a vaporiser, swallowing aspirin every four hours, I slid away from pursuit into the delights of pampering a minor illness. Never was pineapple so sweet: Mme. Zdonowycz changed my sheets, tucked me into them, wound up my old phonograph, played my Mozart arias, and, with her own music, crooned me into absent-mindedness and sleep.

I rose from this bed of small pain after six days, thinner and older. My shaving mirror showed a length of ashy face, a couple of runny blue eyes under a hand's width of seamed forehead, and a mossy top in which silver was driving out richer currency. All floated in an effluvium of exhausted sensuality. "What now?" I asked that marooned ugliness.

It now seemed reasonably clear that Bobbie had made some sort of mistake, or, at least, had been driven by exhaustion to speed up what appeared to him an inevitable situation. The less attention that was called to the whole business, the quicker it would be absorbed in bigger chunks of history. It was time for me to yield, and to take on the world in more familiar guise.

For me, it meant a return to my business life. I telephoned Armand and asked him to lunch with me. I had a notion of making a tour of our European suppliers and entering into negotiations for new contracts with them. Armand said it would be something to discuss and suggested that we do it at Printinière's.

This cathedral of appetite is a dark, oak-panelled room on the Île

St. Louis. In its center, broilers roll on spits, and against one wall, Paris' largest collection of fine cheese lords it like a scale model of a futurama. Twenty copper flambeaux supply the light by which you can glimpse the world's great and powerful at feed. For a quarter of a century, slivers of my heart have been left under those regulated torches.

Armand and I feasted on North Sea crabs, lake trout, and one of Printinière's salads, the feature of which is a mist of shredded nuts dominating a jungle of herbs and grasses. We drank a pale Burgundy taken from a hill Armand knew by sight; but it might as well have been Coca-Cola, and the trout horsemeat, because my reentry into Boisdevres S.A. was stopped cold and quick.

A word about my brother-in-law, Armand Boisdevres. Two years my senior, he looks fifteen years younger. Habit keeps him young, habit and avoidance. What he's had to do, he's mastered, and he ignores the rest. I met him a quarter of a century ago, just two months after the big upheaval of his life. During the last years of the First War, he was engaged to a Normandy girl who attended classes in Paris and lived at the Boisdevres home. Armand's father, Jules Boisdevres, had been a widower for ten years. A deer-like man, gentle, soft, rapid, he deflected the young girl's passion from Armand to himself, and then, flattered by its strength, rejuvenated by it, he ran away with her. He and his son never again spoke to each other. Since then, Armand has been a man without visible feelings. Women marched in and out of his life, but none stayed. My own former friend, Phebe Delattre, stayed the longest, but that was during the war, when for the first time Armand was derailed by a world situation which he could neither slight nor master.

If he had any passion now, it was for appearance, his own and his surroundings'. Like a woman, Armand regarded his apartment as an extension of himself. Every few years he had it completely over-hauled; rugs and tables were swapped, chairs refurbished; there were even new books and paintings. And, by some extraordinary, sympathetic magic, Armand himself would look new. He assisted the magic by restocking his wardrobe, a different color dominating each change. Now it was blue, but I remember years of gray, brown, tweed. Half Armand's age was put on in the war when buying sprees were out. Our lunches, during the year I went up to Paris, were lugubrious catalogues of what he needed and could not buy. Not that lunches with him had ever been bacchanalia. Armand had never been easy with me, perhaps because he associated me with the loss which so closely preceded my meeting and marrying his sister. In fact, only in business talk is Armand easy, for there, knowledge and talent insulate him from feeling.

Over the crabs, he told me, simply and flatly, that I was too far removed from the complexities of the business to be useful in negotiations. "You're entitled to retirement, Sam, and I want you to enjoy it. Even if it were possible, I wouldn't think of asking you to work up what you'd need for something like contract negotiations. These Six Power codes absolutely overwhelm you."

"I need activity, Armand."

"I thought you had so much with your investigations you couldn't keep up with anything else."

"That was the case, but it's changed. It was too complicated for me."

"I always suspected it might be, Sam. The war was an inane misery. I almost wish its history wouldn't be written. I wish everything that happened in it was obliterated."

"I need activity for my obliterations, Armand. That's why I want to travel."

"Then travel."

"?"

"On your own. That's always been a great pleasure for you. You have means. Though we could arrange a special travel allowance for you, make you a travelling emblem of good will."

Stronger men than I have been strung out on Armand's barbed wire. He dealt with me the way I used to deal with Bobbie: the disposer, the one with the whip and the chocolate bars.

We shook hands, and I walked back across the river and through the Tuileries. Snow started falling. I sat on a bench behind the Orangerie, my coat buttoned to the neck. There was almost no one around. School children were in school, babies napped. Over the statuary the trees arched for the snow, arrogant, as if the universe were bestowing itself on them. Not I. A bum on a park bench.

My old friend, Yielding, shivered there with me. How he shortens the life he appears to ease, and how I knew it! The sky tossed down the isolating white; I shivered from inside cold. Since Caen, I had been yielding. Not only myself, but yielding what I'd said I wouldn't, Bobbie.

I got up and pushed toward Metro Concorde, my shoes spooning that city brew of cinder-slush. In a second-class compartment, I was rebuked by the *contrôleur* because of my first-class ticket. Twice in

53

a week, and it had happened perhaps twice before in my years in Europe. I got out two stops early, at Étoile, and went into the first movie on the Champs. It was an American film—*The Best Years of Our Lives*—about three men coming home after the war and finding it difficult to settle down. I was losing myself in it when the intermission came, and the peddlers moved up the aisle with ice bars and chocolate. Commerce: theirs, Armand's, and the guardians of Metro tickets. A penitentiary. I left, walked home, and called Zdonowycz.

"Pack a bag for me," I said. "I'm going off."

"You're a bird. How long this time?"

"Don't ask. Pack. It'll be years."

"You all right?"

"Pack. I'd give you time off to see friends, if you had friends."

A laugh like a pump sucking at a well bottom. "What I need friends, I got you?"

I sat down and wrote out a *pneumatique* to Jacqueline Bargouille. I'd travel, yes, but not just for larks. I had my stake in the world yet, and I was no snowdrop to melt at the touch of opposition.

2

It was not so sudden a decision. Jacqueline Bargouille had been on my mind since Biarritz. I'd thought of her beleaguered underground love a hundred times, translating myself into the hard body of Chaleur and summoning her up, a radiant Montespan. Yet I hadn't written to this radiance who, of all people alive, should have known Bobbie's last years better than anyone. There'd been time to write, and she was certainly as important to my concern as Debrette, but something had sidetracked me, something I'd learned about women during the war.

I exaggerated the extent of my isolation down in the country. I was alone for most of those thousands of hours, but now and then, once every three months, there'd be times in which my days spiralled about women, girls sometimes thirty years younger than I. Something happened to the relationships between Frenchmen and women in the Occupation. Defeat, public defeat, had sunk into people's hearts, men's hearts, for it's men who lose wars. This is what I learned at night from the ten or twelve girls who found my tenderness and need more satisfying for them than the muscular bodies from which defeat had siphoned authority.

Women react to courage the way animals do to smells. Perhaps it's because their troubles too are imposed upon them. I escaped their censure in the war as an outsider, a man who'd done his job years ago and who now had a son doing a similar job. Then too, I was an American, which further camouflaged my weakness. But I grew to fear women then, to respect and fear their judgments; and so after the war, for the first time in my life, I found it easier to be with men. Men act from a greater range of motives and tolerate a greater range of responses. For men, courage is a choice made from many possibilities, and there are many forms of courage. Women are not so tolerant.

Anyway, this was behind the delay in writing Jacqueline. I could face the violence I feared—hoped?—would come from Debrette more easily than I could a single sharp look from Jacqueline. Now, I was no longer exempt from responsibility. I had no excuse to coddle myself. I had a clear mission, and the need and means to work it out.

Behind telling Zdonowycz to "pack" were Armand, and the slush, and the movie with three lovely women ministering to the three unhappy veterans. Coming out of the theater into an ice-gray Paris, I thought, "Yes, I'll travel. I'll head south for a resort beach and walk along the sands in white ducks with a blue foulard tucked into a Sulka sports shirt, the silver in my head gleaming like decorations for wisdom and experience and comfort, walk up to a lovely widow of forty reading on a verandah beside her two children (boy of fourteen, girl of twelve), someone whose single look would say, 'I too am not yet retired, am lonely, comfortable,' and within weeks we'd be off into yachty waters making for Spain, Crete, Tangiers, our abridged lives wound together into endless, interdependent possibilities." Then, just as we were entering the Bay of Naples, I passed a barber shop, and my fantasy switched tracks; but went ahead on the engine of *travel* and *a woman*.

I did not even wait for an answer from Jacqueline, but took a train for Langres the next morning. There, I left my bag in a hotel across from the station and took a taxi to Lepic, a village two kilometers southeast of Langres. The driver left me off in front of the last of the seven houses which make up the town. There was a yellow Bureau de Postes sign over a side door, and I went in there and asked a large, dull-faced girl behind the *guichet* the whereabouts of Mademoiselle Bargouille.

"So you've come already," said the girl. And smiled. It was a face

55

one would have passed a hundred times without noticing, until that smile. That smile, closer to Bobbie's than any I'd ever seen, liberated the whole face, exposed its economy, beautiful, oak-bark eyes, and an autumnal complexion. I'd never seen an ordinary-looking face transformed so quickly. "I should have answered you," she said. "I should have, but probably never would have. I'm glad you didn't give me time to worry about deciding."

She pushed the hinged half-door, and ducked under the lintel. She was almost my height, big-boned, her body a strong base for that thoughtful, pared head. She looked as close to forty as the thirty Jessica had said she was.

Only twenty-two when she'd tumbled out of the sky, this provincial duck had performed like an Arthurian knight. An explosions expert, she could pin a train to a hill or bank it into a gulley, count the bodies in the dark and then show up for a rendezvous twenty miles away primed for the next assault. "Montespan." Disguised by the chicken wire of the *guichet* and her country-isolated years, this was the courier between Chaleur and Bobbie, who'd held their lives in her hand for five hundred days. Captured with the others in the round-up of '43, she was sent to Ravensbrück, where she survived by pinning her identity card to a corpse, just before she was due to go into the ovens. In '45 she and two other women bribed a guard with a promise to testify for him when the Allies came, and then escaped. They walked across Germany until they ran into Patton's army.

In Lepic, I knew only that she'd been a brave courier and had been captured with the other agents. We shook hands, a little shaky from our different knowledge of those times, which this tiny office in the middle of the mud fields clouded into dreamstuff. She reached back through the wire and unhooked a board which squeaked down to shut the office. "It's open two hours a day, and then it's wasted time." Again that smile poured autumn colors into her face, and I had a twitch of envying poor George Towne.

"In here," she said, and opened a door into a small parlor, dark, satiny, musky with preservation. She drew curtains open, and we sat at opposite ends of a sofa.

In retrospect, I can say that I felt something for her that reinforces my wonder about those astonishing cells which transmit temperament as well as shape and color to our children. The underground workings of attraction. Though I cannot strictly recall what I felt in that first ten minutes with Jacqueline which preceded my learning that she was not and never had been George Towne's sweetheart, but Bobbie's, always and from the first week of their meeting. I know that some powerful feeling ran in me toward her, and that it was different enough from any I'd felt before to make me restless with it.

"I suppose," she'd said, "that you want to know if there are any letters from him," and I'd answered, "Only if they have something to do with my son."

A vaudeville routine. She'd come back with, "But you're his father," and I still missed it, and said, "I've never doubted that." "Then every line of his letters would be important to you," and I kept on, "Towne is not that important. I don't want to violate your personal life." Which ended it.

"Ah," she said, softly, "I didn't know that you didn't know," and she picked up my hand, her own harder than mine, her fingers extraordinarily slender and powerful. I could feel her strength seeping into me through them. "It was Bobbie and I," she said. "Never George. I thought that you must have known when I got your letter. Though I wondered why now, after all these years. I'd thought of writing you, years ago, even of coming to see you, but all of us who worked underground were so filled with secrecy that even when there's no need for keeping secrets, we keep quiet. And then what would have been the point?"

So there it was. This powerful, solitary girl had been Bobbie's. He'd not been alone after all. "Are there things you can show me, letters, anything?" Probably swallowing, for it was not easy to think of Bobbie being with such a woman.

"I'll show you everything." She went over to a small desk in the corner and took two filthy scraps of paper out of an envelope and handed them to me. I could not make out what was scrawled on them, so she pointed to one and read it aloud, and then the other. The first, written with something like a fingernail and blood, went "J. darling am fine all love B." Passed along with only a name, it had gone through a thousand hands into Ravensbrück itself. The other, in pencil, was not much different, "Darling Jacqueline, I don't know where, when, how, but it will be. B."

"That's all," she said. "Shall we walk? It's easier to talk outside," and she was up, calm, her eyes a trifle wild, and it was clear she couldn't wait to get out of the tiny parlor where she kept and where she put back the pitiful souvenirs of her love.

3

Up in the hills, walking ahead of a fisty breeze off the mud flats, where hundreds of pigs rooted and squealed, Jacqueline talked without stopping, as if, after years of not talking, she had found in me a version of Bobbie whose listening was not passive and who would not, therefore, smear what still counted so strongly for her. "Bob and I were dropped together. The second Thursday in March, forty-two. We were the first Chaleur agents to drop. We'd had our third stage of training together: codes and Morse work, explosives, obstacle and assault courses, but mostly exercises, with the training staff posing as Abwehr or Gestapo. That night we flew across in a Halifax with four hundred pounds of TNT and detonators. An agent named Peugeot met us and drove us to Pont-Evecque, where we stored the material in the garden of a dentist named Esnault-Pelterie, a grandson of one of the early plane manufacturers. A very nice person. He gave us café Pétain, remember that horrible stuff?" I nodded.

"Bob and I had a funny relationship. We were both young for our age and what we did. Amateurs is a good word for us. Gifted with a job and each other, that's how we looked at it. I don't know who recruited him. There's so much I don't know that I would have known."

"How did you get in?" I asked, mostly to steady her recollection.

"I'd been a governess with a family in Hertfordshire, cousins of my mother. Though better off. I was nothing but a farmer's girl. Here, you see," and she waved around the umber hills and the loud mud below. "I went over in thirty-seven. I was eighteen, but though I'd gone to school in Paris for two years when Mother died—I lived with her sister—I was even more ignorant than most French girls. My mother died when I was nine, so I didn't even learn those things which French mothers are supposed to be so good at telling daughters. Just schoolwork and girl talk, and whatever one learns around here. I suppose a really smart person could guess what life was like from such a blueprint, but when I went over to England, my head was emptier than a chicken's. It was to be for a summer, but my father found the money situation easier with my earning there rather than spending here, so he said I could stay. There were two sweet children, the house was beautiful, and I loved England. Really loved it. It's a rhythm one loves. I'd think of going there yet, if I hadn't heard some of the uglier noises the rhythm can make. But I'm retired now. You see that. If it hadn't come to this, if Bob had lived, if we'd married, had children, had life, who knows?" (Into, through my face, she looked, her old passion hooking in me what she saw of him there; it was actually painful.) "It was the father who recruited me. London made a point of recruiting the unspecialised young for this work. Expendables. That's my view. Anyway, he must have mentioned me to someone as a bi-lingual Anglophile who knew France cold, because I got a call in 1942. I'd left the family in 1940 and was working in the Department of Naval Affairs typing minutes and translating FFI memos. I suppose I first thought about the Resistance then; something in me did take to the idea of it. Why not? I was strong, had lots of energy, and no attachments. I was approached, and I guess Bobbie was, too, about the same time. When we met, we'd each had two training sessions, one down in an estate in Surrey, the other near the Scots border.

"It was one of the strangest lovers' meetings imaginable. In the training camp, we were all kept away from other agents for the first week or so. Then, during an exercise, my job was to pick up some explosives and meet an agent by a plane in a wood clearing about four kilometers from our camp. We were told to have perfect identification because there'd be 'German agents' planted along the route, and if they picked up our trail, they were supposed to take us in. I had on a cloth helmet, a parachute, and carried a great case of mock TNT. At the wood, I was so tired I could hardly breathe. I took off the pack and put it in the bushes. I'd walked about five hours, in and out of patrols, and all kinds of traps they'd set for us. I was angry and nervous, but for seconds at time, I relaxed, not the proper thing to do, but I did. I watched the moon come up and I smelled what I think was boxwood nearby. I suppose it's because smelling is the sense people use least that it's so strong when you're conscious of it. That smell was just marvellous for me, I remember feeling like a girl, as I hadn't for weeks and weeks. I was almost sinking into it when all of a sudden something hard was at my neck and, against all the rules, I screamed. The hand—it was a hand, an arm—stopped moving and that was enough for me to recover. I grabbed it, bent and threw over my shoulders and was down on a body with my pistol at a man's head. I was a very tough girl. He signalled 'enough,' and I pulled him up. The moon was quite bright, and his face shone in it. That was the first time I saw him. You know his face, how it was sort of closed, the nose turned in, the eyes dark and near each other. I guess people call it an intense face, but I thought of it against those open faces of Northerners which seem to keep going beyond their edges into the sky. They don't seem contained by themselves. Even when they're handsome, they seem indistinct to me, at least they did after that first second of Bob's face, which I suppose from that one second became the face I loved. He said, 'It was the woman's scream. I wasn't expecting a woman. I thought you were "Abwehr" because I didn't see the case.'

"That was the first time. If it had been the last, maybe he'd be alive, and I'd have three children. I've had time to think of all the 'ifs': you know, if we hadn't met at all, would I have been happier in the long run, and things like that. Of course it's not over. I'm not dead. I might marry, I might fall in love next Tuesday, but for a time I didn't think I'd ever have any good feeling for anything. I'm hard. I suppose that that's how I got into this in the first place.

"That first night turned out to be a trial run for us. We were going to be dropped together, he as radio operator and Assistant Chief for Chaleur, I as courier. We were going to be closer than I think you can imagine. That kind of closeness melts your skin away; you feel you're getting sunburned when he does, things like that. Siamese twins. But love. I don't know how the chiefs worked that out, whether they planned love to be a part of it or not. But it shouldn't be. There's too much without it, and love complicates. That's well-known. It starts so that you think you can control it, just have it as a treat, a reward for hard work, like sleep, though not so necessary; and then, even when there's so much you have to do there aren't minutes to do it, it's suddenly the heart of everything, the motor, the reason for everything. Everything seems easier to do because you have it. You're stronger, smarter, better. Wrong as it is in your circumstances, bad as it is, it alters everything, the way fog does a field; it makes a new landscape.

"Compared to most lovers, we were together very little, taking the total number of minutes; I mean not only as lovers but just together. But there wasn't an hour in my waking day that wasn't filled with him, and that's how I know how careless of our job it must have made us. Maybe failure is built into love. I don't think anything could satisfy the want Bob gave me for himself. You can be satisfied a hundred ways and yet not be satisfied. But we didn't have time to find that out. And we were probably really together twenty-five or thirty times. I almost feel I can remember them separately. I used to go over my body like a tourist, visiting places where Bob touched me. That sounds terrible.

"But there was another lover. The war, if that isn't too dramatic. I mean, my body is here now, but it's not the same body the war and Bob owned. The Germans can add it to their statistics if they like. No, that's too easy. I tell you, Mr. Curry, I'm having a lovely time walking up here with Bob's father. I'm so much at peace and happy. I'm glad about things, and I haven't been that way. Talking about it makes even the pain sweet somehow. Not everyone's had something to talk about. *J'ai mes ennuis. Enormes*, but I'm for staying around."

4

That night, I took her to Langres for dinner at the Belle Meunière, a bright closet hung over a war memorial fountain set in the middle of a square.

No statuary, but two very live buzzards, we stowed great chunks of the world's treated goods into our holds. "No sir," I told Jacqueline, "you're going to be staying around. Red meat alone will keep you above ground."

Beef grease extended her lips, and then their smile started a sort of harvest dance in her face. It was so pretty, I lost control of my breath and gulped a forkful of beans the wrong way. Gagged, I bleated. She was up, clapping me on the back, raising and lowering my arms.

"I'll have to stay around just to keep you alive," she said.

What power, my back felt as if it had bounced down a flight of stairs. I came back, face draining, breathing deeply. "Then I'll buy you dinner every night. Breakfast and lunch as well."

Out before I'd weighed it, so I counterpoised by becoming excessively paternal, stroked her hand, old, wise pappy-in-law telling son's pretty wife not to worry about the car payments. But I was no father-in-law to this girl. Bobbie's history was behind me, and almost all my feelings were cut off from him. Yet it wasn't desire, or at least was not what I'd have called it. Nor was it avuncular or fraternal. Here was a woman with whom I had community interests. But Bobbie was somehow only a part of these. As for those breakfasts and lunches I'd tossed her way, quick as they'd come out, they stood for some sort of real invitation, a readiness in the kindling before the actual blaze.

"You can't find enough restaurants around here. They wouldn't hold you for two weeks."

"We'll travel. Paris, Madrid, Canberra."

"Kangaroo chops make good breakfasts."

Candles in bottles, wine and music, these lacked, and years, propriety. There was no point. "But I want to ask you about something. Trentemille."

I'd cast it—her?—off. Her face looked as if snow had fallen there. "Dig up a saint's corpse and it'll smell. We'll all smell one day. I can't talk about that priest."

"Jacqueline," and I don't know how much I wanted to know or how much I wanted to keep away from talking about anything else. "Something happened. What could it have been? What was it?"

"I don't know. Truly. If it's assurance about Bob you want, how much would mine be worth? I can't even give you that, only my belief, *my* knowledge. But what's that? Trentemille could just as well have made me the traitor. Any of us. Double agents are common in espionage work. Ideological attachments aren't strengthened underground. You become—what shall I say? International. Not because of the money. Money is the excuse professional agents give themselves to cover their lack of allegiance. But we were amateurs, most of us. If something happened—and it's clear that the Germans did have the mail, they did pick up our agents, they did know our codes— find a professional agent. If it's one of us, I'd guess torture is the answer. And we did not torture easily. I tell you that, contrary to the way people think these days, it isn't easy to extract something from a trained person, at least for the two days of silence to which he's committed."

"Why two?"

"He makes contact every two days. If none is made, all codes and rendezvous which he knows about are changed. Sometimes it's twenty-four hours. For chiefs."

Eight youngish men came into the restaurant. Our waitress whispered happily, "The Cycle Club of Langres." There was a festive-looking table across the room where they sat down after giving us a scholarly survey, Jacqueline as if she were a new carburetor, me, a broken axle. It was further restoration to *my place*, neither a dew-wet foal, an Ajax, nor Hercule Poirot, and in which Jacqueline was not much more than a fading spinster who helped run a pig farm, a flea-sized post office, and who ate two-thirds of her meals by herself, reading a newspaper or staring out at mud flats.

She too felt something. "Let's leave," she said.

We got up, and the Cycle Club moaned en masse. Jacqueline walked out, I shrugged, bowed to the cyclists, paid, and followed her.

She was in the square, her hand dipped into the empty fountain basin. They'd be turning on the water in a week or two. I watched her from the door of the restaurant. There was no moon, but a street light composed the sort of picture you see in photography books, "Woman Musing: Night." Her head was bent to where the water would soon be. "Oh dear girl," I thought, "I wish I could make you happy. I wish I were Bobbie and could make you happy."

She turned around. Agents learn to pick up people's presence by secondary effects, altered reflections and tiny echoes. She was quite something to see. There were echoes of fine things in her. What in the world did she have to do with the Cycle Club of Langres and the pigs of Lepic? Or with me?

We walked half a mile to a taxi stand, and I put her in it and paid the driver for the trip to Lepic. It was only two more blocks to my hotel. At the back window I said, "Jacqueline, I mean it seriously about Paris. I'd really like to help you if you want to come. I'm lonely. And in a way there's no one closer to me in the world than you"—I hesitated—"would have been. I think you should come for your own sake. Don't even warn me. Just come." With her head at the open window, I had a *déja vue*. It wasn't until after she shook hands and said she really might come and I'd walked back to the hotel that I remembered that the feeling came from the time I'd put Bobbie into the London taxi nine years before and he'd smiled in that way which made you feel that no matter what sort of trouble you were in, there was something to hold on to, something that couldn't save you or save itself from being broken but which was worth trying to keep your head up for as long as you possibly could.

PART TWO

"In misery, I chewed at my hands. And they
thinking I did this because I was hungry,
got up and said, 'Father, it would give us
less pain if you ate us: you dressed us in
this miserable flesh, and you can take it back.'"

"I'm returning to the battle,
Since you've branded me a traitor;
I'm no traitor, as God sees me.
But you'll not see me alive again today!"

CHAPTER 7

The governors of the world can be split into those who manage people and those who arrange facts; there's probably a section of the nervous system responsible for the specialisation. I've never been unable to decide where a man excels, and I regard myself as a manager type. Fact-arranging is my bane: I can't think through a balance sheet, and it's hard for me to assemble things. But I know when a man's patience is exhausted, when he wants a favor done. I'm a salesman: the facts I've learned are façade. I do my business inside, and could sell ghosts as well as steel.

In these last years though, I've changed somewhat. The arrangement of facts, the ins and outs of certainty, have become more approachable for me, especially as I have seen them dependent on the people who make the arrangements and believe in them. I've come to think that the only proper description of a situation is one that includes a description of the man making it, but once this old notion of mine is swallowed, I'm ready to deal with the situation itself. Then too, I'm no cynic or sceptic: these attitudes repel me. If anything, my credo centers about that old line "understanding all is forgiving all." That's the big thing.

In the old days, nothing riled me so much as a blockage in managerial progress. Bobbie suffered aplenty from this. I worked him up and down like an umbrella, that is until he returned from two years at Winchester. It was all over then, but in 1935, when I decided that I wanted him at that great seat of public servants—while I joined the graduate department in Washington—I brought it off in typically serene fashion; by buying and selling. I remember him coming down to breakfast a day after my telling him, and through my newspaper, I could feel his resentment grid heating up. But not a word. Bobbie was no slouch at managing himself.

"O.K., lad, what is it? What's up?" I kept the paper between us.

"I'm happy at the *lycée*." He was at Lycée Rollin (renamed now after the maquisard Decour).

"You'll be happy in England also. That's what the good life is, a variety of happinesses."

Grunt.

"No, no, speak up. Don't pig your way through the world. That's one thing an English public school does for a man, makes him articulate. Ever notice how much better English diplomats are than American ones? They speak right to the point, no excesses and seldom deficiencies."

"I don't hope to be a diplomat."

"Every man needs to be a diplomat." I put the paper down and looked fatherly for him, stern but sympathetically attentive. He was sweating, the new hair shone above his lips. Adolescence is not a pretty thing to look at, or, probably, to undergo, though I can't remember experiencing anything uncomfortable in my own.

"Is it possible that you're doing this for yourself? I mean, that you don't want to have me around?" This was said to the floor and hard to be sure of. I made him repeat it, while I took it in. My boy's growing up, I thought, and, God knows, there is some truth in it. One can't live like a free man with a growing son in the house, and though I was not aiming to sublet my nature to the devil, I was at the age when the fire has to be really worked at to be maintained at all. But mostly I wanted it for him, so that he'd have what I've always loved with my Chicago insularity, a British manner, poise, restraint, all these surfaces which I still regard as English virtues.

"No, it's not that, Bobbie. I really don't think it's that."

"Then why, as long as I'm happy?"

"I'm not even sure, but perhaps it's involved with my not getting

66

away from my parents until the war, and then never wanting to go back. I don't want that to happen with us. I want you to miss me a little, always. I don't want you to think of us as people in each other's way."

"Hitting your head with a hammer so it'll feel good when you stop."

"Maybe, but try it. Just one term. Give it everything you have, and then, if it doesn't work, you can come right back to the *lycée*. We'll get tutors, and you can still take the *bac* with your class."

He shook his head a little, said "O.K." and got up.

"No breakfast?"

"I had it."

That night I waited for him till he came home. It was eleven o'clock. He'd had dinner out; I was very free with him.

"Bobbie?"

"They gave me a farewell party," he called in.

"Fine. Come on in a minute."

He came, dressed to the nines in suit and tie. "You look very nice. Who gave the party?" I didn't usually interrogate him.

"Oh, Marcel, Didier, five or six others. The usual."

"You'll see them *en vacances*. It'll be all right."

"That's true."

"I've got something for you."

"Oh?"

"It's my Tuley class ring. I'd like you to have it. That's an amethyst." I handed it over. "It's the only piece of jewelry that ever meant anything to me."

Rings mean a lot to boys of that age. Bobbie smiled that marvellous way of his and put it on, first his pinkie, for I'd had it on mine—though I'd worn it only for the occasion—and then on the third finger, where it fit. "Thank you, Papa. I like it very much. I wish I'd had it tonight," and, though we had stopped kissing for a couple of years, he pecked at my forehead and went off.

That fixed Winchester. This time it had been a few carats of shine and some *ad hoc* sentiment. Sometimes it was a fist under his nose or a boot in the rear end. Bobbie I managed until he grew out of my buying and threatening power, and that I didn't find out about until our trip back to the States in the summer of 1937.

It was my last visit before the war, and though prevision wasn't a factor—I would have bet on Mars growing cauliflower moons before betting there'd be anything more than fists shaken and perhaps a few territorial nibblings—I did want Bobbie to see the country of which he was a citizen before he got old enough to see it without my help, before it altered out of my powers of explanation. I wasn't the sort of exile who finds that distance creates charm, but like most men whose experience hasn't kept pace with their years, it was more and more the past I talked about. Though I hadn't had much time to talk with Bobbie, what I did have was frequently burdened by my American recollections.

We sailed in June, first class on the old *Mauretania.* At the beginning, Bobbie was kind of a lark to travel with. He wore his Winchester blazer, the school tie, and despite his snub, rather swampy face, there was both a nervous alertness and burgher-class confidence in him that drew lots of eyes when we paraded around the decks and salons. We ate together in more festive manner than ever before in our lives, almost two boulevardiers preparing to descend on the evening. The hitch was that we weren't fellow boulevardiers, and we were not quite content as father and son. Both of us had needs, and often needed the same thing.

Our tablemates were a family of four from Whitefish Bay, Wisconsin, the Pennybackers, he a genteel, pleasant man who ran a hosiery plant in Milwaukee, his wife an almost pretty brunette, the daughter an absolutely ravishable beauty of nineteen, a junior at Wellesley, and the son a rude fourteen-year-old whose sole talent was an ability to transform every decent word and gesture into vulgarity. You couldn't call this talent precocious; he was already a master of harsh disenchantment. It was he who brought into the open what was, I'm afraid, a struggle between Bobbie and me that otherwise might have passed without record or consequence.

Elizabeth Pennybacker—I can't recall the set of her beautiful face, but after six meals and two fox trots to my all-time favorite popular song, "Smoke Gets in Your Eyes," I knew that familiar clutch *d'amour* which hid from me years, status, propriety. And then it turned out that Bobbie too was asking if she wanted to walk around the deck, have a drink with him—seventeen, he guzzled like a goat—play deck tennis, watch the movie. "I just promised your father a game," or "I just told Bobbie I'd play rummy, come on we'll play three-hand." Bobbie and I would avoid each other's looks, avoid looking at the girl, dance as much with the mother as the girl, until young Mudmouth Pennybacker came up one evening at dinner with "Which of you Currys is going to walk off with Elizabeth? I'm making book."

68

"Wish I could, Tom-boy, but I'm afraid Liz is reserved for a worse fate." This almost sputtered, the man-of-the-world swallowing vinegar in the wine glass.

Bobbie was worse off, crushed, red. He took to playing Tom-boy deck tennis, snapping the ring back with all his might, trying to whack the head off his thick little neck. Once he managed to trip him so that he came within an ace of falling down a flight of stairs. One remark, and it broke the trip for both of us, a remark that stood for something real, of course.

Fate is contagion of circumstance. In and out of our three months in the States, rivalry infected what we did. In Chicago we stayed with the Showalters, back from Washington, where the end of the NRA had ended his passion for Roosevelt and reform. Recovery was now ungeneralised; it was the old Chicago position of one got it first oneself, and anything after that was a matter of temperamental indulgence. Bahai Temples, Alcoholics Anonymous, palaces on the lake or the Rhine, civic opera houses, or good deeds. The Showalters took us to a Chicago party that I can't believe was typical of anything but itself. Right smack on the Shore Drive in a largish but not extraordinary-looking house that, once beyond the door, became Xanadu. A room the size of Sullivan's Auditorium, where, half a flight down, was suspended the first free-form swimming pool made out of reinforced concrete, that I'd seen. In the pool were islands on which flowers and champagne bottles nudged each other. If you wanted to swim, you went to one of the dressing rooms, got a suit—the women's anticipated bikinis—and then floated away. Movie stars, publicity society, some dots of literature, cowboys, Chicago Cubs, gamblers, the process of invitation must have been by dropping leaflets. The place belonged to a lawyer married to a paper heiress. I never saw them, no one bothered looking. "Bobbie's invited," said Justin, and who was I to question the invitation or to just say no? We wore our bathing suits under our tuxedos, armed with Showalter cautions about infection. "How's it you go at all?" I asked after being commanded into one of the suits purchased specially for us and probably incinerated after, or saved for our next visit.

"The place is so big, it's like going to the beach. Better, because he has filtered ventilation."

One doesn't expect oneself. I mean, you think that certain forms of foolishness are never going to claim you, and two hours later you find yourself floating in a free-form pool, a champagne glass in one hand and an unknown girl in tow in the other. So Rome fell. No wonder the hosts didn't show up; it was the only pleasure fresh enough to touch them.

I'd never really seen Bobbie with a girl, I mean in any way that promised a serious amour for him. I think he had no sexual experience, strictly speaking, but that night, coursing around in that pool, I saw him sporting a look which must be one of the most common my face has worn. The look scarcely altered when he saw me noticing him. Champagne and desire had estranged us. We were a couple of wolves on the prowl. It was no longer a question of sharing one rabbit, there were rabbits all over this creation. Something dies in a father when he sees this. My insides gradually cooled to nothing. I went and dressed and sat inside at one of the bars talking Roosevelt with Justin.

There were just two years between buying him off to Winchester and discovering him sniffing tail in the pool. I suppose a decent father can take such a transition in stride. A decent father being one who isn't himself on the perpetual sniff. My own father had a roomful of defects, God knows, but never did I have to think of him as a tail-sniffer, and that night I envied his genealogical passion and wished I had it or its equivalent.

All during the rest of that trip, which instead of "bringing us closer" served only to clarify our estrangement, I regretted that I had so cut myself off from those southern relatives that they were as abstract as the boxes which enclosed their names on my father's charts. Bobbie should see "real folk" for a change, that was my notion after the party. Now, my notion is deeper, at least different: it's that if I'd taken Bobbie south, and he'd heard from Aunt Zilpah, or, since she was dead, from one of her sons, the sort of stories I had heard at his age, he might not have been so ready to take on that violent world in his own person a few years after. The ugly stories, which were as much of the great world as my southern people knew, were light years removed from Mrs. Mitchell's best-seller, which Bobbie, along with half the country (not including his southern relatives), read that year and which did not derail his boy's view that the energy steaming in his nerves and muscles would best drive the twin motors of war and women.

2

Twelve years after I'd failed to manage Bobbie, I made a southern trip to arrange the facts which had accumulated because of my managerial failure. I went to see August Mettenleiter.

Not to the South of my relatives, but to the European south of

70

orange groves and grape terraces, casinos, olive trees, warm drives in carriages along the violet Mediterranean, this gorgeous *mise-en-scène* of the panting congresses I have engineered in mosquito-swarmed hotels with blond congresswomen from the district of International Beachery. This is the south of visitors, a diversion from action to scenery, a place where the will thins as the blood thickens, and the sole achievement is recuperative contemplation.

This southern trip was not passive, and it did as much as any I made to pry that dark-headed, beringed, tail-sniffing hero-boy of mine out of the vise in which Trentemille's book had fixed him.

The man who eased the grip, August, was Teichmann's interpreter at Avenue Foch, whom I found, as Rampigli indicated I might, through the records of the TMP. He'd been held there for sixteen months after the war, shedding depositions in what the presiding officer termed an "exceptionally open and dignified manner." Then, *gracié*, he'd gone back to the French Riviera, where he'd lived since leaving Austria in 1919.

I wrote to him at the hotel listed in the records, making my now habitual request to come and talk with him about the network. Three days later, I received this note from him:

Dear Mr. Curry,

Although I spent a good deal of time with the Military Tribunal telling what I knew about the Sicherheitsdienst branch with which I served as an interpreter, I am willing to see anyone who, directly or indirectly, suffered through the activities in which I engaged. I must only remind you that what I had to say, I said, and it is in the records.

Avec les sentiments les plus distingués etc.

August Mettenleiter

3

My taxi, a rackety, high-backed Renault, wobbled by a sweep of cypress, thirty ice-green fans of haughty curiosity overlooking the rosy planks of August's villa fifty feet up and fifty yards back from the Mediterranean.

Everyone has a place which truly counts for him, and which he usually carries with him until he actually sees it, when it becomes love "at first sight." August's was my place; if I were a saint, it would tempt my vocation.

"Hold it," I told the driver. "I'll get out here."

I wanted to walk up the driveway for a slow view, and also to damp the possessive heat that house aroused in me. And I'd only seen the back, plus a rock garden spun away from the left side, a rainbow whirl in the most relaxed and emerald *pelouse* I've ever seen, all adrift in morning haze, sapphire and glittering.

A ladder was propped against the right side, and a large man in white ducks and a crimson sport shirt was standing on it hammering at the cornice. I called up, and when he looked down, I said, "I'm Samuel Curry." He came down the ladder, wiped a muddy road down his pants leg, shook hands and said he was glad to see me.

Looks don't promise character, but they are the quickest lead into gratification or disappointment. What caught you about August's was their lack of self-assertion. A good-looking Northern type, blond, blue-eyed, square-headed, pink, these attributes are not those one thinks of in connection with a description of him. What counts in this face is a reflectiveness that shades all the parts; but it is not a reposed reflectiveness. The muscles below the cheek bones are tight, and they tighten the jaw muscles, so that the face seems suspended before a dangerous leap. A face that attunes you to the man the way the actions of other people attune you.

He took my bag, and led me around to the sea front of the house. We climbed two rock steps to a screened porch, sat on plaited summer chairs, and looked out on the Mediterranean, which flickered in violet rectangles between two rows of Florida palm—imported in the thirties—at the rim of August's place. A pitcher of iced tea, with slim ice cubes and sticks of mint in it, were marks of that hospitality which has since become so familiar to me. That first day, despite the glaze with which the house's beauty and its owner's graciousness eased the interrogation, August was for me little more than the enemy, the closest I'd gotten to him since the war. Here he was, the victimizer, sitting back on a sunny porch cuddled right and left with flares of bougainvillea, lighting up a thin, not cheap cigar whose smoke was more substantial than the material remains of Bobbie and his fellow victims. Yet that glaze may have led me to ask, almost immediately, as an indispensable preface to vital communication, the question everyone must want to ask Germans, Why? Was it fear? Lethargy? Ignorance? Belief in a genuine humanitarian version of the program, a purified Europe revitalising heroic legacies?

That August should answer without hesitation, as if it were the question he'd been turning about on his lips for months, but reflectively, as if the answer were not worked out, this speaks for the connection which the two of us, fellow exiles, hyphenated citizens of France, contemporaries, made across the frontiers of reticence.

"At first, it was relief," he said. "Convenience. I'd been interned at Le Vernet in 1939. I was still an Austrian citizen, though I'd been working on the Riviera for thirty years, ever since I left the *Hochschule*. When the Germans came to Paris, they needed interpreters, and I was assigned to the SD right away. I'd always disliked Hitler, but I'd avoided looking at what had happened. Everyone says this, I know, but it's like Indo-China today or Africa. Terrible things are going on, as I sit and smoke. I looked upon Hitler as a child's disease which Germany would outgrow once it felt itself back to pre-Versailles strength. Then too, the group I was with was anti-Nazi. Teichmann was a decent man who used to make fun of Hitler, at least till about 1943, when there was no more fun made about anything. Most of the SD felt itself apart from the Gestapo. They were next door at Number Eighty-six, but they could have been in Poland as far as we had to do with them. The difference showed up in many ways, including the treatment of prisoners. I never saw anyone beaten at Eighty-four, but Gestapo prisoners went off to the camps with relief, if they lived. I did my job, day by day, first only interpreting, then interrogating by myself. It was not so much different from being a waiter or a major-de, or working in the offices down here. Day after day, I handled a job, getting information from men and women whose job it was to keep it from me. I often got to respect their skills a great deal, and they may have respected mine." He took four deep, toxic breaths of the cigar, reduced it to an inch of leaf and threw it into the lawn. "I didn't really feel much till that day in July when Stauffenberg's bomb just missed killing Hitler. Within two hours, we were all arrested, everyone, Gestapo, SD, even Oberg, who was head of the SS for all France. We stood in the courtyard at Avenue Foch for three hours, and the rumor went around that they were throwing sand down across the way in the École Militaire. For executions. Then we heard Hitler making a speech on the radio, over the loudspeaker, crowing about his miraculous salvation and the lunatic revenge he was going to exact, and then, we were released and told to go to the Hotel Raphael for a party. I went. I saw Abetz lead General Stuelpnagel over to Oberg and make them shake hands, and I thought, 'No hand-shaking for me. I was shot in the École Militaire.' Anything but what I had been doing day after day, as if I were clearing a table or pacifying a guest about a bad room. Two days later, I heard that two of the Chaleur agents had been gassed in Treblinka. I had translated the pact which Chaleur and Teichmann had written out, exchanging the arms caches for the lives of all the agents. I'd shown Chaleur the letter authorising it signed by the head office of the *Sicherheitsdienst* in Berlin. It was the sort of thing I went to sleep on every night. I was taking part, yes, but in as mild a way as possible, easing pain, saving lives. So this news, on top of learning that men even more involved than myself had tried to smash the torture instrument, brought my house down. I was too weak a life-clinger to do what I gave more thought to than I would have believed possible, even in Le Vernet: shoot myself. I just went on like a robot till LeClerc's army came and took me. I sit in this house I've waited twenty-five years for, but something inside knows that there'll never be an easy time again."

When Hélène would return from one of her sessions in the confessional, I would detest the cleansed and easy self I could almost smell parading around me. I'd try and provoke the "true self," the unlilylike, soiled self who dared to rebuke in purified repose what I had no way of purifying. That afternoon, I would not let August chew me as his absolving wafer. "Well," I said, "it's at least something to be able to feel uneasy, to feel something. And in such lovely surroundings."

"Yes," he said, without the least note of withdrawal from what he well understood in this. "And that, like everything else, increases what it relieves. Accountability for what one does is what I was raised in, and though I've lost much, I haven't lost that. The rest is setting," and he waved over the gorgeous lawn, so green it seemed a text for newness, forgiveness, forgetfulness of the scarred, the dun, the dead. "Anything can play there, murder or garden parties. The flowers and the sun just make what's there clearer. But saying it is about my limit. You'd think a decent man might give it to an orphan society and go off to Africa with Bibles or medical supplies, but I wrap myself in it and try to understand the few things that happened to me and that I happened to. You see, I'm caught by what I've thrown away. You can alter the statue of a fat man to a thin one, but the other way is much harder. All the proportions have to be changed, and then it may not work. There may not be enough material to make even a thin man. It may be too late for me to come out clean. But I can at least see you."

What the hell, I said. Who am I? I didn't even have a trial, and as for Bobbie, what right have I to stand on his grave and spit on this man? So I said I was sorry, and he said he was glad that I'd put it to him, and we went for a walk along the palms, and it was then that I heard for the first time the name of the other Robert.

4

"Row-bairr." Immediately after saying it, August actually shivered, as if his body were trying to regain what its lips had given away. It had come out in this way: August was talking about the failure of the Chaleur air operations, and I'd said it seemed clear to me that it wasn't the drops which were unsuccessful, but something which happened in the subsequent week. "Yes," he said, "that's the way it was worked out. Otherwise it would have been easy to trace the trouble to our Robert."

"Our Robert? Not *my* Robert?"

When do people say what they don't mean to say? What is "not meaning to"? What have the psychologists left us of intention? August did not *mean* to reveal, but he did. Did reveal and did *mean* to. The fissure was there, never to be closed, and certainly not by what he answered, "Take it any way you want. I can't say any more." We were back at the porch, back in our chairs.

"Why not?"

He shook his head, but again, he wanted to tell more than not to tell. "I talked for a year and a half. The matters are really closed. The people I talked about were dead. Why should I now injure someone living, someone who was doing the same work I myself was?"

"I'm alive," I said.

August got up and walked to the steps which led to the rock garden. He went down and planted himself in that brooding whirl of colored stone, stood there while the sun poured gold on his head. As if the surety of rock would pass into him if he stood there. An odd sight. I called to him after a minute. "I don't want to push you into doing what's wrong, but what happened happened. It has a right to be known. Accountability works for everyone. You shouldn't artificially obstruct people from coming to terms with what they've done. Are people rocks to be arranged for decoration?"

He seemed almost stiller than the stones around him, so that when he spoke, I was a little surprised, as if one of them had. "I suppose I want to be pushed." He climbed the two steps and came over and looked down at me. "When I wrote you to come, I made one agreement about what I owed you, and another for myself. Now the agreements are colliding. To relieve you, I've got to injure someone I agreed to leave alone. I'm a weak man. You're here, and he isn't; and without being afraid, I'll tell you, because I don't like anyone near me to be unhappy because of what I do, and am." He took out another cigar, offered it to me, and then, at my nod, lit it himself, a taste of luxurious suspension before he wrecked his small balance. "There was a man in Chaleur who was also our agent. His code name was 'Robert.' I don't know how true he was to us. I myself hardly knew him. I met him only once, near the very end."

"May I ask the occasion?" I thought I would go slowly, indirectly, until the ease of recollection had opened it all.

He tipped the pitcher of iced tea toward my glass, but I shook my head; information was the only thing I wanted from him now. "Teichmann never trusted him. Why should he? He sold out *Chaleur*, why not us? He told us one day that London was becoming suspicious of him. They wanted him to fly back to be cleared. He was going and wanted to give us the BBC code message which would announce his safe arrival there. Also, he had some 'mail' for us. Now his usual cut-out—his contact man—was one of Teichmann's men—Gretch. They usually met in an empty—literally empty—apartment on Rue Courcelles. This last time though, Teichmann was afraid that Robert might try to kidnap Gretch as a sign of his loyalty to the British, and I was sent along to make this at least difficult. Robert did seem unhappy to see two of us walk in, but he handed over the documents and that was that. It was the only time I saw him."

"What was your impression of him?"

He'd been talking with the cigar in his mouth, the words distinct, though the lips and tongue had not moved enough to quiver a curve of ash. Now, with his lips, he tilted the cigar, and the curve split from its stem and broke on the bricks. "On the surface, he was impressive. Very well-dressed, polite, soft-spoken, sprightly, obviously intelligent. There was something spirited about him, *lustig*, not the least ostentatious. He seemed a man used to being attended to. He was businesslike but unrushed, even courtly. He made a very agreeable personal impression. But I knew what he was, a schemer, a traitor, a liar, a rank adventurer."

"Was he a paid agent?"

"I don't think so. Nor was he 'ideological.' I doubt if he cared about anything more than saving his skin. No, he was a type I've met only in this sphere of life, and then but rarely, someone devoid of principle."

The ash formed, tipped. "Why did you let him go back to London if you thought he might betray you? Or if you thought the British would arrest him?"

"He told Teichmann that he'd be able to persuade London that there was nothing to their suspicions. If he succeeded, then he could return, and we would continue to control his information. Even if he didn't return, his replacement might be using the same landing-fields and letter-boxes. If we arrested him, we gained nothing." He tossed the cigar on the lawn. "Nothing better for lawns. You might think the heat would kill, and I suppose it does some harm, but it unleashes wonderful riches. So there it is. I hope it helps you."

Help. It was something more than help. If a boulder is on your leg, and someone raises it, that's help. The relief is there, but your leg is still bruised and suppurating. What August did was more than this, more than a bandage, a shelter in a blizzard, it was like having love amidst great need, something essential but extra. Bobbie had been possibly guilty; now someone else was guilty. That finished Trentemille.

But why hadn't Trentemille known it? If August's words were "extra," it was because they applied to a wound that was equally gratuitous. "Why didn't Père Trentemille know this?" I asked him.

"I suppose he did know that there was a double agent operating," said August. "But he may have confused the code name 'Robert' with your son's Christian name, and since that fitted in with what he'd learned from others, he didn't pursue it further."

"You didn't use 'Robert's' real name?"

"I never knew it. And remember, I was even more uncertain then than I am now about what to tell. If 'Robert' was a traitor to the Allies, he was, after all, a traitor on my side. I shared what he shared even more than most. He was a Frenchman—though for a long time, I thought he was English—and more than most non-Frenchmen, I am French. France is my country more than any other. If I'd gone the one extra step and become a citizen, I would probably have nothing at all to tell you. My not becoming one is almost a disloyalty in me."

And mine? But I wanted something right away, which was about Bobbie's role in the pact, and I asked him.

"Chaleur made it, and he signed it with Teichmann. A perfectly sensible measure of course for men not in uniform and thus un-protected by the Hague Convention. Chaleur called your son in and told him to explain it to some of the agents while he explained it to others. It was no easy job, as you can imagine. We did not let more than two of them meet at one time. It involved no small strain. And then, it came to nothing, after Teichmann was transferred."

77

He got up again, and stood with his head touching one of the porch columns. Behind him, the vacation colors of the south trembled. "It doesn't do you or anyone any good to know that I'd give anything, everything, I swear even my life, if it hadn't happened."

Today, sitting on the same porch, or one as close to it as I was able to find, I might say something like, "There are compensations. If it hadn't happened, I would never have become your friend," but then this small recompense did not exist, and I said nothing at all. His feelings seemed larger than mine, and I let his statement stand uncontradicted, unrejected, unaccepted, something that had to do not with Bobbie and me, but only with him.

CHAPTER 8

The world, at any rate, is brainless and invertebrate, which means it has no central nerve centers where injuries and pleasures identify themselves and become memory. But I wonder, is there only local, unassembled injury and pleasure in the world, each one constituting a jolting contraction along the world skin, a network catching nothing but itself? X shoves Y shoves Z trips A. Whether you love me or whip your dog, work for bread or steal it, whether Bobbie's lungs smoked with chlorate of cyanide by accident or for single-minded heroism may not deflect another atom in the world's motion. Networks. Brotherly filaments? Links of hatred, causality, coincidence? Mirror reflection? Everything that occurs registers as link, but the registration does not dignify the linkage. Life is uninsurable.

As I tracked the center of the Chaleur Network, my mind kept running along the lines of what I myself had done with Bobbie, a connection of injuries which were linked with my own pleasures so consistently that this network seemed to catch something, and that something was not pleasant to contemplate—the fisherman finding the net around his own shark body. Any view was enough to yank at the linked memories, and like the aging man I still could not *feel* I was, I lived more handsomely, more feelingly in what had been than what was.

The first evening with August—I spent two before going on to Venice for three gawking days at the Biennale—we had dinner at the hotel and watched the last match of the Midi Invitation Tournament. That night I was launched into floods of tennis memories, first the tournaments and great matches I'd watched, then my own playing days, and finally, in the fashion of these late memories, the games I used to play with Roland Trancart, especially the one game I played with him which Bobbie watched.

Tennis was always my favorite game, and Roland my favorite opponent. Like myself, he was a prowler, boulevardier, and sport; married, but available, and always ready for what we called excursions. We used to play every Saturday in St. Germain-en-Laye where they had marvellous courts, a surface not unlike a first-rate *en-tout-cas*, a triple surface of varied clays and ground asphalt which was laid down by hand, square inch by square inch. They'd be dry within an hour after a storm, held their markings beautifully, did not decompose under spikes and were in short worthy of the labor that went into them. It cost a pretty penny to rent one, and, even on Saturday, the price kept the customers down in those hard years. (Despite the great Four and Mlle. Lenglen, tennis was not the great sport it became in the post-war years.) Roland and I played three or four hard sets of singles before lunch, and then in the afternoon played doubles with people whom we got to know there.

The courts were set bowl-like in a grove of horse chestnuts which, from spring through fall, detonated the senses with the perfume and massy beauty of their blossoms. Never much of a competitor, except in occasional games with Bobbie and Hélène, I seldom won our matches. The time I brought Bobbie out, he'd felt like going into the country, and I agreed to take him on condition that he wouldn't disturb us. He'd brought a biography of Lyautey to read and a *cahier* in which to write a draft of his Monday's essay. He was thirteen or so at the time, and a touchy young fellow, but capable of great absorption in work, so I felt reasonably sure that he'd not bother us. Now and then, I could not but notice that he was looking up from his book to observe a point. My stroking became self-consciously precise, and my manners absurd. I wanted to demonstrate decent sportsmanship to Bobbie and also wanted to show him that these Saturday excursions were not into swamps of wasted time but were instead artfully worked out triumphs of benevolent superiority.

This was not easy to do. Roland was a tough player. He had a sliced serve which I seldom failed to return, but which I couldn't control. My returns pulled me toward the sideline and then Roland would bang them down the opposite sideline. It was a sign of my fitness that I survived four sets with him, but I very seldom broke his serve.

My own first serve was a cannonball, a back-straining arch and follow-through; when it was going well, I usually held service. Generally, however, we rallied from my patsy of a second serve, a hesitant, depthless American Twist. Here were the pleasures of our tennis day, for we worked each other back and forth across the court, and enjoyed the strategies of tennis in a way which the smashing net-takers of the post-war period never do. The day I speak of, Roland took the first set, seven-five, each of us holding service till the twelfth game, which I lost on a close sideline call by Roland. Bobbie began looking up more frequently in the next set. I began stroking harder, which threw Roland's tempo off, and I won the set six-two. The third set was very hard fought, and Bobbie would occasionally break out in excitement and call the point. I did not pay much attention to this in the first three games, which I won, but when Roland took his service in the fourth, adjusted to my speed—somewhat diminished—and took the fifth, then took his own on four straight points, one an ace, and finally took the first two points of the seventh, I exploded. The third point ended in what looked like my perfect lob to the back court. "Long," called Bobbie. I wasn't even aware he knew the term.

"What?" I said loudly.

"Long," said Bobbie again. Roland said nothing.

"Are you sure, Bobbie? I saw the chalk."

Bobbie went over to the line and said, "There's a small overflow of chalk here. Look."

This was one of the most perfect courts in France. "It was my shot that moved it there then," I said. "The chalk marks ins and outs in tennis, my boy."

"It was really out, Papa." he said.

"Let's play it again," said Roland.

"No," I said quietly, giving Bobbie a look that I trusted he'd see in dreams.

"O.K.," said Roland. "We'll call it good."

But from then on the game went against me. Bobbie didn't call shots that game or the next. In the ninth game, I aced Roland twice, and began to feel that my rage was becoming operative. The third serve was a tremendous shot down the middle line which Roland missed by two feet. "Foot fault," called Bobbie.

I slung my racket at his head. It sailed over him into a mass of horse chestnut blossoms which dropped slowly over him. The racket was stuck in the branches, ten feet up. I took the wooden press in my hands and walked over to dislodge the racket. Bobbie, seeing me coming, stood up and faced me, his face scarlet. He thought I was going to hit him with the press, but he did not run or speak. My insides somersaulted. I dropped the press, ran over, put my arms around him and apologised over and over while the blossoms came down on our heads.

2

Just as memories cluster around a mastering situation, so it is a common experience to find that once you come upon a name for the first time, you begin to see it everywhere. It's as if a new species had been introduced into existence, one with a rabbit talent for reproduction. Or better, it's like the discovery of a virus behind a variety of apparently unrelated symptoms: after the discovery, you wonder why their kinship wasn't transparent. So after August opened up the existence of "Robert" to me, his name began turning up everywhere. All filaments of the network led to him, and the contradictions that had worried me before seemed from the new vantage point little more than an infant's view of a debenture bond, a diversion to surface, pictorial value. The world began to look like a functioning, meaningful organism, and the meaning was nailing "Robert."

After my southern swing, I went back to the hard benches of the Palais de Justice and went digging through the records of the TMP to see if the virus turned up in them. It did not the first day, but in the afternoon of the second, I came upon the deposition of Wolfgang Kleppa, a notorious Gestapo agent who had infiltrated a network called St.-Juste by making one of its couriers, "La Lupine," his mistress. The Chaleur *réseau* was partly a reconstitution of the remains of St.-Juste, and Kleppa's deposition was an account of those members of the later network with whom he had had something to do. In his thirty-five pages, no paragraph was more vehement than the one which described "Robert."

"Robert" was the keystone of Teichmann's arch: upon him rested Teichmann's control of the network. As a double agent, "Robert" was invaluable; as a man he was a viper. He was as mean-spirited a man as I've ever come upon, a man utterly without scruples, offensive in person, corrupt in morals. He would have sold out anyone for a few francs. His chief characteristic, in my opinion, was a boundless ego which put itself above cause, country, fellow-man, or God.

The other pertinent passage of Kleppa's deposition had to do with the visit of Colonel Wynn-Wyndward to Paris. Kleppa had been told of the visit by his own inside agent, Bire-Taise (a fringe member of a Gaullist network), and when he asked Teichmann to find out Wynn-Wyndward's exact location from "Robert," Teichmann said that "Robert" hadn't told him anything about the visit.

... yet as Air Operations Officer, "Robert" must have known about Wynn-Wyndward. He would have been in charge of the landing operation and reception committee. If he pretended not to know about it, then he must have kept it from Teichmann to cast suspicion on Bire-Taise whom he regarded as a rival. Or he wanted to convince London that he was loyal, for if someone as important as Wynn-Wyndward could stay in Paris without being taken, accusations made against "Robert" would appear to be baseless.

There again, from inside the cancer itself, was the piratical virus. That Kleppa himself was all that he described "Robèrt" as being, did not, in my view, detract from his testimony. Once again, I could not understand how so blindingly clear a guilt had not been immediately discovered and proclaimed.

"Robert" next turned up on the Chaleur side of things. The next Sunday I went to see Madame Petsch, whose address was in the *Geburtstagbuch*. She lived on the Rue d'Alésia across from the Sainte Anne Psychiatric Center where she worked as an attendant. Twenty years she'd been engaged in this work, and during the Occupation, it made an admirable cover for her underground activities. She'd been a "letter-box" for St.-Juste, and then one of the foundation blocks of Chaleur. Seized by the Germans in the round-up of September, 1943, she was sent to Fresnes Prison and then to Natzweiler, where she nearly died of pneumonia, and was only saved from the gas chamber where the sick were dispatched when another woman covered for and took care of her, only to succumb to the illness herself. Madame Petsch contained this catalogue of tribulation in a minute body, surprisingly agile in view of its sufferance and years. She was sixty and had been widowed since her fortieth year.

I saw her after church. Her husband had been a Protestant, and although she had never ceased to think of herself as a Catholic, she went to Protestant services except at Easter, Christmas and Pentecost. "It has something to do with the cleanliness," she said to me. "I am exceptionally drawn to the simplicity and poverty of the services. The church is hardly more than a white room, and the minister is splendid. Protestant sermons are stimulating things to hear week after week. It's become a habit with me." This was not the Danbury Park Presbyterian Church of my boyhood: I never knew a human being dull enough to be stimulated by, or even habituated to those tepid billows of sanctity.

I did not linger in comparative religion, but went to the new heart of my business and asked Madame Petsch if she'd known "Robert," the Air Operations Officer who'd replaced Peugeot.

"Not well, but I knew him." She said this very easily, as she watched her fingers work a white thread out of the embroidered edge of her dress. Then—it was an agent's trick—her head snapped up and her eyes were hard on mine. "Why?"

I'd been thinking of her as an old lady, though I'm now the age she was then and do not think myself markedly older than I was that day. With that movement and question, I turned into the old one of the pair. It took me a minute to realise that I wasn't being accused, only asked a question. "I've got evidence that makes it clear to me that he was an agent for the Germans. I want to get some further evidence before I do anything about it."

She subsided to her thread, studious and remote. Then, "I suspected 'Robert' very early. Without any real evidence at first, just something over-elaborate in his movements. I'm used to the disguises of my patients, and superfluous gestures detach themselves very quickly for me. Then a couple of things happened, and my discomfort with him attached itself to them. I didn't—in a way, I couldn't—say anything about it. I'd only seen him four or five times, and I wasn't really experienced in underground work. As for the network, I knew only the four or five people who used me as a letter-box. But I told Chaleur. That was in March of forty-three. He'd come to stay with me because he'd seen a man he didn't recognise hanging around his street. He never went back, but he only stayed two nights with me. He was so tired, more tired than I'd ever seen him, though it was worse when he came back from London that summer. I know those looks from my patients. But then, I asked him what the matter was. 'There's something wrong,' he said. 'I feel it here,' and he touched his chest. He was so fine a boy, so undemonstrative and simple. He was a great scientist, you know. Once he talked to me about animals. It was wonderful, why they grow only so big, why some have spines, some wings, some fingers."

"What did he say when you told him you suspected 'Robert'?"

"He dismissed it. He said, 'If you knew how many times I've heard accusations about everyone but myself, you'd wonder if we weren't all guilty. Or out of our minds. You could send your patients out on the streets tomorrow in our places, and I think they'd act as sensibly. They may be mad individually, but I think our occupation's mad.' And he said it was like complex nervous systems developing spines for centers and spines requiring muscle tissues. 'Maybe our work requires a certain amount of insanity.' He was partly joking, but I couldn't say anything more. He was so tired."

This was not substantial evidence. "Did you have anything more than suspicion? Or do you now? Did anything confirm your feelings about him?"

"Absolutely." She sat up like a hundred-franc doll, her black eyes popped like a doll's. "When I was questioned at Avenue Foch, the German interrogator, a decent enough man, showed me a photostat of a letter which had been given to me to send to London, and which I myself had handed to 'Robert,' because it was too long for radio transmission and had to go by air. Since the person who'd handed it to me would have incriminated himself if the SD had seen the letter, and since I didn't turn it over to the Germans, simple subtraction leaves 'Robert.' I said as much to the TMP, but Arastignac walks around today, free as—"

"Arastignac?" A band struck up.

"Of course. That's his name. 'Robert's' his code name. Jean-François Arastignac. He's free and prospering. I think he's with a commercial airline. That's the way things go. At least on earth. But there are other judgements."

Judgements. That was the fuzziness in the clear blood of "Robert's" treason. Why hadn't he been judged guilty and imprisoned? Madame Petsch had testified, and one whiff of testimony would have led authority to the whole sewer. But they had more; they had Kleppa. At least. What else, I didn't know, but the next day, right after I got by *pneumatique* Madame Petsch's signed account of what she'd told me, I went back to the records at the Palais de Justice to skim the fuzziness away. Only there, the fuzziness condensed into an alien system of revelation.

3

At Tuley High School, half a century ago, our science teacher, Mr. Harrington, gathered us round his desk to watch him coat a cardboard cylinder with wax and then put it up against a pin which was fixed to another cylinder. Into the second cylinder, our class sang the "Battle Hymn of the Republic" while the pin dug shakily into the waxed cylinder which Mr. Harrington revolved in his hand.

84

After the wax hardened, he drew the pin across the odd scratches of its trail, reversed the megaphone cylinder into a crude amplifier, and listened to the rising, falling squeaks we recognised as "Mine eyes have seen the glory of the coming of the Lord." No record has ever impressed me more than that one. Those sounds came out like colors, and I think the reason was that we knew so well what we had put into the record that we magnified its pathetic reduction into the magical confirmation of our knowledge.

This is the way it was with my reading of the records of "Robert's" hearing before the Tribunal Militaire. Knowing what he was, the facts strode out toward me with the scarlet clarity of my certainty. All that I knew was there, and contrary fact—what I didn't know— was little more than the irrelevant scratches wandering out of the wax with the song we'd sung. When I came then upon the absolving verdict of the Tribunal, it was as if Mr. Harrington had announced that the noise which our cylinder had played back to us was in truth Class 6B's recital of the Gettysburg Address.

That was the immense discrepancy between "Robert's" defense and the judgement. After all, his defense was nothing more than the claim that he had "played along" with the Germans on special orders from London. The single corroboration of the claim was a deposition by Colonel Wynn-Wyndward, the heart of which was four sentences:

"Robert" was an outstanding agent, courageous and intrepid. I owe my life to him, for he knew my whereabouts throughout my stay in France, and he helped me move in perfect safety. To my knowledge, I cannot say that "Robert" ever acted in a manner that was contrary to instructions. Of course, like all agents in the field, he was necessarily given wide latitude.

Though pressed by the *juge d'instruction*, Wynn-Wyndward would do little more than reshuffle these sentences. "Robert's" own testimony was given in what was described in the reports as "a straight-forward manner" which impressed the court. He had removed the Légion d'Honneur from his button-hole before speaking, and his words were similarly unadorned; he was completely absolved of the charges.

The only explanation I could summon up to mortar the space between the charge and the judgement was that the court suspected the British of engineering the whole sell-out, and was under instructions from the very top not to embarrass them. As for London, my feeling was that they did not wish to bear the responsibility for having recruited false agents and of running the entire operation with criminal obtuseness. They, therefore, supported it wherever they could, and here the support was grounded in Wynn-Wyndward's partial view of "Robert," which derived entirely from the fact of his own immunity in Paris. To me the defense was comparable to, say, a claim by Dillinger that his robberies had been worked out in conjunction with J. Edgar Hoover to flush out poor banking procedures in the Mid-west. The exoneration was farcical, and it was clear to me that the records contained but bare hints of the truth.

4

There were, however, some incidental surprises in them, one of which concerned Rampigli and Debrette. These sworn enemies, these mutual denouncers, had each deposed in favor of the other's loyalty and bravery, even while claiming that the other disliked and would undoubtedly slander him. It was almost comic relief, and it so lightened my puzzled gloom that it led me to the first real side-path in my investigation. I decided to tell each one about the other's testimony and arrange a peacemaking reunion at my apartment. I went to St. Lazare and bought a Caen-Paris round-trip ticket for two weeks from the next Sunday, and mailed it with a letter to Debrette. I wrote a similar letter to Rampigli. I did not telephone, because I wanted nothing to interfere with the rush of my gratuitous good feeling. This act did not spring from obligation, entertainment, or even from any contrived "do-goodism." I did it as if there were no alternative. There was no question of irrelevance or inaction, and so for me it was in a way as important as anything else I'd done.

Links. I will not leap to astral networks for explanations, but, returning to the apartment after mailing those letters, aglow with my selflessness, I passed the bus stop at Avenue de Messine-Rue de Lisbonne and heard the croaked syllables of my given name.

Was nature itself praising me? I turned around and, for a moment, didn't notice the blotch of old flesh for whom, thirty years before, I would have spent a year in the galleys. If it hadn't been for a story in the newspapers about her daughter, the wife of a diplomat in Indo-China who'd behaved heroically in a guerrilla attack, I might not have recognised her at all. I had thought, though, on reading the article, how remarkable it was that two such notorious non-combatants as Phebe Delattre and myself should have produced heroic offspring, and I remember daydreaming about a match between the pretty young woman on *Figaro*'s second page and Bobbie, and designing their polite offspring, all shaded from Phebe and myself.

Ten years younger than I, Phebe looked, in my view, ten years older, so wrinkled, spotted, and crooked that my recognition must have gone underneath appearance to let me bring up so quickly, "Phebe, *ma chère* Phebe."

I thought there would be a scene, there at four o'clock while a bus pulled in. Nobody apparently had felt or said "my dear" to Phebe in years. And what a fall that was, thought I, as I took her hand and felt it grab at mine beyond the occasion.

When I'd first met her in the twenties, Phebe had been too lovely to be quite believable, yet so casually beautiful she seemed a natural phenomenon. Her hair was the color of sunny fog, her eyes, a Norman blue which went back to ninth-century ships coming up the Seine, naively clear yet touched with the premonition that they'd soon be assimilated into common soil. Is this exaggeration? Not for this one. A Paramount director had picked her out of a crowd scene in one of Abel Gance's epics—I saw it on a triple-size screen back in the twenties, *plus ça change*—and she went to California to see if her beauty were generally marketable. But Phebe was committed to nothing but change, and California lasted even less time than I did. I'd met her the month before Hélène put the ski pole into her own leg in the Arlberg hills, and all through the thousand gathering streams of that infection, I saw her, here and there, at parties, and once or twice alone. We had friends in common, and I knew her fiancé, a crapulous Breton whose arrogant parents made it so hot for her that she gave up the social ship and started in the films. After a couple of skittery years, she handed herself to Delattre, a cynical old world-beater who let her go her own way and speed. I didn't see much of her till 1931, just before she had another chance at Hollywood, this one even briefer, as it turned out. We crossed together on the old *Europa*, a trip which would have shattered a stronger passion than mine. Phebe suffered a *mal de mer* whose chief sympton was dispatching me on errands over the ship. Our intimacies, their preludes and postludes, were constantly undercut by her shakiness and commandeering. I've never quite dissociated her from bottles of pills and tottering bowls of boiling consommé. And I never really thought of her again as a beautiful woman, even, as was not infrequently the case, when I heard her raved about in that fashion.

Now she was drawing me toward the bus, begging me to accompany her as far as her destination. She met "friends" every pleasant Friday at the Café Lamartine. I was feeling generally benevolent enough to drag along. Her sharp old face pointed me like quarry. "What have you been doing, Sam-son? I'm not much *au monde* myself, but no one sees you. Even after the war, I would hear about you now and then, but for months no one's mentioned you." Her English was marvellous, untarnished by anything foreign but a few throaty airs and depths. It was, I suppose, the remaining camouflage of her vacuity. She was fishing tickets out for the conductor, none, of course, for my fare.

"I'm not around," I said. "I've been on a kind of mission. About Bobbie."

"Bobbie?" Vague and stupid. She used to cuddle him like a grandmother. Finally, "Yes. I'm sorry about that, Sammy. He was a beautiful boy." That, of course, he was not, but what exactly was it that she was sorry about? There was something odd in that agitated vacuum. Could she have heard about Trentemille's accusation?

I asked her if she knew any more than that Bobbie had been killed. "Is there something more?" she asked.

At our most intimate, Phebe had never been a confidante of mine. Something in her prevented any sort of sympathy but a spasmodic, physical one. Her life was a series of contrivances to cover up her cold ego, and she could appear sympathetic just as she could mimic any politician or actress in the world, but even stupid people could see that there was nothing in her to really hold to. On the bus, though, the obliteration of every sign of her beauty offered an illusion of substance that was new to me, and somehow I fastened on to it and poured out Bobbie's story, his heroism, his death in the gas chamber, Trentemille's accusation, and what I had been doing about it.

It took less than fifteen minutes, but it was a tiring account, one I'd not given before, and I turned to her expecting to see her face tense with sympathy. It was astonishingly icy. "If I were you," she said, "I'd leave all that alone."

I could hardly believe it. "What do you mean, Phebe?" I really did not understand what she meant.

"What's your proverb about smoke and fire? The present isn't the pleasantest time of my life, but I could make it into Hell in ten minutes by looking backward. You always did like to sink back on what you'd done, Sam. You had energy, and then wasted half of it digging graves. I should think you'd have learned something. And of all things to meddle with, the war's the very worst."

It was fantastic, a completely gratuitous attack by someone whose role, at the very worst, was to say nothing at all. "I can't consider that sensible advice, Phebe. Suppose it was your girl? Suppose that instead of being celebrated for bravery, someone had accused her of something terrible? What would you do?"

"If it were someone unreliable, the accusation would be ignored. If the accuser were reliable, I would accept it, and live with it as a bitter truth. I have enough in my life to face without facing anyone else's trouble. My life is no one else's. You learned that years ago."

There it was in all its loveliness, the simplest of all life's principles, the one which had supervised my deformity for years. Who was I to be repulsed by it when uttered by a miserable old hound trying to do little more than keep the wind out of her underwear until six feet of French earth did it for her? But there was something else, some drift of misery running under the ice of her ego, and it struck me there and then that just possibly there was more to this than the proclaiming of a principle. Phebe had been notoriously friendly with people in the SS. She may actually have stumbled onto something about Bobbie, and there was no reason in the world to avoid this slim possibility. "Phebe," I said, "do you perhaps know something that pertains directly to Bobbie?"

She got up, half a mile from where she should have gotten off, looked at me with a flood of hatred that washed decades from her face, and said, "I knew you'd come to that. You. You were never one to lean on." She pushed back my knees with her legs and left the bus.

5

Accidents, filaments. That this old truck of passion whom I'd fueled for odd excursions a quarter of a century before should somehow have been in some sort of touch with the network was enough to set my old mystic skeleton quivering like a shorting circuit. I got off the bus at Luxembourg, and climbed into one across the street for my return. "Should it even matter?" I asked myself. "After all, I have my fox, trapped tight. What can be added or taken away? I've got enough right now to take back to Trentemille, if not the courts." But even thinking that, I knew that some curlicue had come into my knowledge. The testimony of Arastignac's defense, which had seemed weightless to me as I read it, now was somehow leaden in my mind. How its plausibility would affect the accusation against Bobbie, I couldn't see. He still seemed clear as air, yet, as the bus chugged along, I became depressed. Just as the case seemed about over so that I could enter such benevolent side-pockets as reuniting Debrette and Rampigli, some decay in what I *"knew"* was rotting my impulse to terminate the case. I had to find out about Phebe, perhaps from

Armand; I would try and see Wynn-Wyndward in London, and maybe Teichmann or other SD officials in Germany. And with this spelled-out intention to continue, my depression disappeared. It's only now that I can guess that it was my own need that did not want the case to end, that my own case had not been settled, my own defecting not been tried. If the verdict on Chaleur had spoken out of a burning bush, I would not have stopped looking.

CHAPTER 9

The Showalters used to call me "our expatriate," until I objected that the term applied to those who found their country uninviting and who went through the world cashing in on their superiority to it. Europe is usually an interlude in American lives, a pleasure wedged into routine. The Showalters overlooked the fact that for me Europe was a form of Chicago, a place to work and raise a family. I came to it accidentally, or, at least, like many Americans, as a soldier, and I stayed for those good American and human reasons, work and a wife.

I was twenty-six when the First War ended. I was instructing at the artillery school at Chateauroux, and expecting to go up to the front. The ending was too quick for me, not that I was rushing toward the trenches, or that I wept when the shots stopped. I wanted to look around Europe. I thought of going to one of the schools that were being set up for soldiers in the Midi, but as I had a little money in Liberty Bonds, I decided to use it for an untrammeled spree. I thought I could last six or eight months on it, and then go back to sobriety and law school. But I met Hélène.

There are meetings and meetings. I wonder if a statistician will ever be able to predict if a first meeting will come to something? I'd like to see the theory that would get Bobby's first encounter with Jacqueline into the same equation as mine with Hélène. I'm not sure I can bring back what counted for me that first evening in the glum apartment she and Armand moved into after the old man ran off with Armand's fiancée. I know that I was in uniform. I've got photographs to bolster that memory. I was a decent-enough-looking young fellow. (Maybe I ought to spell that "feller" to increase the distance between my young self and the compliments I endow him-it with.) In the stiff-backed pose, I'm triangling a leg at the knee for informality, but having your picture taken in a uniform was an occasion few were worldly enough to unstiffen. Now I'm surprised to see that I was light enough then at twenty-six to be listed as blond. Straw hair, slicked under a stiff peak, a nose trying for status although both bulbous and snub, eyes like a weak *tisson*, slender, five-ten or eleven. I'm describing what Hélène must have looked at. Plus—maybe —a little spirit, though I hadn't been in many French homes, wasn't confident of the lingo, and may well have looked stiffer than the photograph.

Georges Sensmesnil brought me. He was a Boisdevres cousin and had been our French liaison at Chateauroux, a competent, rapid, witty man. I wish I could give a decent picture of him. Value. That's what he reeked of. He counted, was honest, a real man, ordinary but refined. Valuable. I loved him, and love remembering him.

He brought me up the street—can I remember it was dusk, my favorite time?—I know it was for dinner, a treat for me. I was living in an eighth-rate hotel, stretching my money, preparing itineraries, but so happy, so relaxed in Paris, I couldn't budge.

Hélène was not the hook. It was Armand. Georges had talked of his great abilities, and his immediate need for a few thousand francs to start a small steel fabrication concern he was setting up around a chunk of *matériaux de guerre* which he'd bought for next to nothing. We'd had an apéritif, the three of us, one February day in the stovesmoke of a little bar which sits exactly where the Cinéma Grevin is today on Rue Bourdalue. Armand made a good impression. A beautiful talker, rich in fact, modest in statement. He doesn't resemble a fox, but his mind is so red and slick that I manufacture a long fox-face out of his normal French one. He outlined his proposal. Was I interested? It was a big risk, I said, the nineteen hundred dollars was all I had. If there were no return in a few months, I'd have to wire my parents for passage money. Either way, I'd have to entrust the investment to him. But at least I'd have a stake in Europe, which was something I wanted. Decision in a week; meanwhile, dinner *chez* Armand.

What hit me first about Hélène? I suppose her looks. She was marvellous looking, all dark around very fair skin, soft and strong. How say it? She was a wise woman, at times. She had unusual patience, again at times, waited out ideas, and then expressed them beautifully without falsification. And then, passion: she had a great deal: much feeling. As we went on together, there was too much. The passion flooded the wisdom and became a monstrosity in her. It was my fault. I goaded her, tyrannised her, praised her for virtues which stuck in my throat, knocked her beauties, which excited me more than I wanted.

I'm exaggerating a bit. If we had x numbers of hours together, the happy ¼ x was worth twice as much as the ¼ x that was hell and the ½ x that just was.

But that day, that evening, she was just there, a largish girl, a very pretty one; and of course, both of us leaked availability. No, I can't do it. I remember almost nothing. There was a maid, but Hélène cooked. No impression. I only know for sure that I don't remember Armand, Georges, or myself that evening. If I sit down and concentrate on my life with Hélène, I think of millions of actions, words, places, but my late memories are governed by disaster, and the memory of Hélène which weighs on me now is the end of what began with that first meeting. By then, there was little wisdom and less patience left in either of us.

It was at Christmas in 1926, up in the Arlberg, twenty years before the mountains had more customers than trees. Hélène and I had gone skiing with Georges and Vilette Sensmesnil. That cold air, heated red gold by the dipping sun, set up such appetite for life, for speed, muscle work, food, drink, and each other that it seemed for our few days the only place life should be permitted. Until, up there, it came to Hélène that there was too much life in her, that she had missed her period, that her breasts were swelling, and that the morning nausea forecast a summer birth.

For me, it was good news, and that for Hélène was the end of whatever joy she might have squeezed from it. By that time, competition was what engineered our time together. Every week we surprised each other with discoveries. It was a rule of the game to be delighted at the other's discovery, and it was real delight at the beginning, but after a while Hélène regarded a new book I'd read, a new game, a new person, a new style, phrase, or insight, as an obstacle to her ascent in life. She measured her ascent against mine, and I responded in kind. Our innovations became a form of chronic exhaustion. Nor did we exhaust only each other, but involved our friends; one consequence of this was that we were regarded as the life of parties. People looked happy when we arrived. "What's new?" was the phrase that accompanied us over Paris. Even our mystic fits, more or less genuine in us, became crazes.

Up on the Arlberg that last vacation, we were as usual playfully innovating and this time in a way which created the frenzied atmosphere that generated Hélène's accident. I don't exactly remember the rules of the crucial game, but I can produce the general pattern the way I can "Now I lay me down to sleep." It started with a mockery of the hotel's "English table," two apple-cheek boys, one standard maiden aunt, and "Mummy and Dads," pink, benign, with voices which issued out of their noses. They were always at table when we arrived, always sweatered and ski-panted for the slopes, and always in the midst of answering "Dads'" questions. Thus, "What are the French, German, and Italian names for Geneva?" "How many Italian lira can be exchanged for two Swiss francs?" "Name four of Thackeray's novels and two of Zola's." "Oh God," said Hélène at this. Our own table was across from the English one, and we spent most of the first breakfast trying to eavesdrop the questions and supply answers. Meal Two, after three hours on the beginners' slopes for three of us, and one on the regular slopes for Hélène, who, no better than any of us, would admit to being a beginner in nothing, Meal Two saw us contriving questions for each other at an Austrian shilling per answer. Meal Three had us playing in pairs against each other with the price of the afternoon chocolate and schnapps at stake. Meal Seven began a running competition in points, the outcome of which would decide who would pay for the ten days. Flushed with cold air, bright sun, Austrian butter, *glühwein*, rum punches and each other, the competition became the focus of the holiday. Questions were prepared beforehand, and under the eiderdowns at night we anticipated ones that would be launched at us.

A new set of living habits forms a kind of blast furnace which takes all of your new energy and then some. Sleep in the frozen heights is crucial, and we were losing it. In the morning, we skied down a snow-packed rivulet to the main house where we ate, tense with lack of sleep and expectation of the Sensmesnil questions. I was especially tense because of Hélène's conduct in the game. She had positive opinions and little information. Almost every one of her answers roused debate. The Sensmesnils were most charitable for a while, but then Vilette began to see that gallantry was going to be more expensive than prudence could tolerate. Georges was suspended between tolerance and his wife's righteous protectiveness, and I was losing my small ability to deflect Hélène's absurd cocksureness. The precipitating exchange concerned contract bridge, which Hélène and I had started playing with the Sensmesnils the spring before when my parents had sent over Vanderbilt's rule book. The issue was something like the penalty for reneging. Hélène responded that there was no penalty, that reneging was only a dangerous strategy. "You penalise yourself, if that's what you mean," she said to Georges, her obstinate perversity all charm and jam.

"Very intelligent," said Georges, "but I'm quite sure there's a two-trick penalty."

"That's correct," said I. "I'll write down your point." We kept a book with two columns.

Hélène's hand was on my writing one. "Don't write it down. The discussion isn't over."

I shook off her hand, smiled and said, "I'm afraid Georges is right this time."

"You're afraid about contradicting anybody else's opinion, aren't you?"

"No, I'm not."

"Then it's a pleasure for you to think me wrong, isn't it?" A sweet tone sheathed her genuine misery and hatred.

I was fed up with her stupidity and arrogance. "Yes," I said. "It's a pleasure to see you revealed as a liar and ignoramus. You've bullied the truth so long, you think you can make murder smell like charity. You're wrong, wrong, and wrong. Your charm will buy you nowhere. You're so stinking mean, every speck of me sings when it shows through."

Before I finished this aria, her coffee cup was in the air and past my dodging ear into the fine English wool on our neighbor's chest. A terrible roar from old Dads, and shrieks from Mummy and Auntie. The little boys were, I think, delighted at this way of ending school. I was prone with apology. I explained that Hélène had been affected by the altitude, begged forgiveness. There was no response but the frozen hatred of injured empire. "I shall find you a new sweater," I said and ran out, after Hélène, who had rushed off. She was sitting on the bench outside the hotel, strapping on her skis, her face all red and piquant, so aglow and fruit-like I could have eaten her with joy. Instead, I raised my hand and swung at her. The night before, we'd walked back across the snow between the *Gasthof Post* and our sleeping hut after dancing for two hours with each other. We could hardly wait to come together. Every star in the hemisphere paraded in those mountains, and the moon looked like a yellow animal running among the peaks. Under the eiderdown we'd been as intimate with each other as we'd ever been in our lives. There wasn't even a questioning session. Now her face stayed still before my hand, and grew a smile where my palm had gashed open on her teeth. Then she was off, sliding down the street toward the lift, and an hour later, shussing down a hill she had no right to be on, she somersaulted, and put the pole through her trousers into her thigh. Not a word did she say about it, nor was I in a position to see it for the pivotal month.

"A suicide," I overheard, as I walked behind her coffin, three months later. I suppose it was; and for years afterward, I hated that dramatizing carelessness which caused her to do nothing about her wound until nothing could be done. All the staphylococci of that willing, pregnant body had contrived a pageant of revenge for me.

Oh Hélène, sweet heart that you were of mine, I watched the headaches, bleeding, vomiting, feverish, sore-swollen repository of filth that you became, as I might have watched my heart extracted under local anesthetic.

And that funeral, your father and brother walking on either side of me, their detestation soaking me so that I was diverted from the meaning of that walk to the cemetery. Not for seven years had they seen each other, their lesion must have been at least scarred over; but the smell of it was fresh and robbed you of their final respect, as I was to rob you a few moments later. And Bobbie. That was also pretty. His galoshes were too big and that late snow squished in his heels. He walked with Nurse Worthington, hand in hand, and I believe he was the only marcher undiverted from the pain of fare-well. There'd been a real tear-jerker in your room, staged by you and Nurse: he'd been carried down like David Copperfield at night, and you, swelling and grotesque, had had a moment of narcotic relief in which to shape his dreams for the rest of his life. What a mixture you were, lovely, witty, wise, harsh, vengeful, egomaniacal. How you'd have appreciated your funeral, your father and brother chained by hatred, your shaken son, and maybe even me, as, at the edge of the grave, I looked up at Phebe Delattre, in black with a half-veil over her perfect face, and indicated to her that I would see her as soon as the funeral was over.

2

It was a week after the encounter with Phebe before I could get Armand to spend an hour with me. Like most managers, he was completely in control of his time. He could persuade a man that he was at his immediate and total disposition, or he could be as in-accessible as the Dalai Lama. It took me four phone calls even to get to talk to him. At any rate, we met, again at Printinière's; I was determined to let my system enjoy itself if I had to erect a Chinese Wall between it and my inquisitorial self.

Armand was an arrangement of blues, the suit like a storming sky, the breast-pocket handkerchief a Fra Angelican peak of hope, the shirt a mere dusk flush in the gray, the shoes a dark suede. Could he have also had on blue underwear? It was a teasing query. Listing the items makes them comic, but in person, he glittered perfection: the human animal on top of its surroundings, Armand, the ecological phenomenon.

His eyes, however, are reddish brown. He did not truckle to iritic dyes or contact lenses, and thus stayed a few feet this side of mania. "Now what about Phebe? I've hardly seen her since the war." This as he spooned up a lobster bisque that purred a tender little sea-song.

"It's about those times I want to know." This between slurps of rapture. The bronzy flames roused blue streaks in his eyes; the bisque had blue shadows. I felt pleased at the cooperation. I'd make my slow way through the blue tide. "About Phebe during the war."

"Is there something special you're thinking of?"

"Yes."

"That you can't ask her?"

"That I did ask her."

A nod. He pushed half a bowl of soup aside. Then he wiped his knives and forks on his napkin one by one and restored them to his place. Although this is a habit, Armand sometimes recalls where he is and controls it. When he doesn't, it means that he's distracted. A good sign.

"She knows something about Bobbie."

"I should think so. Which of your friends doesn't?"

"Something I don't know, which she doesn't want to tell me, something that went on during the war, about the network, or about Trentemille. That's the priest who accused Bobbie—" Armand's eyebrows had pretended to forget who Trentemille was, another good sign, for he forgets nothing, particularly a detail which doesn't affect his own concerns. "I don't know what, but you knew her a good deal better during that time than I, and I wonder if you could imagine what it is."

"I cannot imagine."

"Then do you *know?*" Armand will make "honest" exits on words.

He took up the fish fork and cleaned it once again on his napkin. As if on signal, the waiter brought our trout. Armand cleaned the rest of the silver. He was not in the habit of being pressed, certainly not by me at any rate. "I do not know." Pause. "Anything that would bear on your problem."

I had two bites of the fish, marvelous, clean, toasty, a taste that seemed to come and go like a gull hunting scraps. "But I'd like to know anything, however remote." Armand's addition after the pause was a slip, or a scrupulosity which stood for something in him I didn't recognise. (Naturally I'm thinking of this in the light of what I've come to know. I may not have been so alert at the time.) "Anything which Phebe might know about our Bobbie."

Never before had I given Armand a part of Bobbie. It speeded what might have come anyway. "She knew that Bobbie was the person who had come to me with the message that I must blow up the plant."

"What?"

"That he was in the dark when I opened my apartment door, that he put his hand over my mouth before my hand clicked the switch, that he said, 'It's I, Bobbie. Don't make a noise,' then let me go, put on the light, kissed my cheek, and said before he said another word, 'I have a terrible but necessary thing to ask you, Uncle. There is no choice, so it's more a telling than an asking,' and then told me, told me that the factory I had put together brick by brick, that has every ounce of my thought and hope in it, had to go, that I had to designate areas which would be exploded, that I had to cripple it. If the factory had been a child, he would have used the same words. The plant was my child. And the plant would have been his. That Phebe knew, if that will help you."

I had stopped eating. "Why haven't you ever told me?"

"Because," said Armand, "I was furious at him. I didn't know that I would be able to restrain myself and live with you if I told you how traitorously he treated me. There were hundreds of other plants the underground could have worked with. Ours was not that important to the Germans. It was chosen because its owner was the uncle of an agent. They had an inside track to destruction. Instead of protecting what was his blood right to protect, my nephew handed it over to them."

Armand looked so small, so set apart in his ridiculous blue exclusiveness, that I felt for him as I never before had. Poor lonely old bachelor fanatic, growing this injury in his memory, never venting his anger directly on me, miserable little despot of himself.

"I'm sorry about that, Armand. You should have told me."

He shrugged this off. "I managed. It took them some weeks to force me, 'our Bobbie'" (ice in this) "the most insistent of the forcers. I told no one, no one but Phebe that first night; and I've regretted that weakness."

"I understand."

"Then perhaps you can understand why she was not cordial to your inquiry. Not that she was loyal to me. I suppose it left a bad taste in her mouth."

"Maybe so," I said. Armand was emptied of what he had to say, and, it seemed, of everything else. Never since has he seemed a formidable person to me. I tried to hurry the rest of my dinner to spare him, but even so I enjoyed it immensely, and not only with a divorced system.

CHAPTER 10

"What's the worry?" Madame Zdonowycz asked me the morning of the day I expected Debrette and Rampigli. "That newspaper'll be your tombstone if you stay there any longer. That important, no news is. Not even kings and queens in town." Madame Zdonowycz was antiroyalist in all but attention. She'd caught her first cold in twenty years soaking up snow while she waited for Wilhelmina of the Netherlands to zip around Place Vendôme. "Would they let me in the Ritz WC to dry off? You bet not. Too much blue-blood. That blood don't see no air." Which meant that aristocrats were arrogant and cowardly. I may give a Berlitz course in Zdonowycz one day.

"I've got company coming this afternoon."

"I'll be out."

"I don't want you out. There'll be two gentlemen."

"You sick?"

"Perhaps we could give them a little tea and cake."

"Perhaps we could."

They were due at three. At two-thirty, I nearly told the concierge, Madame Gonella, to tell them I was sick, that they should meet each other at Weber's. But I didn't. There wasn't real reason for me to be uncomfortable. It was, after all, sheer good will on my part. Neither man had to come; in agreeing to, it would seem that it was something they welcomed. Why were my insides jiggling like a music box?

I suppose it had to do with awareness that I was meddling. I've had a life which would have been much the worse for meddlers and snoopers, and I hate this breed of idlers and mischief-makers above all others. That sort of sloth has never been mine. I've had enough life of my own not to need the blood-sucking eavesdropping and nosiness of this crew. I don't spend an hour a year slandering my fellows. But I understand the worms. You spot them immediately in business, letters piled on desks, rushing down the hall, ears twitching at telephone rings. Front, all front. Within their hearts, idleness, envy, fear, great holes to be plugged by shouts and interference.

And with Rampigli and Debrette, this is close to what I was doing. Matching, appointment-making, the camouflage for prying, parasitism. Who elected me marriage counselor, who said the world would turn to dust if they continued their separate ways? The snooper and meddler takes his risk; this meeting might be a disaster. Daggers drawn, the madmen strangling each other. Why not? It would be no novelty for them. Cracking heads with bottles, dynamiting trains.

At 2:50, the concierge's buzz. I sounded the entry ring, and went to the door.

I never saw a more brilliant brown than the gabardine in which Rampigli shot up the stairs, and then, with hardly a "Hello," past me in the foyer, ahead of me into the living room, his monstrous pointer going left, right, then nuzzling the window. "Lovely, lovely place. The père de Gruyère's a man of taste." The turret swung the great gun back and forth. "Splendid view." Nothing could be plainer than a row of Paris three-flats. But at least the reconnaissance was satisfactory. He spread his arms. "I'm ready. Open arms. I have no bitterness. I came a few minutes early to tell you that if anything occurs, it will not be because of my feelings."

This announcement did not blot my trepidation, nor did the bulbous fluorescence above a grin that would have given Fernandel's a run for its money. This man was inflamed. "Why should anything happen?" but uneasy obbligatos shook up the question. "I see no reason for anything but a courteous reconciliation. Which you both want."

"Yes, yes, yes, all lovely," said Rampigli, the facial lights dimming. "All marvelous, but we shall see. This louse is not the most reliable human being of our acquaintance. What I could have said about him, and didn't, sometimes gives me headaches. That one I could have put on a meathook."

Oh, he loved blood. It was literally meant, and relished. I had to reorient this fellow. I got out an eighty-year-old Courvoisier that would have pacified a rhinoceros. I wouldn't have shared a drop with the Queen of England, but I put an inch of it into two of the goblets with which my parents acknowledged my marriage and handed one to him. "Let's hope for better things. Peace, and good will," and I raised my glass.

Two stumpy fingers cradled the goblet, and he slid the brandy past his teeth without sniff or contemplation. I went on a small meathook myself. "Lovely," he said, hoarsely. "Lovely," and held out his glass. I poured him another half-inch of the golden-brown beauty. As I raised my own and worked out another formula of bibulous reconciliation, there was a rap on the front door. Rampigli put the glass on the table, his face dark and drawn.

I went through the foyer and opened the door. Hard, sharp, still, Debrette stood at the door sill, his eyes going past me as he said "Bon jour." There was no sign of that comprehending softness which had put a hand on my shoulder. He was like a suspended dagger fixing a target.

"Rampigli is here," I said. "Inside."

But he wasn't. From the darkest corner of the foyer came his voice, subdued and clear of accent. "*Salut, mon cher* Marcel."

Bubbles are beautiful because they make much of little. The tiny pause in which Debrette waited before going to Rampigli and embracing him had for me a tension of possibility that was a kind of beauty I could not match, and which, I think, must be the sort that men of action know all the time, an imperilled suspension in which possibilities gleam like the rainbow fragments of white light on the delicate lens of a bubble.

They walked arm-in-arm into the living room, and were launched into accounts of their present lives even as I decided to dedicate my precious Courvoisier to the occasion and began pouring it into the goblets.

After one round of the valuable, a white walrus appeared, Madame Zdonowycz in uniform, wheeling a tray of coffee and a mocca cake that looked like a pillbox under assault by frosted tracer bullets. Beside it, the silver coffee urn, sugar bowl and cream pitcher, and the pale blue Limoges cups created a little domestic festival in the room. Urbane loveliness, civilization itself, glowed on the tray, and the two ex-agents were drawn into the field of sweet force and lost to it that part of their own which threatened it. At least, as Madame Zdonowycz poured, sliced, and handed round, the barber and the reconstruction worker were mute. For a minute, the only noise was the chink of Zdonowycz's luxurious service, spoons against cups, forks against plates. Then Debrette said, "It's been a long time since I've lived in decent fashion. I'd almost forgotten that this kind of life went on outside of the movies."

Half-smiling, Rampigli said, "The day they took us in the truck from Sachsenhausen to Mauthausen, they threw us in a shower, then shaved us from head to foot. We didn't recognise people whose noses had been pressed into our backsides for ten hours. Then everyone but a few privileged people like us Italians was told to run around outside. Two degrees below zero and naked. They were saving gas. We privileged ones had to clean out a hut where they'd locked up three hundred people a week before without food or water. I didn't have the strength to turn the key. When we got it open, I came close to passing out. The worst smell in the history of the world. But there was something else. In the corner, a skeleton moved its teeth up and down on the leg of the skeleton next to it. The guard went over and cracked it on the head, and it went down all the way." Rampigli lifted a forkful of mocca cake into his mouth, then, his little finger extended, lifted his coffee and warmed, sweetened, and liquefied the sour-sweet chocolate, and the fair, gold body of the cake.

Debrette said, "I've been more frightened by a look on a guard's face than a whipping. I've been unable to move when there was nothing to touch me, and then worked cool as knives with the Gestapo all around me."

Rampigli said, "Do you remember La Pipette in La Boule Rouge ordering that roast beef without money or points? She couldn't even keep her hands off the waiter. A fifty-year-old redhead," he threw in for me, "ugly, loud, showy, so conspicuous she was never given the least trouble," and back to Debrette, "Remember when she had to spend the night with Borgelgusser. She wet her pants. Oh my God," and both of them bent toward the floor and rocketed up, their throats bulging with roars, eyes tearing, slapping their knees, coughing.

My cake and coffee were in Mauthausen, and I was trying to shake off the munching skeleton. Rampigli sliced a wedge of mocca, big if not hard enough to stop a truck. "But she wasn't so funny," he said. The fleshy destroyer bobbed seriously over that calmed sea of uproar. "The searchlight don't get in trouble, just what it shines on. She was a London error."

This remark was on my frequency; I latched onto it before some other reminiscence, loosened by some other underground source, took them years and miles away. "Were there lots of London errors?"

Even Debrette's cracked jug of laughs had enough left for what wasn't meant to elicit one. "London error is the title of what happened to us all."

"Error may be a kindness to them. They juggled us. Seals and rubber balls." Rampigli's own balancer pointed toward the ceiling. "Heroes with our lives they were, those great men."

"Were they responsible for 'Robert'?"

"Gruyère?" asked Debrette. "Your son? They sent him before he was ready." When could you be ready for Mauthausen? How could they train you for that? "Like all of us."

"I meant Arastignac, the Air Operations Officer after Peugeot."

"He was all right," said Debrette coldly. "Just unnecessary. At least, he knew planes. Unlike the thief."

"I wondered. I've heard things."

"You've heard things about all of us," said Debrette. Old injuries flushed through his skin as if they had a blood network of their own, ready to take over circulation.

I thought, "I'm ruining what I started to repair." That Mauthausen cannibal sat in my head. "I want to take you out to dinner. I know a fine place for celebrations."

They were up, twin springs, more adept at my social trade than I, trained by greater variety. I'd led them by a sidepath back to the fatal highway; I wasn't even a successful meddler. Meddling requires that you do it for sheer love, for itself, for matchmaking. No commissions en route. Rampigli called, "Farewell, and thank you, Mademoiselle," in the direction of my bedroom, not the kitchen, so he got no response from Zdonowycz, and might not anyway. Since the Italians had dropped Victor Emmanuel, she'd lost interest in them.

2

Something in me had been snagged by Rampigli's meandering between Zdonowycz's cake and that starved animal at Mauthausen. It wasn't squeamishness or horror that held me from mocca and coffee, but an itchy recognition of the kinship between such monstrosity and the self-seeking idleness which was its meat. Does every man nourish himself on twisted arms, fires, fights, gougings even while fearing, hating, maybe stopping them, maybe even blotting them out by being in or causing them? Are there men made to inflict, others to alleviate pain? Are there neutrals who stand outside the engine room throbbing with sympathetic ecstasy while human stokers work? I felt with the cannibal, and I felt with the guard who conked him. Which made a jail out of which I wanted to break.

The way out was the way of Chaleur. It was what I had set as my measure. Arrangements of fact. Failure would be the jail of contradiction and self-ignorance, the perpetuation of cancelled opportunity. This was in my head as the three of us walked down toward the bus stop at Étoile, the air dark silver, the way it is before snow, the atmosphere all expectancy, the lights hesitant, stunned yellow or glare white above the houses.

At Printinière's I was welcomed in a way that made these ex-throat-cutters and dynamiters meek with respect, but we were put in the same cove in which Armand had stranded me from the company, and I needed a few shots of vanity-juice to keep from smelling my blood on the red leather.

The menus at Printinière's look like corporation reports, and my guests were treating them with the respect of large investors, with the rapid breath that great prospects bring to speculators. They finished their study and ordered immensely. (Though I have never pinched pennies where appetite was to be slaked.)

After ordering, the restaurant and its high style evaporated for them. They were back in that mazy underground, unloading memories, some of the people I'd encountered in Trentemille and the TMP records, some new: the midget, Pontin-Roustaque who travelled in overnight bags on the racks of the Berlin-Paris train; Lescaudboutille, who pretended to be a mannikin at Charblain; the Mademoiselles Stange, septuagenarian sisters, one in and one out of the network, who went hand-in-hand to concentration camp and gas chamber; M. Bobaut, the baker, who killed his dog by stuffing microfilm down her throat with the Gestapo at the door. All told in that nostalgic heartiness which was their special language, understandable by outsiders, but with a foreigner's uncertainty.

And then, almost before I was aware of it, they were on to "Robert," and a "trial," not the one at which he was cleared of collaboration with the enemy, but one in England which involved smuggling. It was as if one had learned after the war that Hitler had been conducting a policy wheel. Why, though, hadn't they mentioned this when I'd spoken about "Robert?" I asked them.

"What did that have to do with what you're after?" said Debrette.

"Arastignac was cleared of the charge. Just because a man goes around with a loaded rifle is no reason to throw birds in the air for him. The smuggling wasn't important."

"Smuggling is generally considered a serious crime," I said. "I should think it bears directly on the character of the man whom I have good reason to believe is guilty of treason."

"So Arastignac's your pigeon, now," said Rampigli. "Good for you, Papa Curry." The waiter leaned over with a rosy paté, and Rampigli's nostrils became dancing caves. It was ten seconds before he disentangled himself from his appetite to say that Debrette could tell me about the smuggling. "It was all in the papers. In forty-seven."

"I'm surprised you didn't see it," said Debrette.

"In forty-seven, I wasn't worrying about 'Robert' or anything at all connected with Chaleur. I'd never heard the name."

Debrette cut his paté into three sections, then one, two, three, he had it in his gullet. Like exhibiting a garbage disposal unit. A talking one, for he managed to tell the story without losing a jot of the meaty goo. "He was working for an independent airline, running freight around Europe. On one of his routine flights to London, he was stopped by a customs man who was demonstrating the job to a recruit, and who, instead of letting Arastignac through as usual, asked to see what he had in his briefcase. Arastignac tried to ignore the man, but was ordered to stop and open the briefcase. They found about eighty pieces of gold bullion and a thousand-pound note. Ten million francs."

"Not bad for a day's flight," said Rampigli through a mouth-load of paté. He'd been bent into it, and his nose was coated with enough for an evening snack.

"How could they have let him off on that charge?"

"That was something," said Debrette.

"Yes, that was worth it all," said Rampigli.

"London," said Debrette. "Arastignac claimed he'd been given the money by British Intelligence to set up an espionage ring in the event of future disturbances. His lawyer called Wynn-Wyndward for testimony. Then he was released."

A perpetual Lazarus with Wynn-Wyndward as Jesus. "Incredible."

"Oh no, it's right in the papers. Arastignac was said to have comported himself perfectly, removing his decorations, and so on. They don't know that they are stripped off by guards before you enter the courtroom. The newspapers made quite a hero of him. He talked about his long history as an agent, dating from before the war, and got off with a three-hundred-pound fine. The judge said the gravity of the crime was counterbalanced by the importance of the work he had done and was continuing to do. As if he could continue as an agent with his picture over the front pages of Europe."

"It's not a lifetime métier," said Rampigli, finishing up what he'd seen of the paté. "I'd rather barber Australian bushmen."

The waiter brought in three bowls of lobster bisque whose heat must have melted some oblivion-clot in my head. As if *Figaro* lay open in front of me on the table, I remembered the story. I had even discussed it with someone down at the firm. I remembered saying that wartime heroism would lead to peacetime crime. I'd even thought for a trial second that perhaps it was just as well that Bobbie —untrained for anything but war—died before he'd come back to a life of embezzlement. The spoon still at my mouth, I could almost make out a picture of a man in a dark suit accompanied by another man. Arastignac's lawyer? Wynn-Wyndward? Who?

The case had been a part of a day, an amusement among other unremembered ones.

I pushed the soup away. Would the waiter who brought the soup turn out in next week's *Figaro* to have sliced up a village of Gascons or to have devised a serum which would wipe cancer from the earth? There were all sorts of Lazaruses whom time called out of their graves.

If my dinner became a series of feints, my guests tramped through another hour and a half of meats, salads, fruits, cheeses, and tarts. Then we left to walk Debrette to the Gare St. Lazare for the eight-forty to Caen. In a half-trance, I stood by while the two ex-agents embraced and said goodby. I felt like a parenthesis. I was even surprised when Debrette held out his hand and thanked me for everything. Rampigli too shook hands, said he expected me to come to his shop for a trim before long, and then, without waiting to see if I were going his way, loped off down Rue d'Amsterdam. I walked home as it started to snow.

CHAPTER 11

There is a kind of history-consciousness in men that makes them isolate the events of their life more than I think women do, makes them aware of stages, triumphs, losses, defeats. Women are less finicky about time: for them, it may be "the years I was having children," "the years before I married," "the years I worked," but life is generally more continuous for them. Also, women are used to accepting partial success, are trained to disappointment, withdrawal, regret. In a difficult love affair, a man is pressed to the constant possession he cannot have and tortured by its absence until it breaks him, or he breaks its hold. In affairs without obstacles, it is usually the man who feels a falling off, for he requires a history of meaningful rises and falls. Down in the country during the war, I had a view of a large willow tree which curtseyed toward a silvery pond at the rim of a copse. I must have spent a thousand hours looking at it, and I used to think that no man in the world, however important, was ever larger in my scheme of things than that tree. Some men were branches, some boles, some knots, some leaves, some leaf veins, some the smallest grain of the least important section of bark. By reducing the great, I became something. I counted nearly as much as Churchill, sitting out the war, watching a willow tree.

I had a vainglorious uncle whom I visited one summer in Padanarum—South Dartmouth to the mapmakers—near Buzzard's Bay in Massachusetts. He was an Englishman from Surrey who'd married my mother's older sister when he'd come to this country to sell British woolens back in the 1880s. He raced a class boat in the bay, and his son and I crewed for him. The two of us sailed a keelless skiff and had gotten pretty knowledgeable about the clippy breezes that broke off the shore as we maneuvered by oar and main sheet in the bay. Every night after supper, Uncle Randolph put on his fine double-breasted blue suit and strutted to the post office for conversation and the mail. We accompanied him as silent retinue, and in front of his friends, he would pass us each a dime for candy and sarsaparilla as if he were crowning a Derby winner. On board his boat, however, he was Captain Bligh. We never touched a line or said a word on our own hook without receiving a mouth of sailor's curse. Once, half a mile out, we started to fool around, shoving each other and so on. "Out," my uncle snapped. "Out. Overboard, the two of you," and over we went. Eel grass spread over the last two hundred yards, and it wrapped about our legs. I never thought I'd make it. A week after that, my cousin and I were crewing. It was a race, and we were maneuvering for a good start. Uncle Randolph was casting a mean eye at the other boats. He didn't see us heading right for a moored skiff. I said nothing, and neither did my cousin; we tore a two-foot hole in it. Neither that night nor for the next five did my uncle take his walk to the post office. A week later, I broke a rib in a belly flop off the boat, and Uncle Randolph carried me in his arms to the doctor.

He was an inventor, an unsuccessful but resourceful one, and his last years were devoted to finding combinations of flax and other weaving materials which he vainly tried to foist off on the New York textile firms. Finally, he saw that it wouldn't work out, and he decided to go back to England and die there near an unmarried sister who was a registered nurse. His wife was dead, and his son, my playful cousin, had been killed in the First War. In 1935, after my Washington interview, I was in New York about to sail back myself a week later, so it came to me to put my uncle on his boat in Hoboken. I met him in Grand Central Station, a portly, tattered man standing by the gate with four suitcases which were soon joined by thirteen others brought up on a porter's cart. My uncle gave the man a nickel (which I augmented by twenty cents). It took me fifteen minutes to persuade him to check the stuff through to the boat, but we kept the four large suitcases and lugged them around with us to dinner and to a show at one of the Moody theaters on Forty-second Street. The boat was due to sail the next day at noon, a Friday, but my uncle would not board a boat on Friday so I accompanied him across the river with the four suitcases, and we took a taxi to the pier. It was dark as pitch, and we could barely make out the outline of the boat. At the gate, my uncle presented his ticket to the guard, who passed us onto the pier. We boarded the empty ship and came upon an amazed steward who was finally persuaded we weren't certifiable and took us to my uncle's cabin. "Where's everybody?" asked my uncle. "You're the first," said the steward.

"Get me a deck chair," said my uncle, "and set it up there on the quarter-deck. I'll sit out a bit." And there I left him, alone, under a beclouded moon, and made my way back to New York. The transition of my proud Uncle Randolph into that solitary loon, the last stage of his descent via the inflations of Padanarum, was for years the measure of human decline which I felt above all others. The cycle of vanity. I've observed thousands of others; what are newspapers but chronicles of such decline? Even when they deal with the preparatory ascent, you feel it's only preparatory to what really counts, descent. But the deposit of my exiled Uncle Randolph on the ship that would return him home after years of strutting as the patronising Englishman on the American coast shook me up, for our situations were not so different. And his seemed such an abandonment, that I thought, "Watch out. You're in your forties and there's not much chance to pull yourself out." "Out" meant from the pit where I saw myself doing a gladiator job with the Phebe Delattres of my life: it had less dignity than a cock-pit, and we less than fighting cocks. I thought then, "If only I had a noble woman, someone on the order of Hélène, but who would give me repose rather than excitement, who'd offer a place to recuperate and gather strength rather than be the arena for fights and rewards." And I'd thought that many times, even as the possibility of having something to recuperate for drifted away.

2

The day that Jacqueline came was a particularly mournful one. After weeks of waiting, I'd received from Colonel Wynn-Wyndward an answer to my request for a talk with him to the effect that under no circumstances could he reveal any information about the Chaleur Network or the trial of Arastignac. It was a question of policy and entirely out of his hands. He sympathised with the policy and would talk about these privileged matters only under orders.

Success had so spoiled me by this time that I was greatly depressed by the letter. I spent the day staring out the window at a gray sky, the earth's dying head, which spaced the budless, hopeless branches of the Parc Monceau elms and cottonwoods. They were nerves to me, nerves in one old head, stared at by the shaken nerves of another.

At about five o'clock, Madame Gonella came up the stairs followed by the unusual sight which had drawn her to this heroic ascent, Jacqueline carrying two suitcases. Madame Zdonowycz was shopping. "Claims she's been invited," said Gonella. "Thought I'd come see."

"Of course, Madame. Come in, Jacqueline. I'm so glad to see you." And as La Gonella tried to become part of the ménage, I threw in a "Thank you for showing her the way, Madame." Growls and retreat.

Jacqueline wore what must have been her city clothes, a neat, rough suit, and a beret. Very few such displays came to my door, for the least well-off of my occasional companions had a sense of what constituted Parisian appearance, and Jacqueline was totally without it. If, however, instead of the Corbusier chair you were expecting for a gift, you'd received a fine, if dusty, Heppelwhite, you could gauge my happy surprise.

"I thought if I wrote, you'd change your mind. Or I would. I'm no longer recruiting for the network. Only myself. It's not so good a cause."

"I've been wanting you to come, Jacqueline, but I didn't expect you. I'll show you your room," and, as I said the last two words, they became the fact. The room was Jacqueline's, and not as a gesture of hospitality. I don't think Jacqueline was ever a "guest" for me, someone whom I'd invited to spend a more or less fixed number of days and with whom I would embroider a given relationship aware that it would end, as it began, at a given, mutually acknowledged time. Jacqueline did not even seem an addition to the household, a new sofa or a maid; she was something that at last filled a serious want.

But I'm jumping. I could not have said this at the time, though it was, I'm certain, what I felt. Then I sat on the bed, instead of leaving, as I would have with a "guest." She surveyed the room, expressed delight, then put her cases beside me on the bed and unpacked. "It's the way we'd come into people's homes during the war," she said, "expecting what we could not expect under any ordinary circumstance. And they'd understand that our staying was not a personal matter, though it might become that. I'm not that easy now."

"I want you to be easier. Here you have the strongest personal claim." Though I couldn't—wouldn't—have said just what it was.

"I'm easier than I would be anywhere else, easier than I want to be. I've wanted this to cost me something. Uneasiness isn't a big price to pay for what I'm asking here."

"It leads to the greatest expenses."

"Fear of it made me a hermit. Nothing costs more than that. So I'm here, and I've hardly thought about it beforehand. I just packed up. My father saw me and asked me where I was going, and I said I was going to try living in Paris for a while. I'm not even sure that I didn't start packing before I knew where I'd go. If he hadn't seen me, I might have unpacked and stayed in Lepic."

"I think you'd have come sooner or later."

"I don't believe in design. If I did, I think I'd have shot myself. I'd think God had it in for me, and that I might as well get it over." She started to take things out of the bags, asking if I minded her doing that.

I recalled my responsibilities and said I'd leave her.

"Please stay," with a wisp of nervous urgency. "I want to talk with you very much." She had two dresses, one brown, one blue, both ugly. She hung them in the closet, then took out stockings, underwear, and toilet things, all of them unlike what Paris women would have, all of them thick, country stuff. "I've always taken what other people would consider risks, but they've not been brave risks. There's not been real choice, and there's always something to fall back on. Even parachuting. There's just the one second to be scared, and all you have to do is wipe that second from your mind, and the rest of the decision is clear for you. It's just been keeping up with necessity. That's the way it's been for me, going to England, volunteering, going back home after the war, and now leaving it. There's just the one second of doing it, and then everything follows. But I'm dependent. I need ground to fall on. If it's hard, and I break an ankle, that's all right too. That just limits my choice, which is easier. I'm a good administrator, but a terrible planner. You're my ground now, but you can throw me out, and that won't be as hard for me as it would be for other people. I adjust." This said with face turned away, hanging a topcoat, pushing aside hangers as if making room for a queen's wardrobe. When she said "adjust," she may have seen the uselessness of what she was doing, and she whirled, an unnecessarily extravagant movement, but one which put some autumnal life in her face, so that, seeing it, taking it in, I could see how good it was going to be to really take it in, to have her there.

Still, something was odd for me, as if I'd bitten an apple and it tasted like a wonderful pear. I felt nothing in my experience to direct me. Not that there was the faintest possibility of my throwing Jacqueline into the street. The question was how to feel toward her. "If you left," I said, "I'd be all at sea," and the sight that flashed on me was of the eel grass wound around my legs up to the groin after the swim in from Uncle Randolph's boat.

Jacqueline took off her suit coat and tossed it to the bed where I sat. It was a gesture I've watched many times, my heart bouncing with the promise of it: Hélène taking off first jacket, then, together, blouse and brassiere, looking in my eyes as I stared at her, the never-disappointing surprise of her beautiful white breasts, the sweet pillar of the rib cage, and looking at each other looking; and how many times since Hélène, always new and necessary, heads lost in sweaters and slips, and then the throbbing first sight—oh Lord, watching Jacqueline's shoulders go back as the coat came off, the outline of the breasts, I wanted her, immediately, nothing between us. Old man's body, kept up with push-ups, sit-ups, knee-bends, chinning, fast walks, abstinence; still it looked like a football field after a game. I was ashamed to present it, breasts hanging, hairless, bellied.

I looked away from her.

I don't know whether or not she knew my feelings, whether the simple, if slightly unusual removal was calculated to raise my attention. If it were, I would not censure her at all. I know now how acute she is, how organized for accomplishment, and also how decent; but she had tied dynamite sticks to tracks and shot men. She was no innocent in the Paris wood, no matter how rough the material of her suit and the cut of her dresses.

She asked, smiling, how I'd been managing without her.

"Marginally. I've started to drift. It's had something to do with learning about Bobbie and all of you, though I'm not sure what."

She sat down beside me and took up my hand in her strong, skinny fingers, oddly unlike the rest of her body, which, though strong, was full, or, at least, spelled out. She had no right to take my hand then, and if I hadn't been already oppressed by feelings about her, I might have made room for resentment at the patronising rapidity of it. Instead, my own hand dangled in hers like a specimen. "I'm going to get undrifted up here myself, and then I'll take care of you," she said. "I've got a lot to do, a job to find, everything to find."

"Almost everything."

"If you'll allow that. Since I've unpacked, it looks as if I haven't given you any choice."

"It's not a question of choice. The only thing wrong with your speed is that it hasn't given me a chance to say how welcome you are."

Years of novel-reading and movie-going let me see the embarrassment this caused, but she said simply, "I know things are very special here. Thank you for letting me just understand them as hospitality and good will."

It didn't take years of novel-reading to see my flush. I left then, went to my own room down the hall, and lay on the bed. "If every day's going to exhaust me like this, I may have made a mistake," is what I thought.

3

A week before she died, Hélène took what Doctor Robichaud called "a turn for the better." An accurate term for doctors, for they know that final grinding of the life matter which to laymen looks like health itself, a rediscovery of energy and youth. But it is only one of the terms in the unalterable direction. Hélène looked beautiful again. Her eyes had a sweet chestnut haze which, up close, surprised you, for further away her eyes looked much darker and less delicate.

Her body had color, her breasts were fuller, the stomach firm as well as tender. We hadn't made love in weeks and weeks, but we did twice in those two days, and everything we said and did was part of love. My body seemed attached to hers at hundreds of places: when she moved or looked away, I was drawn after her. I read to her, as we sat by the window at opposite ends of a couch. The newspapers mostly. They'd just launched the *Île de France* at Saint Nazaire, and we spoke of sailing on it to New York. Hélène had never been, had never wanted to go to the States, but she talked of it with excitement. Her appetite was good, and I ordered one of the best meals I ever ate in my life from L'Auberge Provençal, and we sat by the window surrounded by silver containers and the southern odors of Provence. At mid-afternoon, we napped. A few hours later, I woke up, feeling a terrific weight inside my chest. It was so heavy, I think quarts of blood had drained down to it from my head. I turned to look at the face which I already knew would have sunk back into the scotched-out glare that would be her last look. She woke up and saw me staring at her, saw what I saw, before she felt its source. Love is fear of loss, and I suppose that I never really felt its power till that moment. Unseamed, unbolstered, taken apart, and inside, nothing but the burden of missing the dearest of everything. I couldn't even say her name, just put my hand on her hair and then her forehead, up and down, slowly, taking its perspiration as the last drops of what would keep me alive. When lovers separate for a brief time, the one going away is lost in preparations and does not experience the emptiness of the one who, left behind, simply sees the hole in his life. As soon as the departure is actual, both are free and lean toward renewal or toward freedom. But this is feeble preparation for final separation. After the hour in which grief ran up and down my body like a bloody animal, I turned stony and would not recognise the fact of Hélène or the fact of love. I buried her then, before she died, and buried love.

That's what I thought of, lying on my bed, knowing that in an hour I would walk into the dining room and find not one but two places set, that for perhaps a very long time there would be two places. Not that I hadn't eaten with one or more people in my apartment since 1945, not that a number of people had not stayed for as much as two weeks, but then there was something fête-like about every meal, flowers in the center, often little gifts wrapped by the silver. Now it was as if I'd had a daughter who'd come back to live with me after finishing college. This is the way I tried to look at it, and I suppose it promoted a snooze because I woke to the lion-tamer croak of Zdonowycz, "You doing some Lent fast? Better get up. Company."

"I'm up. But—if you understand the action—I'm going to wash my face."

The table at which I eat belonged to Hélène's grandmother, an oval Empire monument to Business Triumphant, and Her church, the Eleven-course Dinner. Hélène and I had a few yards sliced out for leaves, and the table fit into a bay, which gives on the brick wall of the neighboring apartment. It was a fine place to put a bay window. I usually sat at a corner which offered the small redemption of a garden at the back of the next house. Zdonowycz had wisely placed Jacqueline there, and I rubbed noses with the bricks. Six candles in two silver candelabra were helped along by two well-shaded lights on either side of an Empire screen which protected the kitchen entrance.

"Madame Zdonowycz ran a small, unsuccessful brothel in Cracow," I said.

"It's very lovely," said Jacqueline. She had a thick brown sweater buttoned over her blouse, and I suppose she'd combed out her hair. Candlelight wasn't the best way to look at her, for it didn't show up the colors. I was just as glad.

"You'll at least become accustomed to it. Even the wall will nod to you. It's one of the few things I know whose harmfulness isn't malicious."

"I prefer it to the pigs. In prison you begin to see anything you want on walls. I'd just as soon face them, especially when I'm in the opposite of a prison."

No, I thought, this is not one's daughter coming home from school, and it is not the file clerk, cigarette girl, or party whore whom you bring home the way a dog brings a bone into the garden. I'd forgotten prison, extermination camp, parachute drops. "Madame Zdonowycz cooks in the East European manner. Thickly. I hope you'll like it."

"If I told you what I used to eat, you wouldn't be able to. And this sole is the Ritz for me. I would say something to her but I don't know how to praise things like food or clothes."

"Maybe that can be one of our projects. I can educate you in vanity."

"You didn't educate Bob that way. He paid almost no attention to what he ate or wore. He didn't really speak much at all, did he?"

"Not around me," I said. "I was not an easy person to get words by. Did he tell you that?"

She kept the fork, tines down, on her lip for a couple of seconds. It was a pretty and girlish thing to do.

"You don't have to tell me," I said.

"I'm remembering." She chewed a huge bite of fish, and I waited. "He said you were always trying to overcome yourself. You always tried to be good to him, but he thought that it was hard for you. He said that you'd be very good to him when you'd read in the newspapers about murderers who'd had terrible childhoods, or when you saw pictures of orphaned Chinese children in Manchuria. He said you were very sentimental, and that it wasn't really a substitute for steady love, but that he got to understand it, and that when he grew up, he began to like your efforts, and then you." She put down the fork and looked at me. "Is it all right to tell you that?"

"Yes."

"I don't want to know things about you that you don't know."

"I'm glad to know anything about him, no matter what. I like to know what he felt. I suppose I wouldn't know if he were sitting here. Most fathers probably never know what their children feel about them."

"Most of your life has nothing to do with your father, I don't care what psychologists say. If I have children—"

"Don't predict," I said. "Don't try. Don't say what you'll do. You don't know. Why should you? You may breathe their breath or eat them alive. You can't say now."

Zdonowycz clumped in, took off the fish, and substituted two plates humped with slices of burnt veal—she carved, and with mad joy, in the kitchen—dropped into a ring of mashed potatoes on top of which were hillocks of lima beans. She should have been a designer of plazas: she has the monumental instinct. I was used to her culinary architecture, but Jacqueline laughed.

"What's wrong, Mademoiselle?" asked Zdonowycz.

Jacqueline pointed to the dark meat, a burned idol in the midst of a May dance. "It looks so wonderful," she said. "I'm so hungry," and by God, they shook hands over it, the Arthurian maiden and the wild boar. It was the beginning of real friendship—good will without sex—and it meant that Jacqueline would really be at home.

After dinner, Jacqueline and I walked to the Champs Élysées, and drank beer in the Pom-pom. Cold and empty, the city seemed full of life to her, and I put off arranging my feelings till bed; and then I went off to sleep, quickly and happily.

4

The first stage lasted about a month. Jacqueline was getting settled.
Then I began to be afraid, and didn't know what of. It's the general
fear you call anxiety, but stronger. There was a real fear in me, and
I could block out reasons for it, though they weren't satisfactory.
The big reasons were that I was losing control of the situation which
I thought I had in hand. I was losing my hold on the case; I was
losing myself everywhere in a way something in me said was not only
dangerous but foolish; and I was jolted, as I have been every now
and then for years and years, by a fear of dying. Usually I'd have
answers for fears like these: I know that formulas don't run the
world, and there are more things in it than philosophers dream.
Things can both be and not be depending on where you stand.
People can be guilty and innocent. As for Jacqueline, why can't
anything that doesn't work harm work well, no matter how ugly
it appears or how ridiculous? Just as you can fear anything at all, a
mouse, a crack in the plaster, a rainy day, so you can love a monkey
or a tree or a woman older than your grandmother. Five billion genes
romp toward your creation, and each of them lies at the powerful
disposition of body weather. As for dying, many's the time I haven't
cared, and if given a choice would say, "O.K. Fine. I'll die."

When he was about three, Bobbie would wake every night about
two A.M. and head for his mother's bed for comfort. Occasionally,
we'd pass each other in the corridor, I en route to the bathroom.
Both too sleepy for words, we'd nod to each other with the
familiarity of polite brothers who spot each other across a room at
a party. One night, as we met, he didn't nod. His lips were shaking,
his eyes wide with fright. "Bobbie," I said. "What's the matter,
darling?"

"Mommie," he said, "Mommie," and he was down the hall, and
I followed and watched him lift the quilt and crawl in with Hélène. I
guessed he'd had whatever kind of dream young children can have
about something happening to Hélène. As I went back down the
hall, I was suddenly hit by it myself, and I actually went against the
hall, into a picture of Hélène and Armand as children, so that the
edge of the frame hurt my ear and I called out, "Hélène," but afraid
to really call out because I was no three-year-old, and my fear of her
dying wasn't permissible. But there I was in the dark hall, staring
down at the shaded bulb we kept on all night in the WC, rubbing

my not-quite-cut ear and sunk in a terrible fear that I was going to lose my beautiful, soft, sweet wife. I don't know how long I leaned against that wall, but my kidneys lost their ache, and I went back to the room and got in on the other side of Hélène and held on to her, held on to her being alive by the little beats of her stomach and heart. And then I felt Bobbie's round little hand holding on also, two sailors on a life raft, and I got out and went back down the hall free of all but the sediment of fear, uncertainty and relief.

Now, I didn't know whether I was afraid of what was or what was going to be. All I knew was that between Jacqueline and me something existed which I could not handle. What does that mean exactly? I can say more easily what it doesn't mean. If I could have picked up our relationship with a handle, no matter how unusual or repulsive, then I could have dealt with it. I mean if there were literal incest or rape or regression to the womb or anything which one hears about as one goes on living, then I feel I could have worked my way into an attitude which wouldn't feed on every moment of the day. As it was, the air was thick with my worry about Jacqueline, my need for her and the cancellation of the need which my instincts urged. I went around the house waiting for her to come back from the city where she went to employment offices as my mother used to wait for my father and me to come home. No, as a man waits in bed for the woman he loves. In no time at all, Jacqueline was the axle of my days. I couldn't take it.

The first month we spent time together like friendly but disenchanted couples. We each read at night, hardly speaking. Occasionally we went out to dinner and sometimes to movies. Jacqueline was gone most of the day, first to the agencies, then at Février, the big winter sports shop on Rue Vaneauleste, where she sold ski outfits.

One night, I came in to dinner to find only one place set. "Where's Mademoiselle Bargouille?" I asked Zdonowycz, who was putting a saucer of leguminous soup in front of me.

"Said she was going out to dinner," said Zdonowycz, as if to say, "What's it to you."

"I didn't know," I said, and felt woozy. "Where?"

"She didn't say, but I'd guess it was a man her age," said Zdonowycz, who was not exactly Talleyrand. I think.

"What's the evidence for that conclusion," I said, stiffened a little by its nastiness.

"She's taking a bath and a long time to dress."

"Baths aren't world events for all women," I said, and won the field. Zdonowycz hauled her great, smelly bones out to the kitchen.

Jacqueline came in and said good evening. She was wearing a dress I'd seen when she bought it, but hadn't seen on her. She'd gotten it at Printemps, but it was a classic dress, and she looked Parisian in it.

"You're deserting me," I said, my voice actually breaking, but lightly.

She clearly knew that it was more for me than it should be, but she smiled the drawing room smile. "It's about time I got my claws off you. You've been tied to a wallflower long enough. Feel free."

"Going far?"

"Near St. Germain, I think. It's a fellow who buys the equipment for our section. Very nice and polite. He was in England when I was there, with LeClerc. I think you'd like him."

"That won't matter. Is he picking you up here?"

"No, I'm meeting him at Metro Sixteenth September."

"In America, one always calls for girls."

"Americans are very considerate people. I'd better be off."

"Have a good time, Jacqueline."

"Thank you." She never called me anything, not Monsiéur Curry, not Samuel, not Père Curry. I was not going to ask her to call me anything either. I didn't get up, didn't look at her when she put on her coat in the foyer, but when she called "Good night" again, I said "Good night," and started to say that I'd wait up for her. This near-error so upset me that I spilled a spoonful of soup on my lap, and cursed like a madman for twenty seconds until the pineapple trotted in from the kitchen with an expression of contempt that would have extinguished the rage of a Hitler.

5

A man can be tangled by circumstance, by his attitudes toward circumstance, by his ignorance, by his knowledge, by scruples or by lack of them. In the next hours, the next days, and then the next weeks, Jacqueline was my Gordian knot; except that the knot was fluid. It formed, dissolved, re-formed. I didn't know how to act, didn't know how to feel, yet acted and felt. I was jealous, then grew accustomed to jealousy, then was renewed by her return to me as the center of her attention. She joined a cine-club, went to libraries, the theater, shops, usually telling me with whom she went, if she went with someone. We ate breakfast and many dinners together, went walking, went to cafés. Spring saw us in Versailles, Fontainebleau, and Chartres, where we stayed overnight, in separate rooms of course. Jacqueline never brought her friends, male or female, home. I never brought my friends home. Home was our lair, and both of us grew fanatical about its integrity, so that happenstance became habit became credo, and we would have regarded someone who stayed there very long as an attempt on our lives. "Impossible," I told myself. "I'll give a party." And imaginary preparations consoled me over Jacqueline's first weekend away: she went up to Antwerp with the buyer "to look at the Rubens'." The thought of her putting her long legs around the buyer was not easy. The party could not hold its own. I went to the Bar Jéri, found a companion, brought her home and took off as I had when I was thirty, feeling myself coming in Jacqueline, feeling her legs on my backside. The whore paid me extravagant compliments, was paid extravangantly herself, and I enjoyed a good but not completely tranquil sleep.

I woke up with the knowledge that I had to get away. Not an unfamiliar solution to a difficulty, and one which older people rely upon almost exclusively, if they haven't already surrendered to medicines and decrepitude. For me there was still mission. I was not untethered from my project. I had not found everything I wanted by a long shot, and though I could have stopped there and felt satisfied that Bobbie had been accused in ignorance and that the real traitor was "Robert," there was obviously much more to learn about, and this provided reason for going any place I wanted to go. It was a decent context for independence. There was much to learn about in connection with Phebe, there was another visit with Trentemille, there were other members of the network to see, there was the need of an explanation for the mix-up at the rendezvous which Rampigli described, there was lots to do. If possible, I wanted to get out of France for a while. I wanted the tourist's cloak, the sense of foreignness, only possible for me in a country whose language I didn't speak. The German side of this story was the real one. Who knew better than the Germans who worked for them and why? But how to get it?

It was then that decision was lifted from me in a fashion which over the years I've almost come to expect. An arrow shows up on a rock, a bush burns, a message talks from a fortune cookie. My bush burned in Brentano's, where I used to go and browse through the Adventure section just in case something about networks should show up. There was a German book on the shelf, *Alle Minen Springen Lassen* by one Waldemar von Bodescher. There was no point in my picking it up. I didn't even know what the title meant, but I did pick it up and on the very first, or maybe it was the second or third page

I looked at, I made out the words "Chaleur" and "Robert" in the very same line. I actually dropped the book on the floor.

One of the international cads who seem to be inextricably mingled with the book business bent down before I could bend, picked it up, and, still bent, smiled at me and dusted it off.

"I'm going to take it anyway," I said.

"That won't be necessary, sir."

"I would like the book."

"Of course, sir. Anything else?"

"No." Though of course there was, an interpreter, but I didn't realise this till I'd actually gotten out of the store and onto the Boulevard des Capucines. I whirled on my heel like a recruit, and ran back. "A dictionary," I said to the cad. "A German-English or German-French dictionary, the best you have. And a grammar. That had better be in English."

"You're really making a little study, aren't you, sir? Perhaps you'd like to begin with an easier book."

"Do you read German?" I asked him. His hair looked like liquefied chunks of coal, a grotesque by virtue of his scalp alone.

"I don't, as a matter of fact."

"Well, perhaps I ought to get help from someone who does."

The face was reordered into semi-civility, or perhaps genuine servility. At any rate, I got the dictionary, Cassell's *German-English*, and a fair-sized elementary grammar, and trotted back to the house.

I spoke a little hotel German in Switzerland, Austria, and Germany before the war. My college language was Latin, this to escape mathematics; my high school language was French. I was helpless in both. That I speak French as well as English is a tribute to attrition, to laziness, for it would simply have been too hard to get on with only English. I've a fair ear for tone, but tenses, genders, vocabulary run right through me. I must have taken up a German grammar once before though, because I wasn't a total blank when I came to it that night. I even remembered the *ich bin, du bist, er ist* pattern. Outside of that, it was all conquest.

Maybe that's why I went at the book this way, instead of merely showing it to someone who knew German and getting him to read whatever portion I needed to hear. Of course, there was the chance that there'd be something about Bobbie which I wouldn't have wanted anyone else to hear, but I could have taken it to Berlitz or some government office. No, I think I needed a sign, got one, and decided to get on with the job myself. Even before I'd read much,

I wrote to von Bodescher in care of his publisher—the book's preface was dated just two months before, so I felt that he'd likely be around, at least among the living—and before I'd read more than fifty pages, two weeks later, I'd gotten an answer from him in French—the language in which I'd written—saying that he didn't know if he could help, but that he'd be willing to see me. Not a warm letter, but if he'd sent a crate of ice with the word "Come" on it, I'd have come. I did want to get out, and though the two weeks were almost Jacqueline-free as I lost myself in the translating, I still felt her hand on my neck, I still woke up sweating with my need of her.

That job of work was one of which I am proud. It was like untying a knot every minute for two weeks, each knot different from the last—though I did begin to see that many were similar. A jungle of knots, and my axes were the dictionary and the week's study of the grammar—though I started on the key sentence and then its paragraph and chapter right away. *Alle Minen Springen Lassen*, an apt title, *Leave No Stone Unturned*, as I chopped it out of Cassell's, though I was unsure whether or not there was a play on *Minen*, which meant both plot and mine. This shows some of my trouble. Those Gothic sentences were plum puddings of reference. If I didn't know more or less where I was going, I could have probably read a history of the movies into them.

But I didn't. There was something there, a gold temple in the jungle, a miniature one, to be sure, but the real thing. Von Bodescher, who was in charge of the German counter-espionage in the north, had penetrated the networks in the Low Countries. He had been in Paris, and was a friend of Teichmann, and there he met an agent of Teichmann's who was a member of Chaleur. He remembered his name as "Robert," and though his description of him did not tally exactly with August's, there was nothing absolutely contradictory there. Later on "Robert" had come into contact with one of his men, "King," a German, who was a double agent. The two agents met pretending to be members of Allied networks, never knowing that they were both double agents. This was one of von Bodescher's comic stories, but of course it was not a book that one stayed laughing with until the small hours of the morning.

It served my purpose, though, perfectly, and when von Bodescher's letter came, I told Jacqueline I'd be off for a while in a way that made me feel the trip was not only legitimate, but essential.

"Watch out for things," I told her. "You're"—and I started to say, "the mistress of the house"—"in charge." I kissed her goodby. On the cheek.

I could feel the knot dissolving. How easy things were when you decided they weren't necessary conditions for anything else you did. The worst part of Hell was unalterability. Even perfection was horrible, if it meant that. Otherwise, why did God make the earth?

Theologically confirmed and pruned, I taxied to the Gare de l'Est.

CHAPTER 12

Bingen stands at the conflux of the Rhine and the Nahe. Ten minutes from the station brings you to a restaurant on the terrace of a castle—Schloss Klopp—where you sit watching another famous ruin, the *Mäuseturm*, thumbing the muscular curve of the Rhine. Well into my sixth decade, ruins had a fraternal attraction for me, were they sufficiently erect as well as ancient. The comfort of two such marvels and the first good Moselle wine I had tasted in years eased the cramping feeling of this visit to the battered ex-conqueror, a feeling that came at the border where a German in uniform had told me what to do for the first time since 1944. A hot Indian summer day, and there weren't ten people on the broad terrace, though it was crowding noon. I was pushing for the name of a soft, shy—inturned petals—yellow silk flower which edged the terrace stones, and which, in small glass bowls on the table, signified an easy balance between the splendors of the natural scene and the human employment of it. Panorama. A word that always came to your lips in this country.

I'd skied here five or six times in the twenties and thirties, mostly in Kitzbühel and Garmisch, had visited the Leipzig Fair, taken a ferry trip down the Rhine with Hélène not long after Bobbie's birth, and that's about it. I never had much business in Germany, though we'd had some dealings with a Farben subsidiary. This trip to see von Bodescher constituted my first business trip, which will explain my sitting on the terrace of a robber baron's *schloss* waiting for one of the minor masters of the most recent robber barony. No, that's too simple.

It was my hours with Bodescher's book that got me through an exchange with the waiter about the *schönes Wetter*, and that accounted for what the *schönes Wetter* augmented, my unbelligerent feeling about Germany, *mein unkriegerisches Deutschlandsgefühl*, as I think the grotesque language would have it. Bodescher had written that he would be very pleased to see me here on the terrace at noon. "Forgive me for not asking you to my house, but my wife is an invalid, and the burden of receiving any but old friends is an intolerable one for her. At Schloss Klopp you will enjoy the famous Mouse Tower where the Archbishop Hatto of Mainz is said to have been eaten alive by mice, a tale which is not dislodged from my fellow citizens' heads by the fact that *Mäuseturm* actually derives from *Muserie*, which you will know, as they do not, refers to 'cannon.'"

Was it fifty years ago that I felt for

> *the Bishop of Bingen*
> *In his Mouse Tower on the Rhine,*

the cruel Bishop who enticed the famished and rebellious citizens into his barn with an offering of grain and then locked them in to die? It had never been dislodged from my head either. "It's the mice," he'd answered, when asked about the cries, and paid the appropriate penalty. I was never much of a bedtime story teller, but this entered Bobbie's small repertory; yet I'd somehow never associated the tale with the Pied Piper or other obvious fictions. Despite the jingling meters in which it came to me from, I suppose, my mother, I told it to Bobbie as I believed it, in prose, as truth. And there it was, out in the sun, gray-black and jutting, a false derivation from *Muserie*.

The dislodger of the tale was at my table before I got the long view I like to have of people I am meeting for the first time. He had a cane and limped. It's my impression that many German officers of his caste do. Is it imperative, as duelling scars were, or as television antennae were said to be back in the States in the first years of the television boom? Or is it simply factual: German colonels and generals frequently suffer leg wounds.

"Mr. Curry?"

"Yes. Colonel von Bodescher?" and I rose and shook hands, the single, unfriendly Germanic shake. He was a few inches shorter than I, a soft, balding man, a bit shy, like the anonymous yellow flowers. He waited for me to motion to a chair, as I had waited for him to assume the prerogative of host and, I think, seniority. We just sat, and for a few minutes talked of the *schönes Wetter*, now *beau temps*, the view, and the defrocked Mouse Tower, after which he said, "But you know this already. And you have other things to ask me."

"Yes," I said, "there are the other things, though they're really only one thing, and that is how the Chaleur Network was penetrated and seized by the *Sicherheitsdienst*."

"When you wrote me," he said with a slow and silky grace with which the yellow flower might have ridden a breeze, "I was surprised that in view of my book you came to me. You know that I had little to do with the *Sicherheitsdienst*, and really nothing at all to do with this Chaleur group."

I did not say that I had not read all of his book, and that I was a little unsure of some that I had read. "You talk about your double agent, 'King,' meeting the double agent 'Robert,' who, in my view, is the avenue of penetration."

"Yes, but as you saw, my interest was in 'King,' who operated in the Low Countries, and whose mission in Paris was something extra. He was simply on loan, as it were."

"Did you ever meet 'Robert'?"

The old neck in his soft shirt arched a little, and was followed in seconds by a reflective and believable "*Nein.*"

"You also mention that you knew Teichmann, who of course was in charge of the *Sicherheitsdienst* unit which controlled the network."

"Yes, I say that I knew him in Paris, where I was assigned for two years, and to which I now and then returned."

This last was said in a manner that was even softer, as if something about the return were not in the admitted line of work. Was the reason for this explained in the book? I took a chance and said, "I see, not on business."

He was surprised, as of course a stranger should be, but he replied courteously, "Not exclusively."

It was time for me to get off his toes. "I would like to get hold of 'King.' Is he available?"

Again the hesitation, as if nothing were sure enough in his world to command wholehearted agreement. "Possibly. I don't see or write to him. I've left the service and so has he. There is not much else in common, nor does the state of our fortunes encourage leisurely reminiscence."

"I need only his address, if you would be so good as to give me that."

"I can give you that," but the assent was less than the hesitation.

I made my face a question, and he limped on, "But a letter had better go along with it. I'm not sure you'd get anything from him without a letter." More delay, and more interrogating silence from me. "I'm not sure that I have a right to give you that."

"Ah?"

"You explained your situation, and I'm not unmoved by it. My wife and I have no children, but I can understand the way the father of a brave son must feel in such circumstance. Yet there is no sure guide to one's behavior here. I'm going to talk it over with my wife, and then perhaps you and I can discuss it."

"I would appreciate that very much, Herr *Oberst*."

He got up then, for it was not easy to find a transition back to the weather or the Mouse Tower, and said that he would call me at my hotel in two hours. Perhaps we could dine together. I thanked him as I got up, shook his hand and watched him wind down the path out of sight.

"Would you wish to order a luncheon, sir?" The waiter stood by with a small menu card, and that particular subservience which is the average German's way of dealing with force.

Roast crow would be just right, thought I. Shoot one down and claim it was the mice. "What do you recommend?"

He grew shoulders, square head, eye-glitter: I'd made him an authority. A short speech about a sauerbraten brought my nod, my surrender. He grew another foot and went off. One o'clock. The sun was passionate. And it sang:

> *Finch' han dal vino*
> *Calda la testa*
> *Una gran festa*
> *Fa preparar.*

Out of the baronial halls, over the baronial loudspeaker, the aria which before all others in the world chilled my blood with its knowledge, the drinking song from *Don Giovanni*, which Chaliapin sang with his face dazzled by diabolic need. "By morning, I've got to swell the list by ten." That rollicking devil's tickle, a great joke for da Ponte, who wrote the libretto which I bought the day I first heard the music in the Paris Opera, but no joke at all, or not much of one, to the man who drove the Don's mania through that music. Hearing it on the terrace at Schloss Klopp was a marvellous treat, a great, joyous pleasure. "My God," I thought. "I must be free of it." For years now, I'd preferred *Figaro*, without knowing till that moment that I'd changed. In *Figaro*, the final scene in which the beautiful countess forgives the count and saves him from the Giovanni-mania is the most Christian music in the world. Better than that: it's the most beautiful.

The waiter brings a red bowlful of *Ochsenschwanzsuppe* and I ask him if by any chance we could hear the final scene of *Figaro*. He too must be in need of forgiveness. He smiles like a fellow man, and we are brothers instead of members of feuding classes, the Served and the Serving, the Informed and the Informants. He will see to my request as if it were his own (which would bring *Orpheus in the Underworld* into the Rhine Valley).

The ox's tail is no ox's tail, as nothing in Germany is what it appears, but it is good soup, and has two grades of heat, its own and the sun's. I'd forgotten how splendid it was to eat *al fresco*. Down in the country, when I'd roast a piece of what might have been a real ox's tail in the grate, I'd have to issue general pardons to all my taste faculties and float above the things of this world. Germany was making up what it took from me there on the Schloss Klopp terrace.

With the sauerbraten, *Figaro*. People will say it was fine to be an American in occupied Germany. Sweet and bitter, bitterly sweet, sauce and music. I curled like the yellow flower in the sun. If a bee had tried me, I'd have given honey. Jacqueline, Bobbie, age, nothing was near me, or rather, I was something else, a compound of what I saw, heard, smelled, ate. If this was illusory, then some of that which counts in life must bear such opprobrium.

An hour later, I was back in my room at the Bahnhof Hotel, soaking my leg in a hot bath. Twenty yards down the hill from the restaurant, I'd taken a tumble, the first in maybe twenty-five years. Down I went, rolling three or four yards, and furious, dirty, swearing, even shocked. I strode the rest of the walk, left word with the manager I was expecting a call, and consoled myself in the tub. I didn't need my father's saws to remind me what life was. I just stewed in a huge tub, face above the water, and little else. Naturally the call came, and naturally I slammed my knee against the tub getting out, so that when I finally called the Colonel back, my voice was wiry with pain. He inquired, I told him that I'd had a fall, but said that it would not stop me from seeing him if he could manage it.

"If you could come here then, I would be happy to talk with you. My wife will not be able to get up, but we can have a useful talk," and he gave me directions, a fifteen-minute walk down the road opposite the castle.

Mid-afternoon was chillier, and my leg was stiff. By the time I reached the Colonel's tiny "garden apartment," I was limping as badly as he. He was very solicitous amidst apologies for the smallness of the place. A dining room table that could seat four, a desk, book shelves, a violet armchair, upholstered, and five straight chairs, all new, this the retirement lair of the Third Reich's Abwehr Chief in the Northwest, and he was lucky.

"I would have called for you," said the Colonel, "but I don't drive. The SS training was rigorous, but it did not include driving. Even *Gruppenführer* had chauffeurs."

"I'd thought you were a regular army officer?"

"I was once, but there was no place in the army which the Versailles Treaty limited us to. One hundred thousand men. When Hausser came to the SS to start the training at Bad Toelz, as many younger men as could followed him. Then later on, I went back." He rose, got a bottle of wine, opened it, and then asked if I would have some.

"Thank you," I said and the glass was there at the "you." "I read that the Wehrmacht represented honorable exile for those who opposed Hitler, and that the SS constituted the core of his support. Did you find this to be the case?" It was not, I suppose, the softened-underbelly approach, but my leg was bothering me and I was reacting to this little fellow as I'd first reacted to August, with some resentment at his security.

He came back with his own glass to a straight chair, picked up his cane and leaned on the knob, which was the oak-brown head of a disagreeable mastiff. He said nothing for a moment, and I was about to go on, when a sound that is represented by "Humph" broke into what I suppose would have been a conventionally circumlocutious account of his own situation. The sound was followed by a series of rapid German sentences, of which I managed to get nothing more than the drift, which consisted of a denunciation of those who used the "so-called split" (*sogenannte Verschiedenheit*) between the SS and the Wehrmacht as an alibi for their own participation in the crimes of the state. "Crimes, yes," he said in French, which meant, I think, that he'd regained control of himself, "monstrous crimes which everybody knew about either because they'd seen and done them, or because they knew that they were needed for the continuation of the regime. I detest those Wehrmacht apologists whose pens are so much nobler than the batons they failed to break in Hitler's face. Stauffenberg and his crew, yes, some of them have less to be questioned about—if they were alive—but curse to Hell the contrived amnesia of those who don't look at their own bloody hands." He held his own white hands out, the cane falling to the ground. "My own are as red as anyone's." For an hour then he talked about the rivalry and cooperation of Canaris and Himmler and Heydrich and Bormann and Goering, telling how each used the other's vileness as cover for his own. "And I knew, but I'd sworn the holy oath we all had to swear, and I did not then recognise anything above that. Ninety per cent of the honorable men of every nation in the world would have done the same. That we take to bed every night with us, and that's what we write on the *Fragebogen*. But men are sieves, and unhappiness can exit with everything else, unless it's part of constant physical pain. I don't ask for pardon. Nor understanding. Nor justice. I ask nothing. I'm not a blood-thirsty man, and I know that. I'm a withdrawn person. I used to lie awake dreaming about violence. I had never been violent, hadn't ever been in a fight, hardly seen one. But I used to lie in my bed imagining that I was in a café with someone who started to insult me. I'd take a beer bottle by the neck, crack the edge on the table, holding the neck tight so that the bottle wouldn't fly out of my fist, and then I'd hold the glass to his ear, trembling at the possibility of slitting him, cutting the vein which no one would repair. So close to violence then I thought, 'From the next moment on, my life will be completely different. From now on I'll be on the other side of life.' In my dream, I didn't need to make my mind up; I could cut or throw away, it didn't matter. Sometimes I worked with the consequences of one, sometimes with the other. Minor pleasures. And then, one day, in the war, it really came about. I had my revolver out and at the neck of a man who had my life in his hands. I stared at his neck: it was slender, wet with perspiration, starting to need a shave. What happened? I stopped thinking, didn't care what would happen, and then, willing, conscious, a little afraid, I pressed the trigger. The blast was the loudest I ever heard. The head split like glass. The inside was fruit. Everything, everything was in it, muck, and strings, and liters of blood, the horrible muck of brain. It was terrible. I thank God for its being terrible, or I would have taken to it more easily than I did. It was never easy for me, but I was changed. I was really changed, just as I'd imagined in dreams, if not the same way. How is not so easy to say, but nobody is quite so much for me, nobody."

What am I, I thought. A confessional font? Why this waterfall? One man goes to another for a few facts and, without warning, becomes the audience of an oration, a lecture, a personal revelation.

I didn't know how to respond. Is it that von Bodescher was threatening me, telling me that he was capable of inflicting dangerous wounds if pressed too hard? God knows, I hadn't pressed him at all. I came on his invitation. I drank wine he'd not only offered, but pushed on me. For a moment, the same sort of suspicion I had of Debrette came to me, and I thought, "He's drugged me. He's off his head. He's drugged me, and he'll lay me out and draw blood from my arteries for his wife fading away, without a mutter, in the back room. Dr. Frankenstein lived on the Rhine. It's a fine spot for maniacs. I'm trembling. My leg's twitching. My eyes are watering."

The Colonel had risen with the bottle and filled my glass. "I'm glad you like it. I suppose one needs a bit of this in him to take an old soldier's reminiscences."

Two-bit Napoleon on St. Helena. "My leg is hurting a bit," I told him.

"I'm very sorry about that. Legs give one a good deal more trouble than they're worth. Though I no longer have a driver."

Well, well, the world is flattening out a bit. I decide that I'll knock on the door I came to enter. "Herr *Oberst*, have you decided that you'll be able to pass on to me the name and address of 'King'?"

He takes an envelope from his inside jacket pocket. "I have a letter to him here. I introduce you, speak of your mission, and ask if he will see you. I can't ask him to tell you anything. That is his decision. I'm no longer in charge of his movements. He lives in Neckargemünd, just outside of Heidelberg, a lovely spot. I wish I could go with you. The Bergstrasse is in bloom now, and you'll have a fine train ride down."

So the battle was over before it was joined. I had only paid the price before admission. I thanked the Colonel as warmly as my condition let me. From the other room, I heard a tiny voice call, "Otto."

The Colonel smiled nervously, got up, bowed to me, and went inside, closing the door behind him. Five minutes later, he was back a bit sunken around the mouth lines.

"My wife wishes to make sure that you have been apologised to for this limited hospitality. Since the war, she has not felt up to receiving company."

"Please, don't let her trouble herself a minute."

"I had her with me in Paris for a short time. It was a mistake. Many of the officers lived very freely. Most had French companions. The German women were frequently resentful. It's a classic situation.

Your man Teichmann was friendly with a very lovely French woman. Delattre was her name. Her husband was on the Bourse, I believe. A very respectable woman. I had her to tea with Teichmann when Amalie was with me. There was a nasty little scene. The Delattre woman had a good deal more chic than Amalie, but she was respectful, naturally. I was Teichmann's superior, although, of course, he was a good deal more important than his rank. The *Sicherheitsdienst* ranks were deceptive. There are signs of power which are not confined to official rank. But Madame Delattre disturbed Amalie's conception of propriety. Amalie wanted to have her green card taken away. It was a most difficult business. I had her sent home, and she has never really forgiven me for that. Among a few other things. Her illness is a token of them. I am obliged to live with it, I, who never indulged in excess."

"I'd better go," I said, blankly. Fantastic. It must be, must be Phebe. I'd *felt* the connection. There it was. It would be Phebe latching on to whatever the greatest available source of comfort was. I'm only surprised she hadn't hooked a bigger fish. Maybe it was to sustain the measure of anonymity she needed to carry on four or five liaisons at once. I knew there was a reason for the tangle. I was most grateful for poor Amalie.

The Colonel went to a closet and got out a twin of the cane he leaned on. "You'd better take this," he said. "You'll need it for a few days at least."

"That's very kind indeed, Colonel. Very generous. I've never used one."

"Why don't we try it together then? I'll walk back to the hotel with you. We'll look like one of those Indonesian huts they put up on stilts over the rice paddies," and the Colonel unleashed a bark of amusement which transformed him. Was it the wine, I wondered. Was ours a fermented Appomattox?

We went out the door and down the street, our canes tapping and flying off together as if we were on parade. The cane, or something, helped, and I walked the kilometer to the hotel without trouble. At the door, the Colonel raised his hand in a British salute, and I shook it when it snapped down. "You've been extremely kind, Colonel. I'll return your stick within the week."

"No," he said, and he was all twinkling. "I want you to keep it. Just drop me a note and tell me what happened with Von Klausen. I've enjoyed your little visit immensely. Maybe you can make a longer stay some time."

Yes, I thought, I'm just getting out in time. The old autobiographer was just warming up. A week more, and I'd have had his mother's affair with the cab driver.

CHAPTER 13

There may have been a factor in Hélène's behavior up in the Arlberg which I have failed to mention, perhaps because I hope that it wasn't a factor. I still believe she knew nothing which could have made it one, but my *je-m'en-foutisme*, raised to whatever noble power the self-saving conscience allows, will not allow its omission here.

It was at the Christmas party at the *Gasthof Post* four days before her accident. At dinner, our first in the dining room, lit candles were on all the tables, and a spruce log fire tossed shadows and perfume around the room. We assembled any nostalgia and holiness left in our systems and sang carols. The innkeeper made a little speech in German, French and English wishing us all a Merry Christmas, hoping we would all feel that this was our home for the holidays. The English table, following Dads' example, called "Cheers," to the English version of this, and this perhaps opened up a small leak in the general benevolence. The Sensmesnils, Hélène and I, drank a lot of schnapps, not more than we were accustomed to drink, but more than early exposure to the heights could accommodate. We were gay and woozy, and when an Italian boy across the way announced that there was to be a big Christmas dance in a hotel down the road before midnight mass, we decided to go.

We walked down the snow-packed road, the moon and the stars as beautiful as I've ever seen them. A very clear, cold night that made us all edgy with waiting for something to condense. Every guest of the eight or nine hotels must have been in the main dining room of the Vier Jahreszeiten. We became part of a table of twenty, none of whom we knew and none of whose faces I can remember. All I remember is that we danced a lot and drank some more. Then suddenly, lines began to form in front of the women, lines of kissing men who moved from woman to woman. Hélène and Vilette stood up and drew as long lines as anyone. Georges and I stood by their side, seeing that nobody took more than a party share. Georges had to pull one pig off by force, an Austrian ski instructor who hadn't had enough time on the hills that day. At ten of twelve, a bell rang to announce mass. Hélène wanted to go. I wouldn't. Georges went with her. Vilette and I watched them go with the crowd toward the bell-hatted church whose stones had been carted up the mountain one by one a couple of hundred years ago.

We walked back arm-in-arm toward the little house across the rivulet, and held each other tighter and tighter. Nothing had ever happened between us, but we knew that we were going to make love. I don't think Vilette had ever been unfaithful to Georges. She loved him a lot. I love him too. I doubt if either of us worried about Hélène. Or, that night, about anyone. Vilette and I had always joked together, but we weren't even really friendly. It was a clear case of unrestraint. By the time we got to my room, we were running. We took off our clothes, looking at each other by the moonlight through the window. We didn't even draw the shades. I can see Vilette's body now. I don't regret that. It was a wonderful surprise, but almost all bodies are when you feel the way we felt. We used no protection; it was completely foolish.

Vilette went to her room in twenty minutes, and an hour later Hélène was in bed with me. I pretended to sleep and would not be shaken awake. This was a rare occurrence. That, and whatever physical signs Hélène may have observed, are my sole grounds for thinking she may have known what happened.

That, and one more thing. When Dads had asked his boys next morning to name a couple of Zola novels, Hélène had said, "Oh, God," and probably in disgust, but her tone and look were somewhat odd, and though I certainly didn't think why then, I think of a possible explanation now. The week before, in Paris, we had gone to the Vieux Colombier to see *Thérèse Raquin,* Zola's play about adultery with a friend's wife. It was the association I had with Zola then, and it might well have been Hélène's—might have fused her feelings about the night before when she could not rouse me to love. It may have grown on her even as we paid especially passionate attention to each other for the next days. And our final quarrel about reneging may have been in her eyes the *coup de grace*: "No, there's no penalty for cheating," she may have been telling me. "Just go on, and I'll do the same. It's just a strategy of life." Maybe that was back of the explosion, and maybe my vehemence was fueled by shame.

I've thought about this only a couple of times since then. The second was when I told Jacqueline that the finest person I had ever known was Georges Sensmesnil, and told her that I'd once slept with his wife. I asked her if it were not possible to care for a friend even as a part of your nature violates him? For Jacqueline and me, this was not an academic question, and we knew it, which made it even less academic. We had reached the stage in which we were aware that we were more than companions, but also each other's confessionals—receptacles for ideas we would never have pumped out of ourselves had it not been for each other—compatibles who fended off each other's loneliness. For people whose bodies are as lonely as their spirits, this is not an academic matter.

The first time I'd thought about it was in my room at the Hotel Bahnhof the night I'd heard about Phebe Delattre and *Sturmbannführer* Teichmann. I'd been turning up "Robert" at the source of all the disease symptoms of Chaleur; now, I was turning up Phebe. Wherever I looked, there was this sullied beauty keeping up the morale—among other things—of the local troops. Armand, Teichmann, Phebe, and myself, a box in which Bobbie had been caught, and for Phebe there was probably as little malice as there had been with Vilette and me that moonlit Christmas morning in the mountains. Simple double-dealing and treachery don't need malice for guidance. Stupidity, feebleness, arrogance, maybe even high intelligence can guide people into it. There are just fewer actions in the world than there are sources of actions. I've heard the expression "God's economy" as an explanation of the amorous visions of saints, or the standard patterns which anthropologists find under differing cultures. Actions are simpler than the thoughts and feelings behind them. So think I, though it was not what I heard from Von Klausen the next day, and it was not what Arastignac thinks.

2

I hired a taxi in Bingen and drove down the Autobahn to Heidelberg and then up the Neckar to Neckargemünd. I got a room in a *Gasthaus* and then asked the owner for the telephone directory. Von Klausen wasn't listed. His address was on the envelope Bodescher had given me, and I asked the owner to direct me there. Neckargemünd is but the elbow crook around the river which flows toward the Heidelberg hand. It is a mighty small place, but nonetheless, the address seemed to be beyond my man. He called in a consultant, an old fellow reading the Rhein-Neckar *Zeitung* over in the corner, and together they examined Bodescher's envelope. I realised that I should have kept the taxi. These men probably hadn't been up to Heidelberg since the turn of the century. They did, however, come up with some sort of solution, which was conveyed to me in a viscous mixture of

German, English and Pointing. My knee felt better, and with the aid of the mastiff cane, I thought I'd walk to what they assured me was not far. It was about noon, a cool, still day, so I headed out along my host's outstretched index finger towards an asphalt road. Twenty minutes later, the sun recollected its pleasure in the late summer, and started boiling heavy fumes from the asphalt. My knee took on a correspondingly active life, and I sat down on the road shoulder sweating pain. I hadn't passed a car, but there was a small house poking its cornice over the next bend, and I collected myself and made for it. A woman who looked like an aging capital "O" answered my knock and question, "Von Klausen?" Long pause. "*Hundert Meters links 'rum.*" I was master of the language to this extent, and moved around the next bend practically supporting myself on the fumes. To my surprise, the human zero had known who her neighbor was, or at least, that there was a house there, for no one answered the knock. Wonderful, I thought, they're away for the month. Then I thought I heard noise in the house and knocked again. No response. Ear to the door. Mice, at least. Perhaps I'd interrupted something. I sat on the single step to wait. I had on one of the lightweight suits which after the war chemists developed and blanket makers designed. It was sent over from Fields, which has had my unaltered measurements on file for thirty years. The sun made for it as if determined to reduce it to the chemicals which had associated themselves in it. I was stewing, my head a brazier churning aches. "What am I doing here?" I actually asked, I mean, aloud, there on the hill road, nothing but insects and a forgetful sun in motion. I conjured up headlines to be translated for the morning's Rhein-Neckar *Zeitung*: SIXTY-YEAR-OLD GUMSHOE ARRESTED FOR LOITERING ON ABANDONED PROPERTY, FRANCO-AMERICAN PHONUS-BOLONUS DIES OF SUNSTROKE ON MYSTERIOUS ERRAND. I was on the fifth headline when a large dark woman, dressed in the stiff, dowdy tweeds of a German bürger-frau and carrying a German market net filled with gummed white-paper parcels and a fat bread, appeared at the bend. I saw with surprise that she was a youngish Negress. Her face had more surprise in it than mine. She spoke in German, and I answered in German that I'd missed what she'd said, could she please speak more slowly, I was an American.

"I'm American myself," she said, in the metropolitan accent of well-bred Northerners. "May I help you?"

I told her that I was directed to this house by a neighbor, and that I was here to see a Mr. or Major von Klausen, who appeared to be away. Could she help me?

133

"Certainly," she said. "I am Frau von Klausen. I'll speak to him. May I have your name please?"

I swallowed more surprise, told her my name and added that I believed there was no one at home. She smiled and went by me into the house. In a minute she was at the door saying that her husband did not recall my name. "Are you sure that you want to speak to him?" I handed over von Bodescher's letter and said that it would explain things. The door was closed. It opened again in five minutes, this time all the way, and I was invited to follow her through a small sitting room into a still smaller bedroom where, on a bed which filled ninety per cent of the room, a ravaged young man with white hair motioned me to a chair which straddled the sill and from which he removed a newspaper and books at the end of his motion.

"I've read the letter," he said in French, in a deep voice full of the repulsive sexual promise of a crooner, but edged now with fury. "I'm retired. Your request is an invasion of my retirement. The part of my life you wish to consult me about is terminated. Completely."

I said that I was sorry to disturb him.

"You know how?" I wasn't sure what this latched on to, so said nothing. "By tripping in the rubble of a house when I was trying to pull out an enamel pot in which to cook soup. After six years of total war and five hundred separate missions. My esteemed wife pulled me out"—he opened his palm at her like a fatigued MC—"in Frankfurt, and got me some of your good American pain-killers; none so good as my wife. My dear wife who is now as loyal a citizen of our Bundesrepublik as any Prussian *Gräfin*. The Americans didn't win quite everything."

Cane in hand, I thought the best response to this oration might be a recital of my own war injuries, but von Klausen's floodgates were opened; he was not after conversation. How was I going to direct him to the matter which counted for me? I tried the ju-jitsu method of using his own force to control him. "My son is no longer a citizen of anything, Major—"

"Herr!"

"Herr von Klausen, because the network to which he belonged was penetrated by your commanders through a double agent called 'Robert' whom you met in Paris in the summer of 1943. I should very much like to know what you can tell me of him and of your meeting." A narrow ledge.

"What have I got to do with your son? What have you got to do with him anymore? This is post-war. You're not dead. He is. As for your double agent, I'd be careful what I assumed."

Once more I coasted on his force, ignoring everything but the ledge. "That's why I'm here. To be careful. To check up. You know something. Suppression of it harms the innocent."

It was a match; he had his hold. "Innocent? Absurd. Since Adam, the word is useless. And in my profession, my former profession, you learn that as the first answer in the catechism. Have you ever seen a three-months-old baby pull a blanket to its eyes and flirt with its parents? Three months! Even the coating of innocence is thin. What do you want? Your son washed clean in the blood of this 'Robert'? Marble-white so you can erect his statue in your living room? I won't help you."

"Then hurt me. Tell me what you know. That's all I ask. My son's name is soiled. If it deserves to be, I want to know. If not, I'll remove the dirt."

"More antiquarianism. You're not much of an American. Names are brand new in our time. Everything begins new every day. That's the only form of innocence that means anything."

Looking at him full length, I said, "I'm sure that you've earned the right to any attitude you want to take, but for an aging man like myself, cynicism looks like the easiest evasion of effort."

He had fine, unhardened, but strong hands, and he spread them, then spread his arms in the dirty white pajama sleeves. A soiled angel. A yawn. The spread arms became a stretch, and with this release of energy, there was a change, whether due to the movement or to his decision to reverse an easy course, I don't know. "Ask what you want," he said. "I don't want to put you off. If I don't want to answer a particular question, I won't."

3

"It was this way," said Klausen, and I'm putting together what he said in answer to a number of questions. "You've read Bodescher's book. It is reasonably accurate. The Abwehr had the entire northern operation of the Allied underground covered *ab ovo*. We operated every one of their radios and directed all their droppings. Never has the radio game been played so well. Naturally this cost something. The English were either idiotic or corrupt, but even in the latter case they had to have some success to show for their failures. One of the successes involved the escape route. Here is where I came in. I have

135

been in espionage all my professional life. An odd profession, but it suited me. I was well-paid, and I am thoroughly professional. I speak to you now from a bed of total retirement in a way nobody ever heard while I was active. Naturally. Not that there isn't a component of exhibitionism in even the most unobtrusive and ideologically motivated spies. Exhibitionism is another form of the camouflage underground work requires. We spies dream of the public explosions which our mines ignite, and in our heads, at least, our own careers conform to the same pattern. As for me, I've resigned, and feel no professional ethic reining me.

"I was called 'King', a cover-name for one of the Canadians who were to extend the Allied network in the north; they were arrested two days after parachuting down because their French was so abominable even German sentries detected a mistake at the roadblock. We ran their radio like a watch. Don't ask me where we learned their code. That does rest in peace. I was telling you of the escape route. I ran much of it, and made quite a reputation with London. They actually mailed me the Military Cross. A rare thing to do, but of course I couldn't come to London to collect it. There was a little scene right here after the war. They sent a major to fetch it back with apologies. I refused to return it. 'I know it is only a piece of metal for your countrymen,' I said, 'but for me it is a souvenir of harrowing times. Of an Ice Age.' He could not persuade or threaten me—there was a hint of that. I have it here." To my surprise, he reached in the table drawer and brought the silver cross out. He was certainly proud of it: he held it as a shy beauty might hold a corsage, and then he returned it carefully to the drawer. "I accompanied forty or fifty British and Americans back to the next link in the escape chain myself. Of course none was ever caught, so you can see that my success was considered one of the highlights of the whole operation. The crux came in the summer of 1943 when London ordered 'King' to return for special instructions. This was it: naturally, we could not release the Canadian. He was still alive under the terms of Teichmann's pact. It was decided that I would go to Paris, make my contact and then, just before I'd have to go to the plane, my arrest would be staged in full view of the contact. I was told by London to meet 'Robert', their Air Operations Officer, in Paris. To my amazement, I was told in the North that we had a double agent named 'Robert' with the French Section in Paris. Could it be that two German agents were going to meet under the guise of being British agents? Absurd, though one gets used to the absurdities of this game, and they become as natural as air. London needed an excuse for putting two network groups into contact, and the cover for them was an explosions job. I was to be—as I am, of course—a demolitions *Fachmann*, and was to examine a cache of stuff with an agent named Rampigli. The group was going to blow up a steel plant which was known to one of them." ("My son," I put in. He nodded.) "The owner was furious and said something to his mistress, who was, it turned out, also the mistress of Teichmann. She carried the information from bed to bed. Teichmann could of course have stopped the whole thing himself, but instead, told me to plant the dynamite so that the destruction would be purely superficial. I told him that the others weren't fools, and that there would have to be at least some real damage. He told me to go ahead, but also said that it was the last job the group was going to do, so I was to get everything I could from them. I asked him if he didn't know everything he wanted from his own man, 'Robert.' 'I can't trust him,' he said. 'He doesn't even have sides. He's a sphere.' I went to the rendezvous at the Café Orléannais, and instead of 'Robert,' another agent came, your son, whose real name was Robert. At the time, I didn't know that there'd been a confusion, but luckily, the arrest was staged in front of Rampigli before we talked to each other. Our Robert probably arranged the mistake, thinking that even if he were released by Teichmann, his usefulness to the Chaleur group was over. I suppose he couldn't claim that he'd escaped in view of the suspicions they already had about him. Anyway the arrest was beautifully staged. London didn't see its 'King,' and I went back north. The other Chaleur agents were rounded up in a few hours."

4

Here his words trailed off and his cheeks bloomed with a remarkably innocent smile. He was looking past my chair, and I turned around to see a tiny, chocolate-cheeked, blue-eyed child at the door.

"*Komm, mein Liebling, komm mein himmlischer Negerlein,*" were his remarkable greetings. The girl sidled by my chair and into her father's arms. "This is Odette," he said. "I might have called her Orianne, but it's Odette, and rightly, for she never stops surprising me. Odette, *sag' Allo* to Mr. Curry." The child said something in German. She was a beauty, a piece of marvellous candy wrapped up in her white father as if in tissue paper. I was quite pleased that the Klausens were being continued so handsomely. The melted father looked at me for approval, and I smiled to show how fine it was.

The former 'King' took the smile as a beggar would a ten-dollar bill. "Your son was a good boy too," he said for repayment. I was touched, at least pleased by the transformation, but I wanted one more thing about "Robert" while Klausen was still not far from what had happened. Did he know, I asked him, what "Robert's" real allegiance was?

Distance piled up in that imperial face, and the little girl slid out of his arms and the room. "I doubt if he himself knew," he said. "Sometimes you don't know from day to day. You're living in high tension every other minute. You're consumed by what you're doing. Allegiance is for those who have luxury. It explains why so many sorts of high living are tied up with espionage, counterfeiting, women, smuggling, piracy. You're like a hot, loose wire that can plug in anywhere, if there's someone insulated enough to handle you. Going from country to country, carrying men's lives and nations' fortunes around like a gambler's pack of cards, you get into all sorts of games. I tell you, the layman can't take the agent's measure by anything he's known. You'd like me to say that this 'Robert' was a traitor who sold out colleagues and companions. I won't. And not just because he was of help to us. I also know he helped the Allies, and took risks in both instances. I can't even say he was more loyal to us than you, or to you than to us. Life lived at the speed he lived it is contingent on itself: every day is filled with risk and threat, and there is no time for strict alignment. These are professionals. And they, *we*, are made uneasy by only one thing, amateurs. And rightly. Who knows if your Robert, your son, didn't do more harm acting 'straight' than this 'Robert' acting—well, as he acted? Whatever his 'allegiance.'

"I've told you more than I've told any Tribunal. I was asked about 'Robert' at his trial, and I denied that I knew him. Why should I harm a living man, one who'd helped my country, and a personable fellow, as far as I could tell from observing him briefly the day I deposed. I got a look from him that I treasure like my medal. He knew I knew, but knew that I understood what he'd done and how he'd lived. We were brothers. I'd be glad to see him. I'd be glad to see any of them. We had such times it couldn't be believed by anyone who didn't have them. Even amateurs would know. Your son would know. I should like to see your son too, Mr. Curry. It's too bad that neither of us can."

CHAPTER 14

Down in the country, I once thought that I'd occupy myself by writing my memoirs. Why not? I could write grammatical English sentences, and there was enough material. I would piece out my own trivia with accounts of the great events which passed me by on both sides of the Atlantic, and with quick portraits of some of the famous men whom I'd seen going by in the street. I once shook Laval's hand at a conference of manufacturers; I said "Good morning," to both Senator Caillaux and Charles Rist of the Banque de France within a month of their scuttling of Blum's government; I overheard Doumergue call his mistress "Madame la Présidente" (he married her a week before he left office in order that she'd have that delight legitimately for the rest of her life), and I even have some inside information about the Stavisky rioters, since a young friend of mine was a cousin of Daladier and told me that Chiappe positively said "*Je serais* sur *la rue ce soir*," not "dans *la rue.*"

Minor views, certainly, even the last, but an historian could add them to a hundred others and come up with a meaningful history of the times. My own disposition is for the anecdote; *the times* are a kind of croissant I took in with my hot chocolate every morning in the form of print. Strikes, elections, diplomatic crises appear in my memory like those defective balloons which hold the profundities of cartoon characters. I don't think this was the case when I was debating about Gifford Pinchot with my father, or even as late as the thirties, when I'd rush to buy the Paris *Tribune* to read the accounts of Pecora's investigation of the financial monkeyshines behind the crash. But then came Washington, and then, like France itself, it was all downhill as far as caring about what happened a foot outside my skin.

I guess the low point of caring came that day in the spring of 1942 when I specifically refused to help in the Resistance. That began at the weekly market at Caleche-de-Meaulivet. I'd bicycled in as usual to buy vegetables, fruit, and potatoes for the week, dodging the occasional German soldier who'd poke his nose in your sack, eat an apple, or look at your papers for his morning's reading. Buying a cabbage from a farmer named Glevin, I was asked by his sixteen-year-old son if it weren't true that I had a house on the Hâchecaille-Caleche road. I told him that I did, and he asked if I would object to a visit from him some evening. I said not in theory but was there anything I could help him with now? There was not; it had to wait. I said that I went to bed early; I was not well. He said he'd come by just after dusk some night. I nodded coldly and said it would be easier if he could let me know when, in case I had visitors. With a manner that I had never before heard in France, he asked me what sort of visitors? "Friends," I said. "That's a rather strange question from a young man." Here his father, a massive hunk of surliness put in, "In these times, strange questions get straight answers. Are your visitors green? is what my son means." This was the country way of referring to Germans. "They have never yet been," I said, perturbed now and unsure what was at stake. "I was putting off your son. I never see anyone."

Two nights later the boy rode up just as I was tuning in to the BBC nine o'clock news program. "Claire?" I said as the door was rapped. My expectation of a visitor was pinpointed to a tri-weekly ten o'clock visit from a magnificent, large-bottomed blonde who'd put my eyes out the first time they'd seen her, standing high up on a ladder putting paint on the second story of her father-in-law's house. Her husband had been recruited for the mills in Ludwigshafen.

The announcement that it was Sylvan Glevin resulted in an inability to turn back the door latch. I pulled at it for close to a minute before it gave. The boy came in and surveyed the room and me; I said nothing. "We need your help," he said.

"Who is 'we'?"

"A group of us," he said, or maybe even "a group of Frenchmen" or "a group of patriots," something sufficiently obscure and dramatic to solidify whatever recalcitrance I felt.

"What do you want of me?"

"We want to meet here now and then. It's way out on the road. It's warm. You've got lights, and above all, there's space to store things. Outside."

"What kind of things?"

"I'll tell you when you've agreed to help us."

I shook my head. I wanted to get back to my English news, and I wanted half an hour to prepare myself—psychologically, I mean—for my hours with Claire. I could not stand this conspirator of sixteen talking of "things" to bury in my retreat. "I shall never aid the Germans," I said, "but I shall never participate in any unofficial illegality. And you are wrong about my isolation here. Two or three times a month, German patrol cars pass here. They shine searchlights right into this house. One day they'll come in. I'm sorry but I can't help you," and I went for the door.

He looked at me as I had never in my life been looked at. Then some sixteen-year-old elegance like, "*Toi, con de putasse.*"

I turned off the news and sat in the dark. When Claire came, a few minutes before ten, I told her that I was ill, and let her put me into bed and rub my back until I simulated sleep.

I was never bothered by Glevin's son again, and when I bought vegetables from his father the next week, the only sign of something amiss was that to my "*Bon jour,*" I received a wordless nod.

2

The Tropic of Sourness is an inside belt for which one needs no visa but ego. I know it as well as any other country of my insides. There are a million entries to it, refusals, the admiration of others, contemplation of oneself, any obstacle to potency or liberty. I entered it for a solid week after my traffic with the noble young resister, Glevin, the world yellowing and greening wherever my eye landed.

I crossed its border again on the train coming back from Germany. It started out in a nightmare. I was looking at a map of Europe, one made out of living flesh, which, as I looked at it, became my Uncle Randolph, not the cashiered eccentric who sat alone on deck at Hoboken, but the blue-suited, injunctive commodore of Padanarum. The uncled map had country-limbs, and they too became people—Klausen, Debrette, August, the Mauthausen skeleton—who reached out for me; I dodged them, but each dodge sent me back against walls, and I was cut and bloody. Then the continent whirled off its limbs and assaulted me, and I woke up, my stomach crawling with sourness, and I just made it to the toilet and threw up. Miserable alley rat that I was, sneaking dreamlike into violence as I had sneaked out of it in life, I'd earned nothing but a blank room and claws at my spine, I, who thought I'd had an Annie Oakley to the universe.

I crawled out of the Gare de l'Est as if I had the brand of Devil's Island on my forehead, and not until I saw the unleafing trees of the Parc Monceau did I even apply for the exit visa from the terrible Tropic.

"Home," I said happily when Zdonowycz opened the door.

"You caught some bug in Germany," she accused, and grabbed my bag. "Sit. I'll get tea. Aspirin. Maybe cottage cheese."

I yielded to her nutty care, and sat by the window, a blanket round my legs, listening to the first act of *Così Fan Tutte* and eased into equilibrium. I was home. But where exactly was that, and what was it? "Where's Mademoiselle Jacqueline?"

Zdonowycz raised her bristles from a cloud of tea steam. "No, you're not dead yet. She's gone to work. Where you think, eleven o'clock on a Friday morning? I don't follow her down the street to the store, I don't need too many pairs of skis this winter, so I'm not there checking up, but—"

"Thank you. I follow you, Madame."

She moved out, but there was a whiff of the Tropic in my nose yet, and I called back, "Has she been in the last few nights?"

"Tuesday night I don't know. You may know, some years now that's a night I don't have to watch where every speck of dirt in the house moves, so I don't know whether she was in or out."

It may not have been worth it. "How about last night?"

"Thursday?"

"In Germany, last night was Thursday night."

"Here too. She was home."

"Anybody call?"

"I wrote it. Monsieur Theillard called twice, I told him you're away. He wants a call from you. Two others. Nothing much."

"Glad to know that."

"A few calls for Mademoiselle Jacqueline, but she was here, so I didn't bother asking her who they was for and what about. All right?"

"Yes, that's fine, Madame. That's all for now."

Knots.

Was I better off now than I'd been before Germany? Who knows? I'd had that hour on Schloss Klopp listening to *Figaro* and watching the Mouse Tower. I'd met Bodescher and Klausen and acquitted myself well enough with them. I was surer than ever, and this time from the inside, of "Robert's" double role, whatever it ultimately was. I had a good cane. I was better off to this extent.

And a few more days had passed out of my life. I didn't know whether this was good or bad.

I went into my room, drew a bath, and sat in the warm water for half an hour. Then I switched to the shower attachment, and let a cool, polite spray clean me off, got out, ripped at my skin with a great towel, did a few aching knee bends—my knee giving me no trouble—and dressed as I used to dress in the days when I stalked the boulevards. I grabbed von Bodescher's walking stick and strolled out. I was part of the world after all.

3

I didn't consciously intend to go where I did go, but there must have been intention beneath the apparent absence of one. I'd never before gone to the Café Lamartine on a Friday, and perhaps only twice in my life at all. But Phebe Delattre had said that this was where she went, and so my long, easy walk brought me there, and there at a front table she sat, not with the "friends" she'd said she met there, but with a friend, with Armand Boisdevres. I saw them both at profile view, and they looked newer and more intimate than they could have looked full face with age veiling the attracting forces.

Was it the habit of old confiding lovers, or something stronger that drew them together? Two cups and two plates of Baba au Rhum were under the tent their noses made; it was a genre picture for Degas—Armand, elegant, bluely constrained, even as he leaned toward Phebe, while she commanded and begged at once, not chic, not shabby, an ordinary elderly woman in a worn-out silk dress, two loops of glass beads around her neck, held up, and then waterfalling over her bosom.

She saw me, and with hardly a turn, with marvellous poise, smiled, as a raiding bee might at his flower, not giving or forgiving, but with a paralysing and extractive power that drew me toward her. Armand got up to shake hands, most unlike him.

"Forgive me, Sam," she said. "Forgive me for the other time. You knew something was wrong," and she was speaking not of something to do with Bobbie, but hinting at the dubious fact, gross and pitiful, that she was still before her menopause. "I was beastly, but the shock of seeing you, along with headache and tummy. It was too much. I snapped at you."

"Yes, join us, Sam. We happened to meet on Rue de l'Abbé. I was checking on Boufflers, who have been very remiss." This was a small steel supplier in the neighborhood, though Armand would never do footwork supervision.

"Well, here we are," said Phebe. "Three very old friends."

The unbelievable gall of the woman. This incredible leg-opener, this everyman's tunnel of love. I could hardly bear to look at her. But it wasn't for this that I was to take a stand against her. I had no place here from which to apply the lever. Germany was my base. "I've just come back from Germany."

"What a traveller," said Armand.

"I've never been to Germany. I suppose it's temperament. There's never been anything there to attract me. I don't like music. I don't like philosophy. I don't care for scenery, and anything else can be found in Austria or Switzerland."

"And formerly in Paris," said I.

"In a way," said Phebe.

"I met a friend of yours from Paris days," I said.

"Oh, how nice." She didn't ask his name. I supplied it. "Ah yes, a gallant gentleman. I met him a few times here and there."

"He says that he was a friend of your close friend, Teichmann."

"Never a close friend, Sammy. Never a close friend, but Germans don't know much about close friendships, so perhaps that's what it means to them."

"I would call their criterion a universal one," I said laughing, and I ordered a glass of Munich beer from the waiter.

"You're in a sportive frame of mind," said Armand. "I'm glad to see travel has done its trick for you. It was, you remember, what I recommended for your doldrums a while back." He looked at his watch without seeing it. "I'm afraid I'll have to be going. May I give you a lift, Phebe? I'll taxi."

I put my hand on his arm. "I must talk a bit to Phebe, Armand. And if you could spare a very few minutes, I'd like to talk to you as well."

He looked again. "Two-thirty. All right. Perhaps ten minutes. Will that be enough?"

Phebe was running her fingers up and down the beads. It made a watery sound, inserted a pastoral note into the nervous little café. Odd that a nervous habit of one person can tranquillize someone else. But her voice was as calm as a summer pond. "I'm glad we have something to talk about after all these years, Sam. I hope we aren't going to resort to sophomoric obliquities."

"I'm sorry about the obliquities. It's a simple enough matter. I may as well be simply direct." They leaned toward me, and then, conscious that the tiny table brought our heads too close together, leaned far back, so that we looked like a tripod which, underneath, supported the table. From the air, we might have been taken for upside-down legs. I thought, "What if we froze like this forever?"

"Well, Sammy," said Armand. "Have you forgotten?" The idea behind this remark was that I was too forgetful to do business of any sort. Armand built up great reserve funds of observation to be cashed in at appropriate times.

"I was thinking about what a peculiar threesome we were."

144

"Ha, ha," croaked Phebe. "Not the Three Graces, perhaps, but not the time to notice it either."

"I mean we've been quite caught up in each other for so many years, it's strange that this is the first time we've been brought together by something outside ourselves."

"I do have to get back, Sam. I'm not retired yet."

"I'm sorry, Armand. What I'm going to ask you is important, but maybe it's not as important as the three of us sitting here."

Armand's face was as pointed, as direct, as unambiguous as the hands of a clock. "Samuel. There are those of us who have time, and those of us who have business which gives us no time. I wish I could speculate about a variety of things, but my life does not permit it. Right or wrong, that's what it is for me. If there is a difficulty, it must be faced or circumvented. There's no choice. If there's no difficulty, then we must meet at leisure with those who we think best improve or beautify our leisure."

"The matter is this: Bobbie told you, Armand, about the plant. You've told me that."

"Naturally."

"You told Phebe."

"Why not?" said Armand.

"And you, Phebe, told Teichmann, who then arrested Bobbie and his associates."

Powder-white, powder-dry, her face, and the beads dripped. She said very quietly, "So you've been waiting, you've been lying in wait, holding your gun on me, waiting for me. You to whom I gave—life. You're a traitor, a swine. I told him, yes I told him. I told him as you'd tell a man it was Wednesday. I told, but not the way you tell. To hurt. The way you tell me, to kill. I didn't tell the way you look at me. Was I to kill Bobbie? Are you telling me I killed Bobbie? Look at yourself, you, famous all over Paris for your disregard of him. Your women—me, brought and flaunted in front of him. It's you who knocked him down. You couldn't stand anyone in your way. You were made to be alone. Lying with me, moaning over me, you were always by yourself, loving nothing but Sam. The American, Uncle Sam, free and alone. You sit there now, dead in your insides, and then claim that I killed your boy. Armand and I."

"It is too much, Sam. Really it is." Armand was shaking. A blue banner in a high wind, or was it my eyes, sweating at her viciousness, while the beads loped up and down on her? "Bobbie was going to have the firm. Everything. I wouldn't, of course, you know—"

"I know Armand. It was excitement for you. But you Phebe, even if everything you say is right, you brought your Teichmann a piece of information, maybe just for amusement, maybe just for a smile from him. I say no more than damn your frivolity to hell. You can hurt me, sure. There's something to what you say. You're not all wrong. I'll let it by. But look in your own mirror, and see your own bloody claws. You've never looked in your mirror. You'll see worse than the wrinkles and bags on you."

Armand: "Stop that, Samuel."

Phebe: "No. Go on."

"Come, just once, know that you've killed someone. I don't know how your girl came out of you. I don't know how Bobbie came out of me. But I never killed for a trifle." I reached out and took her beads and yanked them away, and they broke there, and she slapped me with her ringed hand on the mouth, everyone standing up, looking at us, Armand's hands on mine, and I raised my hand, the beads in them, and I would have stripped her face with them, lashed her, but they held me, and Armand waved for taxis and he put me in one, and Phebe was in one, and I got home, my mouth bloody, my hand on my heart, pumping, body caving and humping.

4

A messy scene, one of the very few of my life. Phebe and Hélène. For someone who has never had a fight with a man, it is not a good record.

I was a little calmer by the time the taxi got me home. I was out before I'd paid and had to be summoned by a whistle that the driver picked up from movies about New York. It took a repetition to remind me where I was. I could not wait to get into bed with a cup of Zdonowycz's soup. And half an hour later, bathed, my lip bandaged, pyjamaed and nursed by a frightened Zdonowycz—after all, where would she go if I débarrassed the plancher?—I sat up in bed drinking a large cup of potage whose heat made my lip first tingle and then purr with ease.

"You start out sick. You come home sick. An old man's got to put his feet flat every step or he's going to take lots of falls. You're going to get lots of falls now, each year more falls. Feet flat, like walking on ice," and she clumped around for demonstration.

"I'd better get a little sleep now, Madame."

"You're sure, no doctor?"

"I'm sure. Thank you for everything."

"Remember, like this," and she clumped out with the cup, shutting the door behind her. If a person clumps around like that, they must be reliable: that is the thought I went to sleep with.

A clumping woke me, slowly, not knowing where I was, and going through four or five places, Chicago, New York, Bingen, then the country, and finally, as the clump became a small knock, I knew.

"Come in," I called.

Jacqueline. "I shouldn't have waked you, but it's dinner time. I thought you'd better have dinner."

The tone was less solicitous than the words, but it was a Jacqueline I'd not seen, someone who seemed to be hurt that I was; there was no better way to wake up than that.

"I nearly had a fall too. There's a little slope we go up on in the store to slide the skis down. You put weights on the skis."

I started to say that it wasn't exactly a fall that bruised my lip, but I thought, "No, that's not for her." I never liked to mix different sorts of friends, and to mix different generations of lovers would be a grotesquerie. "You'd be surprised at the small extent of the damage. It's about the size of a mosquito's eyelid. Zdonowycz is in love with injury."

"If I'd gone down the slope, she would have had a holiday. It's like parachute jumping, but you don't have the advantage of good air and a nice view. Shall I bring supper in? I could eat with you here."

I'd started to get out of bed, but slid my feet back. "That sounds like an offer to keep me bed-ridden."

So we ate on trays, Jacqueline at the foot of the bed, and I told her about Germany. I didn't eliminate a thing. I couldn't just talk about yellow flowers, or the way Frankfurt looked—a great cigarette ash broken on the ground—couldn't stop with Klausen and Bodescher, but told her what they said about Bobbie and "Robert" and then went on to Phebe and how she and Armand had played their part in Chaleur, and then I did go on generation-mixing, went on to what Phebe had been to me, and then what I'd been like, and what Hélène had been like, went into everything, while she sat there eating and my fish chilled on the tray.

"You've got it now," I said. "That's everything."

Her head was back on the bed-board and her feet, in stockings, up on the bed, inches away from my left hand. "It's a lot," she said.

"But what to do with it? What train do you blow up with it? I don't know."

I put my hand around her foot. She has a large foot with a strong, high arch. The veins are clear in it. She moves her toes a lot and the veins dance. I held it tight.

"That feels good," she said. "But you can't decide in the feet. Though you know," and she snapped her fingers, her eyes bright. We had one table lamp on, and when her face lit, it looked like the birth of a jewel, a huge emerald, a brown emerald. "You should go back to Trentemille. You've got enough to go back to him. You don't know why Arastignac did it, you don't know if he told the truth or not about acting under London, but you have enough to explain why Bobbie was thought guilty. You can get a retraction from Trentemille. What do you say?" and she pushed against the board, disengaged her foot, moved it back toward the board with the other and brought her head up close to mine, so close that when I looked at her, I saw the edge of the bandage under my nose.

"You get a decoration for that," I said, and I kissed her on both cheeks, the bandage lessening the contact but not the pleasure.

CHAPTER 15

Two weeks before we went off to the Arlberg on that last vacation, Hélène and I took Bobbie to the circus. Twice a year, for his birthday, and then around Christmas time, the three of us did something conscientiously together. Months of speculation, weeks of planning, frequent postponements, and more outcries and debates than went into international congresses preceded these outings, and I'm not sure whether pleasure was a discernible fraction of the total effort. More often than not, I would forget the day and have arranged something else, a business conference, a drive to the country, or an engagement which I covered up with one or the other of these excuses. The inevitable preface was a fierce debate between Monsieur and Madame Curry.

"Not the zoo again," would be the counter to my first suggestion. And then, for color, "Bestiality is not in demand around here."

A loud Ha, Ha, from Honest Sam, followed by, "I think he's about ready to see a tennis tournament. Richards and Borotra are wonderful to watch, and he'll have a new view of Franco-American relations. You can look at Lenglen's costume."

Hélène never went within a kilometer of an arena or field unless she herself was somehow at the center of it with a new costume or a barrage of rehearsed wit. She had less athletic ability than a steel pier, though she was nearly as strong as one. She did swim like a greasy eel and made a lot of confident noise about skiing and ice skating, but she was basically ungraceful and badly coordinated. The strength of one part of her seemed to work against the strength of others. My tennis suggestion souped up her never placid vocal chords. "Go on. You just go on and watch your Borotorio"—she was always flinging off such brilliancies—"watch your damn ball-thumpers. Not that you need any ideas. It won't matter to you that a five-and-a-half-year-old child sits for three hours watching a pair of leprous cretins slap a white ball back and forth at each other. Why not just put him in front of a flower and head off to one of your whore-houses?"

"You hate these games, because you can't bear to see anyone who can put one foot in front of the other without tripping. And you don't want Bobbie to go because you're afraid he'll see that you're not exactly France's contribution to human grace. He loves sports. Do you know what he asks me about every morning? The baseball scores. And he's never seen a game. That's the only reason I get the *Trib*." (This was the Chicago *Tribune* then.) And it was true. I don't think Bobbie would ever have learned to read English if it hadn't been for the ninety-seven Green Diamond baseball books which my parents crated and sent over a few years later.

"Yes, I'm sure he has an innate love of games derived from your wonderful abilities. Why didn't you work him into asking for the market reports? It'd be better to have an innate love for them."

"All right, darling. What do you want to do?"

Deflation was my great weapon. Hélène took seconds to locate herself. "The circus. We've never taken him."

A minor coup. I'm bored to death at circuses. And even a little frightened at the unhampered egoes whose métier is contempt for flesh. "How about giving him a choice?" I said. It was only a delaying move. Hélène presented the choices with Solomon's caginess.

Triumph restored her color and decency. Bobbie was summoned, was offered a trip to the country, the tennis matches, or—pause, tense whisper—the c-i-r-c-u-s.

So we went, and took ringside seats into which the clowns—I

think Grock was one—jumped with us. I thought Bobbie would hemorrhage for joy. I had my toe trampled, my nose clogged with sawdust, and my blood curdled by Hélène's engineered sweetness.

"Want some grenadine, Bobbie?"

"No more, Sammie," said Hélène. I had been cramming him with the murderous delicacies carted around the place, hot sugared chestnuts, ice creams, sausages worked up from last year's sawdust.

"One more, Mommie." In the lights which spilled into our seats from the arena, Bobbie's face glittered with happiness and repletion.

I don't remember what precipitated the finale, the grenadine or another *glace*, but I remember a couple of muscle-men winding around the highwires when Bobbie leaned over the box and vomited into the arena. Loudly, endlessly. I don't think an elephant could have supplied as much as that little body. Hélène and I were paralysed. There was nothing to do. We couldn't pull him back into the box. We just let him go on, our hands on his back, looking, I suppose as if we were encouraging him. A few hundred eyes shifted from the air to that which had already started to putrefy it. It looked as if Bobbie were a rival act. Other children had been similarly indulged, if not for similar reasons. Catastrophe. All over the enclosure, children and suggestible parents poured their stomachs onto the sawdust, their neighbors' backs, and the slats below which performers, animal and human, waited to go under the lights. The tent reeked like the stockyards in July. People leaped over seats and children for exits, handkerchiefs over faces—which did not augment the orderliness of retreat. We made a slow, tumultuous exit with the rest, while above it all, the trapeze maniacs whizzed on, envied by all.

The next day, right below a picture of Briand signing the Locarno Pact, there was an account of the Circus Riot in the newspapers. Blame was properly assigned to an unnamed—thank God—five-year-old at ringside. Bobbie wasn't told about the account: he had suffered enough. In the taxi going home, I had blown my top at him. "Lousy, inconsiderate rat," I'd yelled at him. "Couldn't you have held off? No little boy on earth has ever caused the trouble you just did. You're an assassin." If he hadn't looked like a bleached sheet, I'd have knocked his ears off. He stared out the window, Hélène stared at me, I at them both. Electrocutions take less than a minute. This went on for the fifteen it took to get home, where I holed up in the sitting room with a bottle of Jacob Beam and cleared the mess out of my head, that is, just after I remembered that it was more or less what I'd asked for.

It was twenty-five years before I went to another circus. With Jacqueline on a Tuesday afternoon. Her store had closed for inventory. After our talk about Germany and Phebe, we were feeling very close to each other, and, once again, discomfited by the closeness. We wanted to be open and easy with each other, but we had not laid the groundwork for ease: we didn't know where we stood with each other, and each day drove us into further complication. Ease leaked away with every move we made toward it. Then embarrassment, formality and withdrawal took over. After a while, conscientiously, one of us would initiate rapprochement. We'd head for a movie, a play, dinner in town. Though never with my friends or hers. Unable to present ourselves clearly to each other, we didn't want to flap our raggedness in our friends' faces. Besides, part of our discomfort was shame and secrecy.

Though I'd withdrawn almost completely from other people, I was almost never lonely. I was busy with love. There was enough distance in it to let me be the companion of the self that was in love, as if it were a child I was worrying about, a daughter who was debating whether or not to marry a man who lived on the other side of the earth.

Once, late at night, I woke up very hungry and went to the kitchen for something to eat. On the way, I noticed Jacqueline's door ajar. I went in. She was lying half out of her blankets, her face slightly puffed and pale. Her hair was tangled and limp, her lips full, almost swollen. I went toward her; six inches away, I felt that wonderful hot sleep-smell of a woman in bed. I put my lips on her cheek, and then, lightly, on her lips. Unlike a woman who is used to being kissed, awake and asleep, who will relax into a kiss or even kiss back in sleep, she moved away. I kissed her again, fully, and she groaned and began to wake, and I hopped up and got out, so full of love for her, I forgot about being hungry.

Jacqueline continued to go out once or twice a week, and I stayed out of her way. All I knew was that there was a group of men and women in their early thirties who went on excursions together, office functionaries, insurance investigators, secretaries, sales people, not a wild group. They went to lectures and belonged to ciné-clubs. I wasn't really concerned. When she went out, it was half-apologetically, half, I suppose, trying to show me that this was necessary. Then the next day, one of us might propose an expedition of our own.

The circus was Jacqueline's idea. There was a huge tent set up on Place Invalides, and a thousand or two Parisians risked simultaneous incineration there every day. Jacqueline had never seen a circus. She said, "Once at school, a gypsy showed up with a bear. Between classes we went into the courtyard and watched it do tricks. The saddest animal, including people, I ever saw. He had puffs of fur stuck all over him, as if he'd made himself up just in time to get the job as bear. He must have been sick. He coughed and rolled his eyes. The gypsy played a harmonica, and the sick bear hopped up and down, and coughed. Not even in time. He's the only wild animal I ever saw, and he was about as wild as a raindrop."

"We could go to the zoo."

"I'm not much on cages. I could have gone to a zoo in England, but I didn't. We don't have to go to the circus."

"I'll never like one as much," I said.

Under the immense tent, we let ourselves get shoved from cage to cage, freak to freak by a fierce crowd. In front of the six hundred and fifty human pounds labelled "Raissa, the Great," Jacqueline suddenly gripped my arm. (I stiffened it to let her know there was strength there.) Raissa, swaying like a suspension bridge in a high wind, simpering and snotty, had touched off something in her. "It's the inside that makes a freak," she said. "You could weigh that much and not be a freak."

"If I weighed half a ton, I might be more oppressed by appearances than I am now."

"Arastignac had an uncle who was two and a half meters high. He turned down offers from circuses. He was an intelligent man, an agent for stamp collectors. Arastignac was quite proud of him. It was what we talked about the only time we ever talked about anything. He wasn't a freak."

For a moment, I hadn't recognised Arastignac's name, and when I did, I thought for a second, "What has he got to do with me?"

One keeps coming back to what one disowns. As if there were freaks of the faculties, as of the body, freaks of concern. Jacqueline and I hadn't mentioned Arastignac's name for weeks and weeks, but it began the same sort of chain reaction that had started after August had first mentioned him nearly a year ago. Though not immediately. Then, he was just a small blemish on our circus day, and I wiped him off.

Half an hour later, we watched a band of white horses scoot into the center ring and run wildly round and round a coruscating blonde

in tights who cracked a whip to signal their turns and reverses.
"Chuchshsh chuchshsh," went the whip, and the spotlights brushed
gold on that skinny menace knifing orders up and down to hooves
which could have turned it and its blonde brain into sticks and
flesh-puddles. Then, the blonde was up on one of the white backs,
somersaulting, spinning, balancing on one hand, and then, quick as
her whip, zipping through the blue air to another charging back,
and then a third. The tent rolled with cheers. Unfettered, undomi-
nated, unwhipped, that's what we thought of ourselves, applauding
the fettered, dominated, disciplined horses and their glittery caesar.
A marvellous act to watch, whatever the reason, and Jacqueline and
I beat our hands with the loudest of them.

Four or five other acts took us out of ourselves that afternoon,
and the day was just such a triumph as the one with Bobbie and
Hélène had been a disaster.

3

Put your wrist to your ear and feel the pounding depth of your
blood. There are times you can join the power of your pulse, when
the air around you is not an easy neutrality, but something keyed
to your wants, when you can tell the world, "Come along, honey.
Things are waiting for us." Out of the Cirque Medan tent that
blonde afternoon, Jacqueline and I walked hand in pounding hand.
As if the wild white horses were charging under us. We swung
across the river at Concorde in matching strides, D'Artagnan and
Queen Christine, the world romping at our beck and whip. Down
at a table in the brasserie between Maxim's and Weber's, we fed
cognac to ourselves and watched the flaring skirts heading for Metro
Concorde after the day's stupefying eight hours. We rocked in the
same boat, rose and fell on the same sights and noises. Did we
defect, forget, drift from that which had stopped our coming together? Or had we been freaks, conscious of roles but not ourselves,
and now freed by the circus, and the dusk, violet and timid, coming
out of the river through the chestnut trees and settling at our table
with the news that it was our time? Not surface, not bogus, the energy
which touched us in that brasserie, my harvest girl, my boy's only love,
and I, young as if I were he. We came toward each other in sympathy,
gratitude, need.

We went next door to Maxim's, consumed the richest slant of the
sweetest cow that ever knew the axe, and walked slowly home, up
the stairs, through the little hall, empty this Tuesday night—had

something in me bought the tickets knowing what was coming?—past the living room, where a single light was all we saw by, and into Jacqueline's room.

"You don't need anything," she said. "I'm almost at my period."

I went into the bathroom. (I don't want to omit anything I remember.) I needed bowel relief, and, despite some trouble I've had in this regard since the war, I knew perfect ease. I washed, undressed, went in where Jacqueline was taking off her slip. Hands over her head, her body in the strapless bra and tiny pants, pink and brown in the small light. Long, wonderfully strong legs and beautiful, wrinkleless backside, her breasts full. On my knees and holding, taking her pants off her feet. She bent over my back, her breasts free now, soft and then stiffening. I had no age but need, I was hard and young, and I leaned up and she went back on the bed, and we were together on top of the quilt, and if she did not come, she did not complain, but was happy, if only because I groaned with it, my hands at her branching legs and at the melting, hopping butt, my face in the heavy breasts, and I within and without her.

CHAPTER 16

I would come down to breakfast and find, usually, that Bobbie had read the paper. We'd had a short struggle about the matter which he won by threatening to get his own subscription. Fourteen, he was interested in the great world, had opinions about everything, all absurd. He was redder than Stalin. He explained the assassination of King Alexander in Marseilles as the result of some "anti-Soviet mission" the poor fellow had been on. The newspapers were printed conspiracies to be read only by trained cryptographers like himself. One morning I came down to see him brooding, almost tearful. I said nothing, picked up the papers and saw a picture of a fifteen-year-old, stretched out between policemen and mourners.

AN ATTENTIVE AND LOVING SON DIES LIKE A ROMAN

Philibert Trisinini, Hypophage of Lycée Rollin, 2nd of 31, came home yesterday from school at four-thirty. After eating a pear and a chocolate tart, he went into his room, undressed, folded his clothes precisely on the bed, drew a bath, and, sitting therein, cut his wrists with the razor that he'd acquired two months before.

154

The stomach had been examined by pathologists, and the chocolate tart and pear had been declared free of any "maddening agents." The elder Trisininis and his professors, Orgélès and de Rampe, of the Lycée Rollin were equally bewildered by the "inexplicable catastrophe." Professor Guillaume Maritontinque of the Institute Psychiatrique de Paris tentatively fixed the blame on the boy's recent reading of a work of M. André Gide called *Les Caves du Vatican*, which contains a description of a motiveless homicide. M. Gide, at Hoseegar for the Conference of European Writers, could not be reached for comment at press time. A picture of M. and Madame Trisinini, heads bent away from the camera, seemed to be staring at an account of M. Georges Bonnet's return from the Soviet Union, which made it look to Bobbie as if the newspaper was blaming the suicide on that innocuous country.

"Was the boy in your class, Bobbie?"

"The class ahead of mine. I knew who he was."

"He must have been out of his head."

Bobbie picked up a piece of bread, broke it in half, and then started doing what I thought I'd broken him of, tearing little bits of it off, rolling them in his hand and flipping them into his mouth. His place used to look like a bird sanctuary.

"Stop that."

He put down the bread. "I suppose everybody feels like dying once in a while."

"Oh," I said. "Is life so melancholy?"

"You know. Sometimes things don't go so well."

"There'd be nobody left on earth if every disappointment produced a suicide."

He sipped at his café au lait, and nodded mournfully. "That darn Bonnet."

"Bonnet? What about Trisinini?"

"It's an Italian name."

"Thank you. And stop that damn picking." He was doing the bird business again. It was infuriating.

"Sorry, Daddy."

I reached my hand across to pat his, and he flinched. I slammed the table. "I'm not going to hit you."

"Sorry, Daddy. I thought you were angry."

I shook my head slowly. "Tell me about Trisinini, Bobby."

But he had to go to school, and I was left thinking, "I'll come home from work and find him in the bath with his throat slit. And they won't have to wire André Gide for explanations." I got up, went to the door, and called out just before he got to the corner. "Hold up. I'll take you in a cab. I'm going early."

He smiled that shivering, melting smile. "I'm meeting Didier at Haussmann. Thanks anyway," and he blew me a kiss.

I blew him one. He was safe for a day.

But I decided to come home for supper, and broke whatever engagement I'd had. Bobbie was gorged with Greek history and eager to spill it. Usually I controlled the conversation, but tonight I let him rant.

"A Greek could stab someone to death at high noon right in the agora—"

"The where?"

"The plaza." Bobbie was no jokester. "And get off free."

"How so?" I said, though God knows how I hate to be lectured by anyone, let alone by something I used to hoist in one palm.

"Murder wasn't a state crime."

"I can't believe it."

"That's right, Daddy. A male relative had to bring charges against the killer. It was a crime against the family, not the state."

"That would save a lot of taxes."

"No, they had lots of courts, even one for animals or objects which caused a man's death. If the object was found guilty, it was taken to the border and thrown across. It was like exile, which was a worse punishment than death for Athenians."

"It's not so bad at all," said I.

"A guilty man would pollute the soil."

"Soil the soil," I said. "Ha, ha."

"I guess so," he said, the lecturing energy a mite diminished. "Jurors in a court called the Phreatto—"

"The what?"

"Oh well, I forget what it did anyway."

I've never learned what jurors in the Phreatto did. "Anyway he had a few good minutes," I told myself. I didn't like all this talk about exiles anyway. And why should poor old Trisinini have to not only suffer his kid's death, but travel to the Porte de Clignancourt with the guilty razor? I yelled for the cook to clear off and then cleared off myself to what I'd earlier cancelled.

156

2

If objects could be tried, they could be judges. The morning after the circus day, I opened my eyes to an oak chiffereau which looked magisterially unfamiliar. Impenetrable and full of doom, it bulked over me with a sentence for which I could not at first find the crime, and then, remembering a possibility, I reached back a foot to see if it would touch another foot in the bed. It kept going without obstacle to the edge. Extended, I let my body sink into the soft, fatigued aftermath of the night's pleasure. I rolled over, and held a pillow against my chest. A matutinal revival followed. Then I jumped out of bed—it was Jacqueline's bed, her room—and made my way to my room. The bed was empty, unslept in, the clock hands embraced at the nine. She was at work. I wished I had work to go to.

In the shower, the water stormed down, too hot, too cold, impossible to regulate. Blistered, refrigerated, I stayed in the spray as if it were a righteous judgement I could not avoid. There must have been a blob of sleep in my brain, for I was telling myself that it was Bobbie who was sending down the judgement. I didn't dare look up at the shower nozzle; in my condition, I might have seen him.

Then, I defended myself. "So what," I said. "I didn't do it by myself. The act is collaborative, even its prelude is collaborative. The desire is there, a fact, but one which comes with its own regulations. Leave me alone," this for the nozzle.

I forgot it was Wednesday and sat fuming in the dining room waiting for my hot chocolate and croissants to show up. Five or six minutes brought nothing. "Zdonowycz. Where the hell are you?" Nothing. And once more, "How about something to eat?"

In the back of the house, a rattle, then a roar, but a roar differentiated into a regulated Polish fury, throaty, curdling. I leaped up, threw the chair against the wall and zipped out of the house before she crawled out of her lair.

I came back in an hour to see the postman handing Madame Gonella the mail. "I'll take mine, Madame, thank you."

Deprived, Madame Gonella slapped a small pile into my hand. Two bills, a notice, and then a letter:

Sir,

I am barely recovering from the shock into which I was precipitated by your outrageous conduct. My doctor is preparing a description of the *observable* effects which will be transmitted to my lawyer with my own account of the incident. I am prepared to go into the courts to see justice done. Let me say that I will not write to you again about this matter, nor do I expect to hear from you *except* about your intentions with regard to it. Some things cannot be forgiven. I regret that a relationship of years standing must end so acrimoniously, but I feel no doubt at all that I am innocent of blame in this and in any other matter with which you have charged me.

Avec des sentiments etc.

Phebe Delattre

Walled in by women, a rubber ball bouncing off their inclinations, that's what I was. Incestuous circus-goers, Polish beasts, itchy-bottomed whores, letter-reading concierges, spikes to take your blood at every liberating move. As for the whore, she had as much chance to get a franc out of me as that oak chiffereau. If she had, she wouldn't have wasted twenty francs on a stamp. She was another link in the fetter with which this Wednesday was circling me. Tonight, there'd be dinner with Jacqueline, and I didn't want to face her. I went up and sat behind my locked bedroom door listening to the lumbering wrath of my hung-over flunkey, my head splitting with indirection.

Meanwhile, under Phebe's letter, there was another, an escape hatch, closed for an unnecessary hour. Finally I opened it. Written on hotel stationery in a hand so cobwebbed with hesitation and blot it seemed like my own heart's hand, it bore the shaky signature of the man who seemed least likely to emerge so quiveringly, August Mettenleiter. He was at the Louis le Grand, a small hotel opposite the Continental, had been in Paris for two days seeing his old stamping grounds (though they were grounds on which he now tiptoed), and he wondered if we could meet. I sprang for the telephone, the saw in the prison cake. He was there. We'd have a late lunch.

"I probably won't be in for dinner, either, Madame," I called to Zdonowycz on the way out. "Convey my regrets to Mademoiselle Jacqueline. I'll see her later."

"Break your neck, old skirt-smeller," and more, which I heard as far as Madame Gonella's cage at the front door.

3

I think it's only been since I've had so much spare time that I've gotten into occasional confusions about objects. You wait for a phone call and begin coaxing a black frog to leap up with the jeweled bell in his head; you sit trying to type a letter and implore the forty eyes observing you to shine with messages; you wait in a restaurant for a friend until the plates and glasses disengage themselves from their function and whirl you into an unlocalizable constellation. Such emigration from the world has happened to me since my days in the country. Sometimes I'd willed it as a way of escaping decision, telephoning, typing, ordering, but now and then it's become the atmosphere of my head. That morning it started with the magisterial chiffereau, and then it disabled me again as I waited for August on a bench across the street from the Rue de Rivoli arcade entrance of his hotel. I was half an hour early, and August probably half an hour late. It was one-thirty, my legs were tired, and the tiredness inched up into my stomach and chest and then all the way up behind my eyes. The sun was focussed by a cloud rim so that it was more like a million-watt bulb than a lake of light. On the bench, I began feeling it like an interrogator's bulb. Grilling. A plain, breezeless day, busses, cabs, a lot of tourists, Dutch, American, and in a few minutes, there was nothing but the Bulb and Me. And the hotel across the street, which had become an immense eye. The arcade was the web under the eye, and some configuration of windows became an iris and pupil. Then, out of the iris, an index finger came, a ledge of nail, the soft double hill of the second joint, the flat mountain of knuckle, an accusatory landscape out of the assumptive, soaking, visibilising Eye.

And the Eye-Finger said, "Curry, you Curry, you and your own son, you and he have had this war of love. Where you should have helped each other through the world, you've tripped over each other's footsteps. It was not intended by nature, law, custom."

To the Eye, I said: who lays down the law? Nature's what happens. I love through and with this son. This son is dead. Burn out a bulb, replace it. I bring love. That's not hate. Love adds, not soils. Who's hurt?

Eye, Bulb, Finger: "Are you alone in the world, old Curry? You set the pace, crack the whip? Everybody a dumb animal beside you, trained to your brain's whims? Can't you stick a plug on your need? Hold? Hold back? There's a world, Curry, outside your years. It's retired you, Curry. So retire, restrain, reverse. Can't you just once in the wide world help it, give way, give in, find more than your will? The knees, Curry."

(Was I on my knees? Stone on my fine flannel pants? Impossible. Someone would have picked me up. Perhaps it looked as if I were tying shoelaces, or picking up a button.)

I: "*Débarrasse-moi le plancher. Je t'en prie. Débarrasse-moi le plancher.* Off my back. It's too easy for you."

The bricks are liquid, a trillion hair-tubes oozing vision droplets.

There on the bench, four slats, three creases in my fine brown flannel, the wood loosening to needle islands, splinters, cab horns, busses, traffic, hotels, the lid coming up the eye, and

BLOT

August's coat. It was August's coat. "*Vous dormez,* Monsieur Curry. *Excusez-moi. Ma montre ne marche pas. Vous semblez un peu distrait. Ça va?*"

We shake hands, he sits down, smokes a cigarette, and I am back. We walk to the Palais Royal and into Vefours, where we order as one can only in the country from which a return home for both of us would be true exile. By the soup, I am out of the hole dug by the accusatory vision.

4

"*Jetzt wohin? Der dumme Fuss*
Will mich gern nach Deutschland tragen;
Doch es schüttelt klug das Haupt
Mein Verstand und scheint zu sagen:

"*Zwar beendigt ist der Krieg,*
Doch die Kriegsgerichte blieben,
Und es heisst, du habest einst
Viel Erschliessliches geschrieben.

"Heine," said August, after reciting it. "Where can he go? He wants to go home to Germany now that the war's over, but he's afraid of the war trials." For whom is this meant, August or me? We are in the little square behind the statue of Henry IV on Pont Neuf, looking over the railing at a *bateau mouche* coming toward us up the river, glassy, packed with tourists like specimens in a tube. "*Jetzt wohin?* Now where?"

I've told August all I've learned since we sat together on his porch, and he's said nothing till now, in the sun, on the little clip of green behind the statue of the assassinated skirt-chaser. "If you're asking me, I haven't decided."

"Just a rhyme," he said. "By another France-lover. I didn't mean it to ask."

"It's all right," but it wasn't quite. My skittery heart wants its friends in their place, patronised by money, or connections, or foreignness, or guilt. The wheel was in the captain's hands, and of the Chaleur enterprise (Subdivision: Penetration, Subsubhead: Trentemille's accusation), I was captain. *Jetzt wohin* was a question I could ask, no one else.

"You've got an impressive amount of testimony," he said. "And one thing about our dear France. It likes life so much that the greater the distance villains are from the events of their villainy, the less likely they are to be punished. *Schön*," he added, looking up, without change in pitch or tone.

It was indeed; the clouds had bunched. They looked like the backsides of white cows, the sun churning butter in their flanks. Below, the *bateau mouche* was starting to pass under the bridge, and some of the bottled victims waved up at us. August waved back. "Running a hotel these days isn't fit work," he said. "Everything is slopped. It has to be. You haven't time to make any one person content. You're supposed to force turnover. It's just in and out, in and out. Hundreds are waiting for every bed. Americans from Germany, Germans from Germany, Belgians—uranium rich—lots of South Africans. Maybe it's the Germans who disturb me. It's been such a short time. But it's myself that's the trouble. I've turned into a palm tree, drinking, doing my work in two hours instead of ten, sleeping. The days are very long. I've envied you having something to work out."

Yes, what I've got to work out, what I've been working out. Things are not so simple, *mein Freund*. My working out has doubled back on itself. I've nearly lost the trail. I could have proposed a trade, his villa for my mission, but it wasn't 1940, and swapping villas with George Sensmesnil was not the same cup of tea as this swap. A villa's the tranquil reward of the finished mission; you don't swap motion for stillness. The chestnut trees puff delicately up the river; I've never noticed birds in them. They're like the Seine fishermen, connected to the river, but otherwise withdrawn. They'd make good judges. I don't, not of August or Trentemille, nor of myself. Whether August was pushing me on because he was bored and discontented with his own life was not the matter at my hand. Whatever the reason for his *Jetzt wohin*, it served as a reminder that in the swarm of my entanglements, there was an initial obligation, if nothing else.

The Seine is so lovely, it's hard to bottle yourself into decision watching its ease. The tourists, under the hot glass of the fly boat, bottled themselves up for packaged exploring. They were on no authentic mission. The chestnut trees were not their judges, just more scenery, a living postcard. Everything was going to remind and judge me until I'd come to terms with what I'd set myself. "I'm going to do something, August. Before too long."

5

Back home, Jacqueline, in a black dress trimmed at the collar with ersatz ermine, was drinking Cinzano. A new dress, which I'd spotted on Rue St. Honoré and offered to buy her; I was denied, and then pleased the following week to see she'd bought it herself, no easy purchase for her. "Hello Sam. Madame Zdonowycz said you wouldn't be back till late." She was *composed*, particularly, sympathetically, deeply, even energetically composed. I came over to her, took a breath and then heart and kissed her hair. She leaned her face back and touched my lips with hers.

"August is in town. I saw him."

"Accidentally?"

"I had a note and called him. He thinks I have a case to go to court with. He'd testify. He thinks Arastignac should go to jail."

She got up and poured me a glass of vermouth, sat me down in the chair with it, and sat down herself on the armrest. "I had a couple of bad hours about us," I said. "Visions of punishment."

"You've got to settle with Bob," she said.

I wasn't sure what she meant. "Go to court? Or Trentemille?"

"That too. I've got to settle with him too. Maybe that's what last night was for."

My insides loosened, dried up, loosened. "I want it to go on. Now, later, any time."

"We won't stop."

That was the simplest thing I wanted, the easiest. That or oblivion. It made a base for settling anything else. The "anything else" was the minimal debt to Bobbie now. We were bottled up in the same boat, Jacqueline and I.

At dinner, Zdonowycz, light years beyond her hangover and my violation of it, almost pronounced benedictions over us. "It's so nice."

"What, Madame?"

She held our plates with the crisped lamp chops, two calorific halos, and paused for thought, while my mouth watered. "Things," was her pot of gold. "Things, things. The air."

We didn't need Zdonowycz to articulate our reassurance. I remember the evening with as much distinctness as our circus one.

Jacqueline, in that new dress, smiling a good deal, and I, feeling as if I'd never had my ethical hangover on the bench across from the Rue de Rivoli. I wasn't lonely, wasn't going to be lonely. We touched each other's hands a lot. I've noticed that men who fall in love late often touch their wives a great deal no matter how many people there are around. I've been contemptuous of it, but now I sympathise. It's not planting a flag on a claim, not saying, "Don't watch my gray hair, just my woman whom I finger for identification purposes." It's that love is touch, and the mind is not silent in love, though it may not be able to work an IQ test, unless they have one for touch. The mind in love thinks in touch, the way painters think in color. Eating, drinking, talking, listening, smelling, love moves toward touch. The rest is all the better for it, meals, talk, odors, all are taken up by love and solved in touch. And then, touch comes, and it too is uncertain, and for moments, there's something unassignable to sense.

We ate our lamb chops and green onions and chocolate mousse, had a bottle-and-a-half of some Chablis, listened to the news and some Irving Berlin songs from Amsterdam, and read next to each other on the sofa. The only interruption was a phone call for Jacqueline to which I didn't listen or inquire about.

I hadn't made love on two consecutive nights for three years, but I felt nothing but happiness till the next morning, when I did not have to reach back my foot, because Jacqueline's strong, full, naked bottom was against mine. Then, half an hour after, I tried to move and couldn't. I was hot, my stomach and head ached.

I've talked a great deal about my cyst operation, my colds, and my hurt leg. Yet I really have been ill very little. A cold a year was about my quota, and as for diseases or injuries, there've been almost none since childhood. Perhaps Chicago's rigors inoculated me from the ills which ambush most men; and as for my life in France, I have never experienced what almost every Frenchman has, a *crise de foi*, mild as such a diagnosis is in this country of constant *crises* and delicate *fois*.

After the second night with Jacqueline, my body simply reoriented itself to illness. By that night, I could barely walk to the bathroom, my legs trembled so. My body, unconscious companion, willing tool, ever-ready sweet shop of delights, my body harbored something that was putting it outside my will. Under blankets, I buried myself from the inner cold until the mad dog within calmed itself, and then I thought, "It's a taste of what 'Gladstone' felt." Not the prime minister, but an agent about whom I'd read two weeks before, an

Anglo-Frenchman who'd been tortured by the Gestapo. No atom of my body had ached when I'd read of the ripping disintegration of his, the attack planned to divide his flesh from itself, and his secrets from his lips. The horror had actually titillated me. Now, as my teeth morsed their helplessness to the rest of my body, I had the feeling knowledge of the war between body and mind which the torturers ignited in their victims. I know that the illnesses I report lack the burning of those willed miseries, that they are but cold, summary, judge's recapitulations of hot crimes, but they moved me, as had August's gratuitous urging, toward the crucial confrontation of the Chaleur case.

More, that post-coital fever reminded me that I was Bobbie's father as well as his surrogate, and also, that whatever I could have, it would be adjusted to what my body allowed; the hope was that the allowance would moderate the need.

Lastly, there was a general sense of the predicament of others. I remember I was lying down when Zdonowycz came in with some tea and toast. I was very weak; it felt as if I were at the bottom of great columns of hot air. Zdonowycz asked me how I was, and instead of saying "Fine" or "Lousy, how do you think?" I said, "How are *you*, Madame?" Tea slopped over saucer. She put both on the night table and wiped the overflow with her apron. Incredible as it is, I had never asked how she felt, not even conventionally. It was because I'd never cared. True, I stayed out of her way on Wednesday according to our quasi-contractual understanding, but as long as she functioned for me, I had no regard to her condition. "I'm a lot of trouble to you," I said.

"Nothing, nothing." Gruff, but no bear, no pineapple.

"Thanks for everything."

"You dying?" It wasn't easy, the land hadn't been plowed in years, but I was responsible. I know her as well as anyone alive. What she had or did on Tuesday nights, I don't know, but the rest of the time, she had me. Her life went into clearing up my messes, filling my stomach. She had no children, her husband had died years before the war, she never got letters, there was only Tuesday night and me. I knew that I would "make testamentary provision for her," but more than such responsibility bound me to her.

I smiled to let her know that things were changing, and lo and behold, she smiled back, though it was stiff, as her facial musculature was unused to the expression; but it was recognition that something was going on, and for the better. It never got much further than this, but there has been no retreat from the advance. I hardly ever think of Zdonowycz as a pineapple anymore.

I said "lastly," but there was an indirect consequence of my illness which was more important than any I've mentioned. Jacqueline caught my bug, and three days after I got up, she lay stretched out white in her sheets, her lips like gags on her mouth, her irises darkened as if varnish had spilled into them, her autumn reds yellowed, then blanched.

I hadn't called young Dr. Robichaud for myself, but I did for Jacqueline. Robichaud is the son of our pre-war doctor, who had lost most of his practise after the war as a "collaborationist." He was a very fine doctor, an expansive fellow full of loud speculation about your ailments and frankly appreciative of the flesh he treated. His son had fought, been wounded in the leg, and returned to the shreds of his father's practise. Now he had a first-rate one. A smallish, grave man, he limped to Jacqueline, took her pulse, raised her pyjamas—her breasts slumped dispiritedly on her chest—ausculated front and rear, took her temperature and then sat on the edge of the bed, head in hands. All this with no word but directions. "Are you disturbed by penicillin?" he asked her. She shook her head. "Good," and he prepared a syringe, turned her over, pulled down her pyjama bottoms—my heart jumping at the sight—and dipped the needle into the beautiful question mark on the right. I turned away. Then he took a culture of throat sputum and nodded goodby. I followed him to the door. "Pneumococcus, I imagine. Lots in the air. A few days in bed. The fever will be gone by morning. The bill to you, I take it."

"Please."

"Very nice," he added, and limped out the door. The 'nice' seemed to mean that he liked the touch of her breasts and bottom, but I don't know. Young men since the war are beyond me. They're remarkably purposive, but the purpose is secretive or even disguised. It's as if they were all members of undergrounds. Robichaud's father would have caressed Jacqueline's bottom with open relish. Rotter in politics that he may have been, he was a fellow one could follow.

The next morning Jacqueline looked rosier, and she ate a good breakfast of slavic *crêpes*, jam, a pear, and café au lait. I read items in the paper to her, but after a while, she stopped smiling, and I, reading. For a few seconds, I don't think she noticed that I'd stopped.

"What's wrong, Jacqueline? Are you tired?"

"Yes."

There are answers that aren't answers. "Would you tell me what's wrong?"

Jacqueline doesn't coquette with her ups and downs. Lilliputian maneuvers are not for someone who's dynamited human beings to death and fallen thousands of feet without losing direction. "I'm going to stop living here, Sam."

Before I'd really been hit with the hammer, I said, "No."

"Not 'no.' Yes. Yes. It's wrong, Sam. It's been worse not to see it as wrong. I can't be everything to everybody."

"You aren't anything to anybody but me."

"My body says I am. That's why it made me sick. That's why you were sick. You're his father, dead or alive. Relationships don't alter with death; only the way you feel about them alters. He was my lover. I can't enjoy with his father what I should be enjoying with him. You took so much of his pleasure in life, and now you want it after he's gone. You've always had it, young, middle-aged, and now. When will you stop just having pleasure?"

Demolition was her specialty. I was rocked toward the ditch; but argument had brought out all the colors sickness had driven off, and she was what I wanted. "I love you. I love you, Jacqueline. That's a relationship. I'm not driving anyone out. This is new."

"I can't think that. Or anything. It's like being in a wind tunnel now." Her fingers were at her hair, but her eyes stayed calm. I believed her because her face stayed whole, thought it was ready to break down. In a way, it had broken down, but an illusion of wholeness was willed there. I reached out and took it in my hands. That large and beautiful head. It raced, it breathed trouble.

The trouble had come from inside though. Nothing was really changed. The bug had been in our bodies before we'd broken down. It was just that we'd yielded to it, as she was yielding to old wives' fears. There was no need to have trouble. We'd come to love each other. You don't abort love. Worse than aborting an embryo, for ours was not an unconscious almost-being. It was the best and ripest of two conscious ones. You don't kill systematically, abstractly, ideologically. What counted was what you did, as long as what you did didn't hurt the living. But then I thought, "It's something else. All the reasoning is camouflage. She's just had it. I'm an old man, and I can't give her the pleasure she knows she can get, or at least not the pleasure which makes up for her discomfort at being with me, and the fear that when I'm gone, she'll be too old to find someone. The rest is made up to cover that."

The long run. I've always hated the idea. Never a planner, I lived like a tepid model of the Von Klausen agent, from day to day. In the heat of things, my small heat. Was she better or worse than I? I couldn't tell; I didn't know her motives or feelings. Did she? Or did they shift from minute to minute? Now, there was a genuine, weeping need in my hands, and then against my shoulders. Her arms were around me, and I was kissing her cheeks and neck and mouth. Every second made us pioneers. Maybe we'd been too easy about living together till now, too much in the routine of husband and wife, though, God knows, my ease dated only from the day of the circus, and so much of what was precious for us came from the secreted abnormality of our condition, the fact that we could be laughed out of existence any day. Was nothing fixed but needs and stale ideas about what was to come?

"I don't have so much more time," I said, not trying to bring her around by pity. I think. And frightened and ashamed of throwing my age up any more to her, "We match each other, complete each other. That makes even a short time too good to give up."

"I don't want to lie and say 'yes.' It wouldn't even be much of a lie. I just don't know anything but that I can't go on with what I have in my head," and she straightened it up, pale and calm. "I've always been able to jump toward my troubles and face them when I arrived, but here in Paris, with you, and all this time around me, I keep meeting myself. I go somewhere, and there's always me doing something. So I've got to act right, or I can't be with myself. Before, I could lose myself. I just can't now. I don't want to hurt you—"

"I'm not sure of that, Jacqueline. You told me I was always taking my pleasures. That sounds like resentment; as if you were trying to hurt me."

"I don't know."

"That's not unnatural. I just want everything said, the whole story. Then, if you've got to leave, you have to. But if we're facing each other in honesty, let's do it all the way, or as well as we can."

"You can talk of it all," she said. "I can't." I held her close. I felt her through her pyjamas, and I lay down, and stroked her, and her legs, through the blanket, were against mine, and she felt me feeling her, and began to move with me, and she said, "All right. It's all right, dear." I took off my necktie and shirt and undershirt and shoes, socks, there's always so damn much to take off, and she just lifted her pyjamas, they were reddish and full of leaves, her body was reddish and a little blotched with white, it grew as the top came over her

167

head, and she was musky, the lovely animal, out of the blankets now, full. Her breasts, full as I looked down, the wide nipples, and the ribs barely showing. I took off her pyjama bottoms, the big, soft but powerful legs, and we were together, my hard, if washed-out, tense, loving body and that marvellous container of it. We came together and came together, minutes and minutes together, and then, over, lying exhausted, breathing hard, she rubbing my back with her hands and my legs with her feet, saying, "Yes, Sam, it's all right. I love you. It's all right," and I thinking, "I don't know if it's what I want at all. Why not stop? Do at least that, and you'll have done something she can thank you for. You'll have done something for somebody by giving up what you want." And I said, "Jacqueline, darling, I love you, and I want you forever, but I'll give it up. We'll stop. The way I feel now, we can stop, and I'll try and keep on feeling this way. We can see each other, but we'll put distance between us. We can try, if that's what you need."

"I think so, dear. I think that's best. I think we've got to try," or was it even trying for her. I didn't know. I was content; she was all around me. I don't know if there's resolution beyond the minute, but for that minute I went along and once again, "Yes, we'll try. I'll help you. I'll make out."

And that was the way it came about that two days later she moved to a room across the river on Rue Verneuil, and we agreed to have dinner together every Monday and Thursday to report on our condition to each other, if nothing else.

PART THREE

"To the face of the child-killing man, I raised
my own."

". . . Those who imagine themselves to be philosophers
turn out to be spies."

"Can it be the moral solitude of traitors that
makes me admire and love them, the need for
solitude being the emblem of my pride,
and pride the channel and proof of my strength.
For here it is that one shatters the strongest
of bonds, the bond of love."

CHAPTER 17

I wish I had scholarly talents, for I'd like to do a study which would determine whether something that I feel about the Second World War is really so. I've read quite a little about the deceptive by-blows of the war, the activities of undercover men on both sides, the spies, Abwehr agents, OSS men, SOE operators, quislings, vichyites, and the blends which make up a large spectrum of neutrality. It's my view that never before can so large a part of war have been determined by men whose actions belied their announced positions, that never before has there been so much deception, camouflage, treason, betrayal, and lying. Whether it be Rudolf Rössler sending the Russians daily reports of the German troop movements, Erickson and Prince Bernadotte pretending to be importers of synthetic oil while relaying locations of Nazi refineries to the RAF, Colonel Stauffenberg leaving his lethal briefcase under the oak table near Hitler's feet, Colonel Montague rigging a body with false invasion plans and letting it wash up on the Spanish coast, Major Yves-Thomas, the Molyneux dress executive performing his heroic Shelley missions under the German noses, Admiral Canaris' debatable sympathies, the Communist cells of East and West, or millions of other "apparencies," every great enterprise of the war seems to have been honeycombed with internal oppositions, aneurysms in the Leviathan ready to split open and disgorge fatally the streams of intention. Since then, neural treason has almost been accepted in commerce, where the buyer's recalcitrance is wiped out by D-days of subtle suggestion, as if internal choice were an antique, toneless instrument. I suppose that students of the Roman Empire will think of the disguises which men had to wear day in and out during the reigns of Caligula, Tiberius, and Nero, but if these are of the same genus, I think that the new species must be recognised or that the sheer scale of contemporary deception deserves novel consideration. Closer consideration than the usual history allows, for history tends to reduce to blacks and whites, so by the time it gets to the shrewd illiterates, it looks like "bunk." We don't have a record of the jokes and good turns of Judas, whereas the underminers of today still live with their clowning and gaiety, and we know that there is sunlight in the darkest acts.

I'm generalising first, whereas I mean this to be inductive, specific. When Jacqueline left me, no, when she decided that the pneumococcus was her hanging judge and moved across the river, I felt curiously liberated, as if my ever-graver weight had become helium and could be contained, balloon-like, only by my getting the Chaleur business over with, by coming to terms with a Bobbie cleared of dirt by my efforts.

I had what seemed to be most of the story in hand. Motives might be debatable, but the events seemed clear enough. What Trentemille had accused Bobbie of was the work of "Robert." Now what was the next step? The assemblage of a case against "Robert" to be prosecuted by the Military Tribunal of Paris? The communication of the facts to the newspapers? What? It was a new sort of decision for me. It had been tough starting out, yes, but I'd been pushed by the shock of the Trentemille book, and the rest of what I'd done was on the order of seeing Towne. I'd travelled, researched, interviewed. Each session had had its own thorns, but in the long run, I had only to listen and record, only occassionally to persuade, accuse, argue. And I had the blueprint. The question now was *building*. I had been deflected for a while by Jacqueline. It was as if a balloon were trying to launch a balloon: my problem had bred a problem. One needs "second-stage" mechanism; I didn't have it.

Bobbie's cause had become the prop of my own sagging needs, a useful occasion. It hadn't been much harder than a trip whose destination faded as one was absorbed by the pleasures en route. But trips needed conclusions; Pilgrim's Progress needed the Celestial City. The point now was to decide. I sat in the Parc Monceau hour after hour, buying ices and letting them dissolve against my palate, thinking perhaps that their cooling would pacify my fevered choices and decide for me. And then it came while I sat by Maupassant's statue, sucking a pineapple-flavored ice—the decision to go to "Robert" himself. Blessed flavor, wisdom of the islands, Zdonowycz's patron fruit.

That would bring the investigation full circle. I'd show him what I'd found and see what he had to say before I brought the material to higher authority. Maybe I could take him along with me, happy to be free of his heavy guilt. The horse's mouth: my father knew that was the place to apply. I'd stick my head right in. The worst that could happen was not so bad. If he bit off my head, he'd really be in for something. He wouldn't do that unless he was insane, a tiger with a brain on fire. That was a risk I'd run with Debrette, and I was up to that again.

He was in the *Bottin*. Why hadn't I looked him up before? Jean-François Arastignac. One of a million entries. A sliver of filth hidden in an innocent name, one that would stand now with the tribe of Judas and Brutus, for selling his brothers, for cowardice, murder, self-worship, a cheapjack narcissist slicing up the world for convenient bites. I worked up a hatred staring at that tiny slot of print. I could hardly control it to type the letter to him (I didn't trust myself on the telephone).

Monsieur:

I have to communicate with you upon a matter of the greatest importance. The subject is the Chaleur Network, and the purpose, that of hearing your explanation of the actions which you took in 1942–43. I am the father of Robert Curry, "Gruyère," whose name has been soiled with mud, which, sir, belongs on your own.

I shall expect to see you one week from today, Wednesday, May 28, at nine o'clock in the evening, at my apartment, Rue Pavier, 32. If this is not convenient for you, I shall call upon you, either at your home or at any place you designate. I wish to find out the truth; that is my chief purpose. If it should bring my son into further disrepute, I would not hesitate in its pursuit. But I believe, sir, that he will emerge exonerated, and that you will be the avenue of his exoneration.

Until next Wednesday then, I remain truly yours,

Samuel E. Curry

I mailed it immediately and the next day I received a telegram: I SHALL BE THERE. J. F. ARASTIGNAC.

It was almost too quick, as if a tree supplied fruit the day after you put it in the ground. My stomach screwed up, and the next few days were wicked; I lost four pounds. By Wednesday morning, I thought I'd have to call it off. Once again I broke into Zdonowycz's sacred precinct and asked for breakfast. Our new ease had tamed her savage Wednesday breast, and though she growled for a few minutes, red-eyed and sweaty, I knew it would be all right.

"I realise it's an imposition, Madame. I'm feeling a bit off though. Just a little tea or chocolate, anything you have around."

A death rattle of Polish curses, but they trailed off.

"I've seen a beautiful brocade handbag in Chartrain's, Madame. I want to get it for you." Zdonowycz carried her belongings in what looked like a black handkerchief, well-used. I'd seen her eying the purses of my friends.

Polish non-curses.

That morning, I rode the clock. In the afternoon, I taxied down to Printemps—Zdonowycz wouldn't know what to do with a Char-train—and paid a decent sum for an imitation brocade purse with a jeweled clip that I knew would set her groaning with joy. Home, I brought out the package. The benevolent rapacity of old age: she looked at it the way grandmothers look at their children's children. And when she took it out of the tissue paper in tender slow motion, I thought, "She'll conceive a bristled brocade handbag."

"You're a baron, Monsieur Curry." The clip was between her two sad breasts, drooping, bristling, I had to imagine them. "My heart thanks you," and so on.

This coasted me till dinner time, and I ate well, a Zdonowycz cheese omelette, a cindery but sweet chop, an occult salad culled from some Polish market which she reached via busses and Metro transfers. A couple of brandy swigs in my stomach, and I was ready.

I knew he'd be prompt; that's an expectation about agents that never failed me. Their souls are trained to clocks. To the minute, Madame Gonella's buzz announced him. I went to the door—Zdono-wycz was reading love stories in her boudoir, clutching her jeweled baby—and stood as he came up the stairs.

Natty, bouncy, a springing stride, sweet-voiced, hand out at me, "I'm very happy to meet you," in English English, refined and easy. A smile that was close enough to Bobbie's to make me think, "He stole that from him too," except that suspicion couldn't last two seconds with the smile. (Was it a requirement that network people should have a smile which extinguished opposition? A last line of defense?) He had fog-gray eyes, light brown hair, about the color of the English cloth he wore, a completely decent countenance, distinguished without being fine or handsome. An educated face. One felt in it a control that was its mind directing the composure, the arrangement, even the size and brightness of the features.

I shook hands, though I hadn't planned to, led him in, brought out the bottle of Cinzano from which Jacqueline and I had drunk a couple of weeks ago, and then, steeling my heart, said, "Monsieur Arastignac, I have the most serious charges to level against you."

No movement in the face, though it seemed to darken. A rigor of serious absorption spread in the features. The face would have done well at a summit meeting. "Please tell me what you have to say. I'm not unprepared."

To listen? To admit? I didn't know. "For a couple of years, I've been investigating the circumstances which led to the round-up of almost all of the agents of the Chaleur Network of which you were Air Operations Officer." He nodded. "It was clear from the beginning that the Germans had penetrated the network from the inside. Someone delivered the mail to *Sturmbannführer* Teichmann of the Abwehr and conveyed the location and identity of most of the Chaleur agents to him." For some reason, I couldn't look at him here, but I felt a sort of glow where he sat, as if a filament were heating. "The person who delivered the mail bore the network code name 'Robert.' You are that person."

I looked up, my eyes getting ready to shield themselves for whatever blaze might be there. But there was only shade, reflection that issued as shade.

"What you say is very serious," he said after a minute, his tone easy but not relaxed. He wiped a crescent of perspiration from the eye socket. I had touched home. "And complicated, so complicated that I don't know if I can explain it. I'm not complicated, but I was involved in a complicated affair."

"A sordid and rotten affair, Monsieur Arastignac. A deadly affair. You sent men who depended on your faithfulness to their death. You sold out. You were a Judas. Why, I don't know. I'd like to know. You're sitting now in the parlor of a man who will never see his only son because you did what you did."

"No," he said quietly. "You have everything wrong. You know I was tried, don't you, that I spent weeks on trial for what you accuse me of. I was completely exonerated. What are you trying to do?"

"You were exonerated because testimony which I have was held back, the testimony of Germans with whom I've talked. You delivered the mail."

"Of course. Of course I delivered the mail."

I was up, my blood running fire. "You lousy, filthy killer. You sold out." I raised my hand. I could have broken his vicious head open, sneak and killer. He pulled down my arm, I raised the other, he pinned both. I sank. He held me up. "Let me alone."

"Sit. You'd better sit."

I flopped. I was out. I looked at him. He stood over me. "All right," I yelled at him. "Kill me too. Kill me." Here I was. I shut my eyes. I stretched out my neck. A hand touched my shoulder.

"Stop it, Mr. Curry. Stop being ridiculous. Listen to me. You have all the facts, yes, but you understand none of them. You've missed the heart of the affair. Listen to me." My eyes teary, sweaty, I looked up at him.

2

I started, Arastignac said, before the war. I was a pilot in training for Air France, and French Intelligence asked me if I'd deliver certain messages, and then, later, asked me to report on a number of things which I would have the opportunity to observe. I was paid well for each piece of work. I took it in stride, and it was some time before I actually thought of myself as an agent. During the war, I was assigned to Air Intelligence, and in May 1940 I went to England as liaison with British Intelligence. I'd spent five years in England as a boy when my father worked there in a restaurant near the Carleton—he's a chef. My English is still fairly good, as is my German. (My father worked at the Berlin Adlerhof in the twenties.) In 1941, Colonel Wynn-Wyndward—he was then a major—of the Intelligence Service requested that I come see him. I went and was told by him that a special intelligence group was being recruited under the Ministry of Economic Warfare. There would be no professional agents in the group, and only some of the central direction would come from people trained for years in intelligence work. He would be one of them. He said that there were great risks in letting intelligence work remain in the hands of amateurs, but it was felt by the War Office that the enthusiasm, bravery, and general intelligence of many young men and women could function best in a group divorced from the more established agencies. He—Wynn-Wyndward—was to be the link between this group and British Intelligence, but no one at all, including the commanding officer of the new group, was to know this. I asked him where I was to fit into the picture. He replied that he wanted a few men in the field who would be responsible primarily to him, at the same time that they fulfilled their responsibilities to the new organisation, of which they'd officially be a part. It was a very dangerous role, for the agent was not only to construct an identity for the field, but had to hide his primary responsibility from his fellow agents in the field. The main thing to remember was that the prime responsibility was to the regular channel, to British Intelligence. The idea was that the new organisation, while it would be accomplishing many things, would serve as a kind of smoke screen for regular intelligence. In a showdown, the special operation was to yield to the regular one. He asked me if I would take the assignment, and I said I would. I was recruited to Chaleur by another officer, went through the training course as if I'd never had any work in intelligence —most of it actually was new to me, because I'd had no work in radio transmission, air operations or explosives—and was assigned as Air Operations Officer to replace an agent called Peugeot.

Three weeks after I arrived in Paris, a German officer stopped me on the street. I reached automatically for my papers—I was listed as an assistant pastry chef, a job which a friend of my father's got for me—when the officer said, "No, Jean. It's I." It was one of my two good German friends, a boy with whom I'd gone to school back in the twenties and with whom I'd visited ten or fifteen times since. Then I made a mistake. Instead of saying, "Christian, *mein lieber Freund, was machst du hier in Paris?*" or something like that, I held off for two seconds to debate whether I should deny my identity. I didn't, of course, but it was too late. I'd made him suspicious. We went for drinks and a meal, and at some point, he left the table for a moment and signalled that I be picked up and my papers looked at. When he returned, the SS corporal who examined my papers apologised to my friend and asked if he would vouch for the authenticity of this "Monsieur Gaston Runge." "Of course," Christian replied, and the corporal left. "I have no option, Jean," he told me. I tried to explain that I had run away from my unit and bought these papers which were turned out by French presses; but my papers were far more official-looking than that. They were perfect. He said, "I've got to turn you in to either the Gestapo or the Abwehr. I won't turn you in to the Gestapo, as I wouldn't turn in Friedrich." (Friedrich was his younger brother, who was killed in Italy about six months after we talked.) "If I take you to the Abwehr, you will have to tell what you're doing. It won't be hard to find out, whether you tell or not," and then he began on a tack which I saw would provide a course for me as well. He began talking about my old ties with Germany, and about the policy changes that would take place as soon as the war was over, which, he felt, would be a matter of two years at the most. I began agreeing, and he brought me in to his commander, Loeffler, at SS headquarters. There was a serious time problem for them. They knew that if they were to make good use of me, I had to be on the streets within forty-eight hours, or all my contacts would vanish, and the codes and letter-boxes would be changed. The same pressure was on me: if I were to become a useful double agent, I had to be on the streets fulfilling rendezvous within the same period. The upshot is I went to work for Loeffler, and when I revealed—gradually, for it's the only way understood among professional intelligence organizations—that I was a member of the special operation, I was transferred to *Sturmbannführer* Teichmann at Avenue Foch. I reported to him from then on. But meanwhile, without telling anyone in the special operation, I informed Colonel Wynn-Wyndward that I had made contact with the Germans, and that I was going to have to show them certain things, but that in the meantime, I would keep them off any regular intelligence operations. Wynn-Wyndward would schedule regular operations to dovetail with the special ones about which I marked time. I tried to protect as many of the special operations as was consistent with protecting the regular ones, but it was soon clear to the Chaleur people that something was wrong. Little was said, but the tone of the network was depressed. Amateur agents are more responsive to conditions than professionals. It made them nervous, and resulted in more exposures than were necessary. Of course by this time, the Germans had them pretty well covered anyway, but if there'd been a period of quiet, if the operations had laid low, then they might have lasted a good deal longer. Your son was a particularly zealous person, Mr. Curry. He was even rash. He needn't have gone to the rendezvous with the German agent. I sent him the message, but I purposely omitted the security check. If he'd been careful, he would have noticed. Anyway, Wynn-Wyndward called me back to London, and I persuaded the Germans that there was some suspicion of me which I had to clear up. I didn't come back to France. I trained other operators in England and passed on my field information and experience. The network was rounded up. I knew all along it was coming, and one of my arrangements with Teichmann was that none of the agents should be killed. He agreed that if the arms caches were turned over, he would secure an agreement from the central headquarters of the *Sicherheitsdienst* to that effect. And this was what happened, although when Teichmann was transferred and lost control of the prisoners, they were killed. I won't attempt to say anything about my feelings here. I knew some of these men and women. I worked, drank, and ate with them. I admired and liked them, yet all along I was endangering them. For a cause we held in common. I won't try to describe my feelings or the strain this put on them. I am a man before I'm an agent. But I was a professional, and not for money, though I was well-paid. What I've told you came out in my trial. I don't blame any one for that, and as you see, I was exonerated.

There it is, your son's innocence and my guilt. I only wonder which of us did more harm in the war? Or does it matter? It may not be a defense; it's just where I stand. I did what I was told to do. I'm very sorry for what happened, but it would have happened anyway. Without me, your son would still be dead, though perhaps Trentemille would have picked on someone else. One can't tell.

3

One can't tell. In French, it's even more anonymous, with the inconspicuousness of the passive blurring its direction. Life is best lived as a convergent figure, not a circle. The heart's wishes come to points, and though points have no magnitude at all, the point of a point is convergence. Arastignac had been my point of convergence for quite a while, and now it looked as if he were more of a convenience than a true convergence, something to rest on before I moved on. How do leaders move or judges decide? How could I decide, looking from a judicial bench on the jaunty fellow standing now at my window, looking about as harmful as a drape. I watched him draw out a pack of cigarettes, light one, and puff smoke out the window, and I watched the smoke make a thousand twinkling dots of Paris life look like a gold grain in rock. Rock that held together a quarter of a second. Arastignac and I, drawn together by the smoke of assassination and slander, fifteen feet apart in a sitting room. He raised his right foot about six inches and curled it around his left ankle.

"Gurdjieff," I said, before I knew what I said.

He whirled around, a crevice of astonishment. "No, but Rinamurti-

Ghode, who worked with Gurdjieff. No one I've encountered can touch him. It's not the objective dance, but contraction and release. Do you—"

"No." But I may have heard the name. I've heard so many of those names. Though you can never say that, because practitioners are like mothers of new babies who get infuriated if they're told that their baby looks just like Mrs. Monahan's baby. "I worked with Gurdjieff stuff some time ago. I didn't keep up with it. I don't suppose I've done any since the war."

"I began after the war," he said. "It's been a salvation." His face was lit up and in motion. The painting had been washed, the crusted varnish skimmed off. I was facing a clearer man, one whose authenticity went below the rapid account of his espionage career.

"Rinamurti began with *mekheness,* the release from responsibility, which trickled down to the West as hypnotism. But he changed during the war. He proceeded to the opposite, to total responsibility in which the practitioner becomes his own guru. The dances are only clues. He's not after the mastery or extinction of the body, only utilisation of it as a calendar for the interior, an ordered reminder by seven postures, one for each day of the week, that the interior must be attended to. You can assume the postures any time. They're inconspicuous; only people who have studied such things will notice them. The point is that you can do this without isolating yourself from ordinary life. But the interior is always there, and the postures are available, like breathing."

Once again, a home lecture. For a moment I resented this one immensely. Who the hell was he to come telling me about mastery of the body after putting my son's on the meathook? Noble motives or not? But like the smoky rock, resentment didn't last. What counted for me then was that this man of action had roots. Klausen didn't have the whole story. Men are beyond their actions as well as their circumstances. It struck me then that maybe action embodies only a small fraction of what counts. Maybe actions aren't the proper ground for right judgements. The courts have to match up innocence and guilt with the swinging arm and the motive behind it, but this isn't enough. Action may be too easy a way into the current, too much a short cut to judgement. Didn't even Debrette and Rampigli realise that when they came together? The actions which had made them enemies were only part of the story. Years before, when I moved like a skimming stone above what counted, I'd sensed now and then that there was something below what I was doing. I'd had

178

some odd calls to the hidden, Steiner, Keyserling, even the Ouija boards, all defective, yes, but maybe arrows into what counts. It's the least expected door that may lead into the garden. None could be less expected than Arastignac, but I could almost smell roses in the room.

"I think I'd like to try them out myself," I said. "Would you show them to me?"

The investigation had come to a fuller circle than I could have imagined.

CHAPTER 18

The next day, Thursday, was a dinner day with Jacqueline. Arastignac had left at midnight, and I'd gone to bed feeling that a large job had been finished. I slept well and woke well, and the morning feeling was that there was another job to do, an undefined but pleasanter one that would last me till I needed nothing else. At breakfast, I read in *Le Monde* that General Eisenhower had said that he might be willing to accept a draft for the Republican presidential nomination, and I thought that here was a man older than I who'd just finished the second of his great jobs, establishing NATO, and was ready now not just to go back to Columbia University but to take on what would be the biggest job of all. Could I? There was a picture of him inspecting a Norwegian battalion, his head leaning toward a Norwegian general with an expression of that courteous availability which persuaded many of us in Europe that he was the best American in France since Benjamin Franklin. Ever since Clemenceau had abused Wilson, I was very sensitive to the important Americans who came to France; I've sometimes felt that the President should submit his ambassadorial choices for my approval.

The Americans in France after this war—I didn't notice them as much when I was new here myself—have been a pretty punk lot, yet despite the fact that not nearly as many eligible Frenchmen lost their lives in this war as in that of 1914, Americans have managed to marry a lot of girls who would otherwise have danced the Catrinette. I have in a way served this cause twice. In fact, if it didn't exist, Georges Sensmesnil would probably not have brought me to Hélène's back in 1919. And today, Jacqueline might not be reduced for company to a salesman of ice skates and her sexagenarian almost-father-in-law. This was a morning agitation I did not want; it even started up the hot wind of Sourness inside me.

Then my left big toe touched my right ankle. Thursday's posture. The wind died down. I sat, newspaper in hand, staring at the sliver of garden beyond the brick wall, my mind not blank but filled with a colorless color and soundless sound. My apartment, my mind's glove, no, the inside of my mind where Le Monde, the breakfast of hot chocolate with its deposit of dead froth rimming the blue cup, the fifty tanned and yellow flakelets remaining from my morning's baked croissant, the dark wood from which Madame Zdonowycz's arm muscles had extracted shine like a king's smile, the window, the tucked brick of the wall, the frame backs of the dining chairs, the billowing emptiness of the room, these and ten thousand other flecks were for some unclockable spell my neural structure, my organs, my self. Inside out, unearthed, embarked within yet not shut without.

Blot.

Weight on me. Depression on shoulder, voice.

"You not getting dressed today? Dreaming, ten o'clock? What's the matter?"

I put my hand to my right shoulder and held Mme. Zdonowycz's even as it shook in surprise. I could feel hair against my palm, flowers feeling the bee's trembling belly as it scoops the pollen.

"You're not sick again?"

"No, I'm not, my dear Madame. I'm all right. I was just remembering something."

I got up and ran a full bath, hoisted my left leg—which had troubled me now and then since Bingen—into the tub and then lay down, thinking, "Not remembering. By no means remembering." I'd been loosed from remembering by the posture. I'd been made stateless, sonless, passionless, roomless; but neither lonely, cold nor discontented. The cake of soap was palm-length and wide, weighty, and had a grassy smell. Unlike most soaps, it lathered on contact. I rubbed it around my head, churned a peruke of sud in the gray nest, and spread it, warm snow down a mountain. I rubbed the cake in my backside valley, raised my legs above the water and soaped the loopy, hairless calves, the soft-veined feet, the thighs, the *verge*, the pelvis, the stomach, the ribs, the chest with its indentation at the sternum from the dive at Padanarum fifty years ago which had broken a supporting rib. I dressed and went for a walk past the École Normale toward Clichy, ate potato soup and a small, charred *bifteck* in a place across from an open auction, where, after, I paid six hundred francs for a swatch of brocade which I thought Mme. Zdonowycz could convert into a noble sibling for her purse. At a book stall, I bought an American novel in French translation—I sometimes tried to guess the original English sentences—and read some of it sitting on a bench near the Chartres Pavillion in Parc Monceau. The book was about a young man waiting to go into the American army, but, like myself, he was strung between the world he'd just quit and the one he hadn't entered, and he had a pile of troubles. They relieved any remnants of my own till five-thirty, when I went home, had a glass of sherry, into which I dropped the yolk of a pullet egg, dressed for dinner, said goodby to Madame Zdonowycz, who was swathed with the glittery cloth and could not answer for the pins in her mouth, took a bus across the river to the Gare d'Orsay, walked two blocks south to Rue Verneuil and came to Jacqueline's.

2

Verneuil is a modest insertion between Rue de Lille and Rue de l'Université, a row of small bars, small restaurants, small grocers, bookstores, vintners, very small hotels, and one or two disguised mansions before which Bentleys and Alfa-Romeos parked.

Jacqueline's apartment was on the bottom floor. On that first visit the door was opened by a large, red-haired dog with a horsy face. At least, this was the first organism visible after the door opened. This proved to be "Duggy," a gift to the owners of the house from an American tenant. It took to me strongly, perhaps out of canine chauvinism, and it was on my coat's top button when pulled off by a girl with hair the color of its own. This was Jeannette, the seventeen-year-old provincial who slaved seventy-five hours a week for the owners of the house, the Chouresnes.

I asked for Jacqueline, just as she opened her door across the hall, saw me and bowed her head. Jeannette's eyes registered this as respect for a distinguished visitor, and familiarity never cancelled this impression.

"I've missed you," said Jacqueline.

"And I you."

"We'll get used to it." As if we'd spent a lifetime together.

"That's what older people are supposed to learn to do. I haven't."

"Another sign of your not being an older person."

No matter how well up in this world a man is, he must sometimes feel that he's being smothered in gauze.

"How did it go?" she asked. I had told her on the phone that Arastignac was coming to see me.

"It went well. But let me wait with it." Nobody takes to such a response; Jacqueline did as well as anyone. She took me over to her bed, which was made up as a couch with pillows, and sat down with me. She looked very large, her shoulders broad in a stiff, orangeade-colored dress.

"Oh, nuts," I said. "I forgot to bring you what I intended." There I'd been out all day buying brocade for Zdonowycz, books for myself, and nothing for Jacqueline's apartment-warming. But I hadn't "intended," for I hadn't thought of anything but Jacqueline herself.

"I have it," and she went into an ex-closet off the ten-by-twelve rectangle where she ate, slept, and entertained, and brought out two glasses of Cinzano. "To your health, Sam," with a motherly look on her face, which was too thick for me. I wasn't prepared to exchange one form of quasi-incest for another.

"That's going to be good," I said. Then I told her about Rinamurti-Ghode and his purifying postures.

"Ridiculous," was her response.

"Probably."

"But you're retired and have a right to experiment."

"Maybe that's it. How about Printinière's?"

"Another cult?"

"A restaurant. One of my old favorites."

"No more Cinzano?"

"Bad for my liver."

On the way out, Jeannette peeked at us from the door across from Jacqueline's. I turned, and for the same reason of clownish discomfort which I suppose had caused Jacqueline to bow to me, I bowed low to her, whereupon a lumpy, wet tongue circumscribed my face. Duggy.

3

"I'm afraid of not striking when the iron's hot," I said to Jacqueline, as we sank into the last course, an oozing Gorgonzola that wrapped up our beef filets, choucroutes, mist-salad, and Gevry-Chambertin. "You know that idiom?" She nodded, eyes a little torpid from our more than amiable feast under the copper flambeaux. "A couple of years ago, I began thinking of new markets for Boisdevres. I thought it would be a way I could demonstrate how invaluable I was. I lit on Chile. They need about a hundred and twenty thousand tons of steel a year and were producing seventeen. Bethlehem and U.S. Steel had eighty per cent of their business, and their converters were almost all American. I saw a profitable entry for us, wrote up a report on it, and was on the verge of sending it in to my brother-in-law, when I happened to pick up the *Bulletin d'Acier*, which I hadn't really read for years and saw that the Chileans had just opened their own plant at Huantichatipek which would give them all the steel they want and enough left over to make excellent converting arrangements with Brazil. My report had the value of a dog's dream."

"It was a good job."

"Two years before it would have been a useful job. No, the crux is to do something at the right time. I don't want to keep hobbling after my opportunities for the next twenty-five years," which perhaps made me sound fifty, instead of fifty-seven. "That's why I went right for Arastignac."

The culinary torpor cleared out of her face. "I've been waiting," she said quietly.

"He said something that you may not take to."

"What was that?"

"The Chaleur penetration was engineered by London. No. Wait." My sales word had gone too far. "Not 'engineered.' British Intelligence had its own operation covering more or less the same ground. If the amateurs' operation worked, fine, but if there were trouble, it was to be thrown up to the Germans. The regular organization had priority."

Jacqueline's face went to war, mannerliness disappeared in it. A Jacqueline I hadn't seen, a stick of dynamite and a gun in her hands. The voice was rigid. "The bone tossed to the dog while Intelligence robbed the safe. And took the loot."

"And took the loot, yes, though the loot was beating the Germans, which meant it was everybody's loot." My defense was meant to restrain her. "That's why Wynn-Wyndward testified for Arastignac. He was the contact man with British Intelligence. He knew what was going on, and he'd made contact with Germans through Arastignac to throw them off Intelligence."

Silence. Waiters' shoes sounded from carpet to planked floor, small clouds of talk here and there in the dark between the flames; our breathing. Jacqueline leaned back against the wealth of leather and faded into shadow. "It's what Chaleur thought," she said. "It's what he thought when he got back from England. I think so too. I don't know about Arastignac. He must be a monster either way. I've done terrible things, Sam, cruel things, taken one by one. I've damaged people, decent ones. I stabbed a sixty-year-old man in the stomach for doing something not too different from what Arastignac did. I reached back my arm and drove six steel inches into his stomach, and slapped my hand against his mouth while my body was flooded by his. I wonder now if he wasn't after the same loot I was. Who knows what side he was on?"

And I, I was on an entirely new side, thinking that she'd spoken of that sixty-year-old man as I would an eighty-four-old. Could I have held off the arcing power of that knife, that arm which had held my fifty-seven years against her breasts? I huffed, sweated, sighed. "Too late for wondering."

"You said it."

"It was a soldier's thing to do."

"*Merde*. It was a rat's thing to do. A bunch of rats. Why we go around moping how we were taken, I don't know. Everybody took everybody. Rats drowned rats. But there were some who worked for love, even doing rat's things. There are rats and rats." She sat up, put her hand on the cheek of mine which was furthest away from her, turned my head around with it, stared into my eyes, her lips within an inch of mine, and said, "You've got to tell what you know."

I said, "How?"

"I don't know. The newspapers, Trentemille. Go through channels. The government is not so cozy with the English. You could force an international protest. Take it up with the American ambassador."

"All right. It's what I've been wanting from you." Some of what I wanted. "Either way, Bobbie's clear, whether Arastignac's telling the truth or not."

"It's more than Bobbie now." With a bit of weight on the diminutive, as if to say that the boy was grown up and stood for more than his own smallness as my son.

"Of course."

"Even if in the long run, what Trentemille said were basically true. Far beyond what he knew about it. That's something we can't wait to find out. The treason of treason. The man I killed could have been a traitor even if he'd been loyally following only French and British orders. I mean he and Bobbie and I might have been undermining while we were obeying. But we can't stop to count that. Life goes on." That Darwin sentence I'd read in Chicago came back: what if life were but one aspect of something much more complex, something that counted more, that didn't need judgement, decisions, traitors? What if Rinamurti saw this and showed us how to go beyond the soiled specifics, the rat race?

The life of my life was going on catechising herself, her face racing once again with the deciduous, lovely colors of the harvest. "What was a Frenchman supposed to do after the surrender? Be a Frenchman and act with Pétain? Be on what we know is the right side? How do we know? Feeling? You had to feel that Hitler was the devil. But suppose you didn't have the basis for feeling? Suppose you were a simple man, someone who'd read only Déat and Doriot?" She leaned against me. "There's no end to worrying about that. You've got to do something if only to see that every rat has to take some poison."

"The poison may be his being a rat."

"A rat that lives like a king? It's the devil that tells you that not doing something is a noble form of doing it." Yes, I thought, these action people hate thought. "I'd better see this fellow."

"Arastignac?"

"I may not even remember him. I thought I saw him in the street once, but I wasn't sure enough to go up to him. I want to know, first and last, if he's lying. I'll be able to tell that."

At least, it would mean another supply of her for me. "I'll arrange it. Over the weekend?"

Shift. "Jean-Marc is driving me to Brittany. He's got a new Peugeot."

"Well, old 'Peugeot' and his friends can wait. How about Tuesday?"

"Madame Z. is out."

"Wednesday? I'll let you know Monday evening if he can make it." That because I was afraid her weekend might go on.

"All right. And we'll go to the movies Monday to relax. I'm not twenty-two any longer. I need cushions."

I liked hearing her talk about getting older. I put my arm around her, eased her back in the shadows, stared at her face, a screen where the huffing torch put shadow, and, as I'd done with others in these same leather booths for thirty years, my body full of love, I kissed her on the mouth.

I didn't go home with her, or, at least, half an hour later, I let her off at the door at Rue Verneuil and went on home in the taxi, lonelier than I'd been since the war, and yet, clear of the worst part of loneliness, dependence on what was undependable. I had a real footing in both *then* and *now*, which is a good deal more than many of us nineteenth-century babies have.

CHAPTER 19

I've read that forty days constitutes a biochemical cycle in the body, an accumulation of sediment which results in a mild depression which the body then begins to flush, until, twenty days later, the chemical juices are whirling in a mild manic phase. I don't know how this gears with the female cycle, which, in almost all the women I've known, has been the chief determiner of moods, or with the social cycles, which can center about when you get paid, when your taxes are due, when you have to put out the magazine or deliver the steel goods; but I do feel that the cycles ride us as much as we do them, and that they're at least as important as those decisions or accidents which seem crucial to us in recollection. I also believe that everyone has an individual cycle which I suppose could be worked out as the combination of his chemical and social cycles plus his level of daring, tenacity, strength, and intelligence. I, at least, have frequently been able to measure important changes in my life with a six-month period. It took me about six months to get used to the army, to marriage, to being a father, to working, to becoming a widower, to retiring, even to finding out about the network. The girls that counted at all for me after Hélène's death usually absorbed me for that length of time, and I know it was six months, from the time that Jacqueline moved across the river to when she moved back, in which most of what still operates my life was prepared for, my job, my relations with Jacqueline and Arastignac, and the final go-round with Chaleur. If you compare my life with that of someone who has daily problems, the six months won't seem busy, but for an aging *rentier* like myself, the time seems thick with event.

Like so many of the events which count for me in these last years, the cycle began with a meal, the dinner with Arastignac and Jacqueline at my house that Wednesday night.

Jacqueline's agent's punctuality had been vitiated by city ease. At least, I had time for two glasses of sherry with Arastignac before she showed up. He'd been reluctant to see her, or anyone else from the network, but he said that as long as the breach had opened with me, it might as well widen. He discussed my progress with Rinamurti-Ghode and was delighted by my report of what he termed "interior purification." His manner was gentle, manly, sympathetic, and—I'm speaking of the whole evening now—nostalgic with a touch of shame, finely, openly, yet subtly amiable. Quite a rope of qualifiers, but each stands for my memory of at least one thing Arastignac did that night, a look, a remark, a gesture.

Jacqueline's exterior is not so refined, and the result of this was that she showed the awkwardness which Arastignac perhaps should have shown. I mean she seemed guilty, and that first hour, after a hesitant handshake, a blushing stumble over the agent's '*tu*,' a patent self-consciousness about the fact that she looked down at him—though less than a couple of inches—and a stuttering attempt at talk about where she worked and lived, she needed the prop of his easy security to stay in the room. He talked about these things without seeming to forget that the real subject was death and betrayal.

As for me, I faded into the wall, the drinks I poured and passed, and the dinner to which I ushered them. When I spoke, though nothing that I said was less relevant to our subject than what they said, it seemed irrelevant, as if I were not magnetisable by the true lines of force. I was first amused, then puzzled, then miffed; finally, I relaxed and accepted the conditions.

Madame Zdonowycz scored one of her few triumphs over the animal and vegetable worlds, a swirling beef ragout, which drew us all into its praise and served as well as anything for the medium in which what really counted for us could begin. Jacqueline began, forkful halfway to her mouth: Was what Arastignac had told me about London's role guess or absolute fact?

"I told Mr. Curry exactly what happened to me. I held back nothing. Whether or not I acted right is not for me to decide. Whether or not London did, I can and, I suppose, should decide, but I can't. I don't know what you want to do with what I've told you. If you make it public, I'd have to decide whether I'd confirm or deny it. I haven't been given permission to tell anyone, though I was never told not to, over and above the usual prohibitions of the work. But I'm no longer an agent. I live an ordinary life, trying to make my way without harming anyone in particular. I was put on trial for the other life, and exonerated. That doesn't mean that I did what was right, but I believe I did. That doesn't make me happy about what happened, and that's why I talk with you and Gruyère's father."

The agent name crawled out of the ragout from the life that was beyond mine; it had been consciously uttered, and Arastignac's answer had been consciously worked out, perhaps even rehearsed before he'd come. It was the result of a hundred hours in tribunal hearings, and it was the way he'd drained the swamp of his old life so that he could build his new one. I don't mean that it smelled of fakery.

The decency and thoughtful hesitation, the propriety and warmth of the tone made it far more natural than the words, set down without any of this, can make clear. Jacqueline had watched and listened like a person on trial for murder. She leaned toward him and said in English, "Have you ever thought about restitution, Monsieur?" She did not *tutoyer* him. "Have you ever thought you could do something for those who were injured by you? Directly, if not purposely."

He put his fork down, his cheek against his fingers, and said nothing for half a minute. "I've thought a million things," he said. "Haven't we all? Didn't you wonder about the families of the Germans on the dynamited trains? It has to stop somewhere. For your own protection. What you do doesn't end with the doing of it, but the decision comes first, and I think you have to stick with it, morally. Only God knows the consequences of his actions, and even he's supposed to let the bad things happen as they happen. No, I haven't done anything for those I've hurt. More than the little I do now, coming here to talk with you and"—to me—"you."

"I don't know what I want from you," said Jacqueline, her napkin rolled in her fist, then raised and slammed against her knees.

"Maybe pain," he said with the same serious ease. "For me, and perhaps for you too. You see me without any marks. It seems wrong to you: I was protected by both sides. Of course I could have been found out by Chaleur, and he might not have waited for London to confirm me. Or they might not have confirmed I was all right at that point. They had a great capacity for making such sacrifices. Anyway, I wasn't touched, and you want me to have been. And maybe you want pain too, because you've forgotten your losses. Pain takes the place of your Bob, and you've lost it. You may want it back."

Silence was the next course. We stopped chewing. Jacqueline and he were fixed by what he'd said. He did not seem someone accustomed to supply such analysis, nor she to receive it. They looked like companion statues of Absorption.

I took a forkful of ragout, to shiver the abstraction; they stirred, ate, even talked, but the evening was keyed by what was indigestible.

2

The portion of our lives that had brought us together was not digestible. It was never digested. What held us together then? Was it the attempt to digest, to soften that which all of us had calloused, Jacqueline and I by turning our backs on it, and our fronts toward, if then away from, each other, Arastignac by erecting a formal

188

monument of testimony upon it? No. There was more than this reflex attraction, but I think that it depended on our awareness that hatred would have made our association clearer and easier than affection. That night there was tension, but little awareness of what we should be to each other; we didn't think that anything much would follow the evening. Arastignac showed Jacqueline what I had been unable to convince her was worth trying, the Rinamurti postures, and the next day he sent us each a copy of the sage's *Testament*, which proved to be a collection of aerated sweets. It did, however, supply the three of us with a base against the drifting past, and when we met again, the week after, we talked about commercial airlines, winter sports equipment, and even Chaleur, cushioned against fear of trivia by the insights into self-oblivion it supplied. The point was that it pointed to what was a larger fact, our mutual sympathy and need.

In those first weeks, there were bilateral as well as general meetings: those between Jacqueline and me went on, but there was also at least one meeting between the two of them. I discovered it in an odd way, although the word "discover" says more about my emotional state than it does about theirs, for there was no necessity on their part to mention meeting nor an attempt to deny it when I did.

It was a week from the Sunday following our first dinner. Despite what seemed to me at best a nominal membership in the Church and an essentially Protestant disposition, Jacqueline went to Sunday mass about twice a month, neither an exemplary attendance nor an exemplary abstention. Since she used to go to the Église St. Germain des Près when she lived in my apartment, I assumed that she continued to go there when she moved across the river. So on Sundays, after her departure, I took my walk in that direction, hoping to see her coming out of church. I had not yet seen her, but that Palm Sunday, I set off from home at eleven, took the slow, sunny walk that was as faithful a pleasure as any in my life, arrived at the Café Royale St. Germain across from the church at ten of twelve, ordered the first bock of the year and studied the *Sortie*. No Jacqueline. Cretinous old fop, I was close to tears. I paid and walked back down Rue de l'Université, crossed to Rue Verneuil, and walked down toward Rue de Bellechasse. By now, I'd overcome the disappointment, and was even laughing, for I had reminded myself of one of the standard Paris Americans of my first years here, Rodman Carpenter, a member of a famous Massachusetts family, who had fallen insanely in love with a dumpy little French girl, a Roman Catholic so pious that her emotional cycle was keyed to the annual rises and falls of the liturgy. Clever old Puritan, Rodman became a close student of the missal, and never made a move without consulting the emotional possibilities of the day's celebration. Fantastic as the scheme was, it succeeded, and on an Easter Sunday, Rodman's passion found its outlet. Christ's Passion, however, survived Carpenter's: a year after he ceased to see the girl, he was baptised a Catholic, became known as Augustine Carpenter and entered a monastery.

I was actually laughing out loud when, fifty yards ahead of me on the street, I saw what appeared to be an ambulatory tree. It turned out to be a man and woman in whose arms were great bunches of palm leaves. They turned in to the Chouresne house, and my laughing stopped. It was Jacqueline and, thought I, the ice skate salesman. I looked in the window as I came to the house and saw that there I'd been mistaken; it was Arastignac.

I nearly went in. Why not? A good friend who happened by, why not? But the usual sac of self-concern, addled further by the recollection of poor Rodman-Augustine and sustained by the rectitude which recalled my agreement with Jacqueline to see each other only Mondays and Thursdays except in emergencies, pulled me past the house before I'd finished debating.

Waiting for the next evening was another chore. I called for her half an hour earlier than usual and took her to a frog-leg place on the Île St. Louis. In the taxi, I asked her if she'd been going to mass.

"I went yesterday," she said. "I'm glad you're concerned about my spiritual welfare." I couldn't pinch up a smile at this. Then, "Imagine who was across the aisle? Our man Arastignac. Very pleasant. Walked me home. I asked him why he bothered with mass when he had yoga. Said he liked seeing pretty girls."

I nodded, grinning like an idiot, at ease but still waiting. That seemed to be all. I tried. "You could have offered him a little lunch."

"I did, but he said he'd just come in to burn his palms. I said that better Catholics than he didn't burn their palms, but he said that Rinamurti felt that any spiritual practise was important if you did it thoroughly and by the rules."

"He's a very decent fellow," I said with all my heart.

3

Another pivotal event of those six months also came at dinner. A month or so after we'd had dinner together four or five times, Arastignac invited the two of us up to see his office. "Just to look it over, and then we can go to a very good Indonesian place down the street."

We had learned—at least, I had learned—almost nothing about his life. He wore no wedding ring and never spoke of a family. The only thing I knew about him was what he had told me that first night. Like true Frenchmen, we spoke about affairs of the world, politics, wines, anecdotes, the sources of mystic strength, and the Tour de France. Also my life, a subject which at least interested me.

I have never lost what may be an American inheritance from European aristocracy, curiosity about origins and circumstance. Frenchmen can go on for years without knowing the names of each other's wives, but I have always liked to appropriate as much of the lives of my few friends as possible. It may be parasitism, but Arastignac's invitation pleased me a great deal. It seemed to me to be on the right track.

Jacqueline called just before I left to say that she was too tired to come, I should pass on her regrets. To my surprise, this did not damage the evening.

Arastignac's office is on Rue de Franc-Bourgeois across from the Place des Vosges. Two rooms with a telephone. No rugs, clean but ugly curtains, a few chairs, a new leather sofa, very ugly, a desk in each room, large filing cabinets, steel, and, the heart of what counted, huge air maps over every inch of wall space. There were lots of offices in the building, but Arastignac's was the only one on the fourth—top—floor whose lights were on at seven-thirty in the evening.

I knocked, and he appeared at the door in rolled-up shirt sleeves, brought me through the dark first office to the second, where a large desk bore the marks of what I can recognise as hard work, a strong light and an assortment of paper piles, each of which was topped by a makeshift paperweight. "An efficient-looking place," I said. "I admire it."

"I'm glad of that," he said. "It's just myself and a Mademoiselle Pilla. We get through a lot of work." He opened a small door in the wall, more like a drawer between maps, took out a bottle of Dubonnet and two glasses. "Shall we have some?"

"Yes, fine. Jacqueline won't be here." He did not seem surprised. "She's worn out." Jacqueline wasn't mentioned again during the evening. It would have been a diversion from the purpose of his invitation. I don't know to this day whether or not they'd cooked it up together.

After the Dubonnet, we went into a little hole of a place down the street, sat on a hard bench under some peculiarly redolent bamboo, were addressed in barely comprehensible French by a fragile ancient, who, in about ten minutes returned practically invisible under a palace of steam which rose from the earthenware pots where all the spices of hell met and married. Over all was the smell of that melange of seeds and palate assassins with which my ancestors have somehow associated me in name. For Arastignac, the juxtaposition was amusing. "Feel at home?" His own face was jostled out of its usual impassivity by delirious anticipation of the culinary explosives. Half-fainting, I nodded. I have never cared for curried foods.

The churned mice and snake butts swilling in their nitroglycerin turned out to be not only very good, but fitting. Fitting because what followed was also as exotically odd and explosive.

Arastignac talked about his business. It was growing. He now owned four cargo planes which made about twenty flights a week, mostly to North Africa and the Middle East on extended contracts; about a quarter of the flights were pick-up jobs. He had three pilots besides himself, and now he was getting hold of two more planes, two more pilots, and wanted an experienced man in the office to handle the business so that he himself could do more flying. "I need an absolutely reliable office man who knows English and French perfectly, someone in whom customers will have complete confidence. The minute after I left your house that first night, I saw that you were the logical man for me. You've had experience with international business negotiations for years, you know the languages, and you're absolutely reliable." My burning insides erupted into a great belch. Blushing, sweating, I put my eyes away from what I feared would be the murderous chastisers of the Orient. Arastignac laughed as if I'd uttered a brilliant witticism. "You're even a diplomat. You've paid them the greatest compliment they've had since I've come here. If they had dinners to parcel and sell in Beirut, we'd have the freight contract like that," and he snapped his fingers. "What do you say?" But he didn't let me answer, for he was telling me what my contract would be: two per cent of all contracts I initiated, and a good base salary, a hundred and sixty thousand francs a month.

I suppose the curry went to my head, for I found myself considering it seriously and immediately. I didn't need the money. I lived close to the income from investments and my Boisdevres shares, and I used up a few hundred dollars of capital a year. Yet one can always use money. Then, too, I wasn't yet sixty, and in some ways I felt livelier than when I was thirty. I always relished going to work for an interesting and pioneering little concern. The early days at Boisdevres had been very exciting ones. Then there was Jacqueline. I never used to enjoy having her come in from work and see me lounging around. Once she'd smiled and called me, "*Flâneur*," when she'd come in and seen me in my dressing gown after a hot bath, feet up on antimacassar reading *Paris Match*. By my old Chicago standards, by any, really, I was a *flâneur*. I'd be ten years younger going to work every day. Whatever fatigue there was in routine negotiations would be more than countered by my feeling that Jacqueline and I were equals in another way.

"It's a good offer," I told Arastignac. "I'll have to let it sink in and then think about it for a couple of days. I haven't really thought of going back to work again."

"Take a week, but say 'yes.' I need you. As you can see, for you become a partner at the outset." The fog-gray eyes shone with welcome and comfort. Neat, unobtrusive, alert, congenial, a perfect partner. Of course, everyone except the secretary was a partner, but it was flattering nonetheless. So flattering that it didn't occur to me till I was on the Metro going home that it was too generous, that the generosity might be paying for something more than my services, that it was the restitution Jacqueline had suggested that first night at dinner.

"Is this always going to happen now?" I thought. "Is Bobbie going to be the silent partner in all my negotiations?" I was like the millionaire's son who's offered all sorts of marvellous opportunities beyond his abilities. Or, if commensurate with them, he can never tell if the offers are genuine. He grows up in an atmosphere of constant solicitation and defense. The girls he meets, even the wealthy ones, act toward him in a way he begins to know is conditioned by the accumulations at his back, the flattering mirror of possession. Much of his energy goes into finding an honest mirror, finding himself. Of course, it's often the beginning of great accomplishment.

My mirror no longer lived *chez moi*. I got off at Metro Opéra. I wanted to see Jacqueline, to ask her advice; to see her. I called from the station. The phone rang and rang, and I thought, "She's with someone. She put me off tonight, and she's with someone." The phone was picked up, and I apologised for waking her.

"I'm glad you did. I'm starving. I went right to bed after work. Just dead."

"I'll bring you food."

"I can . . . Sam."

"I want to see you. There's a real reason," and I ran for the Solferino train, made it, got out there, and on Rue Verneuil ordered a beefsteak dinner and asked the *patron* to bring it up to Jacqueline's place when it was ready. I tapped on her French windows, and she came out, pushed aside the somnolent Duggy and opened the door.

She was in a smock and slippers; her hair fell over her face like Anna Magnani's, and she was as sleepy as Duggy. I kissed her cheek, announced the steak and told her about Arastignac's offer. "Is he buying me off?" I asked. "That's what I don't know."

We sat down on her slept-in bed. She shook herself and said sleepily, "I suppose he can use you."

"Which way?"

She was awake now. "Both ways. He was probably thinking that he'd better get someone, and since you've been on his mind because of—" here the small pause that always came now before either of us mentioned Bobbie—"Bobbie"—and she looked surprised to call him what I called him—"he thought of you. He may not even know that's why he thought of you, but I'll bet the choice pleases him more than he can explain. Not that you'd not be very good, Sam."

"He thinks I'd do, but the other reason is the one that counts. That it?"

"I think it may be. He doesn't have much skill at self-analysis, I'm sure. How could a double agent?"

"I've never thought him a Hamlet. He's too busy."

"Bob and I were busy, but we didn't shoot chickens to get them out of the road."

She seemed excessively sour. "I thought you liked him," I said.

"I do like him. That doesn't alter what he did or is."

The doorbell rang. I went out, took the covered plates and thanked and paid the *patron*, who'd brought them himself. The steak smell must have routed the swirl in Duggy's horsy head. He staggered up, put his paws on my stomach and sniffed the plates. "Get off," I said, "Get off me, you hound," and I gave him a little knee in the throat just as Jeannette's head appeared at her door. "Get him off," I said, "or I'll let him have it." Jacqueline came out, pushed Duggy down, took a plate with one hand and my elbow with another, told Jeannette to go back to bed, and finally snarled some provincial charm which brought Duggy back to his favorite posture and state. "We should have gone out," I said, out of breath.

Jacqueline bounced around, set up a folding bridge table, put on doilies, two wine glasses, and the hot plates. She cut off a corner of fatty steak and threw it out the door to Duggy. "I'll make everyone happy," she said.

Over the wine, she said, "I didn't know you needed a job."

"I could use the money," I said.

She looked surprised, even uncomfortable. Did she think that she'd been "costing me too much"? "I don't need it for money as much as for self-esteem. A man who's earned money all his life gets dependent on sheer earning for self-respect. It's the difference between drinking fresh and city water. Both will do—"

"Neither will do." With smiles. Mine wasn't, after all, so important a matter.

"All right. If you draw money from what your father earned or even what you earned in the past, it's all very well, but it's not the same thing as pulling it in bright every week because of what you've done that week." Especially when you've had a cagy father who'd left you forty-five thousand dollars in 1930 stocks which, without a by-your-leave, became two hundred thousand 1951 dollars. Plus a fourteen-thousand-dollar house, which by your foolish leave, you didn't keep, but sold for that.

"They pay us by the month." More smile, but divisive now. Why? Jacqueline did not seem to want me to work. Or was it to work for Arastignac? Did that have to do with the sentimental reasons which were so strong in us that first night? If so, then was it a mistake to see Arastignac? Or was it possible that she wanted us separated for a reason that was like my desire not to let her know about Phebe Delattre? Would I be in the way of a relationship she might be envisaging with him? Or was having with him? Or, finally, was it that she didn't want Arastignac to find out about us, which, with his nose for information, would not be difficult for him?

Or was it simply what she'd said?

"Those of us who live on fixed incomes always see money in terms of luxury. Extra trips, extra possessions. That is, if we don't have heirs."

The wine, almost dark blue, the way the throat of a storm looks before it opens and floods. Against her face. My heir? She swallowed a half glass of the wine like a cowboy drinking whisky in a movie. Her hand, those extraordinarily slim, strong fingers, the joints as clear as a machine's, on mine, holding it quite hard. "Are you all right?"

"Of course." Though as she asked, I did feel slightly dizzy.

"Your eyes were turning into your sockets."

"No, no." I was breathing a little hard. "I had a bit of dust in them for an hour or so. I just got it out. But I missed what you said." She had said something.

"I said it's because of Arastignac that you don't need to work. He's seen to it that you have no heirs to pass things on to. Working for him would be doubly irrational."

"Yes, I must have caught some of it." It did sound familiar to me; I thought it was my own notion. Why was she throwing it back at me? "That's what I wanted to talk about. You see, I haven't exactly had a great swarm of offers. People don't give away jobs every day to men of"—pause—"advanced experience. Also I'm still a foreigner in France. They need a special license to employ me in any decent job. Even in the States, it wouldn't be easy for me any more. I've lost my feel for conditions there. I don't know the competition. I don't know labor. I don't know money values any more. A business man must feel the currency he works with. That's why the suicide rate triples in times of devaluation and deflation. It's not loss of money as much as loss of confidence in one's ability to handle it. In June of twenty-eight, Poincaré devalued the franc from nineteen cents to under four. I came to work the next morning and found our company treasurer sitting in my office, with *Le Monde* tangled up in his fingers, his head on my desk. It might have been a heart attack, there was no investigation; but the fact was that he had chosen my office to die in, because he considered that American manipulation was back of the situation. The 'One-Nine-Point-Three' was showing between his fingers; I can see it as clearly as I can your eyes. Suicide, sure as you're there. And rebuke. He was adrift. You can't be adrift and be in business. You can't be adrift and do anything, and as I told you once, Jacqueline, I'm adrift. Even more now that you've gone."

"I know that, my dear."

My dear. What medicine for dizziness. For ill hearts. Her hand still on mine, which I turned to hold hers. "I'd better take the job."

"Yes, you'd better take it," she said.

CHAPTER 20

I was in some ways not so far from myself down at *Transport Aérien de l'Europe et de l'Afrique* (TAEA), whose motto was still more comprehensive, "*Nous volons n'importe où. Nous portons n'importe quoi.*" Air transport has been governed since 1944 by my own native hearth; at least the Chicago Convention on International Civil Aviation (CICA) is our business Bible. The rest is bills of lading, duty sheets, registrations of carriers and pilots, contracts, *ad valorem* c.i.f., what we could carry, when deliver, where go—but over all, Chicago; what you could pass over, what signals make, where land. In a month, papers were coming out of my ears, in two months, I had piles of them on my desk, in three, the piles diminished, in four I could calculate the rate of diminishing. "You're a young man," Arastignac told me, and more and more he left the office to me, which meant more flights for him, more returns for all of us. I never went to the field, the other pilots seldom came to the office. The secretary, Mlle. Pilla, was a charming, rotund woman of thirty-five, who said laughing, that her mother had trained her for spinsterhood and she couldn't be happier. A good person, a good worker, we exchanged very few words throughout the week and enjoyed perfect relations.

Most of the air carriage involved special orders, although we had a long contract with an appliance house to handle their overseas shipments of refrigerators, vacuum cleaners, and electric ranges; one with a small vintner who shipped most of his stock to London and Manchester; another with a London shoe firm which shipped theirs to Paris and Brussels; and finally, one with a Tangiers mosaic table and chair manufacturer who sold wherever he could. The biggest headache was arranging full return trips; everybody worked on this. Arastignac bore the brunt of the chore in North Africa, the Near East (very little business) and Italy; I, in the Low Countries and England. This involved ads in the trade papers and follow-up letters. It was the chief variation in what was otherwise routine.

We did very well; as far as I could read the books, on a gross of two hundred and eighty million 1952 francs, the net amounted to twenty-four million francs, of which Arastignac took four point eight million and the five of us split what was left. It amounted to about nine thousand 1952 dollars for each of us, a sum that was not much less than my best returns at Boisdevres S.A., although I am not making allowance for the inflated currency.

It was restorative, this desk-bound, air-cushioned, immovable transport job. The old LaSalle Street glue was oil for my bones. The tone came back to my movements. I had the pleasure of constant usefulness, and the deeper one of an earned fatigue. I remembered what weekends meant, though not a few times I went down to the office on them. The bi-weekly check was color in my cheeks. I put some money on the Bourse, some went to Hornblower and Weeks for market play in the States, and some I earmarked for a place on the shore, August's villa standing for what I wanted. The schedule with Jacqueline didn't irk me: once or twice I was even relieved when we'd finished with Monday or Thursday. I began seeing some friends I hadn't spoken to since the war, an American Parisian named Williamson, who made perfume bottles, and a war-diminished, but still lively Roland Trancart. We went a good deal to the theater, met for drinks, and then, with various men, began a bridge game which met every Friday evening at one apartment or another. Roland and I debated playing tennis again, and once drove out to St. Germain-en-Laye to reconnoitre our old *en-tout-cas* courts. They were no longer there, and the grove of chestnut trees was reduced to a thin alley which led to a public country club, where for a thousand francs you could hire golf clubs and play nine holes, or play an hour's worth of tennis on an asphalt court. We didn't play.

When Arastignac was in town, he and I occasionally drove places, either alone or with Jacqueline. One Saturday we drove down to Saumes, where another Franco-American, Budge Patty, was defending his title in the Beau Rivage Invitational Tournament. His opponent was a Brazilian named Llamos who had the most powerful and inaccurate first service I'd ever seen. Arastignac and I broke into laughter at its violent misdirections. His second service was a tap delivered with the gestures which comedians use to mock homosexuals saying "Oh, you." Patty had been gentle with it for a while, and permitted some rallies, but then he blasted it all over the court. The Brazilian, valiant as well as endless, retrieved no small number of the blasts, but as lobs which were then bombed into still further corners. The Brazilian spun, pirouetted, stretched, and finally tripped, four feet of white flannel blushed with red clay. Our laughter ignited a fuse, and the stands rocked. The Brazilian face was redder than the flannels. Head bent, he held the balls in his hand waiting to serve, waiting for the laughter to stop. We shut up, converted our sympathies, and cheered the Brazilian. He took heart. The first serve started going in, invisible. The tide turned. He took the second set.

But Patty was too much. He sliced, dropshot, lobbed, hit softly to corners. The Brazilian collapsed, the first serve gave way to the tap, and it was all over.

"Your man did it," said Arastignac.

"I was for the Brazilian."

We walked out of the enclosure, which is set at the convergence of three grand routes and a land red with the same earth that made up the courts. An alley of chestnuts led down a hill out of sight. Arastignac suggested we walk there, and we set off. Half a mile away, we were out of sight of the roads, down in a spread of red-green fields, divided by barbed wire necklaces, over which grazed forty or fifty black and tan cows. Seventy kilometers southwest of Paris, and there was nothing but country noise, feathered air. Arastignac said that he spent time in country like this when he was a boy.

"In England?"

"England? No, down in the approaches to the Alpes-Maritimes."

"Your father farmed before he turned to the kitchen?" We sat on an almost purple jut of rock above a stony brook where, fifteen yards away, deaf, or incurious, or simply stupid, black and tan cows lapped trickles of water and licked blocks of salt set on wooden stakes. It was a place that turned you into landscape, quiet and neutral, with nothing paying attention to you.

"My grandfather lived there. I stayed with him a while, because I got rheumatic fever. Then I moved to Grenoble and went to school."

"Before Germany?"

"Yes," he said, quietly. "Before Germany."

The timetable puzzled me, but I did not press him. "I suppose it wasn't easy going to school where you were a new boy. My son was very reluctant to go to England, I remember. You probably had country manners and a different accent. . . ."

"And this," he said, lifting a fist.

"You had to fight?"

"Had to? It was an amusement. There were never enough fights for me. It didn't take long to get *grenoblé*. Like your friend Patty, I adapt quickly."

A cow looked up at us. I suppose cows don't really see beyond the length of their tongues. It stared at us with idiotic, amorous attention, till Arastignac picked up a stone and threw it against its flank. It moved away without audible complaint.

"You do adapt quickly," I said. "I'm more like the Brazilian. I

199

give all of what I have quickly, in one drive, and, if luck's with me, I'm in. I've usually had luck. I don't take well to opposition."

"You wouldn't make a good flier," he said, and turned to me with that self-unregarding smile that seemed to tell you you were a fine person and in general demand. "Nor an agent, I suppose. You have to be masochistic there. I wasn't very good in that way. I think most agents love trouble, and fret when things are going well. Most amateurs anyway. The professionals can always console themselves with limited pleasures, like money or specific operations working out well."

"You think Bobbie was a bad agent? Discounting the fact that he was an amateur, I mean."

He got up and looked at me, wrinkling, to show he was reflecting, though I felt there was really no need and that he believed Bobbie the worst sort of agent without thinking about it. He went down to the brook, knelt, scooped up some water, drank it, and from there called back, "Not the worst."

I got up, and we started walking back.

"Next weekend I'll take you flying," he said. "We've got a little Cessna that's good for short passenger flights, but I fly it for pleasure now and then. You'll like flying that way. It's like today here in the field. You're part of something pleasant, something that's larger than you but that pays no attention to you."

I said I'd be glad to go.

2

Two weeks later. I'm in the air. Literally. Plastic goggles, a tight leather helmet, and a loose, wool-lined leather jacket in whose pockets my gloved hands press assurance into my heart. I see the tip of Robert's leathered head. "Robert," because as he helps me into the Cessna *Deux-Cent-Trente*, I say "Thank you, Robert, I mean Jean," and he says, "Call me Robert. I always preferred it."

It's not a business trip, it's to give me the feel of flying a small plane. Robert has shown me how to operate the stick and will wave when I can handle the plane myself for a few seconds. But in the air, I'm not ready. We have shot up but felt the effort. Air is stuff; explosive stuff, not to be trifled with. A million bees skirl at our nose, propellers; flight is their product, our honey. It feels like a thing, not a state, a way, or a means; something to eat, something sung.

And then such blue, such sun-gold, such clumps of warmth. I look down, I, who want to vomit looking from ten stories. Domestic tranquility, a horse running alone in a field, barns, a gas station, two churches whispering together, then whoosh around, Paris, the Eiffel tower, and around, a train passing houses, tennis courts. I've played there; it's Meudon-Val-Fleury.

A hand waved in the air. "No," I shout. We dive. I go for the stick, but we're up, jerked. He waves, looks around. I nod "No." He nods "Yes," makes a fist, rocks it back and forth to remind me of the stick, and again, down, whoosh, my stomach's a blob of bubbles in my mouth, I'm whirling, but I get the stick and pull, easily, and we're going up, without any dizziness. I bang with my fist on the cockpit, and he takes it. I've flown.

It's not over. A gear change, we're going close to a hundred and fifty kilometers, and then, his hand raised, palm up, like a thirsty mouth, and we plunge down and then come round, all the way, me upside down in the air holding like crazy to the seat, head down and then up, and we're back, he looking around, smiling, and I'm sick, shaking my head "No," and pointing down insistently with a forefinger. And, thank God, he nods and we swoop around and head back to the field.

This is a Saturday. We drive back toward Paris in Robert's Renault. I'm still shaky, but glad, on the whole. We're going to pick up Jacqueline and have lunch with her in the country.

"You didn't like the loop-de-loop?"

"I didn't have time to like it or dislike it. It was too much. Why did you do it?"

He laughs the way men do at those to whom they've displayed mysterious talents, but I do not go along to play the child's role, because, abruptly, it gives me a slap inside my head: he wanted to dump me out, kill me. It's a warm day. I feel icy. "No," I tell myself. "Impossible. There'd be an investigation. He'd be in serious trouble." O.K. I relax.

He's been talking and now asks me, "Well?"

"Sorry. I was dozing."

"I asked whether you were startled when you got the book?" He's serious now, though it's his gentle form of seriousness, a golden courtesy.

"I'm afraid I missed something." We're crossing the Pont-de-Neuilly, coming to the Porte Maillol, a bucolic swish around us. There might be sheep flocks around—my mind runs into an alliterative snag—floating flush by us.

Robert's head looks extraordinarily large. "The Trentemille book. 84 Avenue Foch."

"What about it? I've told you what I think of it."

"I mean when you got it. Did it disconcert you a great deal? I didn't know what the effect would be."

"Of course it did. Why do you ask?"

"I've never known whether it was right or wrong to send it to you."

Into the Bois de Boulogne. Four twelve-year-old girls on horseback, alert, relaxed, hair bobbed out from derbies, then past the Lac Inférieur, where what must be the first canoes of the year squirt around like tan pits. Looking at them past Arastignac's firm, decent profile above the fine brown suit. "I'm not sure I really heard you right," I said. "I'm still a little dizzy from that spin you gave me."

His features seemed to turn into his head, he was so still, so thoughtful at the wheel. "Yes." Very quietly. "It was a most uncharacteristic thing to do. I don't know my motives. I told myself, 'It'll spare him to learn of it this way. From me.'"

Arastignac had been the one who'd sent me Trentemille's book. The trigger, the loop-de-loop. A lethal assault. "Why?"

"The message," he said. "It explained."

"What message? There was no message."

"Ahhh," air leaving the balloon. His face fell in, the fog leaked from the eyes. I put my hand on the wheel. "No. It's all right." He breathed in, the face swelled. "I've never been sure I really sent it. I wrote a note saying, 'Don't believe any of this,' and I signed it 'One who knows.' I wrapped the book, gave a boy fifty francs to take it to you, but the same day I couldn't remember whether I'd put the note in the book. I couldn't find it, so I assumed I did, and I didn't write it again, because I wanted nothing more to do with any of it. It was all done on the sort of impulse agents spend years training to overcome. But there was no note?"

"There was no note."

We drove down Avenue Paul Doumer, past Chaillot and the Grand Palais, over the Pont Alexandre Trois, down Quai Anatole France.

"I thought you might see the book, that someone would show it to you, and that it would help you to know it wasn't true."

"It was good of you to think of that," I said. We went down Rue de Bellechasse, turned left, and were at Jacqueline's. "It doesn't matter now. Your intention was good." But I wasn't sure, am not now sure, and am not sure that he knows either.

That day it seemed to me that the book was sent for the reason he gave Jacqueline that first night, to inflict pain, to distribute his own pain, to parcel out his personal treason.

I couldn't be with him the rest of that day, even when Jacqueline came out, trim and happy, holding back a child's smile, dressed in white linen that picked up Rue Verneuil's small quota of sunlight. I got out of the car and held the door open for her. She got in, and I shut it.

"We can all fit in front," said Arastignac.

"I don't think I'll go."

"What," she said. "Did the plane upset you?"

"I'm a little worn out," I said. "You have a good time," and I wouldn't let them drive me home, but turned and walked away in the direction opposite to Rue Verneuil's traffic so that they wouldn't whirl around and try to persuade me. I had had it for that day.

CHAPTER 21

"Blood," said Dr. Robichaud, and limped over to the window, leaving me shivering in my undershirt, certain now that I should have taken my troubles off like a shot for Chicago and Michael Reese, where doctors did not limp over to windows muttering "Blood."

Robichaud muttered a good deal, a sigh of his own collapse, which nervous patients like myself take as a sign of their own. His father used to roar out his internal debates. His indecisions, equally terrifying, would, at least, leave you the hope he was mistaken, so that after you got out of his office, you could head for Orly Field and Michael Reese, praying you were still in time to undo whatever the old roarer had done to you. But Robichaud *fils*, there you had the bloody spoor of certainty. The thing to do was close your eyes and submit, but it dripped on, and you heard the drippings, "Fainting, vertigo, pulsus tardus, systolic thrill, second right interspace, mitral stenosis, hypertension," on and on, this but the dribblings of the bloody soliloquy. He was at the window five minutes, the sphygmomanometer's rubber onion swinging noose-like as he deliberated. Then, with a slow turn, "You've been upset." An accusation.

"Not particularly." He looked Napoleonic, and I felt like a tenth-rate, exposed Talleyrand. "A little. Yes, there've been a few things."

The look relaxed. I relaxed. "You've got a blood-pressure problem. No salt, low fats, mild, steady activity, walking."

"I walk a lot."

"Excellent. And . . ." pause, and he was remembering, no, showing me that he was remembering the backside in which he had dipped his hypodermic needle months before, "I would counsel, may I even say insist upon, extreme moderation, even abstention from intercourse. It may be that the tension is related to the symptoms as effect rather than cause, but it is implicated in its own causation. Is that unclear?"

"A bit," which it would have been even if I hadn't been caught up in my own aching reminiscence of that same backside. Abstention. The onion swung, and I noticed for the first time a wedding ring. Had Robichaud married since his visit to Jacqueline, or had I simply never noticed the ring?

"You've worried about sexual performance, which tenses you, provokes the vasocontractions which increase the pressure, which brings on the fainting and further tension, and so on, until zoot," and he made a circle with ring finger and thumb and flipped it open.

It was reasonably clear, though painfully superfluous. "I understand. I shall watch my diet. And other things. And I'll try to relax."

"I won't administer any medication now. There is a hexamethonium which I'll introduce if necessary. But remember, there are toxic effects from such introductions; you are introducing paralysis. I want your nature to exert its own recuperative powers. There is no organic defect, I am almost certain. But this constitutes a warning. Heed it."

The fact that the sphinx had spoken at such length was warning enough. I thanked him, dressed and went into the sunshine as if released from Hell. I could feel my heart striking against the rib cage, the blood struggling through the constricted vessels. After a block in the heat, I was faint, dizzy. I leaned against the wall of a building and waited till things righted themselves. I crossed the street to a bistro, bought a bottle of Perrier and drank it slowly. Then I bought another bottle, a small cigar, and read *Figaro*.

I relaxed.

2

"Blood, eh? That's what I've been thinking." Jacqueline, *chez elle,* that night.

"It's systolic, not symbolic, me myself, not me the father."

"I know. You really looked terrible. Those spells of yours were not just the results of our little postures. I mean the Rinamurti." Blushing. "There's inner peace and inner peace, and one means getting run over by taxis and one doesn't."

"Well, I saw him, and here I am. I have to be careful."

"A diet?"

"Everything."

"As for us, that's what we've been doing, and what we want. Isn't it, Sam?"

"!"

"I'm sorry about the rest."

This is the Monday evening after the Saturday in the airplane, and I realise that I left an account of that out of my talk with Robichaud. Doesn't altitude have something to do with blood pressure? I won't go up any more. Then there's something else. The job, but work has always done well by me. I must like it since there's no necessity for it. What's necessity? If I do it, it's necessary.

At dinner, in our little place down the street, I eat soup, an ungarnished cutlet, and yogourt. The *patron* looks worried. A block of a man with a Teddy Roosevelt mustache, earnest, pleasant to be with. Cleanliness is not one of his virtues, and if he sits down during the meal, he should rake off fifty per cent of the bill. "A little liverish, Monsieur Curry?" I'm drinking only Perrier.

"Blood pressure." I'm already used to the diagnosis.

The subject which makes all of us professors, other people's maladies. "Ah, protein. No salt. No dark streets at night. Walk a lot."

I could have saved Robichaud's fee. "Exactly." I motion him toward a seat at the next table. We've finished most of the meal. Jacqueline stares at me for privacy though. (The *patron* has come over now and then since the evening he brought the beefsteak to the house.) I shrug toward Jacqueline in the manner I've never been able to master, and the *patron* goes back behind the bar; but we are under his surveillance.

"I'm getting tired of him," says Jacqueline. "I feel his nose in my backbone."

"We needn't eat here. It's just convenient."

"He's extremely annoying."

I look away from her and notice the veins in my wrist. Bulging with new trouble. Constriction, pressure. My blood. My father. Did the Outer Drive rob him of his thrombosis? Bobbie? Did he escape eighty thousand hours at a desk while systolic thrills regurgitated blood out of his narrow channels? Why was Jacqueline applying pressure to me? We ate for three minutes without talking.

"Let's leave," she said.

"No cheese?"

"Nothing."

I made a sign to the *patron*, who approached. "Nothing more tonight?"

"Absolutely nothing," said Jacqueline.

The *patron* shrugged properly, wrote out our slip, thanked me for honoring it, and said, "*Au revoir.*" Even I felt his look on our backs.

Was it Jacqueline's period? I always knew when Hélène's threatened, but, unlike Jacqueline, she showed it for ten days, pimples, fatigue, edginess, and scratchiness inside. If Rodman Carpenter had adjusted his courtship to Roman Catholic liturgy, I adjusted much of mine to Hélène's. The first week after her period, she was passionate and adventurous, agreeable in the second, reflective and dreamy in the third, stormy in the last. Leaving the restaurant with Jacqueline, I felt that for the first time something ugly had come between us from the inside. From blood.

3

Now perhaps she was worried about me. She certainly had been when she'd come in Saturday evening with Arastignac and found me in her bed covered with blankets. Jeannette had let me in after I'd wandered along the Quai Anatole France for an hour trying to look at books and prints to keep my mind off what Arastignac had done to me years ago and what he might be doing indirectly to me as I walked and thumbed books along the river. My fingers were very dry; I kept licking them. And I felt light-headed. Symptoms. I began to feel faint, but I didn't swoon into one of the quick states that had come over me since the day I'd met August on the Rue de Rivoli. I pulled myself up, got the strength to walk the three blocks to Jacqueline's place and get by Duggy into bed.

I had gone to sleep immediately, blissfully. I was terrifically tired, tired of more than fatigue. I was sleeping *out* of things. If I were ever in truly terrible trouble, I think I could take poison.

I dreamed a great deal, or at least remembered more than I usually do. One dream took place on the *Mauretania*. I was at the captain's table (where I've never sat) between Dolores del Rio and the King of Spain. Across from me, a dark little fellow with a sneer

and a pound or two of gold braid stared at my shirtfront. I looked
down and saw a red blotch on the shirt. It grew as I watched, and
I thought, "I'll be thrown off the ship. Here I am at the Number
One table surrounded by presidents of the Banque de France, kings,
and Miss del Rio, and I'm bleeding on my shirt." I stuck my napkin
up between the studs, but the stain outgrew it. It spread to the
black tie, and then I felt it in my throat. Across the room, something
crashed, and everybody looked away from me. Dolores del Rio had
thrown a champagne glass to create a diversion. I dove under the
table, removed my shirt, grabbed a waiter by the foot, drew him
under, took his shirt and emerged to receive the Legion of Honor
from the captain, who was none other than Robichaud *fils*. Here I
woke up into dusk. Two shadows moved at me, talking. One of
them knelt at the bed. Jacqueline. "Shall I get a doctor?" I couldn't
tell whether she was speaking to me. My mouth was too full of sleep
to answer. "Let me look," said the other, who by this time was
Arastignac. He knelt by her, put a cool hand on my head, took my
arm up by the wrist and held it for pulse.

"I'm all right," I said. "I was just so tired, I couldn't get home."

"Jeannette said you looked terrible. She nearly called someone."

"What time is it?" I asked.

"Seven-thirty. Your pulse seems slow to me. I don't know too
much about it. At least you're alive. It's my fault. I shouldn't have
taken you up this morning." He got up. "And certainly not looped
the plane. You were taking it so well, I thought you'd like something
a little exciting."

Jacqueline got up, brushing my arm with hers. "We shouldn't
have left you alone. How do you feel?"

I felt all right and said so. Jacqueline's touch was full of love. It
was good to have them both there. They were concerned.

"We had a good time," said Jacqueline. "We played golf. I've
never played, and I was apparently remarkable."

"You rent clubs and shoes for a thousand francs," said Robert.
"Do you play?"

"You must have gone to St. Germain-en-Laye." Jacqueline said
yes. "I've been out there. Very nice, but I don't like the game. I
never hit a straight ball. Sensmesnil used to call me The Slicer. The
Chicago Slicer."

Arastignac was taking the Cinzano out of the sideboard, pouring
it into glasses and handing it to us.

"You didn't play eighteen holes, did you?"

"What do you mean?" asked Jacqueline.

"No," said Arastignac. "We just drove a few."

I was relieved and stopped testing him like an interrogator, though I wondered where he'd learned where she kept the Cinzano and glasses. Had he been there since they'd burned the palms?

I swung my legs off the bed, and felt around for my shoes. "Watch your drink," said Arastignac. A glass of Cinzano next to my shoes.

"Jean," I said. "Are you married?"

Silence. The name and the question. It didn't seem extraordinary to me at the time.

"No," he said slowly. "It was not a good idea for an agent to marry. I got out of the habit of expecting to marry, so even now I'm not, and don't think of it."

"German agents marry."

"There are some who marry frequently. There are no rules, or at least more exceptions to the rules than those who stick with them."

It was very hard bending over to tie the shoes. They seemed a mile away, and when I bent to them, something rushed around in my head, a silk curtain started to slide down my eyes. Arastignac bent over and tied them for me. "Thank you, Robert," I said.

He held out his hands. I took them, and he pulled me to my feet. Then he put an arm through my right arm and Jacqueline took the other. They toured me around the room. That cleared things up. Arastignac said, "That's the way they'd walk you around after they'd socked you in the head a few times. That or dump you into a bathtub of ice water."

Something unzipped from my feet through my belly and heart to my head. "Bobbie." I don't know whether or not I said it aloud. "Bobbie, it should be you here." What did Arastignac know about getting socked and dumped in ice water? Hearsay for him. Aloud, I said, "Why did you do it, Robert? What cruelty. You're a good man. You're kind, a considerate fellow. You tie my shoes. You give me a job, when my own brother-in-law puts me out of the firm he couldn't have started or maybe even run without me. I know you're good. You have my boy's smile. You're good, as he was. Fifty times better than I. As a boy, I only took from my mommy and daddy, and there was no love lost between us. I planted myself here away from them because I'd have the foreigner's excuse not to love anything. I loved my wife, but I ground her down. The same with Bobbie. I've had only one dear friend in my life, and I cheated him. I never carried through anything, not even looking after Bobbie, which was my last

208

chance. Here I am with you, who did what he's blamed for, and I've done nothing about it but take your arm and let you tie my shoes. You wouldn't act like that. Nor you, Jacqueline. You carried things out. Miserable, some of them were. You took knives to people, blew them out of their beds. You lied and tricked in a way I wouldn't have even if I'd had nerve, but you're better than I am, and you finished things."

We'd stopped in front of the windows, French windows, with plants in boxes outside, a foot of balcony in front of iron scrollwork. Lights, an Alfa-Romeo, a man and woman walking on the other side. Another day. Each one had hold of my arm. I could let myself go, and I wouldn't be let go. They held me. Duggy yiped: supper. Jeannette said something to him. We said nothing. We looked out the window.

"I didn't have to do it," he said. "I did it. I lived from one minute to the next. That's it. I wasn't afraid. I wasn't cold or hungry. I don't explain it. That'll have to be there between us."

One arm came out of mine. Jacqueline's. She came between us. She put her right arm on my left arm, her left arm on Robert's right one. She held us together. The warm people-smell. The three of us in the dark in front of the French windows. I put my right arm around Robert's shoulders, my left arm around Jacqueline's. I leaned over and kissed her cheek. Robert put his cheek against her other side.

Why not?

CHAPTER 22

There were no more scenes like that for the three of us. Far from being a forerunner of intimacy, it began a disengagement from the burdensome, triangular sense of each other. I was preoccupied with my health regimen and work, Arastignac with frequent flights around Europe, Africa and the Near East, Jacqueline with whatever made up her independence and its counterpart, loneliness.

Yet she and I continued to meet for dinner twice a week, and no one in the world was dearer to me. And perhaps vice versa. The pronoun "us" was as common as any other in our talks; if we spoke, say, of the house on the Mediterranean which my new income pointed toward, we spoke of "our" house. We even described what "we" wanted to Arastignac one night when he joined us, and he agreed to scout around for it on his next lay-over in Marseilles. Indeed he, almost as much as Jacqueline, took what I regarded without the least annoyance as a proprietary interest in my money. After all, who else was there? Some Curry cousin in Tennessee? Clearly not.

I said as much to them one night, and Jacqueline asked me why, since I felt this way about things in general, I didn't go all the way and become a French citizen.

"Bobbie used to ask me that," I said. "He used to wonder why I always spoke of myself not so much as an American as a Chicagoan. I had to work up an answer for him. And for myself, as well."

"What kind of an answer?" she asked.

"Well, for him, it had to do with being a better man for having two allegiances. My allegiances weren't incompatible," which brought my hand to my face to cover what was at least for me an embarrassed allusion to Arastignac's fatally incompatible ones. "I mean Chicago was discovered by Frenchmen, and if Napoleon hadn't sold the Louisiana Territory to Jefferson, Chicago would have remained an Indian village; it depended on trade from New Orleans until the Erie Canal was built in New York. I even told Bobbie that the greatest man who lived in our state, Lincoln, the President, was always tempted by things French, fell in love with and ditched one girl who spoke it, and then fell again and failed to ditch another."

"That's a little bit remote," said Arastignac.

"I poured it on, mostly to educate him. About the rich Chicagoans who bought up the Impressionists, and the Art Institute and so on. I've stayed a Chicago booster. Maybe it's shame at living there so little, at being an exile. He was uneasy about my status with his friends. I am too, I suppose. Anyway I told him that Chicago owed France at least a couple of its citizens."

"Did he approve the answer?" asked Jacqueline.

"I seldom knew about his feelings. He didn't object."

She smiled that Bobbien smile which would have sent me into months of research for a better answer if she'd requested one. What a smile their child would have had. It would have been his downfall probably, for no one could have resisted it.

Although I burdened Jacqueline with American reminiscences a great deal when we were alone, Arastignac held the floor when the three of us were together. And we listened to him with great excitement. He imposed without imposition, modestly as well as fluently, quietly as much as forcefully, and he seldom or never reminisced. It was all present tense. He talked of the week's flights, customers, cargos, incidents with custom inspectors, the weather in Bizerte, the look of the Pyrenees during rainstorms, hotels, meals, beggars, stories about Farouk, the Algerian underground, the Knights of Malta, the Masons. Then, amidst the worldliness, a vapor of the other Robert seeped out, and we'd hear about some Moorish sect that exhibited stigmata en masse, or a twelve-year-old girl in Naples who picked winners in the dog races out of Rome newspapers with a pin, blindfolded, or an account, read in a book bought in Damascus, of Joan of Arc as a witch, a member of a pre-Christian vegetation cult whose emblem was the audition of voices in oak trees. Then, uninterrupted, he would be onto a shoemaker in Barcelona who'd slipped anti-Falangist poems into the soles of the shoes he worked on, and who was now both imprisoned and immortalised by Spanish critics as one of the great poets of Europe, "Though a punk shoemaker." By this time, we'd be at coffee, and Arastignac would excuse himself and head off for what was for us a mysterious world, though so matter-of-fact and unmysterious was his manner that we never felt oppressed by our ignorance of it.

Both of us felt, though, that the core of his stories and interest was the miraculous, even though the story containing the miracle might be hard to disengage, fact by fact, from some of the others. Something in the special restraint of his diction, the absence of gestures, or, who knows, any of a thousand half-visible signals pointed us to what really counted for him. The odder the revelation, the more intrigued he was, and though the evidence was never more than his serious sympathy, it seemed to me that he was looking for the ground work of what was still inexplicable to him in his own actions.

One night, after he'd left, Jacqueline and I had assembled ourselves for our more leisurely exit from the evening's cavern of pleasure. Jacqueline looked particularly lovely in a fine blue dress for which I'd given her a little money. (I supplemented what were the unlivable wages of the store, though I never made specific or regular payments for anything.) I was feeling as much caught up in her as I had when my life was not so full. The restaurant was on the Boulevard de Courcelles, ten minutes walk from the Parc Monceau, and though the natural thing would have been for Jacqueline to take the Metro at Courcelles, I was thinking that it might save her an uncomfortable trip home if she stayed overnight with me. Putting on my coat, I was figuring out the best way to make this proposal, when I felt my coat lifted and then slipped the rest of the way on my arms. I turned around and saw Rampigli's gleaming head.

When I say "gleaming," I don't mean smiling. His face was full of lights which seemed to coagulate at his retina, cheekbones, forehead, and nose more readily than on drier lighter faces, but, if anything, he was frowning, though not at me. "Rampigli, what a surprise. Though this is more your *quartier* than mine, isn't it?"

His eyes moved to mine, and he opened the ripe lips for the smile that made him a more familiar and friendly sight. "I've been watching you," he said, "but I waited to come over." His eyes slipped off mine again, his smile went with them, and I saw that it was Jacqueline, arranging herself at a mirror in front of us, who had aroused his tigerish look. Since I'd been feeling rather tigerish myself, I understood his feelings and enjoyed knowing that I was closer than he to the realisation of what pacifies the tiger. Nearer, perhaps, by virtue of not being a generic tiger, as he clearly was, one who wanted any sort of bone that would satisfy a general hunger, where I was involved with particular satisfactions which could not be redirected or even mollified. Proud of my nearness, I called Jacqueline over to introduce her, forgetting that introduction was unnecessary.

"I saw you"—the familiar—"and 'Robert' together, a big surprise, but to see the *père de Gruyère* between you," and he tongued his lip as if I were a mouthful of filet mignon, "was almost too big to believe." He held out his hand. "How are you?"

Jacqueline took his hand between her own, and smiled in a way that I had never seen, partially in surprise, I suppose, but also in some other way, her lips not parting, her eyes extraordinarily amused, and then, after no small spell of holding hands, saying, "I heard about you, but it was like reading a fairy tale. Of all the ones I didn't think would make it through—you."

Perhaps it wasn't a smile at all. I couldn't place her, nor, in the dim ladle of the restaurant, could I recognise Rampigli; I could gauge nothing but that once again I was irrelevant, outside the lines of force. It was as if I'd just come to France with only Mrs. Liddell's French in back of me, getting words only, hardly ever complete thoughts. Rampigli and Jacqueline reacted so directly to each other that in thirty seconds, my feelings altered from the desire to introduce them to the desire to get them apart, my Jacqueline and that clown with the dirigible nose.

Though, oddly, I wasn't aware of the nose or any other clownish aspect of the barber. It was backstage in his circus. Both of them were backstage, where no spectators were permitted. Being part of the network was entry to an intimacy beyond other relationships. If Jacqueline and Rampigli had walked out into the darkness together, I would have been crushed by jealousy, for despite the absence of conditions which even bushmen exact, I would have believed that they'd be enjoying a communication so intimate that sexuality would be but prelude to it.

"We'll be late," I called to Jacqueline.

She faced toward me, with that same soaking absorption that made me want to ask, "What is he doing to you? Does he have something on you? Is he bound to you?" The expression was very like the one Bobbie had on his face that time down in the country after he'd brought me the meat and chocolate, when he got up and said that he had to go, absorbed, but not by me. "Where are we going?" she asked.

I might have been angry at being shown up, but nothing like that counted. "We have to go." But I don't like to inflict gratuitous injury, or, at least, I like to leave bandages behind. "We'll have to get together and have a good talk, all of us," I threw in, looking at Rampigli.

Jacqueline submitted, and went to the door. I smiled into the barber's teeth and followed her. Then I felt something; I wasn't moving. Rampigli had grabbed the split tail of my topcoat. Astonished, I twisted around. "What, what, what," or some other flooded engine noise came out of me. He bent toward me. A flesh submarine moored at my ear, lips whistled and spat against the external canal. Like having wax gunned off the eardrum. I must have lost sentences before I knew that he was speaking them, and then I understood, "I'd watch that one, Mr. Curry. Legs up to every operator in France. I had the honor myself."

Jacqueline was out the door, and I could see the portal lights sketch her left side against the dark. Ghost stuff. And the stuff at my ear. I spun my head, and the nose just escaped a terrible crack. "You must be out of your head, Rampigli. What kind of dirty-mouthed slime are you giving out? I'd watch my tongue if I were you. There are laws of libel in this country."

His face gaped with innocence, that gross wop. "I thought you'd better know, Père Curry. C'est tout. I thought she might be telling you she was Gruyère's wife. I thought she and that Arastignac might be milking you. We all know you're a man of means. Just the word for warning. If it's just fun, all right, but otherwise, warning."

The son of a bitch had hold of my sleeve. Liar. Coat pervert. Scissors rat. I gritted back everything but, "Hallucinations. Let me go."

I disengaged his hand, finger by finger, gave him a look that may have inflamed his eyeball, and stormed out, put my arm in Jacqueline's and kept storming.

"Whew," she huffed for breath. "What's up? Did he make one of his little proposals to you too?"

"What?"

"The poor fellow's famous. Women fire him. He'll go for a lamp post if he's turned down. He's got pepper in that nose. He can't live ten hours without a session."

"I'll kill him." I meant it. I started back. I was willing to let myself pop the guy in the head. That lousy wop-mop of his, I'd wipe it over the floor. I worked myself up. A great tough I was, who never in my life had punched a man in anger.

She pulled me along. "Come on, Sam. Calm down. He's a pitiful fellow. Sex mania. It means nothing."

"No?" I said. "Listen to the earful he gave me," and I gave it to her.

Big laugh. Right on Boulevard Courcelles. A whore in a doorway looked up scared. Jacqueline's head arched moonward and roared. The whore growled, "Shut your throat. The flics'll pull the lot of us in."

I pulled Jacqueline along. "You're hysterical. This is an hysterical night. There's something atmospherically wrong." I gave a look at the stars to see if everything was under control.

She was shaking her head. "I better go in the doorway with the whore." Another belly roar. I kept pulling her. "No, I mean it. I'll register. That poor rat. I guess he's been itching for years. I spent a half an hour with him once in a ditch. You know, in the morning, waiting for a train to come by. I was lonely. It was cold. He held me. Poor fellow. It was over in thirty seconds. I could hardly get my pants off. I felt like a doctor giving a hypodermic. He asked me another time to come to his room, and I said I was engaged. That was the end of it. Poor fellow."

We walked past the statues of Maupassant and Ambrose Thomas in the Parc Monceau, then down Rue Ruysdael. "Oh," she said. "I've gone by the Metro."

I was dizzy. Where did these people begin and end? What hap-

214

pened to them? I'd thought I was irresponsible. Here was an absolutely decent girl, completely in love, and what happens? She lies in a ditch with nothing to do and opens her legs to the moon and anything that happens to be floating with it. Passion? No. Accommodation? A room and bath for the night? It was pathetic. As for the barber, it was clear something was wrong with him. Jacqueline's explanation served. He had about as much solidity as the space between stars. Vacuous, characterless, he could do nothing but slice up people's heads, assassinate their characters, and chase their women. He was flux itself. Anger at him was dead waste, a child smacking the floor he's fallen on. We were out of the Parc.

"Come home with me." I didn't know then whether I meant for the night, the month or forever, whether I meant that she was to sleep with me or not. I don't know. I know that if she'd said "No" after what she'd said about her charitable bequest to the barber, I might have struck her in the mouth, might never have seen her again.

But she came. And she stayed in bed with me, and without a contrary word, with a wordless yield of sympathy, she made love with me and cancelled the dizzy evening, my jealousies, my hatreds, my fears, and the loneliness she had left me with months before.

2

Two days later, she moved back with me.

Not to a love nest. But for the sake of reasonableness. For economy. For overcoming our common loneliness. For the sake of the present, for life, for human contact, for Mme. Zdonowycz, convenience, sympathy. For marriage. Though this was not mentioned, and not thought of then. By me, at any rate.

And the next months? They passed. Things went on. We worked, we ate, we went out with Williamson and Trancart and a girl of Trancart's named Cecile. Jacqueline went out five or six times a month without telling me where and without my being concerned. Now and then, I went out myself. On weekends, she often went on trips, and sometimes I'd get postcards from places surprisingly far away, Amsterdam, Livorno, and over Toussaint, from Lausanne.

As for the house, not Arastignac, but August found it for me. It was to be available in spring, a fine little stucco house twelve kilometers from the sea and thus within the ten-thousand-dollar limit I'd set for it. Arastignac went down to look at it, pronounced it admirable and signed the papers as my empowered agent.

The job was now routine. I stayed with it only to make enough to pay for the house. With its clear purchase, I was giving myself a present, and would consider that the job had done its job.

As for the network, I'd ceased to think about it. It was, in a way, settled. There'd been no glorious termination, no dramatic finale, just a slow winding up of the story.

Phebe had of course done nothing to follow up her ridiculous threat. I did not see her, nor hear about her. I did see Armand, twice. The first time it was accidental. I had looked in at the office to pick up some letters I'd kept in my file. I frequently reread old correspondence, particularly copies of letters I had written. It is always a pleasure to read a neat typescript of orders one has given, analyses one has made, reminders that one has been active and effective. In any case, I passed Armand in the corridor as I was leaving.

"Sam," he said, and touched me on the arm. Affectionately, no question about it. I was quite taken aback.

I shook hands, and then noticed something even more astonishing. Armand was wearing a sport jacket and gray flannel slacks. He was elegant, but discrepant. "What are you about, Armand?" and I pointed to his outfit.

A smile more released than any I'd ever seen in this master of the indrawn. "Time to relax," he said. "Age."

I shook my head. I was bewildered, and when I looked up he'd disappeared. For a minute afterwards, I thought I'd had another spell. There'd been no recurrence, I'd watched my diet, I was very cautious in almost every way, but still, I wasn't sure.

The next meeting was convincing. A week later, Armand invited me to dinner. I went. He had a cook who had come to him since the war once or twice a week. She cooked superbly and did tonight. We spent the evening reminiscing about Hélène, the early years of the business and our childhood. Astonishing. We were friends. We parted intending to see each other again. And I suppose we shall.

Then one evening, between the New Year and Twelfth Night, I had a talk which changed things. Arastignac was in the office and we went out to lunch at our Indonesian place. I'd become most fond of curried dishes; Mlle. Pilla and I used to lunch there two or three times a month. I felt *chez moi*, and though it had been Arastignac who'd introduced me here, it was I who felt and played the host, asking him what he would like, ordering and preparing to take the check. We never reached that stage though. Arastignac was tenser than I'd ever seen him. We made talk, rather than had it, but it wasn't until he got onto one of his odd discoveries that he seemed to take interest. He had been reading a book about some Guatemala Indians who had been partially converted from the ancient Maya rituals by Jesuits. "They worship not only Jesus, but Judas Iscariot."

"Couldn't they make up their mind whose side they were on?"

"It's a strange system. The anthropologist who described it says it stands in the way of their progress. I don't believe that. Every act of their life is given a kind of personality. They call it *dueño*, and each of their lives has an individual fate called a *suerte*. I think that's an enrichment, not a block. What do you think?" but he didn't wait to hear. He was tracing out the system for me, not as if I were his pupil so much as his disciple, gently, the way he'd introduced me to Rinamurti-Ghode. "There are three important divine forces, one called San Martin *el Rey*, another called Maximon, who's a bundle of sticks and old clothes which they put together at the end of the year and call Judas, and then there's Jesucristo."

"I see. It's just a matter of calling one of the gods Judas, not worshipping Judas as betrayer." The last word held back a moment in my mouth, so when it came out, it colored my face and his.

A little more sharply, perhaps to cover the embarrassment, he said, "No. They worship him in all his aspects, which include betrayal."

"Is it because they know that without him there would have been no crucifixion, no redemption?"

"I think so. Maybe it's also that they see Judas as the god who ages and dies, and who suffers in the world, partly from his own badness. Christ could not suffer from that." He had a long trip to take, this Arastignac, and he prepared well. I felt for him, but against him too. "Every *dueño* is neutral for them, but the acts aren't neutral. If a man drowns, he has an unredeemable death."

"That's not from the Jesuits," I said.

"No. That's where the system is abominable to me. Acts depend on what's behind them. But the worship of the aging God seems healthy to me, the betrayer who acted to fulfill the scheme, who was necessary to it before he existed."

"Maybe, Robert, but Judas was Judas. A man, and an evil one, who sold out for money."

"The money was his excuse. He sold out for the universe."

I don't know what *dueño* was in me. Maybe just as the Indians were confused by their two rituals, so my old pursuit caught up to my new life, and I said what was too obvious and cruel to say, "It makes me think you're simply reaching out to excuse yourself, covering up your own feelings with this, Robert."

Old coals, but burning. A stupidity. Maybe I was covering up my own failure to write Trentemille or the War Office or the newspapers, punishing Arastignac for my own delinquency.

"Is it right for you to speak from the judge's bench?" Without harshness. "My book says that the Judas god was invented to take care of sexual guilt. Here's where all real treason occurs, where the temptations are strong and the taboos also. The Indian world is harrowed by adultery and all kinds of license. The Judas god marks the end of passion, and he expiates their guilt."

The mild Arastignac showed once again the weapon under his mildness. The book in the mail, the murderous loop-de-loop, and now the oblique accusation. Above the spice steam in the dark room, his bloody and treasonable features pretended to scholarly mildness. I remembered Kleppa's analysis of him. "You go a little far. I don't think you're in a position to call anybody else treasonous, including Judas himself. You've spent a good part of your life setting your colleagues up in the shooting gallery. I'm amazed. I thought I knew you. Blaming me for faults which went down the drain before even you were old enough to sell anyone out."

"Is Jacqueline down the drain?" Quietly, as if nothing else were relevant.

"What's that to you? What goes against that? We're single people in control of ourselves. How far are you going to go? What business is it of yours?"

"It is my business," he said. "Jacqueline is with you because you're a souvenir of what meant most to her. She needed something to hold on to. Now she needs something else, someone else, someone who doesn't have an invisible Siamese twin at his side, who isn't knitted to a corpse."

I must have gone open like a chasm, so amazed was I to finally see what I hadn't really come close to seeing. "So it's you she needs?"

"As I don't need, but want her. She's come out of the war and come out of its dead succession. She needs someone to take the long trip with her. You're too far along, Sam. You've put on your son's clothes, you're a good fellow yourself, and so you've tricked her. Yourself too, so it isn't out of malice. It's one of the oldest subjects in the world, and with good reasons, the sexual being just one of them. You don't mix generations without doing harm to one of them."

I was chewing some hot sweet edge of beef, and I cooled it with a whiskeyish root distillation called *taki* of which two glasses put you on a merry-go-round for four or five hours. I took a big gulp, and spoke up with the jolt it gave me. I told him that it was odd he was so sure about matters like this, when about everything else that counted, his credo was uncertainty, living from day to day. "You keep looking for the grotesque events of life to make your own seem straight. To make what you do seem normal. But here, where there's something you want, and your want is just about as charitable as anything you impute to me, here you act with absolute positiveness, drawing on the most hackneyed bromides to support you. I think you're innocent about your own intentions, but once again, Robert— and I'm not raking it up just to throw you off this—your actions are vicious. You'll do a great deal to have what you want, and your claim that others want it blindly is just part of the campaign which started when you first wanted it. Sure I've got a hard road to go with Jacqueline, but what about yours? What makes you think she can live in the same bed with the man who took the real love of her life out of it? And then forced out the nearest thing to love she's had since? Just because, in the nature of life, we've all gotten to see that our mutual affection shouldn't be compromised by what happened ten years ago doesn't mean that what happened never happened and shouldn't be remembered. I've got to eat every day, yes, and I need friends and companions. I like to talk to people. I can't talk to a dead son. I can even go to work for you, because it answers a common need, but here, when it is a question of one of us pushing the other to the wall, what you did adds to what you're doing now, and what you're doing now rips at the old scars. Both bleed, and a man can't survive that much loss of blood."

"What about Jacqueline?" he said. He was warming his hands over the diminishing steam. He wasn't sure. I think I'd touched him. A man who doubted very little was doubting. "Can we just speak of her?"

"Who's to say who'll bring her more happiness? Under the sheets even, who will say? That business is not so complicated and difficult. You talk like Henry Miller. We're not dealing with a mad woman who lives for saturation bombing in her insides. That empress you told me about who wanted her breast apertures wider so she'd be rejoiced in five cavities simultaneously. She'll have, she has sufficient joy," and then I looked sharp at him, for it occurred to me then that it was just possible Jacqueline had complained. Or—and over that oriental mess I could feel slime running in my head—or had she, could

219

she have been *chez elle* to this killer? I looked at him. Bland, unextraordinary, alert, square, fog-eyed, brown-topped. The dark restaurant with the dark men going noiseless in slippers and white dentist's smocks: was it a setting for another duplicity? I could feel my pulses registering the sped-up hammers of my old pump. Oh, I groaned, and reached for the *taki*, a depressant surely. Even as I got it down, I saw his eyes move away, the last two chocolates in a box, his head the *en-tout-cas* surface of a court where I had to lob my will over the unpassable net guarder. But I gripped the dark wood till I couldn't tell whether it or I did the gripping, and then came back, moored to the main event. After all, there was no small supply of what she was inside. This at the "worst." If she could comfort the Italian Avocado in the ditch, cold in the morning while the dynamite waited to breakfast on a thousand bones, then she could bring this benevolent traitor a bit of communal uplift. But there was more to curry than would meet its meat. It would not lie twice upon the same dish.

Where did Frenchmen get their shrug? Atlas feeling the world slide off his shoulders and consoling Hercules with the lie of his returning? It was some dismissal of burden, some coming to terms with what was too much. He shrugged. You can't shoot a man who's sitting on the toilet, and you can't wholeheartedly hate a man who shrugs. It took the heat out of me.

"We'll see," he said.

"We'll do better than that," I said. I was tired of arguing, inside my head and out, but the snake had whipped round in that smoke-screen of truce. The weak and the old can't recover balance so quickly; their best bet is to keep thumping away in the hope of wearing down the strong and young. "Leave her alone."

"That's too much," he said. "The woman's not a hot water bottle."

I slapped the side of my palm on the table. "Enough."

He was up, and out.

"Oh God," I thought, my first thought. "Now I'll have to use my own money for the house."

I called the waiter, paid my own check, told him to put Arastignac's on a bill and gave him the office address. I went home, called Mlle. Pilla, and told her that I wouldn't be back in the office that afternoon. Arastignac, she said, hadn't come back either.

CHAPTER 23

What's the trouble? I ask myself. Many little things, or one large one? A wind stirring up lake water makes fifty moons of one: the illusion of trouble. Calm unripples the water, collapses the moons into the single, bright disc, the great fact in the large sky. My rocking needs latch onto the hundred moons, but in the rare times of self-control, the needs peel down to one inexpressible one; sometimes Jacqueline, sometimes Bobbie, sometimes age, sometimes the grippe, sometimes the mirror recognition that these shards cohere about the treason whose public shape is the sunlit reflection of my inner dark.

Treason—I looked it up—from *traditio*, a giving up.

Eleven years old, I gave up the fiddle, two positions short of the seven, two years of ear torture their own monument, mother publicly moaning, privately rejoicing over the saved two dollars a month, my father minus lines of tension as he communed with the *Tribune*.

Fourteen years old, I sensed that Fingers Sackerman was not the friend to make me more friends in the Right Bunch at Tuley High; and Fingers waited many a long afternoon for me to come by his house, till he got the cold word from this horse's mouth.

Same year, my father was "promoted" to a vice-presidency in the Accident Indemnity Company, but we did not move, have more money or more airs, except in the fair head that imagined the promotion and distributed news of it to selected media, the Right Bunch at Tuley H.S.

Sixteen, I stopped supplying Herschel Grenner with the proper gerunds and participles he needed to remain eligible for the Tuley JV Baseball Team and replaced him as an inferior second baseman, if superior grammarian.

Eighteen, at the University of Chicago, I decided that La Follette had his place, but that Phi Delta Theta was nearer at hand, and that he and Debs would not feel the absence of my supporting voice during the rushing smokers. One year later, I carried a picture of an axed bull-moose in front of Convention Hall, though six months after that, I pulled the lever for W. Wilson of New Jersey, in my heart.

Twenty-four . . . but that's enough of the roast crow. Dispersal of feeling, feeble memory, lack of tenacity, *je m'en foutisme*, what accounted for it all?

Now though, the thing to do was isolate what hurt, and treat it.

Arastignac: under the svelte ease, the manipulating decency, the plausibility, he was a knife, bloody with assault. He shone over my jugular, and I would not now give up, betray, sell out, forget what he had done, could do.

Resolved: I will not "give up." Arastignac, I'd nail. Bobbie, I'd clear. And, thereby, clear myself.

> Father Trentemille:
>
> You asked me for new evidence. I have it.
> You said God Himself couldn't alter the past.
> You have. But you can alter what you've altered.
> You can restore, and, restoring, bring back
> a son's name; though not the son.
>
> You said that you've withdrawn from what I call
> the world. Wouldn't retraction of slander be as proper
> an exercise of your vocation as withdrawal? In fact,
> indispensable to it. If truth rather than charity was your
> guide, now truth is charity.
>
> May I come to see you a week from Thursday?

I wrote this after calling Mlle. Pilla, and took a nap after mailing it. I hadn't taken a weekday nap for a year, and it took me by surprise. It was so deep a sleep, so disordering, like the one in Jacqueline's bed across the river the day of the plane ride, that I woke to Mme. Zdonowycz's door-pummeling in a black fog of worry that I had done something rotten. Water in my face did not help, and even when I walked into the dining room, where Jacqueline sat poised in front of the great torso of my *beau grandpère's* dinner table, and I leaned over to kiss her good evening, I felt askew, strayed from where I wished to be.

"Arastignac called," she said. "He can't make it for dinner tomorrow. I'm sorry. It's been three or four weeks since we've seen him."

"Thank you," I said, and sat down to a watercress potage which groaned with Polish souvenirs.

"What for? Aren't you disappointed?"

"Listen, Jacqueline. How can I say this?" Good bread, fresh butter. I never eat it in America. Like shirts. I never buy shirts there: I have a long torso, and the abbreviated cloth flops out of my pants; I need the English tail. Jacqueline has demanding—beautiful but demanding

—eyes. She held me down. I got back. "Listen, Jacqueline, my dear. I've had it with him. He's not so easy a case as we liked to think. His explanations never quite held, but he seemed a good fellow, and we let them ride. He is a good fellow, in his way, but he holds his way only when it suits him. I never told you that I believe he deliberately tried to get me to fall out of the plane that day. Remember? That's why I was sick. You know he was the one who sent the book. You yourself explained his offer of a job. Now, now," it was a hard part, and those demanding eyes had something else in them.

"You're upset, Sam. You're pale and there are pouches under your eyes. I think you're ill. Don't talk."

She said this for him, not for me. It was true. He had her. She needed him. But when? Of course. There was lots of time. The weekend cards from Marseilles, Amsterdam, Lausanne, and nights I didn't see her. Just last night, and two nights before that. This was more than accommodation.

I pushed the soup away. It slopped over the scallopped bowl and made a creamy island on the cloth. I got up and went to the window. I wish I could have looked far out at stars. Brick wall.

The night before last we'd slept all night together. On the brick wall, I saw her legs arched, closing, the strong legs beyond which she waited for me, by which she drove me to her. At the window, I had an erection. I could not turn around. I talked, my back hiding my embarrassment. "You feel more for him than I suspected."

"Yes."

Jacqueline, I want you. I love you. I want you alone. You'll have all I have. I bring you a long life. The new world, influence, *luxe,* a house twelve kilometers from the sea. My need, my weakness. Mother me. Screw with me. I don't want you wanting elsewhere. Jacqueline. Have some sense. Be like other people here. One thing at a time. Monogamy. I'll marry you. Marry me.

"Will you marry me?" I turned around. In a brown dress which left her neck open and showed the beautiful hills underneath. "I love you completely."

Her hand to her forehead. A big, expelling "Whew." Was I out?

"Wait a bit, Sam. I don't know where I am. Wait on everything."

That was the ticket: she was protecting him. "I've already written Trentemille. I've told him I've got evidence. I want him to publish a retraction and an accusation. I don't say anything will come of the last, but our Bobbie will be out of the muck."

"Our Bobbie," she said, and then, very un-Jacqueline-like, that head was down on her forearms and her back shook.

I went to my knees beside her, touched her head with mine. "I love you. Forgive me. I don't know what for. For everything. It's love for you driving me. I love you."

Her left arm came out and circled my neck, the hand cradled my cheek. She looked up, eyes streaming. The most unlikely woman's face tears ever knew. Rain in the Sahara. I kissed her face, my lips new to the salt. It was as if I'd found her virginal, undiscovered. She kissed my lips.

The door swung open. "What's the occasion?" Mme. Zdonowycz, bearish with a platter of stuffed duck. "Don't like the soup? Love birds. Rabbits. Two days it takes to cook up. All right. Here." The platter down at my plate, the soup plates in hand. She turns around at the kitchen door, comes back, reaches in her pocket, takes out a kitchen towel, wipes Jacqueline's eyes, and goes out.

It does the trick. We came back, smiling. I carve the duck. We gossip, talk books, call up Roland Trancart and Cecile, invite them over, agree to meet them at Café Bobo in an hour.

2

Riding down to the Abbey on the train, I read in *Le Monde* about Queen Mary of England's death. Trains are good places to read about the passing of landmarks: it's the exterior that seems to change while you persist. Yet, every so often, the world seems to break up in a way that lets you see your own wreakage floating on the waters with it. While Jacqueline and I talked with Roland Trancart and Cecile at the Café Bobo, Stalin had suffered a massive brain hemorrhage and died. I remember reading about the Moscow trials in this same newspaper as clearly as I now read Churchill's expression of loyal grief, "She looked like a queen. . . . She acted like a queen."

A rare thing. Did I look and act like a respectable graying gentleman going down to a Catholic retreat to slice up his ex-friend and filicide, the questionable, respectable traitor, J. F. Arastignac? It does not seem so long ago that I got off the landing tug in Cherbourg and called my company into formation, the *Admiral Dewey*, quiet as a defunct rodent in the floating mist: J. Stalin's name had not yet made an appearance in *Le Monde* and Mary of Teck was a young queen.

Four years since I've seen the Abbey. The good soldier Ike has been President for three months and the Russians outscored the American Olympics Team, but the Abbey is about the same in a lemonish sun, and the hotel across the street serves the same fine croissants and cheese omelette, though I do not recognise the handsome *patronne* in the woman who hands me the *affiche* to fill out. Three o'clock, and I'm due to see Trentemille in the cloister at four.

I go past the counter of postcards and medallions. The ancient Père Portier leads me into the cloister and hobbles off for Trentemille. I sit shivering on the stone bench by the waterless mouth of the oriole at St. Christopher's feet. It's extremely quiet, and when two birds caw angrily out of sight, the courtyard explodes with echo. Thin gold light brings blue tints and low reds out of the bloody vines snaked about the cloister columns. I wonder if they bleed in the rain.

Two thin, bent, white-tonsured monks walk under the columns and into the courtyard. One is the Père Portier, the other says, "Mr. Curry. It's good to see you again."

"How do you do?" I say, trying to remember where I had talked with this spectre of concavity, and then to the Père Portier, "Is Père Trentemille busy for a while? He was—" and then I stop, for I see the depleted features in the bone-white face of the second monk begging for recognition.

The air is almost completely out of the basketball. My heart hops at the thought of what had crushed Jo-Jo. "I didn't," and stop again, hold up my hand for the remnant of that bone-crushing hand of his, and take it up easily rather than shake it.

When I let it down, he opens it and the other one like petals, indicating the result of the assault on his body. "I buried myself and then had unsuspected assistance from my own insides. I consider it the right thing, Mr. Curry. The pain has saved me from criminal thoughts."

"I'm sorry for your pain," I said. "It was good of you to see me." What a master of camouflage cancer is, so economical that it needs almost no outside materials. I pray against it.

"I'm glad to see you. I'm glad to see many things that used to distress me. But I shouldn't have shocked you this way. I should have warned you in my letter. You look so well. You seem even younger than last time. We're almost contemporaries now." Which was a secondary chill, for I will swear that he looked ten years older, and emblematically mortal. A rebuke to my mission. "As I wrote you,

I'm anxious to hear what you've found. More, I'm anxious to do what you want me to do. The right thing. To the limits of my ability."

There are a surprising number of ways in which life turns up obstacles. That ease and availability could be ways of obstruction surprised me. Here was a blank slate. I needed only to inscribe my wish on it. Four years ago, there was a fortress around the least assent, and when the fortress turned out to be made of dew, the assent turned out to be worth little more. After all, I had not gotten much treasure out of the blue leather book of secular saints. Now there was nothing but assent, and the original thorn would be plucked out of the flesh. I could say, "Write a public retraction. Send it to the leading newspapers and journals of France accompanied by the evidence which leads you to think that the person who sold out the Chaleur Network to the *Sicherheitsdienst* was Jean-Francois Arastignac, alias 'Robert.' Arastignac can present whatever defense he wishes to make. London can back him up publicly or not, as they see fit, and another few square feet of the world will be cleared. *Fiat lux.*" But not yet.

"Well?" he said, and the voice had some of the authority of that old body strength, "what am I to do?"

I wished I could hear the "drp, drp, drp, drp," of water against the stone sandal of the Bearer. The cloister was remarkably noiseless, a place totally unsuited for decision, or movement. I took a breath, launched myself, and in fifteen minutes told him everything that bore on Arastignac's guilt with the exception of his confession and explanation.

Finished. I looked at him. The black eyes were puffed out of the round, depressed head. He seemed to be studying one of the columns. Had he understood everything? Maybe the cancer had hurt more than his body. Or could he focus on nothing but that?

This wasn't the case. He was digesting, arranging, maybe even checking what I'd said against his own memory. At least, in a minute, he nodded and said that the story seemed much clearer now than it had been. "There were always some things that worried me about my explanation."

Four years ago, that might have blown me up against his great bulk, but now, I had no anger to spare him. "You can repair the damage," I said. "A statement of retraction shouldn't be too much to write. If it is, I can help you with it."

"It's the least I can do. Do you have copies of Kleppa's deposition, and can you get statements from the Germans and Madame Petsch?"

I said that I had Mme. Petsch's in writing and could undoubtedly get the others.

"I believe that what you've told me makes a better explanation of the circumstances, but an historian, such as I was, needs paraphernalia. If you'll be so good as to draft a statement, I can work on that and send it to you for approval. Would that be all right?"

"That would be fine," I said.

A soft bell sounded beautifully, a flowering in the ear. Trentemille got up. "There's service now," he said, "and then our supper. Will you have it with us?"

"Is that possible?"

"Certainly. Please do. It's not the best restaurant in the world, but it's substantial, and you might find it—" he hesitated, whether over "comfortable," "enjoyable," "interesting," I don't know, but then—"nourishing."

"I'd like to," I said. It would be a nice story for Jacqueline.

"The service will be in there," he said, pointing to the church beyond the cloister, "but if you just want to wait in the anteroom to the refectory, you can go straight through that door. It's a brief service. You must be blessed before eating, but that won't take twenty seconds."

That would amuse Hélène, I thought. "Fine," I said. "I'll wait inside."

I walked through the colonnade and an arched door into a white room whose only decoration was a cross, and whose only furniture, a carved oak bench. I sat and waited, and then, in a very short time, looked up at two lines of cassocked monks, heads bent, muttering prayers, filing past me on the bench without looking up. Then another monk, young, bespectacled, entirely bald, came up, introduced himself as the Père Hôtellier and said the Père Supérieur would be there in a minute, that I could kiss his hand or not, as I chose, and that he would bless me with holy water. A portly little man of fifty came in, followed by an untonsured monk who held a bowl of water. The portly man bowed to me, smiled and held out his hand. I went down on one knee, kissed his hand, received water and a Latin blessing, and was led by the Père Hôtellier behind the Père Supérieur past the waiting lines of monks toward a table in the center. I waited standing, alone at the table, which was at right angles to a small table where the Père Supérieur stood. The monks filed in the long room to benches against the walls. High, white ceilings and in the center a pulpit and lectern. The Père Supérieur prayed aloud, the monks joined in. The Père Supérieur sat down, the Père Hôtellier motioned me to sit, and I did. Then the monks sat down. Carts carrying bowls of potatoes, beans and lettuce were wheeled into the room. Bread and wine were on the table. There was no sound but that of monks reaching with terrific speed for the bowls, piling great portions on their plates and gobbling with no small percussion. A monk mounted the pulpit, and in a voice as expressionless as a chugging motor, read in French and Latin incidents in the life of a Saint Niccola, whose forte seemed to be straightening crossed eyes. I ate more rapidly of this at-least-edible fare than I had since I was a child, but when I noticed that the only sound in the room was now coming from the pulpit, and looked up to see that I was the only person of the eighty or ninety in the room who had not finished eating, I bolted the remainder in three bites. My plate was taken up on a tray, the Père Supérieur rose, the monks rose, I rose. More prayers. The Père Supérieur left, the Père Hôtellier appeared at my arm, and I followed, and the two lines of monks followed me. The Père Hôtellier steered me to the cloister. The rest were going back into the church.

"I'd better get back to the hotel," I said.

"Ah," he said with disappointment.

Then, awkwardly, "Howuh, how may, how muchuh?"

"Nothing at all," he said with clear pride, which I trust was matter for repentence later. "Occasionally, people leave contributions, but it is not at all necessary."

I took out a thousand-franc note and gave it to him. He thanked me very nicely. "Won't you wait for Père Trentemille?" he asked. "I'm sure he'll be coming out here."

The knee I'd injured in Germany was beginning to hurt. It was the kneeling down. "I'm not feeling quite right," I said, "and since I've finished my business with Père Trentemille, I think I'd better lie down for a little while before my train. Would you please make my excuses?"

He said he'd be delighted to do so, walked me out to the gate, said goodby and come again.

I limped across the street, walked the one flight to my room and lay down on the bed. My knee pulsed and burned. I covered the right leg with a blanket. In an hour I called down from the head of the stairs to the *patronne* and asked if she would get me a taxi. In half an hour, I was on the train, the knee still swollen, but my insides composed: I had completed what I'd set out to do, and even been blessed for it. The holy setting gave the mission the character of a crusade. At least, it seemed the appropriate atmosphere for conclusion.

CHAPTER 24

It's Tuesday, April 19, 1953, my sixtieth birthday, the birthdays of Marcus Aurelius, Holbein the Elder and Francisco Pizarro, the anniversary of the Defenestration of Prague and the "shot fired round the world." Among other things. I wake at seven-thirty, breathe deeply twenty-five times, pressing my fists against the diaphragm and rolling them up toward the shoulders, perform Tuesday's posture—the ring fingers clasping at the first joint and pulling against each other—do ten knee-bends, seven push-ups, my belly mooning a little on the rug, then take a cold shower. I put on an ivory-cloud shirt from Charvet's, a pale blue tie from Sulka's and a speckled gray suit Morgans sent from Savile Row two months ago. My shoes are from Romano's, twelve pounds sterling; they should outlast my bones.

Mme. Zdonowycz is humming "Dixie" in the kitchen. Tonight is the Polish Club romp, and things will zip along the whole day. *Le Monde* is folded by my place, *Figaro* at Jacqueline's. The latter is rumpled: Mme. Zdonowycz has looked up Princess Margaret's route through Paris.

The household is run by the clock. As Jacqueline steps into the room, Mme. Zdonowycz trots from the kitchen with a dish of *oeufs brûlés*, a cup of coffee, a cup of chocolate and a plate of croissants. They exchange "Good mornings" and Jacqueline kisses me on the cheek, unfolds her napkin, then turns away, and I see her fingers pulling at each other; she'd forgotten her posture. She returns, refreshed, and we smile without embarrassment at the repaired omission, but without comment. Self-consciousness is a perpetual obstacle.

From her dress pocket, she takes out a prettily wrapped little box. "Happy birthday, *mon cher*," and hands it over.

My heart slides, I'm delighted, stupidly delighted. I haven't had a birthday present in years, and then something idiotic from some unmemorable girl. I slip off the ribbon, the paper, and open the box.

It's a ring. It's *the* ring, the Tuley High School amethyst which I gave to Bobbie eighteen years ago.

"It made me forget the exercise, and then remember it," said Jacqueline. I must have been staring at the ring. "I wore it around my neck until I came to Paris. Now it goes back to you."

I try the ring on the third finger; it won't fit. I put it on the pinkie. "I can't refuse it, Jacqueline, but—" and she nods, assuming the end of what I was saying before I knew quite what it was. I went a little further. "That's the way it is with the best things. They're top-heavy. You know you can't deserve them, but you want them so much you think they'll cause you to live up to them." Another nod. It takes away a little from the occasion. In few other respects does Jacqueline ever upset me now, and against the sweetness and sympathy behind the gift, the most personal giving-up imaginable, it's hardly a ripple. A bestowal so marvellous is always loss and gain. When I was about twenty, still in college, my parents were visited by a cousin who'd been a painter and who reminded them of a portrait she'd done of my sister, left unfinished because the girl died at three, the year before I was born. She still had it, she said; would they like it? My parents had forgotten its existence. For the month it took the cousin to go back home and ship it west, they mentioned it five and six times a day. I was home when it came. They could hardly open it, it was like touching a wound. Two square feet of oil paint in which stood the pale blonde head of a not-pretty but animated little girl. My mother and father, usually but two sticks of furniture in the same room, held hands and cried.

It it weren't for the nods, I would have taken Jacqueline's hand, and perhaps cried also. With them, the ring became a discomforting metal band, and I took it off. "It doesn't quite fit."

"It's a little young for you."

"It's tight for the ring finger. I don't think fingers thicken, just get lumpier." I stretched them out and watched the hand tremble a little. Jacqueline took it and put her lips to it. We smiled, and she got up.

"To work?"

"To work."

"We'll have a time tonight."

"I may buy a dress at lunchtime."

"On me."

"It's not my birthday."

"That'd be a fine present for me."

She kissed me on the cheek. "You're a dear fellow," she said.

"Maybe, but you can have me at your price."

She went off to work.

2

I had not gone back to work after the argument with Arastignac, though I was two thousand dollars short of the purchase money. I wrote him a resignation, offering to stay on for a month if he wanted me to: (There is an ethical minimum in business with which the strongest feelings cannot tamper.) There was no response to the offer so I stayed home and worked on the dossier for Trentemille. I wrote Klausen asking him to initial my account of our talk, and, when he did, sending it back without an accompanying letter, I fitted it and the other documents into a running account of my investigation. This kept me from the idleness that might have been filled with what Trentemille had called "criminal thoughts."

I hadn't told Jacqueline what I was doing. I intended to wait until Trentemille's response to the dossier. Cooperative as he had been, he was a sick man, and more, a man who acted on impulses that were alien to my understanding. He might change his mind, and I was tired of promising what I could not deliver. When I'd returned from the Abbey, she'd asked me what happened, and I told her that Trentemille had said he'd think it over. She seemed pleased at this. "I think you realise it's over too, Sam. There's nothing more to do." I gave her my botched shrug. Now, with Bobby's-Jacqueline's-my-ring bringing him back to our minds, I decided to tell her my intentions in the evening, whether the answer came from Trentemille today or not.

At eleven, Madame Gonella handed it to me. "You must be about to take orders, Monsieur. You have a good deal of traffic with monasteries lately." She had long since ceased to be above return addresses.

"About time I looked to my soul, Madame," which boiled up a snort filled with memories of a hundred nyloned legs ascending the staircase which she guarded.

Trentemille was convinced. He would prepare a retraction, a public apology to me, and a full statement of the case which he would circularise through his publisher to the leading newspapers of France. He was happy to see justice done, and to be its instrument. I did not waste time thinking of what he had been the instrument four years ago. If in health, he had spread disease, in sickness, he was curing it. That was enough for me.

At noon, the telephone rang. A voice which, in my ears, was roaring lava: "Come back to work, Sam. We need you."

"Why the delay then?" I said. "You've taken two weeks to find it out."

"I left the afternoon we talked and came back an hour ago. It's the first I've seen of your letter. Pilla is buried under papers. She's weeping. We've lost five commissions. No one's answering letters."

"I'd have come in. She should have called me."

"It's more than an emergency, Sam. You're a part of this now. Don't leave it. The war's over. Nothing is life or death anymore. Live and let live. Let's compete where we have to like reasonable men. I blew up, but what did you expect? You were hammering me to the ground."

"You're a liar, Robert."

"What does that mean?"

"You tell straight stories on top of twisted feelings."

"When have I lied to you?"

"Always, for all I know. Even about Grenoble and your father, for all I know. Maybe you don't know."

"None of that's your concern, Sam, but everything I've told you about everything is true. That's why I don't say much. I've been in lots I don't want to talk about. What I do say is straight. You're trying to break me down."

"No, Robert," I said. "It's you that breaks lives. Maybe there's been so much pressure on you, you hardly know what you're doing. Like Bobbie, but you didn't work it out the way he did. You've spent all your strength on the clean surface. You're still a nice fellow to be with, but inside, you're a killer. I can't work with you, and I'm going to get you. Get you before you get me. Because I love Jacqueline. She's what I have, and if you take her away, you've broken me."

Five thousand feet down in the volcano, the boiled pebble of its heart thumped. On the phone, the ear box translated the thump into the sort of moan a bull makes in its last minute. Then the box winced at the strangled connection.

I waited for Jacqueline in the Parc with a book and a pineapple ice, watching the patient trees holding up against the rushing fury of sap, knowing that whatever lived by the sap in summer would die by it in fall, while they stayed on, year after year, treasured by rentiers and salesmen, dentists and city planners, park commissioners and sanitation men, we fugitives from the pavement.

And I drifted, thinking. Thinking what can a man know about another's life, what especially can a father know about his son's feelings, his—what he was. For five years now, off and on, I'd been finding out facts which would counter the notion that Bobbie was weak and traitorous. And I found the facts, but I do not know what Bobbie was, hero or idiot, or whether he did more harm than good. After all, he didn't obey orders and give Debrette the cyanide pill. He approached Armand when someone else would have hurt the man less. He could have explained more to the prisoners at Avenue Foch. Was he so blind to the network's trouble, so headlong in love that he could do nothing but follow his nose from one minute to the next? Why had he left nothing behind? Why had he not stuck closer to me? Was he brave because nothing really touched him? I haven't really found out anything about these things. I let my son estrange himself from me early and there is no recovering him. What I recover is my invention labelled with his name. Sixty years old today, I am rutted with ignorance and need; and perhaps it's only more frequent illness, an occasional jolting fear of extinction, and general weakness that keeps me from acting exactly as I did twenty years ago, coasting without a hand to the wheel. Yet these last five years have been different, if only that the feelings have been easier transmission fluid for reasoning. They've been more reflective, not that I was ever a foghead, and not that my reflections have not been teased and pushed and strung out by what I've felt. But this part of my life has a second-hand quality which has let me feel more accurately—more conventionally maybe—than when the feelings exploded every hour in my head. I've come closer to being what fathers are supposed to be, and that is not unimportant. And it is despite Jacqueline. No combatant as Bobbie was, I have never really been in a fight; I avoided the Resistance, have been a quick resorter to police and firemen, have enjoyed the red tape which has snarled up violence from approaching me; whereas Bobbie handled violence so familiarly that he wouldn't even have called it that, was tested by his every day, put almost everything at the hour's stake. Yet in handling his last years at second-hand, I staked myself more than ever before; and so, sitting in the park waiting for Jacqueline, I feel that I have bent with winds and am somewhat more than when I started. On the greening city slot, I feel with Bobbie a blood kinship of change and testing, brother as much as father to him, and perhaps his son as well.

Jacqueline got off the bus and walked past the Pavillon de Chartres to the bench across from the statue of Guy de Maupassant, where I sat waiting for her. Under the bronze aegis of that hardiest of love-makers, I offered her the whistle of pleased surprise that with minor differences in pitch precedes a million pick-ups a day in the western world. She stopped, made a circle with right thumb and index finger, winked, hoisted a shoulder, and then came over and kissed me on the mouth.

"I thought you might go to work today," she said.

"Oh no. Did you think that I'd changed my mind?"

"Well, he told me he was going to ask you to come in."

I shook my head at the bronze syphilitic blindly regarding us. "What a rat he is."

"He just wanted me to help persuade you. He said that you had a stupid quarrel. He blames himself for running off and not apologising to you. He needs you, and he thinks, and maybe he's right, that you're happier there, with the work. You're too young to sit in the park waiting for me to come home."

Old sailor-seducer, *fort comme la mort*, you know the savagery of tenderness in appeal. "Don't sell me out, sweetheart," I say, turning from Guy to the composer of *Mignon*.

Her hand on my neck, turning my head around. What strength in the woman's hand, stronger than Hélène's, or did I just feel its strength more against my own diminished stock? The autumn browns stilling the flare red and gorse yellow in her solemn face. "Whatever I feel, Sam, I'll never tell you anything I think is wrong for you. I owe you that. Whatever I feel, I love you enough and wish you to love me enough for that."

Old comforter, old diseased performer, do you hear that? I take her hand from my neck and put it in her lap. "You're with him. Against me. You've forgotten Bobbie, forgotten me. You're looking ahead too soon, Jacqueline." Only the words are harsh. My voice is sinking with love for her. "Don't betray me, Jacqueline."

"What would that mean now?" she asks, head down.

And I don't know what it means. Is she to stick with whatever I need and want? To act according to her own feelings? To feel as much sympathy and love for everyone as she can feel and then ride with the strongest feeling? To act "rationally" in the light of her needs and obligations? Where do I fit in? Where Arastignac? Where

Bobbie? Where those atoning, recuperating, hermit years with the pigs in Lepic?

I take out Trentemille's letter and hand it to her. When she finishes it, she says, "Is it as clear to you as it is to me why you're doing this?"

"It's what I started to do, five years ago, what you knew I wanted to do the first day we saw each other. I'm clearing one honest man's name. To do that, I've got to involve another man. About my own feelings, I don't know."

"I know."

"You know lots. All right. Maybe. But what he wants to do to me now is what he did ten years ago to all of you. He's got good explanations now, as he had then. But what about his feelings? Do you know them?"

"No," she said.

A fat boy of fourteen or so, carrying four or five books, has walked by us to the statue of Maupassant. He touches the bronze jacket, then bends his head toward it, perhaps to verify it by smell as he had by touch. Then he backs up to our feet and sits next to me, his eyes, two yellow-green bulges, gaga with wonderment. I move away toward Jacqueline, who gets up. I follow, after a quick stare at the odd admirer, and we sit down near the statue of Gounod facing the Musée Cernuschi. A half moon, unlit above the museum, is scared by scooting lizards of cloud. We say nothing for a minute. Then, "He wants me to give you up. He says he's better for you, younger, and free from—from what we're not free from."

She didn't flicker. It was no surprise. Of course. Naturally. They'd talked, had come to some agreement. But what about her living with me? "Am I wrong, Jacqueline? I'm telling you only what he told me. That was the quarrel. It isn't that we were disposing of you at a conference table. I love you, and we're together; he knows it, and wants us apart."

"And that's why you went to Trentemille."

"It played a part."

"Not a decent one."

"Maybe."

"You be true to one thing, Sam. Let our business work itself out, but don't mix it with Chaleur."

"They're the same, Jacqueline, and I'll stay with that, even if it means that something happens to us." I meant that when I said it, though I don't know what would have happened if Jacqueline had said she'd live with me if I denounced Bobbie as a traitor in every newspaper in France. But this was not far from it. By not clearing him, I was denouncing him, though only in my old fashion, as a passer-by.

"They're not the same," said Jacqueline. "Though if they are for you, maybe Arastignac sees more truth than you think."

"That's unfair."

"I don't know. I've got no strong notions about anything. I never have had. It's always been easier for me to do than think. I left you once for good reason, and came back because it was easier. But the reason hasn't changed. Good or not. And there is something now that there wasn't then."

"Arastignac?"

"Yes. I've been with him. We've gone to Amsterdam and Lausanne and Africa. He's an interesting and decent man. You're dear to me, dearer than anyone, I suppose. You picked me up from the pig sty and gave me a way to come to life here, but Sam, if the two of you are going to force a decision on me, I'll have to think everything out as clearly as I can. You see, Sam, it's not as if I were passionately, unalterably attached to either of you. I've had that, and I won't have it again. My insides won't support it. I trained in Lepic not to have it anymore. It's especially hard on me to be forced to choice, and you almost take away the possibility of choice. You leave me only you to choose, and though it might be you anyway, the necessity is an oppression." I have to listen hard, almost at her mouth, she talks so rapidly and quietly, nervous, but with a sunken resignation that makes her pale and lightless, a blotch against the careful greenery of the park. "Maybe what I've said will be enough to disenchant you, and him too, and I won't have to worry about choice at all. I'll end up with my winter sports colleague and talk fabrics and promotion techniques between love-bouts. Maybe it doesn't matter. It was easier in the network. There was a job that took everything and it counted, or you believed it counted for something important. You say that's the way it is with what you're doing now, clearing Bobbie. All right. Go on with it as you would if I weren't around."

This wasn't a full stop, just a station en route, but where, neither of us knew. She couldn't decide, and said things to unsettle my decisions. How did one get to be a statue in the park but by deciding. Though this was no high-grade bunch of statues, and maybe they didn't have to contend with knowing that nothing was absolutely sure. I had things to stick with now, Jacqueline, if possible, and a debt to Bobbie; I wanted to clear everything away from them. But it wasn't clear. And they were not so clear. Maybe not having my way with Jacqueline was the payment of the debt. Maybe. Maybe not.

"I don't know what to do either, Jacqueline."

It was dark and the moon had color now. "Happy birthday, Sam. Maybe it'll all come clear over the candles. Madame made you a cake." She took up my hand and kissed the little finger where, this morning, the ring had been.

PART FOUR
EPILOGUE

"O reason not the need . . ."
"To understand all is to . . ."

CHAPTER 25

In May, 1955, I'm on a hill two hundred yards above the villa where I've lived for two years. I can see the Mediterranean, bluer than any camera will ever record. To the right of the house is a garden in which, this weekend, Jacqueline will pick the fruit from which she and Mme. Zdonowycz will make tarts. To the left, four men are laying down an *en-tout-cas* court on which Roland Trancart (who is putting up a third of the cost) and I will try and pick up our game. They lay down the mixtures handful by handful, layer by layer. An almost indestructible surface which dries an hour after a thunderstorm. It's a luxury here in the Midi, but it's one which suits me. I earned the money for most of it.

It is my own hope to be dry after thunderstorms, whatever these may be. The next five months may bring a few. Jacqueline is four months "gone," and will have to stop commuting from Paris and stay here to prepare for the baby, which will be born in the Hospice Obstétrique du Sud, eleven kilometers southwest of here. She may feel rusticated, spending all her time here, though there are no squealing pigs, and the Riviera has attractions of which Lepic cannot boast.

I am not sure whether or not the child is mine. If it is, I enjoy the pleasurable distinction of having been potent for half a century and of engendering sons—or children, at any rate—forty years apart. If the child is someone else's, Arastignac's or even the young man's in Winter Sports Equipment, I shall take great pleasure in raising it under my own name. Such "tolerance" is not the *sine qua non* of every successful marriage, but it fits my case, what I believe, what I've learned. So far. In any case, we won't name the child Bobbie.

Not that I've forgotten Bobbie. Often his life seems to have been lived as an indictment of mine. Often not. I do not know the decisions he made, and though I guess at his bravery, and though I loved him and love his memory, I do not know from how many levels deep his decision came. He was, like so many of the men I've met in these last years, a man of action. I am not, and I do not value the stands which these men take as much as I did the day, just four months ago, in which I read Trentemille's long-delayed account of Chaleur in *Le Monde*. That day I congratulated myself for the blossoming of a plant I'd long tended; but that night, I remembered some of the thousand things that went into that sensational bloom and felt a little as I did those nights when I used to go to Bobbie's room and apologise for my morning's behavior to him.

Not much came of it. Arastignac appeared before the military tribunal and was again released. I'm beginning not to care that he's free. In fact, Jacqueline says that he may come down here in a few months, and, if so, I'll see and talk to him.

I have nothing to do with anyone else I met in the course of investigating Chaleur, except August, with whom I have a good talk about once a month at my place or at his.

When I come across a book or article about an act of the World War II underground, a blur rises from the page, and I imagine hundreds of possibilities behind each of the acts celebrated. After all, one can't even guarantee that we'll have good peaches on our trees for Jacqueline and Mme. Zdonowycz to preserve. How guarantee the acts of agents?

I haven't gone back to the United States, and I'm not sure that I ever will. So far, I've not felt the need for moving around. The Showalters are coming to Europe this summer and will spend a week here. They'll satisfy my curiosity about Senator McCarthy and Chicago gang killings.

It's remarkably tranquil down here. I don't say more than that. I'm still but sixty-two years old, and that isn't even retirement age in most Western countries. I am reasonably energetic and alert, and

I consider that I'm still available if any interesting business offers come my way, or if an exciting excursion is proposed. I probably wouldn't be up to another mission. Though I don't regret for a moment that I undertook Chaleur. Nothing would be the way it is here if it weren't for Chaleur. I'm not saying that this is all to the good.

Much of what happiness I have is connected with marriage to Jacqueline, but I have resolved to let her do what she wants. What else is there to do? Shoot her? We get on very well, and I am looking forward to the child. I hope to be a more controlled father than I was, if only because there is less to distract me. In any case, I have enough to live with and for.

About the Author

Richard Stern graduated with honors from the University of North Carolina, and went on to earn an M.A. from Harvard and a Ph.D. from the University of Iowa. Since 1953 he has written and published a wide variety of work, including short stories, poetry, translations from Italian, German, and French; criticism, articles, interviews, and two novels, *Golk and Europe: or Up and Down with Schreiber and Baggish*. An assistant professor of English at the University of Chicago, he is currently in Rome on a Guggenheim fellowship.